THE ART OF OBSESSION

A Frankie Johnson FBI
Local Profiler Thriller

Lori Lacefield

Cover designed by Nick Castle, Nick Castle Designs, UK

Edited by Rachel Keith

Lori Lacefield
Visit my website at www.LoriLacefield.com

Printed in the United States of America

First Printing: October 2021
Open Book Media, LLC.

ISBN-13 978-1-954457-09-6

CHAPTER 1

Escape or die was the woman's only thought as she burst through the tattered screen door of the old farmhouse, clattered down the broken steps of the front porch, and ran into the overgrown meadow nearby. The five-foot-high grass reeds lashed at her face and arms like whips as she fled, but she didn't care. She had to get as far away as fast as she could and find a safe place to hide. She knew that if he found her, he would once again render her motionless, powerless, completely at his mercy. Which would mean only one thing—death.

Naked, her muscles aching and her wounds bleeding, she ran in a zigzag pattern through the heavy night fog, hoping to thwart her predator. Sweat poured from her brow and her lungs heaved, begging the sticky Carolina air to reach them. Behind her she heard another slam of the door as he exited the house. When he howled her name into the darkness—"Anna," long and drawn out—she collapsed to the ground and clasped her hands over her ears.

Shut up, shut up, shut up.

She couldn't stand the sound of his voice anymore. Once, she had trusted that voice, had even considered him a friend, but not now. He was sick. Obsessed. More than she ever could have imagined.

How did I miss his true intentions?

He screamed again and her entire body quivered. She had to get up and run. Run harder. Run faster. She had to make it out alive. But which way was out?

The scent of blackberry, honeysuckle, and stagnant pond water invaded her senses as she peeked through the reeds to examine her options. To her right were low grasses, swampy with recent rain; to her left was more meadow extending to an old barn. Straight ahead a thick line of hickories, oaks, and elms rose like monuments to the gods, their leaves shimmering silver beneath the glowing moon.

That way. It was the only option.

She got to her feet and, with a second wind, surged toward the trees, hoping they would be her salvation. As she ran, her steps pounded the earth like drum beats and the walls of her heart rammed against her chest. She wondered if he was behind her and, if so, how far? Could he see her beneath the light of the moon?

She had made it to the edge of the woods when, unexpectedly, the images before her began to waver and spin. At first, she wanted to blame the sweat that streamed down her face, but as her legs grew numb, she quickly realized that was not the cause. During her struggle to escape, her pursuer had managed to stab her with a needle before she yanked it out, and it was clear now that some of the drugs he'd injected must've made it into her bloodstream.

No, no, no.

This isn't happening.

Her fear raged, but she kept moving. She had to run until she emerged on the other side of this hellish world. Find a road, find a driver. Someone, anyone, who could help her. But halfway into the woods, she knew she could go no farther. The sting in her lungs was too great, the pain in her chest deep. The view before her went out of focus.

She wrapped her arms around the trunk of a tree and forced herself to remain standing. Her breathing became labored, and the objects in front of her took on unusual colors and forms. Trees bent and twisted like animated beings, their branches and leaves seeming to float in midair. Through the brush, she saw the silhouettes of two people and wondered if they were actually there. With the sights and sounds of nature fusing into a kaleidoscope of sensation, she could no longer tell what was real and what wasn't. She started to scream but stopped, fearing it would only serve to notify her pursuer of her location. Instead, she said a silent prayer.

Help me. God help me.

High in the treetops above, an owl hooted in response, but she couldn't discern its message. A crow soon joined in, cawing as if to warn her, but it was too late.

The moment she imagined the two human forms emerging from the fog and motioning for her to come forward, she felt his hands latch on. His guttural scream pierced the night, an outburst that sent the owl and the crow fleeing from their branches. The force of his weight drove her to the ground and the two apparitions back into the fog.

Crying, Anna clawed forward, tasting the salty tears that ran down her cheeks. Strands of brown hair stuck to her face as she blindly searched the woods in front of her, looking for a way out. She forced out a powerful scream of her own, hoping the two former illusions would hear and come to her rescue.

They did not.

Pain exploded in her shoulder as he yanked her to her feet. The sutures holding the incisions together on her chest ripped, and she bled, soft red drops falling to the earth. He shoved her in the direction of the house, but she sagged to the ground, both unable and refusing to proceed. She knew if she went back that she would die, that this would be her death march.

She hugged the moist earth and gripped a cluster of lavender wildflowers inches away, sensing that their color and fragrance would be the last beautiful thing she ever experienced. She had started to pick them when he crushed them into the ground. He clasped his hand over her mouth to muffle her cries, threw her over his shoulder, and carried her away.

As the distance between her and the trees grew, she reached for them one last time, words of dismay soft on her lips. *No. God no. I was so close.*

Back in the farmhouse, he took her to the basement and returned her to the same cold table as before. He bound her wrists and ankles, tighter this time, and she felt the pinch of another needle breaking skin. Her consciousness began to ebb, and when it did, she had a revelation: that this nightmare, more typical of a dream, was real. She had made the crucial mistake of trusting him, and now she was going to die.

This thought stayed with her as she experienced her last hallucination, of a single hand wiping a circle of dirt from the basement window and two frightened faces peering within. In her mind she heard the words she wanted to utter and placed them carefully in her mouth, but they fell motionless on paralyzed lips.

Help me.

CHAPTER 2

Frankie Johnson's eyelids twitched hard and fast as the images beneath them flashed in her dreams. She was back in the Carolina mountains, stepping over boulders and brush as she climbed the steep terrain. It was the dead of night, with only the stars to guide her path, and one misstep could send her careening off the cliff to her right. She planted her boot firmly into the earth and hoisted herself up, then repeated this pattern two more times before abruptly stopping. A scent foul and unnerving raised the small hairs on the back of her neck. Animal or human? She decided by its rank acridness that it was most definitely human.

Him. It has to be him.

She focused on the crest of the mountain and trained her ear on the night, waiting for the crack of a stick or a brush of earth to inform her of his whereabouts. Two owls conversed and a stream trickled in the distance; otherwise, it was quiet.

Where was he? Up there, beyond the edge of the mountain, or concealed in the nearby brush? She imagined his face peering over the edge above, the glow of the moon casting him in silhouette. He'd be smiling, with a .45 aimed at her head. Yet it wasn't the gun or even death she feared; it was what he would do to her before he killed her. The pain and torture—how he would enact his revenge, just as he'd done with his prior victims. Cutting, carving, stabbing then slowly watching her bleed out, all for his viewing pleasure.

As if the past had heard her fears, she looked down at the four-inch scar that decorated her abdomen. The wound had reopened. Blood oozed across her shirt. She watched the stain grow, then heard his familiar cackle arise from the shadows. She ripped the Glock from her holster and aimed, refusing to back away. She wouldn't stop until she got her man.

She hoisted herself up another foot. Then another.

A twig snapped beneath her boot.

Her eyelids flickered rapidly as she closed in.

"Show yourself!" she demanded.

His laughter echoed across the rugged terrain.

She focused the gun on the ridge. Her hands trembled, but she promised herself that this time she would shoot without hesitation. There would be no second-guessing Bureau policy, no allowance for self-doubt. She had to kill him or he would keep returning. He'd already made it clear he wouldn't take no for an answer.

"Show yourself!" she yelled again.

A presence—large, dark, and powerful—appeared over the edge and descended quickly toward her. She pulled the trigger, but the image scattered into thin air, like dust. She hesitated, confused, until his hands latched on to her shoulders and he wheeled her toward him, his breath hot upon her face. The edge of the knife blade glinted in the moonlight.

"Miss me?" he asked, just before the knife sank in.

Frankie awoke with a start, flinging her arms and legs and letting a small, unnatural sound escape her throat before sitting up. For a moment she stared at the blackness beneath the pink eye mask she wore, then clutched at her heart to make sure it was still beating. It was.

It took her another second to realize a sound was coming from her right. She ripped off her eye mask and rolled over to see her phone vibrating on the nightstand. She grabbed it and squinted at the illuminated faceplate. The caller was Davidson County sheriff John Brenner, ally of the Charlotte, North Carolina, field office and her friend since they'd worked together the previous year to solve a serial rape case. She tried to imagine why he'd be calling in the middle of the night and couldn't come up with one, so she decided to answer.

"I'm sorry it's late," Brenner said.

"No problem. Trust me, you did me a favor."

"Still not sleeping?"

"No, I am. The doctor gave me these pills, but..."

"Bad dreams?"

"The worst."

"Well, you might prefer them to reality once I tell you why I'm calling. I've got a dead girl in Lexington, and..." His words choked off.

Frankie waited. He didn't answer. Finally, she asked, "and what?"

"And I think you'd better come."

CHAPTER 3

The minute he saw the flashing red lights ahead, he eased off the gas. A quick escape was necessary, but the last thing he needed was to be stopped for speeding. The woman's blood still stained his scrubs and the latex gloves in his bag. Shards from the rollaway mirror she'd toppled on him in her attempted escape had embedded in his body. He needed to get off the highway and find a place to clean up, preferably a place with a restroom outside.

He knew of a gas station off a nearby exit that, like its round sign and old star logo, was an antique, built in the 1950s and constructed of cement. More gas station than convenience store, it offered only sodas and chips from a lone vending machine inside, the smell of oil, diesel, and tires emanating from the adjoining auto shop. The guys who worked the counter weren't clerks but mechanics, with stained blue shirts and greasy black fingers. Tonight the boy on duty had blond hair as slick as the oil leaks that spotted the pavement out front, and through the station's window, he appeared to be half-asleep. If the boy knew what was good for him, he'd pretend to be sleeping even if he wasn't. After tonight's events, the man was in no mood for games. His hair was soot stained, his clothes were slick with blood, and his hands smelled of gasoline. He'd like nothing more than to take out his anger on anyone that crossed his path.

He avoided the lighted pumps in front of the station and parked in back, then grabbed the duffel bag from his trunk and hurried to the restroom. To his frustration, the door was locked. He poked his head around the corner. The blond kid inside yawned and scratched his head. There was no way he could sneak in and remove the key from behind the counter and avoid the boy and the video camera. He would have to wait until someone else came along and intercept them and the key when they exited the restroom.

But how long would that take? He couldn't afford to waste time.

Fortunately, he didn't have to wait long. An aging tan pickup soon weaved into the parking lot, nearly taking out the pumps. Unfortunately, it contained three teens, two boys and a girl, and he'd dealt all he'd wanted to with delinquents tonight. Just the sight of them made him want to kill them, especially the girl, who slid from the truck with her shirt in disarray and shorts baring her ass.

So when she appeared from the station moments later with the bathroom key jingling from her drunken hand, he briefly considered shoving her in the trunk and finishing her off. He quickly thought better of it, however. Impulsivity and sloppiness weren't his style, nor was wasting time on such a slut. It was too easy to make mistakes when acting under emotion, and God only knew how many he'd already made tonight.

Those damn kids. It had taken months to prepare for Anna—the selection, the courtship—and within a matter of minutes they had ruined it all.

Duffel in hand, he waited in the shadows as the nymphet inside did her business and slurred a Miranda Lambert tune. He was careful to avoid the glare of the one streetlight as she swung the creaking restroom door wide and staggered into the night.

She jumped at the sound of his words.

"The key," he said. "Could I have the key?"

She turned, wobbling on unsteady feet, and squinted bloodshot eyes into the darkness. He again thought how easy it would be to take her—but he stopped. When her hand reached forward, he snatched the key.

A whore. Easy prey. Not his type.

In the restroom, he removed his clothes and stuffed them into a garbage bag along with the bloody latex gloves and surgical tools. The lighting was bad, a single naked bulb burning from the ceiling, but it would have to do. With tweezers, he carefully removed the glass shards from his hands, face, and chest, then he washed the wounds with soap and water. He changed into university sweats and running shoes, cleaned the restroom with disinfectant, and discarded the garbage bag in the station's dumpster out back. In twenty minutes he was back on the interstate.

Close to Charlotte, he passed an unmarked police car with lights flashing, heading the opposite way. He wondered what the authorities were doing at the scene, whether the fire had been put out, and most importantly, whether the boy had survived. He and the boy had struggled, and the boy had seen his face. If the little urchin was alive, the man would have to deal with him and soon, even sooner than his vengeance would warrant.

But not now. Right now he needed to return and solidify his alibi, just in case they came looking for him. He doubted that would happen. He'd planned his escape as carefully as his seduction, but he'd never had to use it before.

Nothing had ever gone this badly before.

CHAPTER 4

A jump into black slacks and a white blouse and a forty-minute ride up I-85 later, Frankie arrived at the scene. She'd driven a half mile down a one-car-wide dirt road, headlights glaring at vegetation taller than her vehicle, before finding the abandoned farmhouse near Lexington, North Carolina. The smoke from the fire still hung in the air, dulling the beauty of the impending dawn.

Parking the black Dodge well back of the dozen police cars establishing the perimeter, she quickly ascertained a search was under way—officers barking orders at their lesser counterparts, flashlight beams sweeping behind the trees bordering the property. As she approached, a sheriff's deputy stopped her with a raised palm and a command to halt. "Identify yourself."

Frankie produced her credentials. "I'm looking for Sheriff John Brenner."

His eyes lingered on the ID only half as long as they lingered on her, stopping too long on her chest and her cinnamon complexion before moving up to meet her eyes. She'd started to issue an *Eyes up here, pal* statement when he jerked his head over his shoulder. "Through the meadow to your left. I'll radio ahead."

Frankie slipped between the squad cars, squinting as each round of red and blue lights left flash points in her vision. The house, or what was left of it, was barely visible from where she stood, hidden by a long untended field.

Walking through the meadow, she experienced what she termed the eye of evil, a brief eerie calmness in the center of chaos, like the eye of a hurricane. In moments like this, she sensed the joining of the physical and the spiritual worlds, nature emerging from the backdrop and transforming into a communicative entity. This time was no different. She felt the tendrils of the grasses peck at her legs, the fingers of the southwest wind massage her left cheek, and a resonant voice whisper in her ear.

Evil had crossed this spot tonight.

A sleepy-eyed officer soon appeared to greet her. Speaking quietly, as if out of respect for the deceased, he informed her of the sheriff's whereabouts and pointed her in the right direction. Frankie retraced his dew-soaked footprints and found the sheriff standing on the south side of the former structure, his lean six-foot-two frame and shock of white hair silhouetted by the rose-and-indigo sunrise. She could tell he was distressed, his bottom and top lips twisted around each other as if he'd just eaten something sour.

Frankie stepped over a pile of broken glass and extended her hand. "Sheriff Brenner," she said. "I phoned Agent Andrews to see if he could come as well, but he's out of town." She spoke apologetically, assuming he'd rather work with Ben given her screwup on the serial rape case they'd worked the year before, but he quickly shut her down.

"I called you, didn't I?"

She cleared her throat. "Yes."

He turned to look at the remnants of the old house. "I do wish our reunion was under better circumstances. My team has been here gathering evidence for the past two hours, but the scene should still be fresh. You'll do fine on your own."

"I appreciate the offer—and the vote of confidence."

"I'm not going to lie to you. It's a rough one, Agent Johnson, a real mess. I don't like the feeling I get. It's why I called."

Beneath the scent of smoke that drifted through the remaining wood slabs like fog, Frankie could smell the raw earth underfoot, fresh wildflowers blooming among the high grasses dripping with dew. She plucked a handful of lavender petals near her feet and examined them. It seemed cruel, the burgeoning of new life so close to where life had been taken. "What kind of feeling?"

He shook his head. "I'll let you determine that for yourself. I don't want anything I say to bias your opinion."

That was Sheriff Brenner. Always thinking procedure. Nothing to taint the case.

"Anything I need to know beforehand?" She noticed a yellow crack of light seeping through a broken window near the ground, crime techs crawling around inside. "The basement?"

"It's where the body was."

"Was?"

"It's been moved." He pointed toward a patrol car some thirty yards away, where a shivering girl wrapped in a blanket stood speaking with two officers. "Her boyfriend attempted to rescue the victim from the fire. Brought her from the basement and up the stairs to outside. He's in the hospital with severe burns."

"What's their story?"

The sheriff scratched his head, leaving a two-inch tuft of hair sticking up to flap in the breeze. "We weren't able to get much from the boy. He was in bad shape when we arrived. According to the girl, they were in the woods doing what teenagers do best when a woman, identified as the victim, ran toward them. She appeared disorientated, on drugs or drunk. The two got out and started to help her when a man emerged and became violent. They hid during the confrontation, then followed the couple back to the house."

He pointed to the window. "They cleared a spot in that window to watch. By then the woman, who appeared unconscious, was strapped to a table inside. We're not sure what happened after that, except that the boy tried to rescue her. The boyfriend sent his girlfriend to get help. She called 911 from her cell phone as soon as she got back to the truck."

Frankie looked back at the structure, sensed a gnawing in her gut. "What do you think happened while the girl was gone?"

"Given the place was in flames, I'd say either the perpetrator discovered the boy's presence, or the boy tried to stop the perpetrator from whatever he was doing to the victim and the perpetrator set the place on fire. Either way, he did it purposely. He doused the victim and the basement with gasoline."

That was Sheriff Brenner too. No slang for a by-the-book kind of man. It was *perpetrator*, not *perp*, *unknown subject*, not *unsub*. Like most law enforcement, he also referred to the deceased with the more impersonal *victim* instead of using their name. Frankie preferred to use the latter when she could as a reminder that, for the individual—and her—it was personal.

Of course, right now, they didn't know who the victim was.

He continued. "There's medical equipment in the basement, and judging from the cuts on the victim's chest, she's had some recent surgery. What, we're not exactly sure. The body is ... damaged."

"Fire?" she asked.

He nodded. "The boy, name of Miguel Herrera, was only able to mumble between pained breaths that he brought the victim up the stairs and attempted CPR. They injected him with high doses of pain medication after that and flew him to a nearby hospital."

Frankie grunted. "I've been on that ride. Feel for him. Miguel's a hero." She looked back at the girl, mascara smudged across her cheeks. "They get a look at the guy, the perpetrator?" His language, not hers.

"The boy probably did, but the girl ..." He shook his head. "She didn't see him at all in the basement, and when they were outside, it was dark, foggy, and she was scared."

"Race?"

"She thinks white."

"How about a car? A license plate?"

"Nothing. But we're searching for tracks. He had to park a van or truck out here somewhere. He didn't get here in a car, not with all that medical equipment."

Frankie sighed. Medical equipment. Surgery. What the hell were they dealing with here? None of those things belonged in a farmhouse in the country. "Well, let's hope they find something."

She knelt by the basement window and looked through the same spot Miguel and his girlfriend had hours before. The basement was alive with activity, one of the crime techs taking photographs, another examining burn patterns on a wall. "Who owns the house?" she asked, knowing full well it would have been one of the first things the sheriff checked, despite the hour.

"Neighbors say a man in Georgia. Inherited down the generations from his great-grandparents. He pays the taxes on it but not much else."

She stood. "Any indication the perpetrator was living here?"

The sheriff didn't answer. She observed his left eyelid twitch and sensed his uncertainty, the doubt he had formerly expressed. "Sheriff?"

He sighed. "There was a generator. We found it out back. And there was food stocked in some crates in the basement and women's clothes, size four as best we can tell from the few tags that remain."

Frankie clicked her tongue against the roof of her mouth. Food and a generator meant that the killer had been living—or planned to be living—on the property. The clothes likely belonged to the victim.

In her mind, she recorded her first thoughts. *Preselected the scene of the crime. Knew the property was unoccupied. Planned to stay on the premises. Brought his own medical equipment and supplies.*

She was starting to understand why the sheriff had called.

"Where's the body?" she asked.

The sheriff pointed to a transport about twenty yards away where one of the sheriff's lieutenants and an assistant from the medical examiner's office stood. "He's ready to take her to the morgue, but I wanted you to see her first. The assistant didn't like it, but that's too damn bad."

Lucky for him, in North Carolina, investigating officers ruled the crime scene. Lucky for Frankie too. Typically profilers like her and Ben saw evidence only after the fact, through photographs, autopsy and tox reports, and other records, so getting a chance to examine the scene—and the body—firsthand was a gift.

The ME's assistant opened the back door of the transport and slid the victim out.

In Frankie's five years with the Bureau, she'd never found seeing a dead body a forgettable experience, and this was no exception. As soon as the assistant unzipped the bag, an odor like cauterized squid consumed the air, and Frankie had to take a step back. Yet the smell paled in comparison to the sight. Only portions of the woman's face, arm, and torso had gone unharmed by the fire—the rest was blackened and bubbled, like coffee left on high at the bottom of the pot too long.

Damn.

She saw the sheriff look away.

The woman was white, and Frankie estimated her to be in her mid-twenties. The fragments of brown hair and a mole on her left cheek were the only other clues to her identity. "We've had no reports of a missing white female in the past week," Frankie said, "but maybe someone isn't aware she's gone." She glanced at the sheriff. "No identification of any kind inside?"

"Nothing yet," he said.

Frankie removed a small flashlight from her pant pocket and clicked it on. She inspected the woman's feet, legs, and pelvis for any sign of wounds prior to the fire, but nothing appeared out of the ordinary beyond the damage from the fire itself. The exposed bone and sloughed skin made Frankie's stomach do a 360. In normal circumstances, death at least brought the knowledge of a life well lived, but in this situation, it was simply tragic. This was a life cut short, just as Lianna Wakefield's had been in Frankie's last case. This young woman would never get to experience any of those moments that made life so special, and that made Frankie extremely angry.

She proceeded to analyze the victim's arms, feeling the eyes of the lieutenant and the ME's assistant subtly regarding her. She knew what they were thinking—the body belonged to the medical examiner, not her. Maybe if she included them in the conversation, they wouldn't be so put off by her presence.

"Did she have any broken nails? Any defensive wounds?" she asked the assistant. He'd already bagged the hands so Frankie couldn't see her fingers.

"Not that I saw offhand. Fingernails were intact. Short and dirty but intact."

"Well, hopefully that dirt will contain some DNA."

"They'll be scraped at the morgue," the lieutenant said, as if Frankie had insinuated that the ME would overlook such a matter.

Her head twisted toward the man. He was six-four and dark haired, with lips too full for his gaunt face. He wasn't the lieutenant who Frankie had worked with when they'd investigated the serial rapist. *He must be new.* "Meant nothing by it, my man. Simply an observation."

He glanced at her, his eyes briefly penetrating. She knew the look well, the quick piercing stare under lowered eyelids, the one that said she was too young for the job, too female for the job, maybe even too African for the job to suit the man's taste. She imagined that when she departed, he would issue a more overt statement, something about cream in his coffee or cinnamon and sugar. Having dealt with his kind over the last five years, she'd heard them all.

She saw Sheriff Brenner send him a disapproving glance, an *I'll deal with you later* look. The lieutenant cast his gaze elsewhere.

She returned to the body and inspected the woman's chest, which had the smallest amount of damage—at least from the fire. The surgical procedures the sheriff had referred to were another matter. The woman's breasts were missing, and it was clear to Frankie that she'd undergone a mastectomy. A curved incision ran above her ribcage, about six inches long. The incision had ripped in places but several sutures remained, green and black and intertwined, like braids in a kid's hair.

She called the sheriff over. "Did you see these?"

She waited for him to slip on a pair of glasses. Grunting, he motioned for the lieutenant. "Did our guys get a detailed photo of these?"

"I'm sure they did but ..."

"Get another, just in case," Brenner ordered.

The man obliged, this time without any smart-ass remarks.

Frankie slipped inside her head now, speaking to the analytical part of her that sometimes felt like a separate entity. *Burning. Why?* Only to cover the crime. *Surgery, including a mastectomy. Was it for sacrifice? Religious ritual?* Right now this didn't have the feel of any of that. *Personal vengeance, sexual sadism?* The autopsy might prove the latter if it existed. *And the sutures, what do they mean?* Was it possible the unsub hadn't planned to kill this woman, but wanted to experiment on her like a guinea pig? Possible, quite possible, because stitching her up only to kill her soon after didn't make any sense.

Frankie added more notations to her mental profile. *Skilled in medicine and/or surgery. Burning only to cover the evidence.*

She stepped back, clicked off the light. "You can take her now," the sheriff said.

They watched the ME's assistant load the young woman back into the transport. Frankie and Brenner had started to leave when the sheriff's deputy who'd formerly greeted Frankie in the meadow approached from the house. "Sir, one of the techs wants you to see something."

The gaunt-faced lieutenant trailed her and Sheriff Brenner to the house. After Brenner gave a brief tap on what remained of the basement window, the tech walked over and showed them an item. It was about an inch long and black, with a distinctly sharp edge.

"What is that? An arrowhead of some kind?" the lieutenant asked.

"Maybe," the sheriff said. He looked at the tech. "What is it?"

The tech reached down with a pair of tongs and pulled up another find, a cylindrical black-and-gray object about six inches long. He pointed at the shiny black item, then at the tip of the cylindrical object, as if they belonged together. "Homemade knife?" he questioned.

"Or a scalpel," the sheriff said.

He and Frankie exchanged a glance.

She felt her stomach pull, retreating like a prairie dog back into its hole. Her mind scribbled additional details. *Brought his own tools and equipment. Reacted logically when discovered by the teen—gathering tools, pouring gasoline on the scene and the victim, destroying the evidence.* Then the part she didn't like, what she knew the sheriff had sensed as well.

Calm, planned, and organized = experienced.

This was probably not the killer's first time.

The sheriff nodded to the tech and mumbled a thank-you. He took Frankie's arm and walked her to her car. "I'll send you copies of everything I have," he said. "I want the Bureau's help on this, yours and Ben's."

"We'll do everything we can." She hesitated before opening the car door, unsure if she should say anything more. "This one went all wrong for him, Sheriff. If he'd been left to proceed uninterrupted, that woman might never have been discovered, evidence never left behind. He made mistakes. That's good for us. It may be our only chance to stop him."

The sheriff's pale-blue eyes narrowed at her choice of words. "*This one?* You're certain about this? You don't think we could be wrong?"

Frankie glanced across the meadow spreading north under the emerging light of a new day. She shook her head. "No, Sheriff, I do not. You were right to call us. What we have in there is not a first offender. What we have there is a career man."

CHAPTER 5

Frankie sat at her desk in the Bureau's North Carolina field office, set in southwest Charlotte on a gated campus surrounded by an expansive lawn. The move to suburbia from the higher target uptown had occurred a few years earlier, as it had in other cities across the states post 9/11. Frankie had been in Charlotte since her graduation from the academy, and in those five years, had tracked the activities of a domestic terrorist group known as the Triangle of Terror, investigated members of the Mara Salvatrucha, and participated in the bust of a Hezbollah cell, but she'd never investigated a killer like this one—a man who carved and chiseled his victims to his liking, then disposed of them like bad art projects.

As she considered the traits of the unsub they sought, Agent Ben Andrews appeared at her office door, looking, as always, like a cover model for *GQ*, his cobalt-blue eyes sparkling beneath full eyebrows and thick black hair. Since she'd joined the Bureau, Agent Andrews had been her mentor, both officially and unofficially. For her, he was a catchall guy—a teacher who sharpened her skills, a peer to bounce ideas off, and an ally for support. They'd also become good friends, and she couldn't imagine Fed life without him.

He rapped twice on the wall only as an afterthought. "I hear you caught a bad one. Something about a dead girl and a fire?"

Frankie swung to face him. Though her tiny office was a replica of every other one in the building, it was the most uniquely decorated, with posters from *Show Boat*, *Cats*, and *Hallelujah, Baby!* framed and hanging on the walls. Signed by the cast, including her mother—a New York stage actress—they usually brightened the place. Today, however, they appeared an odd contrast to the gruesome photographs and reports scattered across her desk, everything they had on the victim, now identified as Anna Jamison. "Sheriff Brenner called me in the middle of the night. Didn't like what he saw. He wants our help."

Ben took occupancy of a corner chair. "Ours, or yours?"

Frankie was surprised at the hint of offense in his tone. "Vicks said you were in Fayetteville. What were you doing there? Don't tell me you're still trying to trace the Imposter. You need to let it go."

"I know, but I can't. I'm going to get that son of a bitch. I'll never stop until I do."

Frankie shook her head. "Obsess much?" She popped the last quarter of a stale sugar doughnut into her mouth and chased it with black coffee.

Ben wrinkled his nose. "Dunkies. Breakfast of champions."

"Works for me." She licked her lips.

"Maybe I am obsessed, but I was already in Fayetteville working another case so I just pulled double duty. We're surveilling a new militia there with ties to a white supremacist group. We think they're planning something big."

"Great. More KKK wannabes. Just what we need in the world."

"Hey, I don't like them anymore than you do." He sniffed at his armpit. "I've taken ten showers since returning from their camp, and I still can't get the stink off."

"That explains the extra dose of Polo taking over my office."

He smirked. "So what've you learned about the case? Give me the lowdown."

"Make that both of us."

In tandem, they turned to regard Manny Vicks, the suited six-foot-one former Marine with a shaved head who'd previously headed up Major Crimes and been promoted to assistant special agent in charge of the Charlotte field office two years before. Like he did most days, Vicks was leaning in the doorframe of an office, eavesdropping; today the office happened to be Frankie's. His typical stern mood—as indicated by a single deep crevice that ran the length of his forehead and dipped into a V above the bridge of his nose—was more than double its usual depth.

Frankie wiped the remaining sugar from her hands and got down to business. "Anna Jamison, age twenty-six, fourth-year medical student at the University of North Carolina Chapel Hill. Engaged to Brian Schaefer, a fellow medical student. By all accounts the two were madly in love, applying to residency programs in hospitals in the same cities. Coworkers say she left work last Friday at noon for a rare weekend off. Parents confirmed that she drove to their house in south Charlotte and stayed Friday evening. They say she gave no indication of anything being wrong. The mother says they spent five hours talking wedding preparations—flowers, the cake, even the possible inscriptions on the napkins."

Ben frowned. "What do you mean she gave no indication that something was wrong? Was there something wrong?"

"Yes," Frankie said. "Apparently, Anna was preparing to ditch her fiancé. At least that's what a letter found at her residence indicates. They discovered eight different printed communications plus some poems. The correspondence with this secret love goes back four months, beginning in January. The letters never reference his email or mention his name, though, and none of them are handwritten except her last one, which is odd."

"Married?" Vicks questioned.

"Quite possible," Frankie said.

"Her computer?" Ben asked.

"A laptop. Gone. They're checking her social media sites and known email addresses, but so far they've found no record of this other man."

Vicks pulled at the goatee on his chin. "What else?"

"Saturday morning, Anna ate breakfast with her parents, then headed for SouthPark mall. She was due to have lunch with a friend at two p.m. but phoned her at one fifteen and stated she was having car trouble and wouldn't make it. Instead, she said, she'd see her later that night."

"Did she?" Ben asked.

"Yes. According to the friend, Anna arrived at the bar just after six p.m. and stayed for an hour. The friend said Anna acted strangely. Finally, Anna told her she planned to call off the engagement. The friend was floored. She hadn't heard a word about this other man."

Ben pulled at his pant leg. One of his feet began to agitate.

"In addition to the friend who saw Anna Saturday night, we have three other sightings. An elderly couple at the mall reported seeing a man with thick glasses help Anna with her car in the parking lot. That was at one p.m. Saturday afternoon, shortly before Anna called her friend. Then Anna's neighbors in Chapel Hill said she arrived home Sunday with a blond woman around two p.m. According to them they left two hours later, suitcases in hand. So far the sheriff's department has had no luck identifying the blonde. Lastly, we have a convenience store clerk who remembered Anna calling to check flights to New York from her cell phone while she purchased a pack of gum. He said, quote, 'She was hot'. That was at four thirty p.m."

"Any activity at the airports? Raleigh, Charlotte, Greensboro?" Ben asked. "She could've met up with this mystery man at any of those locations."

"They're continuing to look, but so far they've come up empty. None of the major airlines report a flight booked in her name, yet nobody has seen her since. It looks like she just disappeared after leaving the convenience store."

"What about the boyfriend?" Ben asked. "Seems to me he would be the obvious suspect. He finds out that she's leaving him, gets pissed off, end of story."

Frankie nodded. "The sheriff's thought also—especially with the fiancé being a medical student and the surgery performed—but he was on shift or on call the entire weekend. Coworkers confirmed he never left the hospital, only took periodic naps in one of the break rooms. He left several messages on Anna's cell phone beginning Saturday night that started out normal but became increasingly urgent when he didn't hear from her. By Monday, he was frantic, especially after he received a call from her parents saying they hadn't seen Anna since Saturday morning. On Tuesday, he went to her apartment and found her cell phone and the handwritten note about the other man. Sheriff Brenner said he's devastated. They haven't completely excluded him, but I don't think he's our guy."

She paused as Ben processed the information, cracking his knuckles like peanuts at a baseball game. She was used to this display—his fidgeting—almost legendary now in Bureau circles. She imagined the synapses charging inside his head, dissecting, categorizing, and filing away all the pertinent details like a human PC.

"Tell me more about what you saw at the scene," he said.

Frankie filled him and Vicks in. The two teens, the interruption, the medical equipment, the generator, food, clothes, and the oddest part—the mastectomy.

"All of those things speak to advance planning and a calculated motive," Frankie said, "not a boyfriend who just found out his girlfriend was cheating on him. In that scenario, I would expect a murderous rage. This was calm and highly organized."

Ben nodded, but he was analyzing her, she could tell. "What else is bothering you about this case?"

His questions were typical mentor Ben, always seeking to test her responses or make her probe deeper. She wondered if he was really asking or just auditioning her in front of Vicks. He knew how badly she wanted to become the Charlotte field office's lead profiler and work with the National Center for the Analysis of Violent Crime and the Behavioral Analysis Unit. Her misstep on the serial rape case last year had set her back, but her work on the case involving the district attorney's daughter had put her in line again. It hadn't hurt that Sheriff Brenner had reached out to her personally, too.

"The fact that he had a plan in case something went wrong," she said.

"And why does that bother you?" Ben asked.

"Because, once again, creating a plan involves thinking ahead. And thinking ahead usually means he is practiced and careful, which indicates experience."

"We don't have any other victims with this MO," Ben said.

"No. At least none that have been found," she said.

Ben raised an eyebrow. "Have you looked?"

"I've requested lists from NCIC and ViCAP of cases involving missing medical personnel, of arsons or fires at unoccupied homes or property, and of crime scenes involving medical equipment or procedures. We'll see what happens. But my gut ..."

She glanced at Ben, knowing he disliked that word and preferred to stick with facts, but said it anyway. "My gut tells me that if the two teens hadn't interrupted the scene, this unsub would've kept the victim as long as possible. And when he couldn't any longer, or when he was finished ... doing whatever ... then she'd just disappear."

Ben started to interject, but Vicks interrupted. "What did the autopsy reveal?"

She handed him the report. He glanced at it, then handed it to Ben.

"It's preliminary," Frankie said, "but it appears the surgery was limited to the mastectomy. No other signs of cutting or sutures. Also, there was no evidence of any sexual contact—no rape, no semen, and no DNA—not even under the nails. The tox report won't come back for a couple of weeks, but the ME believes the cause of death wasn't the fire but a lethal amount of anesthetic. There were no signs of burning or scarring in the lungs. Anna died before the fire was set."

Ben frowned. "If he killed her peacefully instead of letting her die in the fire, that means he cared for her. He didn't want her to suffer. But then why the mastectomy? To what purpose?"

"I agree it seems contradictory," Frankie said. "The surgery represents taking her womanhood away, and the lack of contact leads me to believe that sexual gratification wasn't his motive. Yet, if our unsub is the man she was leaving her fiancé for, then these acts seem inconsistent. At this point, it's very difficult to understand the motive."

"What are your next steps?" Vicks asked.

"Sheriff Brenner's team will continue to interview Anna's friends and family and comb through her credit cards and phone records. They'll also follow up with the other evidence from the crime scene. We're all anxious to speak to Miguel Herrera, of course, but his doctors said it could be days or even weeks before they can bring him out of his medically induced coma. I told Brenner I'd investigate the medical angle. I have an appointment with a surgeon tomorrow." She turned to Ben. "You want to come?"

"You go," Vicks commanded. "It's time you prepared to take over as NCAVC coordinator anyway. I need Ben to remain on this militia."

Frankie nodded. She forced down the hard lump in her throat. *Shit, did that just happen? Did Vicks say I was going to take over as coordinator?* If she nailed this case, she could make a strong argument for it.

Vicks turned to Ben. "You, this new militia—I don't like them and I don't trust them. They're recruiting heavily and they have plans. Find out what they are. Focus on the militia. Understand?"

Having warned Ben to forsake his diversions, Vicks departed.

Raising his eyebrows, Ben folded the autopsy report and slapped it on Frankie's desk. He revealed two empty hands, palms up. "All yours," he said, "Ms. NCAVC. How does it feel? Do you want me to get you a sash and a crown?"

He must have sensed her apprehension, because he rose from the chair, rounded the desk, and grasped each of her shoulders. "You were there at the scene. You already have a sense of this guy, his handiwork. You know what to do. Go with what the facts tell you. I trust you on this. And if you need anything at all, let me know."

Ben started to leave but stopped in the doorway and turned. "Find him, Frankie. Hunt him. Because if this guy is a repeat and he didn't get to complete whatever he set out to do, then take my word for it, he will. He'll seek out another victim, and soon."

Frankie took a deep breath. She'd just been handed her first solo case. The path to the Behavioral Analysis Unit stretched long and winding in front of her, and she didn't know whether to feel elated or terrified.

She could not screw this up.

CHAPTER 6

Frankie scheduled time with the surgeon through Carolina Medical's public information officer, who told her of the man's graduation from UNC, his expertise in general and emergency surgery, and his participation on the board of the Miracle Project, a popular children's charity. So when Frankie arrived at the ten-story brick building two blocks from the hospital, she did what she always did—imagined the person she was about to meet—and decided he was a distinguished, salt-and-pepper-haired white man in his late forties. Instead she got a six-foot-one African American wearing scrubs who, she was nearly certain, was the same surgeon who'd performed her emergency splenectomy nine months earlier.

Backing up just beyond his view, she double-checked the nameplate beside the door—Dr. Lawrence Banks. Was that him? She'd been under heavy sedation after the knife attack, and his name wasn't exactly what she'd been focused on at the time. What she remembered most was how Ben had teased her relentlessly about dating the doctor after her release from the hospital, which made her break out in a sweat.

Shit. This surgeon—not to mention Ben—was totally going to think she'd arranged this meeting on purpose.

She watched him thumb through a heavy journal and replace it on a bookshelf while humming a soulful tune. It was something old-school—Vandross, maybe. His ample desk, a polished walnut affair, held tidy mounds of manila folders, a single dark-green lamp, a personal planner, and a fern in need of water. She waited until she'd composed herself, then knocked lightly and stuck her head in the door.

"Dr. Banks? Special Agent Frankie Johnson with the FBI. Is this a good time?"

As he turned, the doctor's reaction to her was the same as hers had been to him, his dark-brown eyes landing then freezing, his voice attempting words but finding only silence. He briefly checked his planner, noted something with his finger, and furrowed his brow. "Johnson, you said?"

"Yes. Did the public information officer inform you about my visit? I was under the impression that she'd set up a time for us to speak."

He simply stood there, a dumbfounded expression on his face.

"You don't remember me," she said. "That's okay. It's not like I'm your only patient. You removed my spleen several months ago after … an accident." She smiled, although she was a trace disappointed. She'd hoped he would remember her.

"No, I do," he shot back. "I do remember you. The name just didn't connect. And that was hardly an accident. A man tried to kill you."

She felt a slight flush. "Well, if it's any consolation, I'm surprised to see you too. When the PIO provided me the background of who I was supposed to meet, I expected to see a middle-aged white man with a pair of bifocals perched on his nose."

He flashed a wide grin. "Funny, so was I." He picked up the planner from his desk and showed her his entry. "When the PIO called me, I penciled it in as I heard it. I never connected it to the name I knew you by, which was Frances."

Frankie examined the entry, stood back, and chuckled. The entry read *Frank E. Johnson, two p.m.* "So much for stereotypes. Shame on us. We should know better."

"Yes, we should. Like John Lennon said, reality leaves a lot to the imagination. We should expand our boundaries."

She studied him. *Nice. I'm not the only one who likes to quote people.*

He motioned toward a leather chair opposite his desk. "Please, have a seat, Agent Johnson."

While he settled in behind his desk, her eyes wandered to an open closet where a cream silk dress shirt, pair of olive slacks, and expensive watch dangled from a hook. She briefly wondered if a wedding ring resided in a pocket or on a shelf, then reprimanded herself. She was acting little better than most of the men she met, the ones who introduced themselves with their dicks and followed up with a handshake.

Get yourself together, Johnson.

"How can I help?" he asked.

"We discovered some medical equipment at a recent crime scene and I was hoping you could tell me about the items. I have photographs." She unfastened the clip on the envelope she'd brought and laid the pictures on his desk. "Any information you can provide would help. No detail is too small."

He shuffled through the pictures. "Most of this is standard equipment. Surgical table, lights, EKG monitor, gurney. I'm not sure what I could tell you that would be useful."

"What about distribution?" she asked. "Any way we could track the purchaser?"

"Unfortunately, these items are available from hundreds of supply companies."

Frankie sighed. "That's what I was afraid of." She dug out the photographs of the sharp black object and cylindrical item. "What do you make of these?"

He slid aside the other pictures and picked up the new ones. Interested, he put on a pair of glasses to inspect them closely.

"The one piece almost looks like a rock someone sharpened into a knife-like object," she said, trying to be helpful.

"Not like a knife," he said. "It *is* a knife. A scalpel, to be precise. I can't be certain because it's just a photograph, but the blade appears to be obsidian. You can buy obsidian scalpels, but they're not FDA approved."

Frankie scooted closer on her chair. Obsidian? That sounded rare. And rare meant easier to trace. "If it's not FDA approved, why would a surgeon use it?"

"Because it's about five hundred times sharper than a steel blade. Obsidian is made from volcanic glass. Next to diamonds, it's the sharpest cutting material available and provides a precise cutting edge. Clean, not ragged, so it leaves less scarring. At least that's what the experts say. But they're far more expensive than disposable scalpels."

He swiveled toward his computer. "Most surgical tools are a dime a dozen, but some are one of a kind. They're invented and patented by a doctor or medical company, so they often have a proper name associated with them." He reached toward a shelf that contained several medical texts and handed Frankie a stack of catalogs. "You can get an idea from these."

Though the instruments in the catalogs all looked the same to Frankie—glossy colored images of retractors, rakes, elevators, and forceps—she understood his point. Several were supposedly exceptional, boasting a different design to ease part of the surgical process.

"But obsidian is truly unique," he said. He stopped typing and turned the monitor toward her. He tapped the screen. "I only see three websites offering these scalpels, and two are international. The one in the United States is actually an archeological site, a company that recreates tools used by our primitive ancestors." He turned to her. "It's based in Virginia. I suppose you could give them a call."

She wrote down the phone number and email address.

"What type of surgeons would lean toward using an obsidian scalpel?"

Dr. Banks swiveled back to the computer. "According to these sites, cardiothoracic surgeons are the primary base, followed by plastic surgeons. I only know of one colleague, Dr. Kenneth Whitman, who uses obsidian and he's a cosmetic surgeon. This site says obsidian should only be used on soft tissue, areas that are delicate and prone to scarring."

"Would that include a mastectomy?"

The doctor's face stilled. He grew quiet as he focused on the screen. "Um, I'm not sure. Possibly. Is that what the Bureau is interested in these days? Mastectomies?"

Frankie could tell by his demeanor that he was uncomfortable. Mentioning details of the crime would only increase his discomfort, yet it was necessary if he was to provide helpful information. "Unfortunately, yes. We discovered a young woman at this particular scene, and it appears she'd recently undergone a mastectomy."

He forced a lump down his throat. "Would you like a glass of water?" Without waiting for an answer, he fetched two small cups from a water cooler, filled them up, and gave her one.

Frankie wondered if she should continue, although she couldn't imagine that any surgeon would be squeamish around crime scene photos given what they saw daily. "I was also hoping to get your take on something else, but ..."

His eyes widened. "What is it?"

"Photos of something else we found on the body. I don't think the photographs are too graphic, but ..."

Dr. Banks swished the water in his cup. Frankie sensed he had something to say, but he remained quiet. "It's fine. Believe me, Agent Johnson, there are few things you could show me that could rival the horrors I've seen in the ER."

"Okay." She started to hand the photographs across the desk, then retracted them. She knew closing the proximity between them might only add to his discomfort, but she needed to clarify what was in the photos. "Do you mind if I show you?"

Rising, she rounded the desk, bringing the lamp with her, and clicked it on. "See this? This is a curved incision to the underside of what used to be the right breast, and these are what we believe to be sutures."

Their shoulders briefly touched as he removed a small magnifying glass from his desk, examined the photos, and frowned. "Yes, they are sutures. Ones with an interesting chessboard pattern. I haven't seen these before. You wouldn't happen to have a sample?"

"I do, but it's in evidence."

"No problem." He examined it in more detail. "Do you have a clearer photo of the nipple area?"

"I think so." She sorted through the photographs and found a larger shot of Anna's upper torso. It was more graphic than the close-ups—revealing some of the burned and sloughed skin—but at least it didn't show her face.

The sight gave him pause. "Fire?"

Frankie nodded.

He took a breath before going in for a closer examination. As he studied the picture, he moved it in a circle. "I take it this surgery wasn't done for health reasons?"

"We don't think so. Why?"

"Typically, for cancer patients, what is performed is a simple or radical mastectomy, involving removal of the nipple and areola and possibly lymph nodes and muscle tissue. What was performed here is known as a subcutaneous mastectomy. It's not recommended to treat cancer, as the nipple and areola are spared and more breast tissue is left behind."

"In fact, I'm not sure if I would classify this as a mastectomy or a full-reduction mammoplasty. This anchor pattern under the breast more closely resembles breast reduction surgery. That could be why the surgeon was concerned with scarring."

Frankie jotted down notes. "How about the sutures? You said they were interesting? How so?"

"The pattern itself. Also, there are no drain tubes that I can see, which is odd." He turned back toward the computer. "Let's see what we can find."

This time they scoured the goods together, his fingers flying through key words and images. Their shoulders touched again, and the air warmed between them.

What is it? Why now? The last time she had been in a relationship was over two years ago; it had been nearly eight months since she even noticed someone. So why this, why now, especially when they were looking at photos of a dead girl?

"You ever had surgery?" he asked. "Other than the splenectomy?"

Head displaced in the clouds, she snapped her focus back so she didn't end up stammering something ridiculous. "Besides my tonsils, just once. You?"

"Knee." He stopped typing and lifted his pant leg to show her the scar. "Tore my ACL in college. Ended my football career, but at least I was able to run again. Left quite a scar, though."

"Impressive."

He raised an eyebrow. "Not as impressive as a fugitive with nowhere to go but through you. When it comes to scar competition, you win."

Their laughter echoed through the open door, earning them a disapproving look from a passing nurse with a permanent scowl and a glare to match.

For the next several minutes, they searched various sites but didn't find a match.

"Well, just because it's not popping up doesn't mean it doesn't exist," he said. "Tell you what, I have to do rounds now, but let me do some research and get back with you. In the meantime, you may want to talk to Dr. Whitman about that scalpel."

He cleared his throat. "Of course, you'll have to give me your phone number if you'd like me to contact you."

Frankie removed a business card from her purse and twirled it between two fingers before handing it to him. "Business," she said.

He cleared his throat. "Yes, absolutely."

They both knew it wasn't so.

CHAPTER 7

The militia group calling themselves the New Patriots gathered by the dozens in the open field outside Fayetteville, arriving on motorcycles and in trucks new and old. They were predominately white, male, bearded, and tattooed, and, although Ben disliked stereotyping people, were largely of a particular political domination. If you asked them, they would tell you that they loved their country, their freedom, and their Second Amendment rights but hated taxes, government, and the liberal media.

Which was all fine in Ben's mind—and the FBIs, for the most part—as long as they didn't take to blowing up buildings or harming people who didn't believe in the same ideals they did. To Ben, that was the problem with all these fringe groups. No matter where they were on the political dial, they started out as networks of people with shared beliefs but soon developed the notion that the rest of the world needed to think just like they did. And almost all of them used some form of religion to back up their message. With the right text and the right preacher, they could justify anything, including riots, bombings, and outright genocide.

It was the FBI's job to prevent that from happening, which meant tracking such groups and making sure their agendas didn't start taking on dangerous overtones. One of the best ways to do that was to put in an undercover agent, and for this operation, Ben had chosen his latest field trainee, Special Agent Tom Trimble. Tom—or Tommy, as the agents called him due to his boyish looks—had been with the Bureau for only eighteen months, but he'd done well in other ops to date. Plus, his feigned innocence would play well in this circumstance, where the leaders were looking for recruits to mold and shape. He was a young man with no cause and no direction, and they'd love nothing more than to provide him with his special place in the world.

Ben also believed that having Tommy succeed in this op would finally punch Ben's ticket for a promotion to supervisory special agent. For the past five years, Ben had shown the Bureau his talents for grooming other agents and leading high-stakes ops, and he was ready to move up in the world.

Tommy's normally clean-cut appearance was a no-go for this operation, however, so for the past few months, he'd worked hard to transform himself from the kid on the cover of *Mad Magazine* to a raging redneck with hair to match. Agents at the office had taken bets on whether he could grow facial hair, and most had lost money. Tommy now proudly displayed a respectable four-inch beard along with a matching mustache and ponytail. The biker's jacket, dirty jeans, and wallet chain he wore added to the overall package.

From inside the van that they sat in near the perimeter of the field, Ben gave Tommy the once-over and nodded his approval. He was even a bit jealous. His own undercover gigs were always white-collar, investigations that required a suit and tie and a neatly groomed appearance. Frankie had told him he was too pretty for gritty undercover work, and unfortunately, she was right. When it came to posing as someone else, Ben would always be more JFK Jr. than Al Pacino. Frankie could put on street clothes and fire up that New York accent and no one would know she was a federal agent, but every time Ben put on a motorcycle jacket and jeans, he just looked like an actor in *West Side Story*. Frankie had once said she expected him to break out in a dance routine at any moment.

Ben picked up a set of binoculars and looked across to the open field, where two volunteers were directing those arriving to park. License plates representing the entire East Coast dotted the landscape, but the Carolinas, Florida, and Georgia dominated.

He sighed. "Let the Confederacy ride again."

One of the other two men assigned to the surveillance, an agent known as Big Al, grunted. The other, the techie of the group, paid no attention as he finished setting up the microphone and body camera on Tommy. He made Tommy turn in a circle to make sure everything looked good.

"Okay, get on out there and do your thing," Ben said. He fist-bumped his trainee as Tommy exited the van. "Just remember I'm counting on you."

Outside, Tommy strode toward his motorcycle and put on his helmet, then spoke to test the microphone. "Is it not the definition of irony that we're spying on a group of people that have banded together precisely because they're paranoid that we're spying on them? They see us as an intrusion on their freedom, and we in turn infiltrate their camp with microphones and cameras."

"Hey, be careful you don't turn into one of these guys," Ben said.

Tommy laughed. Stroked his beard. "That would really make you look bad, wouldn't it, partner? Grooming one for the enemy."

Ben huffed. "Might as well put me in the gallows."

"No worries, boss. I got your back." He straddled the bike, revved the engine, and was off. A minute later he joined the crowd in the open field. Ben and the other two agents went to work listening, watching, and recording the conversations and video.

Ben considered what Tommy had said. The Bureau was supposed to be impartial in protecting individual freedoms, yet they were charged with investigating all these groups and keeping everyone safe from anyone who went too far or became too obsessed. But who decided what that meant? Sure, it was easy to say Christians couldn't become clinic bombers, Muslims couldn't become suicide bombers, blacks couldn't burn down neighborhoods, and whites couldn't take down government buildings, but somewhere among all that was a thin line separating free speech, the right to bear arms, and the ability to congregate from the rights of the larger society. Working for the Bureau—or any law enforcement agency—these days was like walking a tightwire with a pack of hungry lions below just waiting for you to slip.

The rally turned out to be an all-afternoon affair. Between speakers, bands played, beer flowed, and flames rose from open barbecue grills. After three hours, Ben wondered how many southern rock tunes he would have to endure before the day was through. A man could take only so much.

Ben switched between watching video and listening to various conversations until a heavily tatted, extremely pale bald man stepped onstage. The man, known as Cloud, was the head of a neo-Nazi group called the Skinners, and, despite his fluffy name he was as mean and vile as they came.

"Heads up on this, Big Al," Ben said. "Use whatever you've got to find this guy's followers. I have a feeling we'll be seeing them in the future. The more we can identify now, the better."

Al responded with his normal grunt.

The speech Cloud proceeded to give lived up to the hate his group was known for, as it was loaded with slurs and attacks against all those they despised: immigrants, socialists, commies, gays, hippies, and liberals. When he went on a particularly nasty rant that used the N word with abandon, Ben could see Big Al—who happened to be black and a former Alabama offensive tackle—grow angrier by the minute. The taps on his keyboard grew so loud that Ben worried he was going to punch through it.

When Cloud finished spewing his wrath, Ben reached over and squeezed the agent's shoulder. "Why don't you take a break?"

Big Al removed his headphones and took a deep breath. The whites of his eyes glowed furiously. He shuddered as if he were trying to shake off the filth. "Every time I get an earful of this shit, I think ... how are we still here, man?"

He got up. "I need some air."

His footsteps rocked the floor of the van as he exited the back. Ben was glad they were stationed behind a tree line far enough away that Big Al wouldn't be seen—even happier Big Al wasn't in Cloud's vicinity. Otherwise Big Al might give the head of the Skinners a special lesson in race relations.

The crowd, now well past the legal limit of intoxication, continued to cheer the speech long after the man had stepped away from the mic. With Al on break, Ben joined the other agent in watching and listening as Tommy made the rounds.

"Mark my word, this country is going to burn if the commies try to take our guns," a soft, chubby man with a deep southern accent said. The alcohol he'd consumed, in combination with the hot sun, had reddened his nose and cheeks so much he resembled a clown.

"Let them try. I'm locked and loaded," a younger, far more buff man in a Guns N' Roses T-shirt said as he pumped a keg and filled his cup.

"They take our guns, then only the criminals will have guns," Tommy said, participating in the rant. "Makes no sense."

"N***, got plenty of guns. I'll be damned if I'm letting them rule," the guy shot back.

Tommy carried on with similar conversations and interjected himself into various groups until he landed in a prized circle. The video from Tommy's camera showed only a part of the other man's face, but Ben recognized him as the leader of the New Patriots. Nicknamed Patton, he was a former Army Ranger who was rumored to have deep ties with the KKK and Aryan Brotherhood.

Tommy didn't waste a moment striking up a conversation with him. He praised the man, the rally, and the slate of speakers he'd organized. "Most sense I've heard in all my lifetime," Tommy said in a practiced slang.

"It's our mission to defend our house," Patton said. "Our way of life is under attack now. We must protect our own. Our families. Our God. Our country."

"I'm here for you," Tommy said. "I'm not former military like you, but I know how to fight, and I shoot pretty good. Also ..." He paused and lowered his voice as if he were letting this small handful of patriots in on his secret. "I'm good at documents. IDs, badges, passports, clearance. I can make anything you need."

One of the men in the group grinned. He put a hand on Tommy's shoulder. A second man standing next to him slapped him on the back. "Hell yes, brother. That's what I'm talking about."

The former Army Ranger took interest. "Good to know. We'll be in touch if we're ever in need of your services. Be sure you give Bill here your contact info."

Tommy gave a nod and did as Patton instructed. Then he uttered a "Nice to meet you guys," gave them a wave, and slipped back into the crowd. He'd planted the seed, and that was all he needed to do. Pushing any harder would only make them suspicious. They would never ask him to produce anything without checking him out first anyway, and it could be months before they gave him a task greater than forging a driver's license or an employee badge. But that was okay, because patience was one attribute the FBI had in buckets. So much so that it often drove Ben to the brink of insanity.

"He's doing good," Ben said. "Striking the right balance."

The other agent nodded. "He went a bit too hard earlier on a conversation surrounding the upcoming NASCAR race in Concord, but most of the time he's shown interest without asking too many questions. Still, you should know there's been a whole lot of side chatter about that race. When I get back to the office, I'll work to single it out from the other conversations."

Ben frowned. That wasn't good. The race was Charlotte's big Memorial Day kickoff to summer, and it would be a packed house. "No specifics? Maybe they're just planning to attend?"

The agent shook his head. "Sounded like more than that. There was discussion about a pit crew and a garage. Tommy was trying to dig, but he didn't get far. Maybe he'll have more insight when we get together tomorrow."

Ben tried to pay attention as Patton took the stage, but his thoughts kept going back to the chatter the other agent had referenced. What the hell would these guys be planning at a NASCAR event? Not to put too fine a point on it, but NASCAR was about the whitest event a person could attend outside these rallies, so what beef would the New Patriots have with them? Ben couldn't imagine, but he decided an extra call to the head of security and a visit to the track would be worth the effort.

CHAPTER 8

The colleague Dr. Banks had referred Frankie to was lean, with baby-fine platinum hair and eyes the blue of winter frost. Yet beneath his soft exterior existed an underlying strength in manner and build, one that reminded her of a swimmer's knifelike ability to slice through the water without so much as a splash. He kept the cuffs on his pinstriped shirt buttoned, his slacks pressed, and his shoes polished, revealing a man concerned about image. That he had his degrees expensively framed and prominently displayed also revealed a man proud of his accomplishments. His office was modern and decorated in tones of brown and blue, containing a Scandinavian-style desk, a bronze sculpture, and abstract art. Yet not a single picture of a wife, child, or friend appeared anywhere. If Frankie had to guess based on first impressions—and of course she had to—she would bet Dr. Whitman to be a man of little emotion, with confidence bordering on arrogance. Whether she was right or not remained to be seen.

He hesitated a moment upon greeting her, then motioned her to a thin, flat chair. "I apologize," he said. "I purchased them because I liked the contemporary design. Little did I know that contemporary also meant uncomfortable."

His southern accent was pronounced but smooth, creating a very subtle layer of charm. A local. Now that she'd lived in North Carolina a few years, it was easy to separate those who'd been raised in the area from those who'd moved in later in life.

Frankie took a seat. Indeed, the chair was uncomfortable, an oddly curved back with a lack of padding that made Frankie wish she had a little more padding of her own—not a wish she had very often. "Thank you for taking the time to see me. I had to coerce your assistant into giving me fifteen minutes of your time. As she tells it, you're booked out months in advance."

He tipped his chin proudly. "Yes. I'm sorry if it was difficult. Now, what procedure are you looking at having done? I can usually guess what a client is interested in before they ask, but you're such a beautiful woman," he said. His eyes wandered over her body. "It must be something only your intimate partners can see."

He said this with such nonchalance that Frankie didn't know whether to feel flattered or aghast. In his line of work, she guessed, checking out the clientele was part of the job. "Sorry, I guess your assistant didn't explain. I'm with the FBI. I'm here on business." She showed him her creds. "Special Agent Frankie Johnson."

His eyebrows rose so high they nearly joined his hairline. "The FBI?" He gave her another once-over. "My, but agents have changed for the better." He leaned forward and smiled. "I bet you're a woman who always gets her man."

She returned his smile but didn't respond. *Yes. Yes, I do.*

"So how can I be of service, Agent Johnson?" he asked, eyebrows lowering. "I can't imagine why the FBI would want to speak with me."

She squirmed in the hard chair, once again trying to get comfortable. "I recently spoke with a colleague of yours who said you had experience using a type of scalpel I'd like to know more about."

She took out the evidence photos of the cylindrical object and sharp, shiny black blade and pushed them across the desk. "The blade is obsidian? I understand it's not largely used, so I was hoping you could tell me more about it."

The moment he saw the photographs, his entire demeanor changed. As he picked up one photo, his other hand selected a pen from his desk and began to twirl it between his fingers. "Obsidian scalpels. These are what you—and the FBI—are interested in? Why? May I ask?"

She didn't want to go into too many details, but since she'd already informed Dr. Banks of the situation, she saw no reason to hold it back from Dr. Whitman. "We discovered this at the scene of a recent crime," she explained. "A very disturbing crime, I might add. I could really use your help."

Like Dr. Banks, Dr. Whitman registered some alarm. His visible stress increased as he twirled and clicked the pen repeatedly and frowned. "I see. Can you provide details?"

"I'm afraid not. What can you tell me about it? Dr. Banks mentioned obsidian was used most often in cardiothoracic or cosmetic surgeries, like those you perform."

Dr. Whitman continued his silence, his eyes never leaving the picture. "Dr. Lawrence Banks? Is that who provided my name? Interesting."

The corner of his left eyelid twitched.

Frankie furrowed her brow. There was something bothering him, but she didn't know what. Did it have to do with the case, Dr. Banks himself, or the fact that Banks had given Whitman's name to Frankie?

"We often play in golf tournaments together," Dr. Whitman added, picking up on Frankie's concern. He clicked the pen two more times. "And he's correct. I use an obsidian in many of my surgeries. It's extremely sharp and carves through tissue with great ease."

Carves through tissue with great ease. Those words brought back the vivid image of Anna lying in the back of the transport—cut, burned, and bagged—and a heavy anger weighted Frankie's chest.

"But the biggest advantage of an obsidian is that it leaves minimal to no scarring," he continued, "which is the preferred result. Face-lifts, rhinoplasty, tummy tucks—if you want your patients looking their best, then leaving a mark is taboo."

"What about breast augmentation or reduction?" Frankie asked.

He leaned back in his chair, the soft leather whirring. "Yes. Why?"

"That's what was done to the victim in this case."

He set the photos down, pushed them back to her. "Oh."

"Where do you order these scalpels from? They must be fairly rare?"

"Yes, they are. I get mine from a supplier in the UK."

He returned to his pen, clicking and twirling.

"I understand they aren't FDA approved," she said.

The clicking stopped. "That doesn't make them illegal."

She raised an eyebrow. She hadn't meant her statement to be a challenge, but he clearly didn't like her insinuation, whatever he believed it to be.

"They just don't hold well if lateral forces are applied," he quickly explained. "An obsidian scalpel can break easily and leave fragments in the wound if a surgeon is not careful. A surgeon must practice to become skilled in its use. I learned about obsidian blades during my plastic surgery residency at Johns Hopkins."

Johns Hopkins. One of the degrees on the wall he'd had expensively framed. The confidence bordering on arrogance was holding true. The verdict was still out on his lack of emotion. She did notice that in addition to medical texts, his bookcase contained several titles on religion and ethics. The man had opinions, or at a minimum, he liked the debate.

She briefly studied an oil painting that caught her eye, a naked woman surrounded by myrtle, roses, and doves, all in abstract. It seemed oddly erotic for a medical office, as did a perpetual-motion device on his desk with both the male and female symbols.

"Do all surgeons learn about obsidian scalpels during their training?" she asked, still not quite able to tear her gaze from the artwork.

"It isn't part of the required curriculum."

"I assume the number of surgeons using them nationally would be fairly small? Even smaller regionally?"

He thought. "Yes. In the hundreds, maybe less."

Frankie nodded. Her adrenaline stirred. This scalpel, this was the way to find Anna's lover—and her killer—she was certain of it. The unsub, as careful as he was, had made a crucial mistake in leaving it behind.

"Do you know any surgeons in the Chapel Hill or Raleigh area who use obsidian scalpels? Maybe you've had a discussion with someone or received questions? Or is there a group board where you can exchange ideas or talk about issues with its use?"

His demeanor darkened. "No."

His posture had gone rigid, telling her he didn't like where the conversation was going. But why? Did he know of someone and didn't want to tell her? Or was it because he used the blades himself?

"That's okay," she said, offering a faint smile. "Given the obsidian's rarity, the suppliers' purchasing lists should narrow the suspect list considerably."

He frowned. Her use of the word *suspect* had gotten his attention.

He took a moment to gather himself. "I get the feeling that you believe a surgeon—one of my colleagues in this profession—has committed this crime you're investigating. Am I correct?"

She had to be careful what she said now. Given Dr. Whitman's use of obsidian scalpels and the small community of surgeons like him, it was quite likely Dr. Whitman knew the unsub, or he could even be the unsub himself. Although the odds would be against it, she couldn't rule out anybody at this point.

"Given the facts in this case, yes, we do believe the suspect has medical experience. However, he may not be a licensed surgeon or doctor. He could be someone with an interest in surgery as well."

His lips thinned as he appeared to think about what to say next. "And this case, does it concern Anna Jamison?"

Frankie perked up. Anna's death had made the news, of course, but his interest piqued her curiosity. "Yes, why do you ask?"

"I knew her. She was a patient."

Frankie had to pick her jaw up off the floor. "She was? What did she have done?"

"That's private, but she wanted to look her best for her upcoming wedding."

Frankie squirmed. "How many times did she come in? When was the last time you saw her? How well did you know her? Why would she come here to see you and not some surgeon in Chapel Hill?" She tried not to dive into interrogation mode, but the questions just flew out. In front of her was a surgeon who used obsidian scalpels and had known Anna Jamison as a patient. It was difficult not to treat him like a suspect or make him feel he was connected to her case in some way.

He waited for her to take a breath before answering her.

"She came in for the first time about six months ago. Her mother lives in the area and is also a patient, so I assume that's why Anna came here as well. I believe the last time she was here was about a month ago."

"How well did you know her? Did she speak of her fiancé or ... anyone else?"

He picked up his pen and began to click and twirl it again. It was clear that for him the pen was akin to a stress ball, a mechanism he used to calm himself. "Not to me,

I'm afraid, although I understand why you're asking—the rumor that Anna was smitten with another man."

He trained his ice-blue eyes on Frankie. "Do you think this is the same man who hurt her? Who performed this ... surgery on her?"

"That's what we're trying to find out."

He nodded. "Well, I can certainly appreciate why someone could fall for her. She was a beautiful, smart, vivacious woman. I asked her out to dinner once myself before I knew she was engaged." He sighed. "It's just a tragedy what happened to her. I was stunned at the news of the fire. The kids, I hope they are okay?"

"They're surviving," Frankie said. "Under the circumstances, I think that's the best they can do." She started to ask another question when the doctor's assistant came in and announced to Dr. Whitman that his next patient was waiting. She gave Frankie a side-eye and left the door open.

Damn. Just when things were getting interesting.

"I guess our time is up," she said. "But one last question. Just out of curiosity, where were you a week ago Sunday between the hours of four p.m. and midnight?"

Dr. Whitman put a hand to his chest. "Am I a suspect?"

"You use obsidian scalpels. You knew the victim." She cocked her head.

His lips thinned. "Goodness. Well, I can tell you that I was home that night and the next several. I'm in the middle of a remodel. Trying to be a real do-it-yourself guy."

"Was someone else with you?"

"I'm afraid not."

"And the following Wednesday between the hours of nine p.m. and three a.m.?"

He shrugged. "Asleep, and also alone."

He didn't have an alibi. Yet he'd willingly admitted an attraction to Anna, which a guilty man wasn't prone to do. Still, she'd have to keep Dr. Whitman on her radar.

He walked her to the door.

"One last thing ..." She pointed to the painting. "Does that represent—"

"Aphrodite, yes. The goddess of love and all things beautiful. I think of her birth as what we do here. Make people into the gods and goddesses they've always wanted to be."

He turned and looked her over, as if he was once again checking for flaws he could fix. "If you'd like to discuss it, or the case, I'd very much like to take you to dinner."

The invitation caught her off guard, as it did his assistant, who stood nearby waiting impatiently. She gave Frankie a disapproving look.

"I appreciate it, but right now, I need to focus on discovering who did this to Anna—and why. I will find her killer." She said it partly out of determination and partly as a warning, but his pale eyes didn't waver.

"Yes, I believe that you will. You're the woman who always gets her man."

CHAPTER 9

Frankie and Ben departed the office at one thirty to grab a late lunch on their way to their next mission, a tour of the Charlotte Motor Speedway in preparation for the upcoming Coca-Cola 600, a NASCAR event that would pour an additional hundred thousand people into the city of Charlotte. For the next week, fans would arrive via plane, caravans, and motor homes to tailgate in parking lots, take the hotels hostage, and send local beer sales through the roof.

The rowdiness of the fans however wasn't the Bureau's concern. Their focus was— as it had been with every event post 9/11—terrorism, and being prepared for an attack. The city had long ago created a multijurisdictional task force to deal with such a crisis, but for an event of this magnitude, every officer in the metro area would be on alert. Today, Ben was to provide a briefing to the speedway's officers on the latest federal chatter, including a warning about the new group his team had been surveilling, and assist in reviewing the area for any security concerns. Frankie went along to help.

They parked in the VIP area where the manager of security greeted them. "We'll meet at the top of the hour for the briefing," he said. "Before then, I'd appreciate it if you'd do a once-around-the-track for any concerns and examine the clubhouse seating and suites." He slapped blueprints in Frankie's open hand and handed a two-way radio to Ben. "Anything new of interest from your side?"

"You'll like it," Ben said. "Government has upped the threat assessment based on regional chatter about an attack on a large-scale event."

"Well, that narrows it down," the security manager said, his ample belly jiggling. "A large-scale event on Memorial Day weekend. Where do we begin?"

"Don't shoot the messenger. We'll see you in forty."

Ben and Frankie gave the blueprints a cursory glance before setting off on their assignment in a golf cart, Ben driving. "Tell me what you've got on the Jamison case."

Frankie informed him about her meetings with Dr. Banks and Dr. Whitman but halfway in, noticed Ben wasn't listening. A wry smile covered his face.

"What?" she asked. "What is that?"

He laughed as he swerved the golf cart around a large pothole. Frankie had to grab the side and hold on. "You didn't remember the doctor's name? A likely story."

Damn. She knew he'd think she'd set it up. "I didn't know. I swear."

"Girl ..." He threw up a hand.

Frankie tried to maintain a serious face, but couldn't. "I knew you wouldn't believe me. You sound just like my mama."

"Mama is a smart lady. Mama knows bad acting when she sees it."

Frankie slugged him. It only made him laugh harder. His thick, black hair blew in the breeze. He turned to her and winked. "Did you at least get his number?"

"Shut up. I'm not talking to you."

She waited for him to have his fun and turn back to serious matters.

"Did you check into this Dr. Whitman?" he eventually asked.

"Not yet. I've been busy, and I got big news this morning. ViCAP got a hit on the green-braided suture. Case of arson in Hendersonville, a barn that burned down two years ago."

Ben whistled. "No body, I take it? Anyone missing?"

"Not that I know of, but I'm heading to Hendersonville tomorrow to speak with the detective who worked the case. Maybe he'll have an idea."

"Was that the only hit?"

"On the suture, yes, but regionally, ViCAP listed more than fifteen arsons that took place on unoccupied property in the past three years. Seems we have a few jurisdictions looking for an arsonist but not a serial killer."

"Fifteen?" Ben talked over the wind as he accelerated. "Let's hope they're not all related. I'd hate to think this guy has been active that long without getting noticed."

He stopped the golf cart at one of the lots and examined the placement of the parking cones. He radioed the security manager. "What's the required distance on these cones? Looks like you could drive a truck right through gate number one."

A squawking sound came over the radio. "Part of infield access. We'll check it."

Ben shook his head. "I hope so."

After doing a once-around of the entire track, they parked the cart, checked a maintenance shed, then took the elevators up to the clubhouse seating and suites. Ben shined a flashlight behind one of the many food service counters. "Damn, I don't like these places. Too many vendors with too many employees. Too easy for terrorists to get their guys behind the scenes—ticket takers, delivery guys, food servers."

Frankie glanced down at the track; she had a nice view of the finish line. She watched Ben buzz around, feeling his restlessness grow. It never took much to get him roused: his four whiny sisters in Boston, the car doing fifty in the fast lane, the hypocritical politicians and preachers speaking their minds on television.

"Not to mention all the motor homes and campers they allow on the infield," she said. "How in the hell do you protect such a place without a constant contingent of officers, K-9s, and metal detectors?"

"You don't," Ben said. "And even if you did, it wouldn't protect you from the guys outside in the parking lot, or the guys flying overhead. Where there's a will ..."

She huffed. "Remind me not to attend any more major events."

"What about missing persons?" he asked, returning to their prior subject.

Frankie grimaced. Little depressed her more than combing through missing persons records, but in this case, it had been a necessary evil. In the previous year alone, over 600,000 cases of reported missing individuals had been entered into Bureau records, and although the majority of those individuals had been located, 2,079 remained missing. In total, the Bureau had 87,500 active missing person records at the end of the year. Given the statistics, Frankie couldn't help but feel the good guys were fighting an impossible battle. She wondered whether, if she had kids, she'd ever let them leave the house.

"Two possibilities using the same parameters as the ViCAP search," she said. "One was a radiologist who left a similar letter behind to her family as the one that Anna did, but she died in a hit-and-run accident just days later, so she doesn't fit the profile. The other is an oncology nurse from Hickory who went missing last year. The report says they suspect the husband, but my instincts tell me otherwise."

Ben shouldered open a reluctant door and checked inside. "Instincts are like farts, all gas without substance."

Frankie grunted. She shined a flashlight in his face. "Nice. Is that from Ben's guide to deep thoughts?"

"I have many wise sayings."

She smirked. "Call it gas if you want, but I have great instincts and you know it." She poked a finger in his chest and raised an eyebrow. "What about that new guy you were all atwitter over that I warned you about?"

That Ben was gay was knowledge only Frankie and a few others possessed. She'd urged him countless times to come out to the Bureau, as the Office of Professional Responsibility could see his hiding as a blackmail risk, but Ben wasn't ready. Though the Bureau had made headway with homosexuality in the past decade, as it had with women, Ben still felt revealing himself would impede his career path.

Ben followed Frankie from the room with a fallen bottom lip. "I wasn't atwitter."

"Please. I've seen hummingbirds with less twitter."

He chuckled as his shoes—his very polished shoes—shuffled across the floor. "Okay, yes, Casey was a little off-center."

Frankie bit the cap off a bottled orange juice and spit it away. "He was the freaking Leaning Tower of Pisa."

For the next two minutes, they laughed as Frankie now took her turn teasing him. It felt good to ease the tension of the week, if only for a moment.

It ended when they came upon two men tinkering with an electrical box.

"Hey, you there," Ben shouted. He approached and showed the workers his creds. "What are you doing? You have a work order?"

One of the men produced a mustard-yellow paper and handed it to Ben. While Ben examined it, Frankie asked them to step away from the box and stood by, resting her palm on the butt of her Glock. The two men shook their heads and muttered in a heavy accent, but they complied. After Ben received confirmation over the radio, he handed the paper back to them. "Okay, you're clear. Sorry for the inconvenience."

Frankie gave the men another once-over before joining Ben. "Legit, huh?"

He shrugged. "At least on paper. Like I said before, anyone can be employed."

They headed to the next suite to begin their inspection. Frankie decided a change of subject was in order. "Tommy said this New Patriot group is bad news."

Ben looked beneath several seats before raising his head. "White supremacists disguising themselves as revolutionaries? Yes, I'd say so. And word is they're planning something during this race. That's why I had to come today. I can't let that happen."

Frankie stopped searching the seating area. It bothered her how Ben always took things from the collective *we* to the individual *I*. "Not taking it personally again, are you?" she asked, genuinely concerned about the amount of pressure he put on himself. "Don't forget we work as a group. You've got Tommy, Big Al, and the other agents to back you."

"So says the woman who ended up alone in the mountains with a killer and is promising personal justice for Anna Jamison now."

She smirked. "I relied on you to get the message last year when I didn't think through the consequences of my plan. You showed up. I trust you'll do the same if it ever happens again. And I'll be there for you too. That's what a team does."

Ben's smile faded. He clicked off the flashlight and took a step toward her. "But I almost didn't get your message, Frankie. Truth is, we got lucky. Group efforts are great, but if you go out on your own—especially if you go rogue—you'd better be ready to finish the job alone. That's all I'm saying. That's why I make it personal. Sometimes all you've got is you."

She studied him, wondering where this was coming from. What was he saying? That he wouldn't back her up anymore once she was appointed NCAVC coordinator and he was an SSA? For four years she'd had Ben's back when it counted most, and she'd like to know she could expect the same from him. There had been times she'd seen his loyalty to the Bureau outweigh his devotion to team members—it was one of the few things she didn't like about Ben—but he'd never turned on her. At least, not yet.

He'd started to walk away when she grabbed his arm. "Just promise me one thing," she said. "You'll still be there if I need your advice and support. You won't leave me hanging."

He stopped. "Of course. Why would you think otherwise?"

She started to say more but decided against it. She'd said what she needed to say.

CHAPTER 10

He was growing impatient waiting for the last of the office staff to depart for the night. The obese clerk was taking her damn sweet time, organizing her paperwork into three evenly stacked piles, and watering a yellowed philodendron and wilted African violet before finally heading home for the evening. He felt sorry for the plants, office pets trapped with their lonely, overattentive master. He bet she was the sole employee sorry the day had ended, the only one who had nothing but another night of watching inane sitcoms to look forward to while the rest of the world participated in their lives. Had she not been so uninteresting, so patently plain and abhorrent, he might have sympathized with her plight, but she was, and so he didn't. She was not the kind of woman who harbored his attention.

Not like Anna Jamison.

Standing at the window with his arms crossed, he mourned Anna's loss while watching the woman exit the main door six floors below and waddle across the street to her dented Honda. Once she was gone and he was alone in the office, he singled out the small jagged key on his ring and opened the lockbox he kept beneath a hidden panel in the bottom drawer of his desk. The aroma of lavender wafted out as he lifted the lid, reminding him of the doctor he could not refuse.

He removed the photographs of her, preop and postop. He shivered at the first picture, the beauty of her naked body lying immobilized on the table. He recalled how she'd looked so peaceful sleeping, happy to be with him, then so frightened when she'd woken up. She had lurched against the restraints and begged him to release her, but he'd whispered and held her until her tears had stopped. Later, she'd said those triumphant words—that she loved him and would stay with him—and oh, after all the months of courting, how he'd wanted to believe her. So he'd undone the restraints and guided her to the mirror to show her what he'd done, and how beautiful they looked together.

See my beauty. See what I have done?

But she hadn't seen the beauty. Instead, her cheeks had sagged and a repulsion she couldn't hide had filled her eyes. She'd become angry, attacked him, and run.

Why? Why had she done that?

He stroked a finger across a second photograph, this one taken of Anna as she'd dined with her parents the evening before they were joined together. She'd looked so lovely in that particular shade of blue, her sandy hair and jewelry shining like she was royalty.

Finding her engagement ring among the other treasures in the box, he slid it onto his pinkie. If only she'd worn it for him, and he a matching one for her. That he hadn't gotten to finish with Anna didn't please him, but neither did her trickery. She'd been lucky he'd killed her with the anesthetic instead of letting the fire have its way with her. In the past, he hadn't always been so understanding.

He searched through the box and chose a cloth necklace belonging to one of his former girls. This one, for instance, had not died so well. After flirting with him for months, she too had tried to run when he'd decided it was time for them to be together. He recalled how the rain was pelting the windshield when she charged from the moving vehicle, how her body rolled and tumbled across the railroad tracks. Then she—wet, a blur between the wipers and dull headlights—ran limping down the lone country road, trying to escape. But he taught her a lesson. If she didn't want to be with him, then she wouldn't live to be with anyone else—that was his rule.

The news said at least two other vehicles had run over her before one driver finally realized it wasn't an animal in the road but a woman.

He closed his eyes. *Stupid girl.*

A rush of anger overtook him and he fisted the photograph in his hand. He loved Anna—loved all his girls—and yet they'd all tried to leave him. After leading him on for months, they'd turned and denied him, refusing to accept him. And every time, his mother's words would echo in his ears.

No one could love you. No one ever will.

The memory of his mother made his blood rage. He envisioned her standing in the kitchen in her sunflower-yellow dress and apron, looking so damn prim. She was baking cookies, humming a hymn, part of her endless preaching. Seeing him, she ordered him to join her, to stand on the stool and help mix the ingredients.

No. No more. Not ever.

When she issued the command a second time, her eyes narrowed into thin reptilian strips. To defy her, he took a step back and stripped his clothes off, the act she most abhorred. It would earn him a beating, but it didn't matter. He was sick of her judgment and control, disgusted by her bright colors and clown-like face that masked the true woman inside. His hatred of her was greater than any pain his body would bear.

She stormed to the utility door, apron flying, and motioned to his father. Moments later the rumble of the lawn tractor died and his father's footsteps crackled on the gravel drive. His father, a burly man who smelled of alcohol and a three-day sweat, ducked beneath the doorjamb and thundered across the wooden floor. "We got a problem here?"

As he drew the belt from his pants, his eyes bled fire, though whether from the sin of rage or whiskey, it was hard to tell. He raised his fist to the sky and started preaching: *God created man to live in His image. You are His reflection. Every time you rebel, you blaspheme God. You are a product of the devil. Release this evil spirit at once!*

While his father proceeded to beat the devil out of him, his mother hovered in the corner and prayed for her child's salvation. For ten minutes, twenty, the lashes stripped his skin and parts of his soul—his very evil soul—until his father was spent. When it was over, his mother closed her eyes and uttered a *Thank you, Jesus* while he stood there bleeding on the kitchen floor.

Reliving the humiliation, he crumpled the picture of Anna until one of the sharp edges cut his finger and he bled. He wanted to kill his parents all over again.

The computer in his office flashed a local news bulletin, bringing him out of his daze. He had his settings adjusted to signal him anytime there was breaking news about Anna.

The sheriff who'd found Anna suddenly appeared on-screen. He gave an update, stating that they had new leads but nothing they could talk about yet. He said the family was devastated and noted that the FBI was assisting. The news channel showed the remains of the old farmhouse, then switched to a reporter standing in front of the police station. After the reporter provided an update on the medical examiner's findings, the station returned to the sheriff for a final comment.

But the man didn't hear a word he said.

Because behind the sheriff stood the woman who'd visited the other day. He'd been in utter admiration of her then, but planted statuesque there to the side of the aging sheriff, she looked like a queen, her honey skin glowing and almond eyes shining. He narrowed his focus to admire her when she turned right into the camera and winked at him. He closed his eyes, momentarily unbelieving, but when he opened them again, she repeated the action.

Yes, there it is. She winked!

She was talking to him. Signaling him.

Forgetting all former thoughts of his bastard parents, he slid into his office chair and pulled the computer monitor close. He stared intently at the image of her, placed a finger on her face and trailed it down her the length of her body.

What do you want to tell me? I hear you. I'm listening.

As they finished the press conference by taking questions from reporters, she did something he would never forget. As she turned on a heel to leave, she cast a final gaze over her shoulder to acknowledge that he was watching.

He caught his breath. *She's sending me a sign.*

He sat back and put his hands together in prayer. The other day he hadn't been certain if the feelings she'd aroused in him were mutual, but now there she was, giving him her message that yes, indeed, it was true.

Oh, my love. I hear you. I see you.

He'd start preparing for her right away. Alas, there was still hope for love.

But first he had to take care of that other annoying detail. He couldn't risk waiting any longer. He had made mistakes—the scalpel, the sutures, leaving evidence behind—but nothing compared to a witness. The boy could wake any day and ruin everything. First, he'd take care of the boy, then he'd take care of his new love.

CHAPTER 11

rankie had always found the western part of North Carolina stunning. Raised in Queens and DC, she'd hadn't had much early exposure to nature, so the first time her father took her for a drive on the Blue Ridge Parkway from Virginia into North Carolina had been like a trip to a magic land. With multicolored trees, fog-covered mountainsides, and wildflowers blooming unhindered, it had always brought her a sense of serenity and oneness. Yet today felt different. All that foliage seemed suffocating and isolating. It was possible the same man who'd stalked and killed Anna Jamison had hunted here as well.

Because it was after hours and Mrs. Hatcher was out of town, Detective Daniel Hatcher had asked Frankie to meet him at his residence nestled in the hills away from town. Many people used the homes here as summer residences when they sought to escape the heat and humidity farther south, but Hatcher and his family clearly lived in this house year-round. A half cord of cut wood remained stacked in the backyard, unused from the mild winter, and two bikes and a big wheel occupied the lawn and driveway out front.

She rang the bell, and a minute later Detective Hatcher opened the door. Dressed in jeans and a T-shirt, Hatcher still gave off that cop vibe, with broad shoulders, a barrel chest, and precision-trimmed gray hair. Given the young ages of the three kids sharing a bowl of macaroni and cheese in the family room, Frankie guessed he had started his family a bit later than his counterparts.

"This here is Cory, Billy, and my daughter, Hannah," he said, his words running together as if they'd been parked on a hill with no way to keep them from crashing into each other.

The children turned to look at her. Two boys, around nine and seven, barely took notice, but a dark-haired girl, the youngest of the three, curled into herself and smiled. Her big brown eyes were laced with some of the longest lashes Frankie had ever seen.

"She's a little shy," Hatcher whispered. Which didn't appear to be the case for either Cory or Billy, as they opened their mouths to gross each other out with the sight of their chewed food, then fell backward into the couch, giggling.

Hatcher sighed. "Let's go in the kitchen. I promise I'll have better manners."

They passed through a dated living room with paneled walls and carpeting into a small kitchen that was equally old-fashioned. He pulled a chair with a country-blue cushion out from the dining table for her to sit on. "Now, tell me, what's your interest in our arson case two years ago?"

"You've heard about the case in Lexington? The one where the perpetrator courted the victim and took her to live in an abandoned farmhouse before he set it on fire?"

He nodded. "Who hasn't? Terrible, just terrible."

"Before her death, that victim had undergone a surgical procedure at the hands of our unsub. There was a green-braided fiber discovered on her person which turned out to be a surgical thread. On ViCAP, you reported finding a similar fiber in that arson case."

The detective flinched like a man who'd been backhanded after reaching up a waitress's skirt. "A fiber I assumed was from a piece of clothing or carpet. Not a surgical thread. You sure?"

"We think it's related, plain and simple," she said. "There's evidence at the scene that makes us believe the killer has acted before."

"Like?"

"The organization and planning. He pursued the victim for four months, sought out abandoned property, and brought in his own tools and equipment to do the job, among other things."

"You're talking about a multiple, a serial?"

"Yes."

"How many others?"

"We're not sure. This may be the first we can link based on the surgical thread. Problem is, we have no victim that we know about. No missing persons."

The detective rubbed his chin, frowned. The lines on his forehead deepened. "That may not be true," he said. "Hold on a minute."

He rose from the table and went into a small office nook adjacent to the kitchen, where he booted up a computer and tapped keys. Frankie didn't realize she was holding her breath until a few minutes passed.

The printer whined.

When he returned, he removed his reading glasses and handed her a piece of paper. "We had a missing person report filed right about then on a Melanie Higby."

Frankie quickly scanned it. She was twenty-nine, a brunette with a big smile and green eyes. She didn't work at a hospital, however, as Frankie would've suspected, but at a flower shop. "It adds up," she said, "except the occupation. Wait, where is this flower shop?"

"Right across the street from Pardee Hospital."

Frankie tapped the paper. "So not an employee of the hospital, but I bet she delivered plenty of arrangements to the patients there."

The detective nodded. "She was well known by the staff."

The incessant buzzing in Frankie's chest was joined by an equal weight of dread. This was one time she hated to be right. "That's our girl. Tell me about her."

He rejoined her at the table. "From what I can remember, we suspected she left on her own. That's why I recalled it, once you mentioned the Jamison case. Melanie Higby had a suitor too."

Frankie's heart sank. "She did? Did this suitor send her letters, poetry?"

"Yes, I believe he did." He sighed. "I can't believe ... I didn't even think ..."

"You have those?"

"If they're not in evidence, the girl's mother should have them."

"The mother, where is she?"

"In a nursing home." He explained how the mother, who had Parkinson's, had needed the daughter to take care of her. After Melanie disappeared, the mother had asked a friend to bring her to the station to fill out the missing person report. "She was adamant that her daughter wouldn't take off without explanation, charming lover or not."

Frankie brushed her sweaty palms across the top of her pants. She had to be careful how she phrased what she was thinking. "Yet the Hendersonville PD bought the theory that she abandoned her mom and left her to the hands of the state. Why?"

She wasn't trying to be accusatory; she simply needed the whole story. This unsub was doing something to make these women leave without even a good-bye. It was difficult to believe he could be seductive enough to have convinced Melanie and Anna to leave loving families, and yet it seemed that was exactly what was happening.

She watched as Detective Hatcher sorted through the innuendo in her statement before he offered a shrug. "I figured he was a charming man, offering a better life. Melanie didn't have a history of relationships, and she was none too enamored with being her mother's caretaker. She'd lost a lot of weight recently and was ready for a new life. I expected her to call her mother later, but she never did. By the time I suspected there might be more to it, I didn't have a lick of evidence to follow up on."

At least he'd kept it to the first person. He wasn't blaming anyone else. And Frankie couldn't say that given a similar scenario, she wouldn't have suspected the same thing. It was hard in this day and age to identify who might disappear intentionally.

"Her mother, can she talk?"

"She has good days and bad, but I haven't seen a day when she was too sick to talk about Melanie. She refuses to die until she finds out what happened to her daughter. If she doesn't call us monthly, one of the nurses at the home does. She's relentless."

"No, she's just a mother," Frankie said.

At that moment, the little dark-haired girl entered the kitchen, dragging a teddy bear by one arm. Sliding between the table and the chair, she hooked an arm around her daddy's waist and pulled herself into his lap. Detective Hatcher melted under the attention. Frankie hoped that when she had kids, she'd have a girl so sweet on the world.

He hugged her for a minute then kissed her on top of the head. "Do Daddy a favor and go get your pjs on and get ready for bed. I'll be up to check on you in fifteen minutes." The little girl muttered an "Okay," then brushed a lazy hand across her sleepy eyes and slid back to the floor. Her bare feet slapped across the linoleum, the teddy bear hanging by one arm dragging right behind her.

Frankie watched Detective Hatcher look after his daughter, knowing exactly what he was thinking—at one point, Melanie Higby had been that age. One day Hannah could be Melanie Higby.

He rubbed his tired face before he turned back. "What do you want me to do?"

"First, get me copies of those poems and letters. Then reopen the case. Let's find Melanie Higby."

CHAPTER 12

The next day, Frankie traveled to speak with Ryan Dearborn, husband of the missing oncology nurse in Hickory, a city sixty miles north of Charlotte. Ryan was forty-seven, with gray temples and aqua eyes, and despite what the police believed him to be—a wife killer—he welcomed Frankie in. He sat across from her, legs uncrossed, fingers intertwined, eyes vacant. His two daughters, ages ten and twelve, each claimed an arm at their dad's side.

"What happened that day?" Frankie asked.

"We went to Lake Hickory for a picnic—me, Em, and the girls. It was her idea. The kids were excited. A few minutes after we arrived, Emily said she forgot the mustard and took the minivan to the nearest convenience store."

Dearborn curved his hand into a fist and held it tight. "She didn't come back."

Both of his girls cuddled closer to him. They were protective, eyeing Frankie through suspicious doe eyes. They could be a tool the man was using to convince her of his innocence, but given their age, and the amount of acting she'd seen in her life growing up with her mother, she didn't think so.

"I waited four hours before I finally called the police. I kept thinking she would show up with an explanation—a flat tire, traffic—or at least call me. I left a dozen messages on her cell phone. I knew something was wrong by the time I called the police, but I didn't want to frighten the girls. I was certain she'd been in a car wreck."

The layered guilt in his tone was like molasses, thick and immobile. He was punishing himself for not calling earlier. Maybe they could have found her. Four hours? He'd given his wife a good head start. This was one time patience wasn't a virtue.

He hung his head. "I never imagined that she would've been abducted. I mean, what are the odds?"

Frankie nodded. *Abducted* was his word. But was that what had happened? Or was this a man who wanted her disappearance to appear like a kidnapping or couldn't accept that his wife had left him?

"They found her phone in the minivan?" she asked.

"Yes, unfortunately, because the police said if she'd taken it with her and left it on, there was a chance of locating her."

"Cell phone pings. It's proved a lifesaver in many circumstances," she said. "Either your wife knew that and didn't want to be found, or her ... abductor ... made her leave it behind. How about her state of mind? Nothing seemed out of the ordinary with her before all this occurred?"

He nodded harder than necessary. "Yes, as I told the police, she was very depressed the previous night. She didn't sleep at all. She cried on my shoulder and told me she loved me. I kept asking her what was wrong, but she just shook her head. The picnic was her idea. She wanted to spend the day with us."

Frankie frowned. In her estimation, that type of behavior sounded like a suicide, not a murder. She wondered if she could be wrong about Emily having been a victim.

She regarded the thin, brunette girls, who seemed frozen. "Mr. Dearborn, could I speak to you privately for a few moments?"

He looked at the two. "Girls, why don't you go watch one of the new movies?"

They slid off the couch, understanding that the adults were dismissing them so they could talk. Once they settled in the other room, Frankie continued. "I know this is a tough question, but is it possible your wife committed suicide?"

He swung his head from side to side. "No, no way."

"People do strange things when they get depressed."

"You don't understand. She was squeamish about death. She'd call me in every time there was a spider in the house. She couldn't kill anything, let alone herself. The police—believe me, they did a thorough search. They wanted to find her, mainly so they could convict me, but that didn't matter. The fire department searched the lake with sonar equipment. The sheriff's department scoured the entire park. The townspeople came out in droves, enough so they could cover every square mile. Nothing."

Frankie nodded. In her preliminary research, she had found what he was saying to be true. He was displaying honesty by not leaving anything out. The police had even suspected that he'd hired an accomplice to abduct his wife and killed her later.

"And before you ask about the murder-for-hire theory, that's ridiculous. How would I know she would go to the store? She's the one that suggested going, not me."

Question answered.

"Okay, one last thing. Was it possible your wife was leaving you?"

Dearborn shifted, uncomfortable. "No. Maybe. I don't know." He sighed. "The police said I made those poems and letters up, that I created those as an afterthought to cast suspicion somewhere besides me. They said if it had been a real love affair, the letters would have been traceable to a real address, a real person."

Frankie froze, feeling like the proverbial deer in the headlights. "Wait, there were poems?" She flipped through the police report. "The report doesn't mention any letters or poems."

Frowning, Ryan walked over to a secretary in the hall and removed a folder from one of the drawers. "Here, I kept them."

She shuffled through the papers, read. Much of the language was the same as what she'd seen in Anna's letters, expressing the unsub's outpouring of love, but it wasn't until she came across an ode to Emily's beauty that her heart did a deep dive. The verses were identical to those given to Anna Jamison except that the names had been exchanged.

Frankie tried to breathe, but her lungs couldn't get air. This was big. There was no way Ryan Dearborn would pick the same ode one year before Anna had received it and print it with his wife's name. Frankie had her first solid evidence that the same unsub who'd lured and murdered Anna Jamison had acted before.

They officially had a serial killer on their hands.

"You only found these after she disappeared?" Frankie asked, still breathless.

He wrung his hands. He seemed reluctant to talk about it. "No. I mean ... most of them, yes, but two I found earlier. I confronted her. We argued."

"What did she say?"

"She swore to me that she didn't know who they were from. She said one was left in a sealed envelope at the nurses' station with her name on it, and the other one was in our mailbox, but hadn't been mailed."

"You didn't believe her?"

"No. I accused her of having an affair. In the months before she disappeared, Em was having a bit of a midlife crisis. She bought a sports car. She talked about us traveling to Italy. She even got her breasts enlarged. The affair—I assumed that was just another escapade and I demanded that it stop. But she insisted she didn't do anything wrong. She even acted spooked by the letters. She felt like someone was stalking her."

He buried his face in his hands. "My God, I should've listened to her. She was asking for my help, and instead I accused her of something horrible."

Which was probably why Emily had been afraid to bring it up to him again when she received more letters—and why she'd been fearful the night before she left him. Had she known who her admirer was? Or had she just suspected the man would be coming for her?

Frankie's thoughts whirred.

"Did she happen to leave you a handwritten letter telling you she was leaving?" she asked. Both Anna and Melanie had left a handwritten note behind, explaining their love for a new man. Anna had even told a friend.

His face reddened. A subtle nod came seconds later. "Yes. I found it in the van. But she didn't write it. I mean, it was in her handwriting, but it wasn't ..." He sighed. "How can I explain? The words used weren't her words."

Frankie understood. "What did the police think of that note?"

He huffed. "It was the one thing they agreed with me on. They said I wrote the letter as part of this attempted cover-up they thought I was staging."

"Do you still have it?"

"I have a copy." He got up and retrieved it. "She left it in the driver's seat."

Frankie read it. It was scarce a note as any, a simple apology followed by her expression of love for another man. She could see why the police thought it was a ruse—it was written as if Emily's leaving was no more substantial than going to the store with the intention of coming back later.

She studied it, now wondering if these women were leaving voluntarily. If Emily hadn't really known her admirer, maybe Melanie and Anna hadn't either. But then why would they willingly write a note and go along with their abductor?

Were they being threatened? Coerced?

Ryan picked up on her disturbance. "What? What's wrong?"

Frankie attempted to gather herself so she could tell him about the link to Anna, but she didn't have to. The sallow skin near his eyes and cheeks sagged. "Oh my God. You think Em might have run off with the same man who killed that girl in Lexington—that medical student? She left a note behind to her fiancé, didn't she? They printed one of the poems he gave her on the front page of the newspaper."

Ryan Dearborn curled into his lap and began to weep.

Frankie reached over and rubbed the man's shoulder. "We don't know that. Ryan, we don't know that. But ..." She reviewed the letters again, shook her head. "I'm not going to sugarcoat it. There are similarities in the language. Are you certain your wife never mentioned anyone new in her life? What about the witness reports that say Emily left the convenience store with a woman? If Emily had been in trouble, would she have called a friend?"

Tears streamed down his cheeks. The eldest daughter poked her head around the corner, concerned for her father. "No, no one," he said. "I spoke with everyone she knew. The woman was just some stranger in the store, as far as I know."

He wiped his eyes. "Listen, I've thought about this so many times." He glanced behind him to see if his daughter had retreated, kept his voice at a whisper just in case she returned. "Even if she left me, there is no way—no way—she would ever have left Jen and Jan. They were her entire life. There was no man—or woman—in the world who could take the place of her kids. Understand?"

Frankie did. And, she felt certain Ryan Dearborn was right. It was difficult enough to believe that Anna Jamison would voluntarily leave her fiancé, and Melanie Higby would leave her ailing mother, but for Emily Dearborn to leave her kids? No amount of evidence could convince Frankie of that.

Ryan grabbed Frankie's hand. "Please," he said, "find my wife. I didn't kill her."

CHAPTER 13

Frankie stormed up the two flights of stairs to her office, no patience to wait for the elevator. She wanted to shout the news to Ben, to Vicks, to anyone who would listen. They officially had a serial killer on their hands. *How many other victims are there? How soon will he charm another?* Question after question raced through her mind.

Reaching the third floor, she flung open the door and charged through the matted gray cubicles, ignoring greetings and a question about Miguel Herrera's progress. She bypassed the kitchen and the smells of burnt coffee and popcorn, on a mission to hit up ASAC Vicks. She needed resources, maybe a task force. She needed to contact the BAU. But as she rounded a corner on the way to his office, she could hear a commotion of enormous proportions brewing. Some of the voices she didn't recognize, but one she did—it was Anna Jamison's father, and he was not happy. A city weekly had published a second poem given to his daughter before her death.

"I want to know who keeps leaking information to the media. They're making my daughter's death into tabloid fodder and the sheriff up there doesn't care. I want whoever is doing this fired!"

The man's skin was a fiery scarlet normally reserved for stove burners and the tips of branding pokers. The flesh beneath his eyes was pulsing and swollen, like boils ready to burst. Across from him, Vicks appeared little better, his trademark scowl and neck vein prominently displayed against flesh bordering on the shade of a beet. Frankie didn't know what kind of pull Jamison had exercised to get inside the Charlotte field office and in front of Vicks, but it had to be something—his finger was solidly in the middle of Vicks's chest.

As soon as Ben caught a glimpse of Frankie, he made a little whipping motion with his head. She stopped and started to retreat, but not before she caught the barrage of outrage that flowed next from Jamison's lips. "I want to know what you're doing to find this man. This man is a killer of women and you give me what? A female agent?

Young, inexperienced. You really think a woman is the best person to handle this Romeo? He'll probably charm the pants off her too. Is that the best you can do for me?"

Ben tried to intervene. "Sir, listen, you're grieving right now and you're highly emotional. Believe me when I say we're doing everything possible to assist the sheriff in this investigation. Despite what you believe, he is aware of the leak and is investigating the matter."

Anna's father wheeled. "Don't patronize me, son. Yes, I'm grieving. Yes, I'm angry. My daughter was butchered by a psychopath. Time is running out."

Frankie took a deep breath but held her tongue. Part of her wanted to lash out, but she understood that the man's angry words were coming from a hurt place. She could tell Ben also understood, although the man's flippant *son* comment hadn't set well with him. She watched Ben open and close a fist at his side, attempting to maintain control.

The door to a nearby conference room flew open, and four additional men spilled into the mix of humanity gathered on the floor. Frankie knew two were Homeland Security, but the others were strangers. Vicks's personal assistant rushed after them, looking at her boss like a panicked dog who had failed to protect him.

One of them spoke. "ASAC Vicks, pardon the interruption, but this is a most urgent matter." He held up a binder with a bright-red label. "New chatter has come across about Sunday's race. We must assess this situation right now."

"My daughter's death is of the utmost priority," Jamison said.

The DHS agent turned toward Anna's father. "Sir, with all due respect, I'm very sorry for your loss, but if we don't assess this latest brief, we could have five or ten thousand dead by Monday. Understand?"

And with that, it was open season on Vicks. At once, voices rose—one over another—resulting in sheer pandemonium. Vicks let them go at it for a minute until he spread his substantial arms and yelled, "Enough!" His voice, deep and baritone, silenced the room. The entire office of agents stood at attention.

"You four, back in the conference room now," he ordered. "Mr. Jamison, take your concerns up with Sheriff Brenner. Agent Andrews, I don't know what it was you initially came to ask me, but ask me tomorrow."

"Resources," Ben muttered. "I need more—"

"Later," Vicks shouted. Ben stepped back.

Jamison stepped in front of Vicks as he started toward the door. For someone who wasn't in law enforcement, he was a brave soul. "Just tell me you will assign more resources to my daughter's case," he said. "There must be someone else. Please."

"Look, I'm telling you, Agent Johnson—"

"Is here," Frankie interrupted, shoving her way between the cadre of white men, and feeling like the whole of minority America trying to get attention. Ben tried to grab her arm as she brushed by, but she jerked away. The feisty part-Cajun from Queens had arrived to the party. "Sorry I'm late to such a fais do-do."

Jamison brushed a hand across his face. Sweat pooled on his brow.

Frankie wheeled toward him. "Sir, can I ask you a question? Anna was studying to be a doctor. You believed in her skills and abilities, did you not? To the point that you would put your life in her hands?"

He pulled his chin in, doubling the flesh beneath it.

"I'll take that as a yes. If your daughter, as a trained professional, was assigned a critical patient, and the patient's father stormed in and demanded this young woman be removed and a man brought in, how exactly would you respond?"

His shoulders dropped. His cheeks sagged. He cleared his throat and looked away.

"Exactly. So, being the trained professional that I am, you should know that I've been busting my ass on your daughter's case, and not only have I found a way to identify potential suspects through a single piece of evidence found at the scene—I found two other likely victims of the same unsub."

She slapped the two case files into Vicks's hands. "Both worked at or near a major hospital, and local authorities believed each of them disappeared due to other circumstances. The police thought one, like Anna, left her current lot in life for another man. Police in the second jurisdiction blamed the husband. The husband, however, told them he believed his wife was abducted by a man—a charming man who wrote his wife poems and letters. Sound familiar?"

Frankie didn't wait for either Vicks or Anna's father to react. Instead, she turned on a heel and headed the other direction. "I'll let you two take stock of that on your own. In the meantime, I'll notify the BAU and see if they're ready to get involved and get to work on building a profile right away."

She wheeled back around and snapped her fingers. "Oh, and I asked both jurisdictions to reopen those cases and instructed them to search for any reported arsons in the area at the time the women disappeared."

She met their gazes. "We good?"

They all stood, staring, mouths slightly agape, and for once ... speechless.

She pushed the door open to the stairs and exited, resisting the urge to flip them all off. A Voltaire quote came to mind: *It is difficult to free fools from the chains they revere.*

She added silently: *Especially when those fools are men.*

CHAPTER 14

Frankie uncorked a bottle of wine and poured herself a glass. The minute the first drops touched her lips, she felt the tension melt. It had been a grueling two weeks since the discovery of Anna Jamison's body, and all she wanted to do was eat a decent meal and get some rest before the whole thing exploded in round two. She knew that as soon as the media picked up on the other victims, there would be no rest.

The BAU had shown some interest in the case when Frankie presented it to them, but they had reservations with there being just one body and an incomplete crime scene for analysis. The BAU liked to work in threes, and if Frankie produced three bodies and three completed crime scenes, they felt they would be able to create a far more relevant profile of the unsub law enforcement should be seeking. For now, they asked that Frankie keep them informed of any new updates. They were very important and very busy. The agents of *Criminal Minds* wouldn't be getting on a plane and flying down in their private jet. This was reality.

After cooking up a pot of Louisiana court bouillon, one of Frankie's favorites among her grandmother's many recipes, she nudged Bones from his spot on the couch and fell into the cushions. Bones shook off the rude awakening and paced around Frankie's feet—until he realized she had food. Then he quickly became loving, brushing against and between Frankie's bare calves.

She offered him a piece of red snapper. The gray tabby mewed.

While she and Bones shared dinner, she flipped through the various news channels, seeing if any of them had caught wind of the latest developments. She stopped when she ran across Sheriff Brenner conducting his latest news conference. He appeared tired, with thick black bags beneath bloodshot eyes. Most sheriffs Frankie knew would welcome the daily attention and exposure a major case would give them, but Sheriff Brenner wasn't one of them. He held the unique perspective that if a crime was committed in his county, he wasn't doing his job.

After the release of the second poem, Brenner had cracked down on his team and promised to fire anyone who disseminated further information. It was vital that they keep a lid on the remaining evidence so the unsub wouldn't know what they had when it came time to interrogate him. There were still the cracknut headlines to admonish— *Boyfriend Cuts Out Woman's Heart to Keep It Close to Him; Alien Conducts Surgical Experiments*—but overall, he had tightened the ship. For now, Brenner let the media know the sheriff's department was following up on evidence and interviewing witnesses. To Frankie's relief, he kept her recent discoveries of the potential new victims quiet.

The news cut to Anna's father, who stated he would not rest until they found his daughter's killer and brought him to justice. Now, in front of the cameras, he affirmed his belief that the sheriff's department, with the assistance of the FBI, was doing everything possible. It was a far cry from the picture he'd painted the day before in Vicks's office.

Unfortunately, his confidence wasn't shared by Sheriff Brenner, as the physical evidence in the case continued to yield less than earth-shattering results. The tire tracks at the scene belonged to a common tread pattern sold standard on utility vans. They still hadn't been able to identify the blond woman seen with Anna on Sunday. And no DNA had been recovered from the fire other than Anna Jamison's. Frankie was holding out for the purchase lists of obsidian scalpels, but even those were proving hard to get, especially from the international suppliers.

They'd all become momentarily excited when Anna's car was found at a rest stop off I-40 west of Raleigh, but a sweep of it had produced surprisingly little. They'd uncovered a service receipt in the glove box for an oil change early Saturday morning, yet no record of repair existed for whatever later car trouble Anna had experienced that day. No nearby garages or mechanics reported servicing her car, nor had she used AAA, although she was a member. Frankie wondered if the man with the glasses in the mall parking lot had been able to rectify the problem.

The truth was, right now, their main hope resided in Miguel Herrera—in obtaining his physical description of the unsub and his testimony about what had occurred that night at the farmhouse. A phone call from his doctor earlier in the day had sounded hopeful; she felt that within the next couple of days she'd be able to remove Miguel from the ventilator and lessen the pain medication so he could speak with the police. Frankie needed to compile a profile of the unsub so that once it was coupled with a description, they could seek out the killer before he struck again.

No time like the present.

Finished with dinner, Frankie washed the dishes, poured another glass of wine, and turned the television off. She retrieved two posterboards, a stack of Post-it Notes, and a box of pushpins. In the living room, she took down a large framed lithograph of *Graffiti from the Elevated 7*, an homage to Queens, to clear one large wall. Then she tacked up the posterboards. This was her whiteboard, where she did her best profiling. She needed to let her mind explore options, both the probable and improbable. In the office, the more farfetched ones could bring the occasional roll of the eyes, but here she just allowed herself to explore. One never knew when those ideas might reveal a killer.

Truth was stranger than fiction.

She tacked up photos of Anna Jamison, Melanie Higby, and Emily Dearborn, then stepped back and took a deep breath. Bones rounded the coffee table and jumped up on the ottoman, ready to assist. She needed to get into the heads of the unsub and his victims to uncover the motives that sewed them together with so much thread.

She started at the highest level—race and gender—and immediately wrote *white male*. In addition to the limited, albeit sketchy, witness testimony stating that the unsub was a white male, statistics surrounding cases involving white women led to the same conclusion.

Next, she considered education and occupation and wrote *college educated, medical school, perhaps a graduate*. Because of the surgery and the precision of the suture ties, Frankie felt certain the unsub had training in the medical profession. Whether he was a doctor or surgeon or whether he worked in another capacity remained to be determined, but his organization and detailed planning told Frankie he was highly intelligent.

For age, she wrote *thirty to forty-five*. Given his education, career level, and prior experience, he would at least be in his thirties, but with his ability to attract twenty-something women, she didn't think he would be older than forty-five.

For marital status, she wrote *single*. The time required to court the women and establish a relationship, search for a suitable property, and plan and organize their time together made her certain he didn't have marital or family obligations at home. As for the victims' marital status, one had a boyfriend, one was married, and one was single, so that clearly wasn't an issue to the unsub. To him, they were all available.

The next profile attributes depended on three factors. First, was the relationship between the unsub and these women real or fantasy-based? Second, did the victims leave with him voluntarily, or were they forced in some manner? And last, did the unsub truly love these women, or was the real motive hate?

Frankie had lost many hours of sleep thinking about these questions.

On the surface, it appeared each relationship had been real and the women had gone with the unsub voluntarily. In Melanie's case, Frankie could see that possibly holding true, but for Anna and Emily, their falling for him—and leaving their families—was more alarming. How charming would a man need to be to make an engaged woman leave her fiancé and a married woman leave her husband and children?

The answer was, a great deal.

The man likely owned his home and lived alone. Also, because he was powerful and charming enough to lure his victims, the likelihood of him being anything other than a doctor or surgeon was low. He spent most of his time in an urban hospital but traveled to other hospitals, perhaps in a teaching capacity, searching for victims. The other possibility was that the victims were all previous patients of his, as Anna had been with Dr. Whitman.

She immediately pushed the thought out of her head. One of the keys of developing a good profile was not to have a suspect in mind. Otherwise—as Ben had warned her countless times—you'd find yourself doing a personality analysis and not a profile. It was easy to come up with reasons your suspect's behaviors and motivations fit the crime, rather than justifying why the crime pointed to a particular behavior. If Whitman became a suspect to pursue, it needed to be because he fit the profile and not the other way around.

Frankie stopped writing for a moment to consider this unsub's motive. Bones studied her from the back of the couch, his tail gliding back and forth. What was driving this man to pursue these women—love or hate? The poetry, letters, and courtship spoke of love, but the removal of the breasts indicated hate. In essence, he took their womanhood away, indicating a need for power and control. So, did he feign his love for them only to strip them of their dignity later? Or did his love grow angry once the women displeased him?

She considered Sheriff Brenner's description of Anna and her attempted escape the night she died. Would that have triggered the unsub's anger?

In either scenario, the answer was yes.

What would have made this man hate women? The most common reason was an abusive mother, followed by rejection. A woman or women who had degraded him and punished him, both physically and mentally. Yet, if he was driven by hate, she had to wonder—why no rape? Rape fit this profile. The unsub they were searching for had kept Anna under his control for at least three days, and by all appearances, he hadn't touched her sexually. Why?

Maybe because he couldn't. Maybe he was impotent or dysfunctional.

She added a note, then read through the entire profile.

Profile #1: Real Relationship/Voluntary Leaving/Hatred.

White male. Age 30-45. College educated, medical school graduate, doctor or surgeon. Single, lives alone, owns his own home, works in a major urban hospital but travels or has connections to other hospitals, possibly in a teaching capacity. Incredibly charming, attractive, and intelligent. In need of extreme power and control. Pretends to love but secretly hates women, particularly his mother or former girlfriends. May be unable to perform sexually. Potentially abusive/sadistic.

Charming, good-looking, and intelligent. A prime candidate for attracting women. Unfortunately, also a prime candidate to be a sociopath. Just like someone else she used to know.

She studied it. It was good, but it contained some flaws. Most men with the need for that kind of power hunted vulnerable women, and Anna, Melanie, and Emily didn't fit that mold. All three of these women had balanced careers, family, and community obligations. And *sadistic* didn't describe how Anna had died—with an overdose of ketamine, presumably in an effort to be merciful, now verified by the tox report.

Frankie took a sip of wine and stroked the cat's back. He purred. She felt her eyes narrow. She created a second column and changed the motive. How would loving the women instead of hating them change the profile?

In this case the unsub would have a strong, unfulfilled need to be deeply loved because his mother had likely withheld or been incapable of love. She might even have put him up for adoption or abandoned him. He pursued women relentlessly, but no amount of love and romance could fulfill him. Yet with love, the removal of the breasts was difficult to explain. Why take their womanhood away? Was it an attempt to return them to a prepubescent state, make them a virginal bride? Possibly, although in this scenario, she would've expected the two of them—pursuer and pursued—to have already had sex as part of a real, loving relationship.

This profile still spoke of a need to control, but at a different level. The sex was also an issue. Just as the autopsy had shown no evidence of rape, neither was there any sign of consensual sex between Anna and the unsub. So he was waiting; he withheld physical intimacy until his future love was perfect. Or as before, he couldn't perform.

Profile #2: Real Relationship/Voluntary Leaving/Love.

White male. Age 30-45. College educated, medical school graduate, doctor or surgeon. Single, lives alone, owns his own home, works in a major urban hospital but travels or has connections to other hospitals, possibly in a teaching capacity. Incredibly charming, attractive, and intelligent. In need of deep, abiding love. Loves and courts these women but grows angry when they don't please. Mother incapable of love or abandoned him. May desire prepubescent girls or be unable to perform sexually.

Possible, but also faulty. A child raised without love would likely grow up angry and sadistic, or self-conscious and insecure. Frankie saw neither scenario capable of producing a doctor, let alone one so charming and self-assured that he could persuade a mother to leave her children.

She was about to dive in again when Bones hissed and twitched his tail. He stared out the front window and let out a deep, unhappy sound.

Frankie walked over to check outside, but she didn't see anything of note. *Probably just the neighbor's terrier peeing on my bushes again.* She returned to the wall and flipped all three attributes on their head.

Only one word was needed to describe this profile—*abduction*. A man with a fantasy or fetish who stalked his victims. Frankie often questioned whether Anna, Melanie, and Emily had truly left of their own choosing or whether the unsub had forced them to leave. But if the unsub had abducted them, how did she explain Anna informing her friend she was leaving her fiancé for a new man? Or Emily crying the night before she left, as if she'd wanted to tell Ryan that she planned to leave? How did she clarify the letters written to their families in their own handwriting, expressing their apologies and celebrating their new love? To Frankie, it could only mean that the unsub had threatened them in such a way that they had risked telling no one—not even when Anna had met her friend Saturday night, Melanie had visited with her ailing mother, and Emily had slept next to her husband the evening before. In essence, the unsub had held them hostage mentally before he abducted them physically.

But how?

Although it still seemed likely this unsub was a doctor or surgeon, given the mastectomy and his knowledge of scalpels, he could also be someone who wanted things he couldn't obtain himself, both the status of doctor and the women such men attracted. This meant he could be any medical professional in a hospital setting, which, in turn, changed the education and living attributes of the profile. This unsub wasn't necessarily a college graduate, but he may have aspired to be, might even have attended college, and obtained medical training. This unsub would also likely work at the same hospital where he searched for victims. He was more likely to rent than to own so he could pick up at a moment's notice and leave when things turned bad.

Profile #3: Imaginary Relationship/Involuntary Leaving/Hatred.

White male. Age 30-45. Some college with medical training. Single, renter, works in the same urban or regional hospital as the victims. Average looks. Fantastical or fetishistic elements. In need of extreme power and control. Love letters and poems are only a decoy to hide his real intent. Hates women, particularly his mother or girls that have rejected him. May be unable to perform sexually. History of stalking in adolescence. Potentially abusive/sadistic.

Frankie thought this option interesting, but again, it had defects. She wouldn't expect this unsub to be the highly organized, calculated offender represented at Anna's crime scene. A man who wanted things he couldn't have would lack patience and therefore display more impulsivity. Also, this unsub would need to have enough presence or be enough of a threat that the women would follow his directions rather than seek help.

She stood thinking for several minutes. Again Bones interrupted, a deep reverberation coming from his lungs. He crouched on the edge of the couch as if he were about to leap at the window.

Frankie glanced out to the curb and this time saw what had Bones in such a ruffle. A woman stood on the opposite side of the street, staring directly at the house. It was dark out, so Frankie couldn't see her face, but she didn't appear to be anyone Frankie knew from the neighborhood.

What the hell is she doing? Casing the joint?

Frankie remained in the window until the woman turned and walked away. Afterward, Frankie shut the blinds and patted Bones on the head. "Yeah, she was a little creepy, dude. I'll give you that. But she's gone now."

She got back to work, flipped the last attribute.

This unsub was an abductor of a different kind. An abductor from a distance— stalking, obsessive, even an erotomaniac. What Frankie knew about erotomania was limited to textbooks and case studies, but she knew erotomaniacs tended to love their idols from afar, and poetry and letters were one of their favorite forms of communication. They believed fully in their fantasy that their idol felt the same way about them, and often sent them secret signs expressing their love. If the object of their affection was involved or married, the erotomaniac rationalized how the person wanted to be with them, but couldn't because of their obligations. Although the majority of erotomaniacs never became physically dangerous, those who did posed a danger not only to their idol, but also to anyone else who might be seen as an obstacle to the two of them being united.

Frankie thought this option interesting, as the erotomania could explain the poems, letters, courtship, and selection of a new home for the unsub and idol to live in together. If it led the unsub to explicitly threaten the women's spouses, family, or children, it could also explain why they would have left with him and not sought help.

Profile #4: Imaginary Relationship/Involuntary Leaving/Love.

White male. Age 30-45. Some college with medical training. Single, renter, works in the same urban or regional hospital as the victims. Average looks. Fantasy obsessive or erotomaniac. In need of deep, abiding love. Believes fantasy is real and object of his desire returns his affections. Loves and courts these women but grows angry when they don't please. Mother incapable of love or abandoned him. May desire prepubescent girls or be unable to perform sexually. History of stalking in adolescence.

Bones came back and hunched his back against her hand, seeming to agree that the option was interesting. However, Frankie still had concerns. One, erotomaniacs often pursued their idols over years, not months, and those pursued often complained of stalking or harassing behavior, even initiating restraining orders. Two, erotomaniacs were not usually highly intelligent and possessed low self-esteem, so once again, imagining one so highly organized and careful in planning and preparation was difficult. Also, the majority of erotomaniacs tended to be women, at a ratio of ten to one.

Frankie felt her eyes narrow again. She changed the gender.

Although it seemed unlikely, especially when it came to exerting control over the victims, they couldn't rule out the possibility that the unsub was a woman. Anna had last been seen with a woman, as had Emily.

Profile #5: Woman—Imaginary Relationship/Involuntary Leaving/Love.

White female. Age 30-45. Some college with medical training. Single, renter, works in the same urban or regional hospital as the victims. Average looks. Fantasy obsessive or erotomaniac. In need of deep, abiding love. Believes fantasy is real and object of her desire returns her affections. Loves and courts these women but grows angry when they don't please. Mother incapable of love or abandoned her. No sexual contact, same gender. History of stalking in adolescence.

Below the five profiles, she added her prior observations.

Preselected the scene of the crime. Knew the property was abandoned. Planned to stay on the premises. Burning only to cover the evidence. Brought his own tools. Reacted logically when interrupted by the boy, gathering tools, destroying the evidence. Calm, planned, and organized = experienced.

Frankie backed up and reviewed the board. She took a sip of wine. The truth was, some of the components of each profile made sense, whereas others felt incongruent. It would've been helpful to have a completed crime scene, but they didn't, so deciphering the unsub's true motivation was an incomplete process at best. Still, this was better than nothing, and in each profile at least a few of the unsub's attributes were similar. Her efforts would help them narrow down the list once they obtained Miguel Herrera's physical description.

She glanced at her watch. It was late. Ben's comments about her workaholic tendencies echoed in her head. She had started to turn off the lights and lock up for the night when her cell phone rang. It was Allison, one of the analysts from the field office.

Frankie felt a twisting in her gut. "Allison, what's up?"

"I know it's late, but I thought you should know. The hospital called. Miguel Herrera just died."

CHAPTER 15

Frankie ran from the visitor parking into Carolinas Medical Center as fast as she could. The place was busy for a Friday night, one ambulance in the ER bay and the scream of another approaching. At the entrance, Frankie pushed through the crowd and jumped into the elevator just as the doors were closing. The pace of her steps must have indicated she was on a mission, because the nurse stationed at the ICU desk jumped at Frankie's succinct words. "I need to see Dr. Birnbaum now."

Dr. Nancy Birnbaum, she of the stout body and brunette hair streaked with gray, emerged moments later through the door to Miguel Herrera's room. She wore black slacks and a lab coat and looked like she'd been hit by a bad case of the flu. "Agent Johnson. I know you're disappointed. Trust me, I am as well."

She took Frankie by the arm and led her to a visitor's lounge furnished with an array of chairs and a well-worn lime-green couch. She offered lukewarm coffee, but Frankie declined. She wanted to get down to business. Their last hope of identifying Anna's killer had just died, and she wasn't in the mood for chitchat. "What happened?"

"I wish I could offer you an explanation, but at this juncture I'm afraid I don't have one. Mr. Herrera took a turn for the worse at approximately nine p.m. this evening and went into respiratory failure within the hour. I could speculate, but I won't. Anything I could say would be premature at best."

"You said he was getting better. Just this morning you told me he was making progress, that you'd be able to remove him from the ventilator so he could speak with us this weekend."

Frankie knew her accusations were out-of-bounds, but she couldn't help it. Miguel Herrera's testimony could've helped stop a killer. Now, others could die.

"It was true. He'd been improving steadily the past week. His vital signs were stable, his pain manageable. But burn cases are fragile. A simple infection can prove disastrous. Pneumonia can unexpectedly set in."

Dr. Birnbaum stuffed both hands inside the pockets of her lab coat and sighed. "Agent Johnson, I'm so sorry. I don't know what else to say. I promise you a thorough explanation just as soon as I have one."

Frankie marched about the room with her hands on her hips. "We'll need an autopsy, a tox report. We need to know what killed Miguel Herrera. He was a witness to a murder—the only witness." She halted just inches from the doctor's face. "Are you certain there were no unauthorized visitors in his room?"

"There has been a police officer stationed outside his door since he arrived. We've been under strict orders—essential personnel and approved family only. The officer said only medical personnel have visited today. However, we will view the security tapes."

"I'll want to see those. How long will it take?"

"I can have copies sent to you by Monday."

Just then, the door to the lounge opened and Dr. Lawrence Banks appeared. "I heard," he said. "What happened?"

To Frankie's surprise, he wrapped his arms around her and offered a hug.

"We won't know until we review all the records, but you know how touch and go these cases can be," Dr. Birnbaum said. "Things can turn around very quickly."

Dr. Banks nodded. Sure, he could be empathetic, but he didn't have a murder case riding on the boy's memory. Not only had Frankie wanted Miguel to live because he was a heroic young man, but she didn't want another victim to succumb to their unsub.

She paced, feeling helpless. She had hoped that with three potential victims identified, the purchase lists, and a witness identification, they would be able to quickly narrow down their list of suspects. But without Miguel Herrera's testimony, they would be working without a vital piece of information. The purchase lists would take processing, the subsequent interviews would take resources, and that would give their killer the most valuable resource of all—time. Time to create an alibi, and worse, time to take another victim.

Frankie didn't know whether to cry, scream, or pound a fist through a wall. She wanted—no, needed—to solve this case. She glanced up, pleaded. "Did he ever say anything, anything at all, during his brief moments of consciousness?"

Dr. Birnbaum shook her head. "I'm afraid not. I'm sorry."

A nurse entered, spoke softly to Dr. Birnbaum, and pointed to a small group of people near the front desk, including a short Hispanic woman who had wound her purse strap between her fingers so tight her knuckles were white. Dr. Birnbaum turned back to Frankie. "I'm sorry, the family has arrived. I must go speak with them."

When the door shut, Dr. Banks reached for Frankie's hand. He squeezed. "I know I'm supposed to be all business, but I can't help myself. I sense your disappointment."

"You have no idea." She sat down, dejected. "The truth is, our whole case was riding on Miguel's identification. The physical evidence has proved too generic to narrow down to individuals. This perpetrator, he'll kill again, and he's very good at hiding his victims. There's no guarantee we'll get another chance to catch him."

"Maybe I can offer you another chance." He looked at his watch. "It's late, but the Midnight Diner is always open. Come on, join me, and I'll tell you what I've found."

CHAPTER 16

It was nearing eleven thirty p.m. when Frankie and Dr. Banks arrived at the Midnight Diner. In the distance, the skyscrapers uptown shimmered, oblivious to Frankie's mood. The Midnight was notorious for its late-night crowds, a place where concert attendees, factory workers, and policemen shared conversation over burgers and fries. Tonight seemed to belong to several teen couples, who were out after their prom or graduation party.

The waitress, a heavyset, middle-aged woman whose breasts were about to pop free of the top buttons of her blue-and-white uniform, poured each a cup of coffee without asking. "Whatcha having, sweethearts?"

Frankie was in no mood for food but, since sleep wasn't an option, ordered a grilled cheese sandwich. Dr. Banks opted for the shrimp and grits.

When the waitress departed, Frankie spoke. "What have you got for me?"

But Dr. Banks didn't reply. Instead he drew his coffee to his lips and concentrated on luring Frankie in with his eyes. And they were gorgeous eyes, chocolate satin wrapped in black feathers. "Did I mention you look beautiful tonight, as always."

"You've only seen me twice."

"That qualifies as always."

Frankie felt herself blush. She tried not to be swayed by his words or his physical appearance, but it was difficult. She brushed the napkin across her lap.

"Were you out earlier, when you got the call?"

"No. I was home working. Creating a possible profile of our suspect."

"Friday night home alone? Does that mean there isn't anyone special in your life?"

She sighed. Anyone special? What could she tell him? In her five years with the Bureau, she'd only dated other badges, and most of those had been flings. She was, she'd determined, hot sex on the side, not someone men wanted raising their kids and washing their underwear. She thought about telling him this. Instead she said, "I date. You?"

68

"The same," he said, too quickly.

A quiet contemplation hovered between them. Frankie examined two teens covered in piercings and tattoos as they slid into a booth. The boy was unusually gangly, possessing moderate acne and wearing a One Republic T-shirt. The girl's messy purple hair reminded Frankie of a troll doll she'd once had. She wondered whether, if she and Dr. Banks ever did connect, they could overlook the real tragedy that had brought them together.

Like an omen, an ambulance screamed past outside, its lights flashing and siren blaring. A second followed. Frankie remembered Anna and Miguel, and her thoughts returned her to the matter at hand. As they'd left the hospital, she'd seen Miguel's mother hit her knees, and it had driven a stake through Frankie's heart. Her son had stepped forward to help a stranger and paid with his life. Now it wasn't just Anna's family counting on her to stop a killer.

The waitress came and placed their food on the table. Frankie stared at it, unsure if she could force anything down. How could she eat when a murderer was on the loose?

"I know you're struggling, but try to eat. It will do you good. We can talk shop afterward." Dr. Banks drowned his grits in hot sauce. "May I ask you a personal question? You can say no if you like; I only ask because your beauty is so unique. What is your heritage? Who are your parents?"

She sighed. Maybe a little diversion would do her good. "My mother is French African American, my father is Irish and Italian. My grandparents are what I like to call European blend. What that makes me, I don't know. I usually just check the *other* box."

To her relief, this made Dr. Banks smile. "I think it makes you an American, just like the rest of us," he said. "Was it hard growing up? I mean, your name is very white." He laughed. "It's also very masculine, hence my surprise at your arrival at my office that first day. There must be a story."

Frankie smiled, remembering his notation of *Frank E. Johnson*. "With my middle name, Ayanna, my heritage is ethnically questionable, but without it, it's white. I believe my mother gave me my father's name intentionally, although she'd never admit it. They weren't married, so she had a choice: Johnson or Doucevay. By giving me my father's name, she separated me from her Louisiana ancestry, which she associates with slavery. So, whether it was intentional or not, I was more accepted by the white community."

"You grew up in Louisiana?"

Frankie shook her head. "Queens. Summers in DC. But my mom grew up in Louisiana, and my grandmother made sure to hand down her Cajun influence." She bit into a thick layer of melted cheddar cheese. Grease from the bread covered her fingers. "What about you?" she said between bites. "Where did you grow up?"

"Tyron Hills, here in Charlotte. Raised by a single mother, just like you."

"Did you know your father?"

He shook his head as he chewed. "No. Left right after I was born. Guess he didn't like what he saw." He laughed, but Frankie could tell it was a sore subject.

"My mother never married. The men in her life were either abusive, drunk, or both. My older brother took it upon himself to look out for me. He wasn't the best role model, but he was my brother. I looked up to him."

"Where is he now?"

He concentrated on his grits, avoiding her eyes. "Prison. Doing time for armed robbery." He paused before looking up. She could see he was waiting for her reaction.

"It happens. It's not your fault."

"Yes, that's what they say. But seeing as he was committing the robbery trying to get money to help me pay for medical school, I can't help but feel responsible."

Frankie winced. "I'm sorry. You see him?"

"Occasionally. When I get the chance."

"And your mom?"

The tiny lines around his eyes tightened. "Dead."

"I'm sorry." She changed the subject. "What made you want to be a doctor?"

He set his biscuit down and carefully cleaned the crumbs off his hands, one finger at a time. He seemed to think carefully about what he wanted to say. "I saw a lot of bad things growing up. Tyron Hills wasn't what it is now. It wasn't new condos and restored historical homes, you know? It was drugs, and violence, and death. I saw things no twelve-year-old boy should see. Friends. Relatives. They died young."

He surveyed the glittering uptown lights. "I just decided that after all the shootings, stabbings, and overdoses, maybe I wanted to do something else with my life."

Frankie studied him. Somewhere between his words and distant gaze, she could sense he wrestled between an obligation to his old life and a desire to never look back.

He took a deep breath. "Sorry. You didn't need more depressing talk tonight." He moved his plate aside and reached inside his pocket. "Maybe this will make things a little better." Blowing open the top of a small envelope, he slid two fingers inside and pulled out a curved needle attached to a braided green-and-black thread.

"You found it," Frankie said, feeling a spark of hope.

"It wasn't easy. It's not commercial. At least, not yet. It's in the clinical stages of research and development. Johns Hopkins is leading the study. I don't know if that means anything."

Frankie felt her brow furrow. She thought about Dr. Whitman's shiny framed degree hanging on the wall of his office. "What are they testing, exactly?"

"It's an absorbable suture. I'm guessing that's why there were no drain tubes used with the mastectomy. Apparently, the material can act as a sponge and absorb fluids."

"I'll need a list of doctors participating in the study."

"I tried, but no go. Maybe you'll have better luck."

She nodded. "I'll get it. Given that we have no possibility of a visual ID of our suspect now, this might be our last chance. Hopefully, between the purchase lists of the obsidian scalpel and this, we'll get a name match. If I can find a name, then I can start finding a link between the victims."

Dr. Banks's eyes widened. "Victims? You found others?"

"Potential victims, technically, and it's not public, so keep it under wraps." She told him about Melanie and Emily. "If I could come up with a way to find others who disappeared but were never reported as missing, I'd possibly have more."

"Why wouldn't they be reported? People don't just disappear."

"Ah, but they do," Frankie said. "And if it appears voluntary, then it's possible, even probable, they won't be reported as missing. The last victim, Anna Jamison, told a friend she was leaving her fiancé for another man. If she never shows up again, then who's to believe it was anything but her choice?"

The waitress refilled their coffee. Frankie sipped and observed Dr. Banks start to speak before stopping himself. He appeared to be fighting with something heavy and dark, hanging above him like a bat in a cave. Finally, he spoke.

"I want to tell you something. Need to, actually." He twisted a napkin around his fist. "I feel badly I didn't tell you before. Truth is, I didn't know how, under the circumstances."

Frankie stopped breathing, feeling the second bomb of the night about to drop. Here it came. He was married. He was involved. He was gay. They would be relegated to friends just like her and Ben. She prepared herself. "What is it?"

"I knew Anna Jamison."

CHAPTER 17

Frankie shot a glare like fiery knives across the table, what Ben called her laser daggers.

"I know, I should have mentioned it before," Dr. Banks said.

"How? How did you know her?"

"I met her at an alumni event. A fundraiser. I'm a UNC alum."

"Half the state of North Carolina is a UNC alum. You just happened to be at the one event where you could befriend the one woman who happened to end up a victim of the one crime I happen to be investigating? How is that so? When was this event?"

"Like eighteen months ago. Before basketball season the prior year. I only remember because I asked her to a game. UNC versus Duke. It's a big rivalry. We went to that one game. She was dating her fiancé, but it wasn't serious yet. Their relationship only got serious afterwards." The pace of his words and the pitch of his voice increased rapidly as he spoke, disclosing his nerves.

Frankie leaned across the table. "You *dated* her?" she said, emphasizing the word like it was a crime. She felt a sharp pain in her stomach and wondered how she could feel that—jealousy—for a dead woman.

"No. I wouldn't call it a date. We went to a basketball game. We were Tar Heel alums. We were playing Duke. It's a big rivalry."

"Right. You said that." Frankie threw her napkin on the table. "This is bad. I can't talk to you anymore." She started to slide out of the booth.

"Wait." He grabbed her arm amid curious onlookers, including a couple of police officers sitting nearby. "Don't do this. I didn't think. I made the wrong choice."

Frankie hesitated. "I have to ask. Why didn't you mention it?"

"It was circumstantial. It didn't seem pertinent. And I didn't want you looking at me the way you're looking at me right now," he whispered. "Like I'm a killer."

Her heart thrummed. She pointed a finger across the booth. "Did you know? When you looked at those photographs?"

He bobbed his head, exasperated. "I thought about it, but the mastectomy, that detail wasn't in the news. It was a few days later when I realized it was Anna."

"When was the last time you saw her?"

"Not since February."

"Phone calls?"

"No, I've never called her."

"Texts? Emails?"

"Sometimes. Sure."

"Have copies?"

"Maybe." He scratched his head. "I don't know. I've probably deleted them by now."

"Where were you Sunday, May ninth, between the hours of four p.m. and midnight?"

His jaw dropped. He squirmed in the booth. Frankie saw one of the officers frown.

"Do I really need to remember that? I can barely recall what I did yesterday, let alone nearly three weeks ago."

"I think you'd better."

Over his shoulder, Frankie met one of the officer's eyes. A busboy passed between them with a tray of clinking dishes and a dirty towel thrown over his shoulder.

He writhed. "Sunday I play basketball at the gym in the late afternoon. It's a league, so it's always the same time. I usually stop for Thai on the way home. I can get you the receipt."

"Anyone who can vouch for you later that evening?"

"After I left the gym? No, I don't think so."

Frankie remained silent, continuing to scrutinize her dinner companion. The tiny muscles near his eyes twitched. He fidgeted with the spoon on his saucer. She didn't care for being made a fool of, and right now she felt like a clown.

"Look," he said, "I'm sorry about not mentioning Anna to you, and I'm sorry about your witness. I hope locating the suture makes up for it in some small way. I want to find Anna's killer every bit as much as you do."

He glanced across the table. "She was my friend."

Frankie tensed. Everything about Dr. Banks's body language, words, and pitch indicated he was telling the truth, but with so much at stake and her emotional attachment, she wasn't sure she could trust her analysis. She turned her attention back to the suture thread. Holding it in her hands provided her with at least some confidence that she would find Anna's killer.

"Look, it's helpful," she said. "It is. It means a new direction. It means I may not have to go back to the girl and ask her to undergo hypnosis to remember what she saw. Her parents are adamant about her not getting involved."

Dr. Banks frowned. "What do you mean, the girl? What girl?"

"What?" she asked.

"You said the girl. What girl?"

Frankie stilled. She considered his words, staring at him as if they were suspended there solidly in the air. *The girl.* A light went on and she remembered—they had not released information about the girl to the media. No one knew about Miguel's girlfriend except those on the inside.

She started to speak, then stopped. She tilted her head.

Across the aisle to their left, a server slipped and dropped two cups of coffee, making them rain against the tile floor. The clatter and chaos matched the sudden confusion in Frankie's head.

How could she have missed it? Had she been so obsessed by the news that the doctor had known Anna that she'd overlooked a crucial revelation? The conversation of their meeting replayed in her mind. *It's just a tragedy what happened to her. I was stunned at the news of the fire. The kids, I hope they are okay?*

Kids, in the plural. Frankie muttered under her breath, cursing herself. She felt her heart thunder in her chest. She slid from the booth. "I have to go."

Dr. Banks called after her. "What? Why? Frankie, wait."

She turned to him as she opened the door. "Dr. Whitman. He knew about the girl."

CHAPTER 18

Frankie raced through the streets of Charlotte early the next morning, anxious to get to the office. The rising sun cast a large orange glow across the Bank of America tower, a constant reminder of the power the financial institution yielded over the city. In her office, she settled in with a large latte and got to work. All night long, she'd replayed Dr. Whitman's words and actions in her head, and this morning she had a long list of questions she needed to answer. She wanted to find out everything she could about Dr. Whitman and any relationships he might have had with Anna Jamison, Melanie Higby, and Emily Dearborn before she called in Sheriff Brenner and his team to conduct an interrogation.

She started with a full background check, including criminal history, aliases and addresses, family members, and known affiliations. If he was their unsub, she'd expect him to have a few priors—perhaps of stalking or harassment—but other than a few speeding tickets, his record was clean. His family members were equally sparse, a handful of names associated with Kenneth's at various addresses. The first real revelation was of his parents, a doctor and a teacher, who'd died in a car crash when Kenneth was just thirteen, leaving him an orphan. With no close relatives to assume guardianship, he'd entered foster care at a home in Columbia, South Carolina, where he'd remained through high school. Five years later, he enrolled in the University of Maryland, where he continued through medical school. His residencies included stints at Johns Hopkins and the University of North Carolina.

Frankie thought about his degree on the wall. *Johns Hopkins.* Where he'd learned about obsidian scalpels. Where doctors sponsored research on an absorbable green-and-black braided suture.

She picked up her cell phone and called them. Frankie told the young woman what she needed—a list of physicians and surgeons participating in the research study— and after some arm twisting, the woman said she'd have it for her by the end of the day.

The second thing she ordered was his credit report. She couldn't get detailed account information or a charge history without warrants, but the report at least informed her of his mortgage, car, and student loans, along with his credit cards and balances. She wasn't at all surprised, however, to find his credit as neat and polished as he was.

Frankie conducted a full internet search, seeking to learn all she could about Dr. Kenneth Whitman. She wanted full access to his emails, social media accounts, and phone records, but again, that wouldn't happen without legal justification, and what they had on him so far wasn't enough.

Several listings online mentioned his name, mainly reviews from patients and descriptions of seminars he'd given at conferences. One article discussed the pros and cons of using obsidian scalpels, another showed the before and after shots of tummy tucks, and a third dealt with the emotional and sensitive nature of discussions with intersex patients. This last one surprised Frankie, as she hadn't even considered that part of his profession, but it appeared he was quite well versed on the subject. That could explain the oddly erotic art and objects in his office. Maybe those items put his intersex or transitioning patients at ease.

Frankie noted that Dr. Whitman also traveled throughout the region consulting on difficult plastic surgery reconstruction cases. Two of her profiles stated the unsub might travel or have connections to other hospitals, and Dr. Whitman fit that description. Now that she knew he matched the behavior, she wanted to know how Emily and Melanie had crossed paths with him. It was quite possible Emily had been Whitman's client when she'd had her breast enhancement done, and a phone call to Ryan Dearborn confirmed her suspicion. She'd gotten the implants in January, five months before disappearing during the picnic.

That made sense, but what about Melanie Higby? Had she encountered Dr. Whitman at the hospital across the street from the flower shop where she'd worked, or had she also been a patient?

Frankie called Detective Hatcher to see if he could answer her questions.

"Cosmetic surgery? Yes, now that you mention it," Hatcher said. "Melanie lost quite a bit of weight the year before she disappeared and had to have the excess skin removed. Her weight loss and new dating activity was one of the reasons we believed she may've left on her own."

"Do you know what surgeon she saw?"

He didn't, but promised to call the nursing home and ask Melanie's mother. Ten minutes later he texted the answer: Dr. Kenneth Whitman.

Frankie felt her mouth turn dry. One client-victim relationship could be coincidental, but three? There had to be a connection.

Frankie sat at her desk and pondered this information. The red joker on the stage poster for 52 Pickup frolicked in a way she didn't appreciate. He seemed to be mocking her. She didn't see Ben or ASAC Vicks standing in her doorway until Ben cleared his throat.

"Woman deep in thought," he said in his best caveman imitation. "Is it man or beast that bothers woman?"

"Man," she said. "Dr. Whitman knew about the girl."

Vicks's eyebrows shot up. "We excluded that info from the media, didn't we?"

"We did, yes," Frankie said. "No one but those at the scene would know that Miguel Herrera's girlfriend was there."

"But Miguel was being treated at the same hospital Dr. Whitman practices," Ben said. "You don't think Whitman could've learned about her through the other doctors there? A casual discussion in passing?"

Frankie shook her head. "No, because we didn't inform doctors or staff of the girlfriend's presence at the scene either. There was no need. She wasn't injured, and she was told not to visit him for her own safety."

As she proceeded to fill them in on her conversation with Dr. Banks after learning of Miguel's death and her realization of Whitman's slip, Vicks's frown and Ben's cringed lip didn't even faze her. She'd already spent the better part of the day chastising herself for her mistakes.

"And before you both start in, understand that I've already spent considerable time calling myself clever names—both for missing such an obvious clue and for mentioning it to Dr. Banks. So save your air."

Ben looked disappointed. "Well, that's no fun. Couldn't you at least tell us some of the names you invented?"

She flipped him off, then continued. "I've spent this morning looking into Dr. Whitman's background." She updated them on the details of her many conversations, including the discovery of Melanie's and Emily's cosmetic surgeries. "In many ways, he fits the profile. He's a white male, age forty-two, well educated, a plastic surgeon. He's single, works in a major hospital, and travels to other hospitals. He's also highly intelligent, graduating magna cum laude from the University of Maryland."

"What about his childhood?" Ben asked.

"It's interesting. He was raised in Spartanburg but was placed in a foster home in Columbia after his parents died in a car crash at the age of thirteen."

"An orphan?" Ben said, his voice rising. "That could lead to a whole host of issues: stress, anger, abandonment."

"No history of stalking or domestic violence?" Vicks asked.

"Not on record. I'd like to get ahold of his college records or talk to a campus advisor. I feel if there was a time these behaviors started, it would be then. Or even earlier, maybe high school."

"Are the foster parents or other relatives still around?" Ben asked.

Frankie scanned the list. "There's an aunt—his mother's younger sister—and his grandmother. I found their names in his parents' obituaries. Betty Sue Taylor also comes up as a possible relative. Given her age and the address in Columbia, I'm thinking she could be his foster mother. No record of a Mr. Taylor though. Another lists a Mary Campbell at an address in Maryland, but that was while he was in college. An old girlfriend, maybe?"

"Why didn't the grandmother or aunt take custody after his parents died?" Ben asked.

Frankie cocked her head. "I don't know. One of many questions to ask the foster parent. Hopefully she can tell us something."

Ben combed through the papers on Frankie's desk. "Uses obsidian scalpels, did a residency at Johns Hopkins where this suture is in clinical studies, and three potential victims were all his clients." He whistled. "Not looking good for Dr. Whitman."

"It's still all coincidence unless we get physical evidence that ties him directly to these three women. It would help if we could locate the other bodies," Vicks said.

"Hatcher said this morning that he and the NCBI were working on getting ground-penetrating radar to the arson site where they discovered the green braided suture. There's been a few hang-ups but he said they would get it done. He'll let us know if they discover any remains," Frankie said. "I haven't heard anything on Emily's case. May have to twist a few arms."

Just then, one of the analysts came in and handed Frankie a fax. Frankie quickly scanned the list of participants in the absorbable suture research study. "There he is," she said, flicking the page. "His name is sixth from the bottom."

Vicks nodded. "We have enough to bring him in for a talk. Bring Sheriff Brenner up-to-date and tell him to pursue the warrants for any other evidence needed. Judges aren't usually the nicest when it comes to tossing the house of a respected citizen, so my guess is he'll have to work to get them. And update the BAU. See if they have any thoughts. Good work, Johnson."

Their conversation came to a halt when Ben's sidekick, Agent Tom Trimble, interrupted. "Sorry for the intrusion, but we've got a situation at the racetrack."

CHAPTER 19

With Tommy unable to join Ben at the track due to his current undercover work, Ben and Frankie raced to the speedway in Concord, where they were greeted by the security manager they'd spoken to before. At the time, he'd seemed little concerned about the government's threat assessment or the New Patriots, but now he wasn't so sure. A small backpack with a homemade bomb had exploded in the car garage assigned to the only African American driver in the upcoming race, and a not-so-subtle racial message had been scrawled on the wall: *Die N****.

Ben knew this driver had been the supposed target of attacks previously—including one in Alabama the year before where a noose had been left dangling from the garage door. In that case, however, the FBI had determined that someone had created the noose to assist in pulling the garage door up and down and that no harm had been intended. Not so with the noose left here this time. This one was a blatant message, complete with a little stuffed black doll hanging from it, the rope around its neck.

And this time, the driver was more than a little shaken up.

"This is bullshit," he exclaimed, pacing the width of the garage in a red-and-yellow uniform matching his car. "They could've hurt one of my team, or me. How do I know they haven't tampered with my car?"

"We're going to check it out," one of the mechanics said, wiping his hands on a greasy rag. "Don't you worry. We'll go over every hose, belt, nut, and screw."

"It will take too much time. The race is tomorrow."

Ben stepped in to reassure him. "I'm sorry this happened to you. I assure you we're going to get to the bottom of it. Can you tell me what happened?"

The driver, who went by the nickname Bobby B, explained how he and two of his mechanics had arrived at eight a.m. to find the back door open. "My lead mechanic went in to check it out. He didn't see anyone or anything suspicious, so he opened the bay and *blam*, smoke everywhere."

The smell had been putrid, equivalent to that of rotten eggs.

"Thankfully, there were no nails or pellets used as shrapnel," the bomb tech who remained on the scene said. "Looks like they just wanted to scare someone." He glanced at Bobby B. "Somebody trying to get you to drop out of the race?"

Bobby B grunted. "I'll be damned if I let these Confederate assholes run me out of town. They just amped up the competition. That's all they did."

Ben noticed Frankie studying the noose and the doll hanging awkwardly from it. She mouthed words he couldn't hear, but that was probably for the best. He could fill in the blanks.

"Who has access to this garage?" she asked.

"Just me and a few members of my team," Bobby B said.

"Somebody forget to lock up last night?" she replied.

"No," his lead mechanic said. "I did it myself."

"Cameras?" Ben asked the head of security.

"Guy with a backpack, loose jeans, and a hoodie drawn tight around his face entered the garage at approximately two a.m. this morning. He had a key, but how he got it, I don't know. All I can tell you is he was white, medium build, and about five foot eight."

Ben sighed. *Great.* That described about half the guys who stood in the garage right now, including one who had a backpack slung over his shoulder nearly identical to the one that had held the homemade bomb. He quietly wondered if this could be the work of someone inside Bobby B's own crew. Maybe this was the work of the New Patriots, or maybe it was just an orchestrated stunt. Despite the Alabama incident having proved to be non-malicious in nature, Bobby B had received a huge amount of publicity from it, and even a new sponsor or two. It wouldn't be the first time somebody had construed such an act to gain attention.

Frankie seemed to sense what Ben was thinking and set her stony gaze upon him. "Don't even," she said.

"What? I didn't say anything."

She pulled him into a corner. "You're already suspecting the driver?"

"Can't rule it out," he whispered. "Like that actor who staged his own attack."

She gave him a look that said she wanted to cut off his head and impale it on a stick. "So now every black person who's the victim of a hate crime is faking it? I bet you wouldn't even think that if he was white ... or gay," she said, poking him in the chest.

He sighed. He wasn't trying to be racist; he just wanted to be thorough. He started to respond, but after thinking it over—especially the gay part, which hit close to home—he decided he didn't like his answer to her question. The chants and rants of the recent New Patriots' gathering echoed in his head. After hearing all of that, how could he doubt that racism was still alive and well?

"I hear you," he said. "I apologize."

Choosing to get out of the way of her accusing stare—which felt like a part of some Cajun curse she was reciting in her head—he took to examining the scene along with the crime techs, who were busy gathering evidence. He sauntered outside and glanced down the row to the other garages, where the competitors and their teams were preparing for the upcoming race. He noticed that, while some individuals stood in the road watching the investigation with immense curiosity, others occasionally poked their heads out to check out the fuss. Most looked concerned, but Ben swore he saw more than a few smirks and smiles before going back inside.

He returned to Bobby B, who stood by his car like a protective parent. "You have any enemies among the ranks?"

He grunted. "Outside the track, ninety percent of the drivers are friends. On the track, we're all adversaries. Race car drivers are hypercompetitive. We talk a lot of smack. Some of it's real. Some isn't. If you can't keep up with the big dogs, then you get run over. You get it?"

Ben nodded. He did get it, all too well. In his youth, he'd been a ferocious competitor in windsurfing and sailing until his tactics nearly cost an opponent his life. Now he put all that energy into battling the bad guys. It required the same determination and mindset, but he got to protect people instead of kill them—at least most of the time.

"You get any other personal threats lately?" Frankie asked.

He sighed. "To tell the truth, they've been on the increase ever since that incident last year in Alabama. The slurs, the nasty diatribes on social media, the bumps and rubs on the track." He shook his head. "You'd think the national focus on race relations would create more of a conversation. Instead, people just dig their heels in harder."

Ben glanced toward a blonde in tight jeans and a sleeveless red blouse headed their way. Even though her eyes were hidden behind sunglasses, it was clear she'd been crying. Her face was puffy and swollen.

"This is my girlfriend, Gigi," Bobby B said as she joined them. "They've been rough on her, too. The trolls on social media, they call her names I couldn't make up in my wildest dreams. Last month some asshole handed her a package of milk-chocolate candy with vanilla cream in the middle and told her that's what our babies were going to be like."

"Jesus," Ben muttered. He felt his face flush.

Frankie snorted.

"People can be so mean," Gigi said in a deep southern accent. "It just makes me sad. Most of the time I ignore it, but sometimes it gets to be too much."

"In all that online chatter, do you remember seeing anyone who declared themself a New Patriot? Did you see any posts tagged with hashtag NP?" Ben asked.

Bobby B tipped his head back. "Now that you mention it, yeah. I didn't know what it meant. I thought it was just some new text acronym, like LOL or OMG." He offered a half laugh, but Ben could tell that, beneath the attempt at humor, it disturbed him. This was what Frankie always tried to explain to him: how difficult it was for people of color to live with an extra layer of fear that white guys like him didn't experience.

Double that for women.

"Who are they?" Bobby asked.

"A group based in Fayetteville we've been keeping an eye on. We might want to look through your social media posts and read some of the commentary, if you don't mind."

"Feel free. I have a staff member who administers all my sites. He'll get you whatever you need."

"Appreciate it," Ben said. He handed Bobby his card. "If you see or think of anything else, give me a call. I'll be here during the race too." They shook hands. "Good luck tomorrow. We'll be cheering for you."

Ben and Frankie walked back to their car, leaving the techs to do their work. "I don't think this was an inside job," she said. "I'm leaning toward your new friends."

"Probably right, but I'm worried one of Bobby B's own team could be involved. The New Patriots could've enlisted someone on the inside. I'm sure they'd like nothing more than to make a big splash at a NASCAR event."

"Well, let's hope this is it and it isn't a precursor to a larger event tomorrow," Frankie said. "I'm glad you'll be here. Unfortunately, I won't be able to join you."

They weaved through the collection of law enforcement vehicles. "No? Why?"

"I just got a voice mail from Sheriff Brenner. He asked Dr. Whitman to come in for an interview, but Whitman is refusing to speak to anyone but me. Looks like I'll be spending tomorrow preparing for a showdown."

Ben raised an eyebrow. "You sure you don't mind going it alone? I know we talked about backing each other up, but I'd never forgive myself if the New Patriots tried to make a move and I wasn't there."

"I know. You need to be here. This is your case. And I need to be in Lexington with my case. Like you said, I've got to be prepared to go it alone."

Ben smiled. "Let's go get the bad guys."

CHAPTER 20

Frankie phoned Dr. Kenneth Whitman and scheduled the interview for Monday afternoon at the Davidson County Sheriff's Department. She made certain to call it an interview and not an interrogation and emphasized that Whitman would be speaking only to her. Oddly, he sounded pleased that she'd called and promised to clear his appointments.

When he arrived, Frankie led him to the interview room, an unremarkable gray space devoid of windows and distractions. Other than a small table and two matching chairs, the only item inside was a video camera hanging from the corner ceiling.

He took one look and grunted. "Not exactly the Ritz-Carlton, is it? Next time let's try a glass of wine and a quiet table in a corner, shall we?" He dusted off one of the chairs and sat.

As before, Dr. Whitman had dressed to impress, wearing pale-gray slacks, a pinstriped gray and lavender shirt, and a royal-blue tie. He wore his thin blond hair neatly combed and smelled lightly of cologne. Frankie, in a navy-blue suit, sat opposite him.

"Thank you for coming in," she began. "As I stated on the phone, we're speaking to everyone who knew Anna to establish their relationship and whereabouts when the events with Anna unfolded, for the record this time. I'm only on a fact-finding mission here. However, I want to let you know, you can have a lawyer present if you'd like."

She made sure to refer to Anna's death as *events* and not *murder* and mentioned a lawyer to alleviate any suspicion that he might need one. No point risking him lawyering up.

"I'm happy to speak with you," he said. "No attorney necessary."

Frankie acknowledged his statement and proceeded. She started the interview with questions Dr. Whitman would have no reason to lie about so that she, as well as Sheriff Brenner and his detectives—who were all watching from another room—could establish his baseline behavior. In particular, she wanted to ferret out any habitual reactions or movements they might otherwise consider deceptive—like his habit of clicking and twirling his pen—as well as determine his personality type, which would help shape her interrogation strategy. Once she completed the baseline, she moved on to more pertinent subjects.

"When did you first meet Anna Jamison?"

He took out a small piece of paper from his shirt pocket. "I looked it up. It was in early December of last year—Thursday the third, to be precise. I know you asked before and I didn't answer, but she wanted to slightly reshape her nose and lift her backside, which are very common requests from young women these days."

Frankie made a note of it. Not that it likely made any difference, but everything counted in a murder investigation. "What was your first impression of her?"

"I thought she was beautiful. I didn't believe she needed any work done, but like most women—and more and more men these days—she focused on small flaws disproportionately."

"In our brief conversation before, you mentioned asking Anna out."

"Yes, I did. But that was before I learned that she was engaged. She wore a rose-gold engagement ring. It was small. I didn't notice it at first."

The ring. Frankie didn't recall anyone mentioning Anna's engagement ring as part of the evidence found at the crime scene or at her apartment. Where was it? Had she hidden it somewhere? Or had her killer kept it for himself?

And now Dr. Whitman had mentioned it.

She felt the small muscles near her temples tighten, like a fist.

"Did you continue to pursue her after you learned of her engagement?"

"No. I wanted to, but … I guess you could say we had a meeting of the minds."

Frankie cocked her head. "What does that mean?"

"We understood there was an attraction between us, but out of respect for her engagement, we couldn't carry things forward. She had already committed herself." A slight smile. "She knew I loved her. That's all that mattered."

Frankie's eyes went wide. She sat up straight. "You *loved* her?" She couldn't believe those words had come out of his mouth. For someone reluctant to talk before, he was certainly candid today.

She scooted closer to the table. "Dr. Whitman, were you having a relationship with Anna?"

"No. As I said, we were just friends."

She felt confusion arch her brow. "So, just so I'm clear, you were not involved with Anna and yet you felt like you *loved* her?" If no relationship existed, then his emotions seemed extreme, maybe even fantasy-based as her fourth profile suggested, which could explain his motive.

Seeing her response, he settled back. "Maybe *love* is a strong word. Let's just say she was the type of woman I'd like to marry someday. She was attractive, bright, and vivacious, and I am a single man."

This might have lessened Frankie's suspicion in another conversation, but not this time. The question was, just how desperate for a wife was Dr. Whitman? *Enough to stalk, court, and lure a young woman to play house? Enough to become Frankenstein creating his own bride?*

"Did you ever write Anna poetry or letters expressing your feelings?"

He frowned. "You mean like those they printed in the paper?"

"Yes, exactly like those."

He thought. "Do you think she liked poetry?" he asked. "She never mentioned receiving any such items to me. Do you think she told her fiancé about them?"

His random inquiries gave Frankie pause. Asking questions with additional questions was a common diversionary tactic. "Did you write Anna those poems and letters?" she asked again, more firmly.

The pen came out of his pocket. He began to twirl and click it. Looked her straight in the eye. "No. Of course not."

Frankie made note of the stress indicator. She thought he was lying.

"What about emails, texts, or phone calls?" she asked. "Did you and Anna talk?"

"Only regarding upcoming appointments and to connect after the procedures, which is standard. You can check my office accounts if you don't believe me."

She already knew it was true. The emails and phone calls traced to Anna's accounts had proven to be a source of frustration for Sheriff Brenner's team. If Anna had been involved in a new relationship in the months prior to her disappearance, she hadn't spoken to the individual via her regular email or cell phone. The sheriff's team had identified all incoming and outgoing addresses and phone numbers, and none had led to a new male contact of any significance.

"Can you tell me again—for the record—where you were Sunday, May ninth, the day Anna was last seen?"

He let out a deep breath. "Like I told you before, I was working at home. I've been remodeling this old house. Making a home for my future wife."

A deep crease appeared in his brow. "Do you really consider me a suspect, Agent Johnson? I mean, I told you how I felt about Anna. Why would I harm her?"

"People kill for love all the time, Dr. Whitman."

His smile disappeared. The pen stopped twirling.

Frankie slipped out a file folder from beneath her notepad. "Let's shift away from Anna for a moment. Do you know this young woman?" She removed a photo of a brunette with wavy hair and bright-green eyes and slid it across the table.

He glanced at it, and his eyelids tightened. "Melanie? I know her, but not well. We went to lunch, had coffee a few times when she came to town. She owns a lovely little flower shop in Hendersonville. Why?"

"She was a patient of yours?"

"Yes. She'd lost considerable weight and needed some excess skin removed."

"Did you find her attractive?"

Dr. Whitman stared at Frankie oddly, as if he was trying to determine why she would ask such a question. "Yes, I suppose so. Once the surgery was done, she was quite stunning. I pride myself on my creations. Why?"

Frankie wanted to shudder at the way he'd referred to the woman—as a creation—but couldn't show her disturbance. "Did you love her, too?"

His face darkened. "We just went to lunch, had coffee."

"When was the last time you saw her?"

"I don't know. It's been many years."

"Two years," Frankie corrected. She removed a photo of Emily Dearborn. "How about this woman?"

"She looks familiar. I think I helped her with her car once when it wouldn't start."

"I mean as a client," Frankie said.

"Okay." He studied it some more. "Maybe a tummy tuck or what we call our mommy makeover?" He put down the picture. "I'm not sure."

"Breast implants. Early last year," Frankie said.

He sighed. "I'll take your word for it. But I don't understand." He gestured with his hands. "What do these women have to do with me? With Anna?"

Frankie felt her eyes narrow. *Does he really not know, or is he playing with me?*

"What if I told you that both these women are missing and believed to be dead, like Anna? What would you have to say about that?"

Dr. Whitman slowly put a hand to his chest. He opened his mouth, but no words came out. He squirmed for a solid minute, trying to figure out how to respond. "I don't think I'd have anything to say about that. What makes you think they're dead, or connected to me?"

Frankie removed copies of the poems and letters given to Anna, Emily, and Melanie and put those that were similar beside each other. "First, these, which were given to each of our victims. See the similarities?"

Dr. Whitman picked up each one and read. As his forehead alternately creased and smoothed, his lips moved silently. He pulled and groomed his tie so many times Frankie thought he might strangle himself.

She could see his mind working and questioning, but questioning what? Was he fearful that they'd found other victims and linked them to him? Or was it something else? She wished she could climb inside his mind and read his thoughts.

"Do you recognize the works?" she asked.

After his visible brain battle ceased, he abruptly set the papers down and pushed them away. "No. I'm sorry. I don't know anything about them."

He crossed his arms defiantly.

Frankie slowly picked up the poems and put them back in the folder. "I guess it could all be a coincidence, but with the obsidian scalpel we found at the scene ..."

"An obsidian. One of many," he said. "I looked into their use, and obsidian scalpels have national U.S. sales upward of two thousand units."

Frankie inwardly smiled. He'd just revealed that he'd researched the sales to know his risk as a suspect, but she would let that thought rest for now. She wanted to continue exposing the evidence. "As I was saying, it could be coincidental, but then there is also this."

From her pocket, she removed the small envelope Lawrence had given her with the needle and green-braided suture. "Tell me, Dr. Whitman, have you ever seen this type of suture before?"

He reached out and took the material, twisted it between his fingers. Frankie sensed he wasn't pleased to see it but attempted to act unaffected. "Yes, it's part of a clinical trial I'm participating in, which I assume you already know. I presume you also know there are hundreds of surgeons participating in the study."

"True, but not hundreds that knew Anna Jamison and Melanie Higby," she said. "See, these sutures were discovered on Anna's body—right beneath what used to be her right breast. And a similar suture thread was found at the site of a fire in Hendersonville around the same time Melanie Higby disappeared."

He set the suture down. Stared at Frankie. In general, direct eye contact was a good thing, indicating truthfulness, but right now Dr. Whitman had a bit of a deer-in-the-headlights look—angry at her accusations, fearful of being exposed, or both.

She spread her hands over the evidence. "How do you explain this, Dr. Whitman? Three of your patients, all courted by the same man, who wrote the same poems and used the same tools, all presumed dead. The connection has to be you, or someone you know."

For the next several minutes, Dr. Whitman squirmed and shifted in his chair in an unending battle to get comfortable—much as she'd done in his office—but Frankie didn't think he'd find any relief. The evidence was starting to pile up and the walls were closing in.

She waited for him to settle down before she proceeded. She hoped that he was ready to move into the next interrogation phase after anger—that of depression.

Frankie conveyed her best empathetic look. "How do you feel about love, Dr. Whitman? Why haven't you married?"

His chest rose and fell with tepid breaths. "Well, love is complicated, isn't it? You meet someone, have hopes. Then discover they aren't what they appeared to be."

He studied the pen in his hand, which he gripped with white knuckles. "I have been in love many times. Not all of them have worked out. Some relationships were very hurtful." He glanced up. "I'm sure you understand."

His eyes held a message she couldn't quite interpret, as if they were sharing a private moment. "Sure," she said. "We all get our hearts broken. Tell me, who hurt yours? Does she have a name?"

"I wouldn't say there was just one."

"No? How about Mary Campbell?" In the background check Frankie had run on Dr. Whitman, Mary Campbell was the only name that had appeared as an association of his in adulthood. She'd had the same address while he was completing his medical residency in Baltimore. Frankie assumed they'd lived together for a time.

His reaction was not what she'd expected.

He nearly choked, then started to laugh. "Mary, my goodness. It's been so long since I've heard that name. To tell you the truth, I'd forgotten about her."

Laughter was often a stress response—a way to make an uncomfortable situation less stressful or appear less significant—and Frankie found it telling.

Forgotten? I don't think so. "She was an old girlfriend?"

"No." He waved her off. "Just the sister of a friend who stayed with me for a time. There was never anything between us. Never. She's nobody."

The pen in his hand began to twirl and click, twirl and click.

He was like Pavlov's dog ringing a bell.

"When was the last time you spoke to her?"

"I haven't."

"Do you think I could call and talk to her?"

"If you can find her, sure. She'll tell you the same thing. She's nobody to me."

Frankie stared. *Maybe, but I don't think so.*

"You know, if you're that interested in my dating life, I'm happy to give you some names. They can tell you I'm not the monster you think I am."

"That would be helpful, actually, thanks."

Frankie provided a piece of paper and he scribbled out two names before handing it back to her. She took it.

Now for the final shot.

"Okay, last question. In our first conversation, you spoke of the two teens who happened upon Anna's death. *The kids, I hope they are okay.* Your words?"

He shrugged. "Yes."

"Kids?"

He squirmed, clicked his pen. "Yes, kids. Why? What?"

She leaned into the table. "Dr. Whitman, how did you know about the girl?"

He hesitated, uncertain. "I don't know what you mean. Wasn't there a girl?"

"Yes, but that detail was never released to the media."

For the first time in the interview, Dr. Whitman stopped blinking. "I'm sorry, I wasn't aware of the media exclusion. The family told me about the girl."

Frankie narrowed her eyes. "They told you? When? Why would they do that? Endanger the girl?" She felt a rush of anger. *He's lying. He has to be.*

"I'm a plastic surgeon. I was examining Miguel Herrera's case to see what we could do to treat him cosmetically should he recover. The family brought the girl to the hospital and tried to pass her off as a cousin, but it was rather obvious she had feelings for Herrera. They didn't think I was a threat. Why would I be?"

"Because Anna died at the hands of a surgeon—a surgeon just like you," Frankie said. She felt her final point slipping away, when the revelation hit her. "So the family told you she was Miguel's girlfriend? What else did they tell you?"

"That's all."

"Then how did you know she was at the scene of the fire?"

Internally, she smiled. Even if the family had informed him that she was Miguel's girlfriend, that didn't equate to her being present at the crime scene.

The flush across the doctor's face extended across his forehead, his ears, even his scalp. His mouth opened, closed, opened. He veered toward the camera and back to Frankie. He pointed a finger in her face, his focus unwavering. "I didn't hurt Anna. I loved Anna. You've got this wrong. All wrong."

"Do I? I don't think so."

He shuffled wildly before he suddenly stood. "I'm sorry. I thought you and I had an understanding. I was mistaken." He straightened his tie and smoothed his shirt. "If you have any other questions, you may speak to my lawyer."

He tipped his hand to the boys behind the camera. "Have a good day."

CHAPTER 21

A strange wind blew from the northwest the next morning, the kind that said a change was coming and trouble was on the way. The temperature was eighty-four and it was only nine a.m. By midday, it would near the triple digits, and by late afternoon, the sky would turn a dark grayish-green, then transform into a deep purple bruise, as if the gods had given it a black eye. Angered, the clouds would howl and release their fury with wind, rain, and pounding hail. Frankie hoped to drive to Columbia to visit Whitman's foster mother, Betty Sue Taylor, and return to the city before getting caught in the wrath.

Overnight, she'd played back her interview with Dr. Whitman, seeking additional cues of deception in his testimony. Those times he'd picked up his pen and played with it were clear signs of his stress and discomfort, but Frankie liked to slow things down via video and concentrate on voice, word choice, and pitch as well as actions. Only then could she see the subtle signs she'd missed in real time.

After a thorough analysis, she'd come away with three observations. One, Dr. Whitman had readily offered his feelings about Anna—now a dead woman—and spoken of Melanie and Emily in the present tense, which were both things a guilty man was not inclined to do. Two, she felt certain he wasn't lying about his association with Anna. They had been friends. If their relationship had been real, he wouldn't have been able to contain his ego and would've told the world about it. And three, he was lying about the poems and letters and Mary Campbell. Dr. Whitman might've said she was a nobody, but Frankie didn't think so. She needed to find out about their relationship and what may've led him down a darker path.

Today, she hoped his foster mother could answer some of those questions.

After a ninety-minute drive, just as an ancient church bus clamored to a stop in front of a neighboring house to pick up a handful of teens for vacation Bible school, Frankie pulled in front of Betty Sue's modest brick ranch home. The first thing that struck her about the place was how neat it was: the yard freshly mowed, the rosebushes trimmed, and the flower boxes filled with petunias. If she was expecting a beast of a woman who'd turned little Kenny into a monster, the yard wasn't a good sign. Frankie guessed the woman who lived here would be just as tidy and charming as her yard.

She was correct. Answering the door was a petite woman with silver-gray hair and manicured nails. Her face was aged but pleasantly so, the extra crow's feet and deep lines telling of a person who enjoyed laughing.

As if she'd read Frankie's mind, Betty burst into a smile. "You must be Miss Johnson. Welcome. Please, come in."

Frankie hadn't been called *Miss* in a while, but she liked the formality and the woman's pleasant accent. She stepped inside and inhaled the cool air, a welcome relief compared to the sauna outside. During the drive, the car's air conditioning had begun to whine, and she wondered how long it would hold up. The late spring heat wave had taken a toll.

"Tea?"

A single nod and Betty went to the kitchen and removed a pitcher of tea from the refrigerator and poured it in a tall glass filled with ice cubes. Frankie didn't have to ask if it was sweet or unsweet. She'd learned the past five years that there was no such thing as unsweetened tea in the South. Occasionally she would request it just for fun, however, to see the appalled expression on people's faces.

Betty returned and handed the glass to Frankie, then led her to a living room furnished with an ivory couch and two wingback floral-print chairs covered with pale-blue pillows. The entire house carried the scent of one of those plug-in air fresheners. "We can talk in here."

Before she sat, Frankie studied the framed photographs of several children adorning the wall.

"My children," Betty said. "I've fostered twelve of them over time, some just for a short time before they were adopted, others until they were old enough to be on their own. None are my biological children, but for me, they've become mine just the same."

Frankie thought it odd the way the words spilled from Betty's mouth as if they were little rubber blocks of letters she bent, twisted, and rolled with her tongue before releasing them into the air. She caught herself tilting her head, as if the right angle might make her better able to understand the woman's southern words.

"You never had children of your own?" she asked.

"No. My husband passed early with cancer, and I never remarried."

No wonder only one foster parent had come up in the search. "I'm sorry."

Betty Sue briefly raised her hand. "It's okay. What is it they say? God laughs when men make plans."

"How true." Frankie turned toward a corner shelf, where several other photos, not one a bit dusty, sat. She picked up one of a young Dr. Whitman. He was maybe fourteen. "One of your children was Kenneth Whitman?"

"Yes, Kenny. One of my favorites. A bright boy. Good in school. He became a doctor." She straightened as she said this, indicating her pride.

"Yes, he did." He may also have become a serial killer, Frankie thought, but she kept that thought to herself. "He's quite successful."

Betty's eyes sparkled. "That's good to hear. To be honest, I don't know much about his life. He sends me flowers for my birthday and a card at Christmas but never comes to visit." The pull at the corners of her lips told Frankie how disappointed she was by that, by his no longer wishing to be a part of her life. Betty perched herself on the edge of a couch cushion. "I hope I can help you, but you probably know more about him than I do at this point. Is he in some kind of trouble?"

Frankie took a seat next to her and placed the glass of tea on a coaster. She thought of the best way to answer. "I'd rather not elaborate on the facts, but it is possible that Kenny is involved in a situation. I'm here because I want to learn about him and his past and help him if possible."

She hoped that by referring to Dr. Whitman as Kenny—not as the man he was now but as the boy Betty Sue remembered—she would make Betty feel more comfortable in providing information.

"I tell you what," Betty said. "Let me get some of my photo albums. They always help refresh my memory."

Frankie watched the petite bundle of energy whisk into the bedroom empty-handed and come out with an armload of pastel-colored albums. Frankie caught two as they slid from her grip and set them on the coffee table. Betty flipped through several albums before landing on the pages she wanted, pictures of summer vacations at the beach.

"Kenny loved the ocean," Betty remarked, as she handed it to Frankie.

"I see that." Frankie flipped through the pages of old pictures, pre-digital age, looking at the younger Kenny on boogie boards and body surfing, wondering what could have turned such a happy teenage boy into a man who performed unnecessary surgical procedures on women. There didn't seem to be any moments of darkness on these pages. "Who's the other boy in the photographs? He and Kenny seem to be close."

"That's Perry. He was another boy I fostered for a time. He was a year older than Kenny, and the two had a lot in common. Both lost their parents—Kenny's died in a car accident, Perry's in a fire. At one time, they were like brothers, but they grew apart as they got older. Kenny hung with the popular crowd, and Perry never quite fit in. He ended up dropping out of school, worked as a mechanic, and lived above the garage last I knew. I think Perry was jealous, you know, of Kenny's looks and smarts."

Frankie looked at the photographs again and thought that odd, because in her opinion, it was Perry who was better looking and more athletic. Kenneth, on the other hand, often appeared moody, especially in his later photographs. "He didn't like getting his picture taken," Betty explained, tapping a finger on the photo. "Teen angst, I guess."

Frankie continued through the pages, little Kenny growing up before her eyes. "So Kenny was popular. Did he have any problems outside of school? Any bad habits like bedwetting or fire-starting? Did he ever hurt animals or like violent movies?"

Betty placed a hand on her chest. "Oh no," she said, frowning. "Nothing like that. Of course, he was sad about his parents. Sometimes I'd hear him cry at night, but he never showed any signs of depression. He adjusted well."

Frankie sighed. So far, little Kenny wasn't fitting the profile of someone who would turn into a serial killer. "What can you tell me about his parents?"

"I didn't know them, but the state told me his father was a doctor and his mother a schoolteacher. She taught Sunday school too. I had no qualms at all about taking him in. They were good Christian people. Kenny knew his Bible well."

So the parents were religious. In Frankie's experience, a religious upbringing could be good or bad, depending on the intensity or fervor with which it had been presented. More than a few serial killers had experienced a religious upbringing that had manifested in antisocial behavior. "Were his parents strict?"

"Again, I couldn't say for sure, but it was clear Kenny had been taught to behave. He was polite and followed the rules. I don't recall ever having to punish him."

"Do you know why Kenny's grandmother or aunt didn't adopt him?"

"Yes, the aunt had cerebral palsy and her mother was taking care of her full-time. She didn't think she could handle both her daughter and grandson. After the car accident, it was all her mother could do to keep it together."

That answered that question.

Frankie sipped her tea. "Kenny was in the car crash along with his parents, correct? Did he ever suffer any residual effects from the accident? Any physical or mental difficulties?"

Betty shook her head. "Other than a deep scar on his right shoulder and another on his thigh, nothing I could see."

Frankie stared at the photograph still in her hand. "It sounds like Kenny adapted very well and you provided him a great home. Yet you said he doesn't visit. Why?"

Betty quieted. She grabbed her tea and took a long, slow sip before speaking. "No. Truth is, Miss Johnson, I haven't seen him since he left for college. I think ..." She leaned close, whispered. "I think it just brings back bad memories for him. Here, in Columbia."

Frankie raised an eyebrow. Finally, an indication that something was amiss. *Bad memories.* Something had occurred, something that might have turned Kenny down a darker road and prompted the sullen face Frankie saw in the later photographs.

"It was his girlfriend, Tammy Kay. You know about her?"

No, but Frankie was certainly interested.

"Awful story. They were in love, those two. Sweethearts all the way through high school. She was a cheerleader and he was president of the science club. Not your typical match. But they planned to attend the same college and talked about getting married."

Betty swiped at the legs on her periwinkle slacks. Took a sip of tea. Set it down. "One night, Tammy left cheerleading practice, and there was a man hiding in the back seat of her car. She didn't see him. He forced her to drive out to the country at knifepoint, and, well ..." Tears swelled in her eyes.

"I can look up the case," Frankie said, getting the picture. "Did she live?"

Betty grabbed a tissue and dabbed at the tears. "Barely. The animal beat her so badly that she had a series of strokes. It took years of physical therapy and counseling before she was able to resume a normal life."

She sniffled. "After it happened, Kenny went to see her every day. Stayed most nights too. He reached out to Clemson and USC to see if he could switch his college plans from Maryland, where his father had attended. He couldn't stand the thought of leaving her."

"A couple of months went by like that, Kenny at the hospital, still making plans for their future, then one day ..." She shrugged as her eyes went distant. "He packed his things, headed to Maryland, and nobody ever saw him again."

Frankie frowned. "Nobody? Did he call?"

"No. No call either, not even to me." She rubbed her hands together as if washing them free of disappointment. "As I heard it, Tammy broke it off. Said Kenny didn't need a handicap to take care of all his life, someone who couldn't give him love or children. He was so hurt. To face a second tragedy at such a young age. It was like everybody he'd ever loved died."

Frankie felt an involuntary shiver. The woman didn't know how right she was.

Betty Sue examined the ceiling and sighed. "I don't hold it against him for not visiting. It's understandable, the way he felt."

But Frankie could see that she did hold it against him, just a little. This hadn't just been Kenny's pain; it was her pain too. This woman had loved and cared for Kenny, had taken him as her own when no one else wanted him, and she felt as abandoned as he did. For him to have done that to her, the wounds must have run deep. He must have left South Carolina believing he was deeply cursed, that life could hold nothing but bad things for him here.

The question was, had these events in his childhood caused enough damage to make him a killer? Or had something else occurred later to make his life—and actions—take an even darker turn? What had happened next in Kenneth's life? At the University of Maryland? In medical school? Those questions needed to be Frankie's next steps.

Frankie stood. "Well, maybe one of these times, he'll come around. Don't give up. I hope I didn't resurface any troubling memories for you. I'd like to keep in touch."

Betty walked her to the door. "I hope that you will, Miss Johnson. Because I really can't imagine that Kenny could be involved in anything bad. That simply wasn't the young man I knew."

Outside, Frankie turned her eyes toward the sky. The sun was still shining, but the clouds, and the subsequent storm, were starting to build.

CHAPTER 22

The time and temperature on the sign outside the bank now read one thirty-four p.m. and one hundred two degrees. The car's air conditioner whined louder than ever and blew only hot air. Driving one-handed, Frankie used her other hand to rummage around in her gym bag in the passenger seat to remove a towel. She dabbed at her face and neck as she drove, cursing the sun as it baked through the windshield at every stop.

Before leaving Betty Sue's, she'd decided a quick search for Tammy Kay was in order, and she was surprised when the woman's name popped up with an address just ten miles away. Given Tammy's former relationship with Kenneth and the impact it might've had on him, she decided to make another stop.

The address listed was in a gritty part of Columbia, an area with more than its fair share of crime and poverty. Frankie swerved around potholes and upended asphalt until she found Tammy's apartment building, which sat next to a long-closed gas station with boarded up windows and a cement culvert decorated with graffiti. The building, a solid brick structure with barely-there windows, made Frankie nauseous. She could only imagine how hot it could get inside, which likely explained why the majority of residents were sitting outside on the stairs or the shaded lawn. The adults fanned themselves while the kids splashed in a puddle of water created by a hose with the water pressure of a spit bath.

She parked the car and left the window cracked. As she got out, old and young alike turned their heads, suspicious of the stranger in a pantsuit obviously sporting a gun. A posse of young men posted at the top of the stairs outside the entry quickly found other places to go. Two moms shuffled kids playing hopscotch off the crumbling sidewalk to let her pass.

No security code was necessary for entry. The hallways were dark, with only the occasional flicker of a working bulb to light her path. The place smelled putrid, like dirty diapers and fish left in the trash too long. Past door after door, she could hear the residents' lives unfolding—*Judge Judy* on the television, a toddler crying, a spousal argument.

And fans. So many fans.

Door 14C seemed quiet until Tammy Kay—or rather, what was left of her—opened the door. She was a skeleton of a woman, maybe an ounce north of a hundred pounds, with bristled blond hair and bad skin. The left side of her face still carried the residual effects from the strokes, especially her eye and lips, which hung at unusual angles.

The woman sized Frankie up, making no attempt to hide her disdain. "Who are you and what do you want?" Her voice was hoarse, likely from years of smoking. An ample cigarette stench wafted from inside.

Frankie showed Tammy her creds and asked her if they could talk about her case.

Tammy huffed between chapped lips. "My case? What case? Statute of limits or whatever took care of that long ago. Wasn't a case and never will be a case."

"It's important. If we could just talk."

Tammy shrugged. "Whatever, come on in. Not like I was conducting brain surgery or inventing the next atomic bomb anyway."

Frankie stepped into a tiny smoke-filled apartment devoid of light. Two small windows were open, but it was a single box fan that oversaw cooling the place. A cat appeared from the bedroom and rubbed against Frankie's leg. She petted it and took a seat at a small kitchen table. Tammy sat on a well-worn bench just to the side of a window.

"You wouldn't think I'd end up like this from a rape, would you?" she said, using what remained of one cigarette to light a new one. Her words, like Betty Sue's, tumbled around before coming out, but with an extra slur, like she'd had a few shots of vodka with her cigarette.

"You had a stroke. The doctors say why?"

"He beat my brain to mush. Swollen and shit. They said I was lucky to be alive. That means I'm supposed to be happy and grateful, right?" She took another draw off the cigarette and blew a trail of smoke out the window.

"I know this is difficult, but I need details about what happened to you that night. I'm investigating a series of homicides that might be related to your case."

"I'm not dead. How could they be related?"

"I understand, and I'm not saying your attacker is the same as the attacker of these other women, but there could be a connection."

Tammy studied her through her one good eye, smoke drifting. "Whatever."

Frankie turned the chair around to face her. "Tell me about the rape."

Tammy remained where she was, staring out the open window. Frankie imagined it to be her favorite spot, where she could gaze past the splotchy grass and tall pines to the magical what-if, a place where she was a doctor's wife, a mom to three small kids, and a member of the PTA. The difference between where she'd landed in life compared to Kenneth Whitman couldn't be more stark.

"He didn't rape me—at least, not in the way you're thinking. First, he … felt me. Dry humped me, hard. But I didn't feel an erection. I told him just to do it, to get it over with, and he got really angry and started beating me, like it was my fault."

"I don't understand. You said you were raped."

A little bit of the fear that still resided within Tammy Kay surfaced through an involuntary twitch at the corner of her good eye. "I was, but not in the typical way. I guess because he couldn't … do it, he used the only other thing he could find: a branch from a tree. It was sharp, splintered. Tore my uterus all to hell. Left me sterile."

When she drew on the cigarette again, her hand shook.

Frankie glanced away and drew a long breath. Her legs reflexively crossed, and she had to swallow the warm vomit she felt surface. She couldn't imagine the pain.

"Can you tell me anything about the man that did this to you? What he looked like? Distinguishing scars, tattoos, anything?"

"No. He put a pillow case over my head and kept it on the whole time. I think I knew him though. I told the police. Something about his voice. He was young, I know that. He didn't have any chest hair and had a lanky build, like boys are in high school. They had me look at the yearbook, but nothing really popped out for me."

She stroked the cat as it ran under her legs. "I couldn't stand the thought of going back to school after it happened. I kept imagining he would be in the hall with me, or in class, watching and laughing. I still get the creeps thinking about it."

"When it happened, you were seeing someone. Kenneth Whitman?"

Her eyes briefly lit up, then went distant with memories. Back to staring out the window. "Yeah, Kenny. Poor Kenny. Everybody he loves dies."

Frankie raised an eyebrow. Tammy was the second person to have said such a thing.

"You didn't. Why did you leave him?"

"Oh, but I did. I did die. I couldn't look at him anymore, with that pitying look on his face. I hated everyone, even started to hate him. I didn't want to be responsible for making his life miserable, having a wife who looked like me, unable to give him kids. Before, it was all we talked about. I told him to go away."

"According to Betty, he was heartbroken," Frankie said.

"Mama Betty? She still living?"

"Yes, and she seemed pretty fond of you. Cried when she told me about you."

"She was nice. Real nice."

Tammy's eyes grew moist. "Kenny was so sweet. The sensitive type, you know? The funny thing is, I didn't really want him to leave. I was having a bad day, in pain, and just confused. We'd fought before and he'd always come back. I didn't really think he'd go to Maryland. But he did. And he never looked back. Not even a phone call."

She picked at a nail and choked back tears. Started to laugh. "Can't blame him, though. Who would want to go through life with a bitter, used-up, hag like me? Hell, I don't even want to be with me."

"Tammy, don't," she said. "What happened to you was a tragedy, but it doesn't need to define you."

Tammy doused a cigarette and quickly changed the subject. "He wrote me poems. I kept them. You want to see?"

Frankie's heart nearly exploded. Her mouth went dry, and a nervous energy gathered in her core. She could feel the muscles in her face contort into various shapes. "Poems? Yes, I'd like to see them."

She watched as Tammy removed a stack of magazines from the top of a chest that doubled as a coffee table in the living room. Frankie could see fine linens and china in the chest, along with a family Bible, and she knew at once it was a hope chest, everything Tammy had held onto from her past. Frankie wanted to ask about her family but let it go when Tammy handed a stack of papers to her. Frankie unfolded the sheets within and started to read.

> On that first day I saw you,
> Instantly I knew
> We would be together,
> Our love would be true.
>
> I will build you castles,
> Should you be my queen
> We will raise a family
> Across fields of green

Juvenile, and frankly, what Frankie would expect of a teenager. Two similar poems followed. The fourth one, however, turned her knees to gelatin.

> It lies not in our power to love or hate,
> For will in us is overruled by fate.
> When two are stripped, long ere the course begin,
> We wish that one should lose, the other win;
>
> And one especially do we affect
> Of two gold ingots, like in each respect:
> The reason no man knows; let it suffice
> What we behold is censured by our eyes.

Where both deliberate, the love is slight:
Who ever loved, that loved not at first sight?

"I know this one. Marlowe." Frankie said. They were the same two verses written to Anna Jamison and leaked to the *Charlotte Observer*.

"I'm not sure. Some guy that was born the same year as Shakespeare. That's what I remember Kenny telling me."

Right. Christopher Marlowe and William Shakespeare, both born in 1564. A good year for poets, and for tragedies.

Frankie skimmed several other poems, most of them juvenile like the first few, until landing on "Go, Lovely Rose!" This was one of their unsub's favorites. He'd given this entire poem to Anna, Emily, and Melanie.

Go, lovely Rose!
Tell her that wastes her time and me
That now she knows,
When I resemble her to thee,
How sweet and fair she seems to be.

Tell her that's young,
And shuns to have her graces spied,
That hadst thou sprung
In deserts, where no men abide,
Thou must have uncommended died.

Small is the worth
Of beauty from the light retired;
Bid her come forth,
Suffer herself to be desired,
And not blush so to be admired.

Then die! that she
The common fate of all things rare
May read in thee;
How small a part of time they share
That are so wondrous sweet and fair!

"Nerdy, huh?" Tammy said, reading along beside her. "But I loved them. I thought they were sweet." She glanced up. "Ma'am? You okay?"

Frankie looked at her, saw her not as the victimized forty-year-old but the sixteen-year-old waiting to be victimized. Frankie was no longer sure Tammy's attacker wasn't the attacker who'd killed the other three women. The poem had been written by Edmund Waller, but what were the odds that the same one would be given to Tammy and all the other victims? It had to have been Kenneth.

Frankie suddenly felt like she was handling something unclean, the beginning of a lifetime of obsession and death. She put the poem down, wanted to wash her hands.

She thought about her profile of the obsessive fantasy-based lover. Dr. Whitman was suddenly checking several of the boxes, including ethnicity, age, being fantasy obsessed, his need for deep, abiding love, and his mother abandoning him. But what of the last part about desiring prepubescent girls or being unable to perform sexually?

She needed to find out more about that last part.

"Tammy, did you and Kenny ever have sex?"

The woman sat back, distrustful of the question. "What's this about? Is this about Kenny? Kenny wouldn't hurt me. Kenny wouldn't hurt anyone."

Frankie wasn't her mother. She was younger than Tammy. "Yes or no?"

"Yes."

"And he never ..."

"No," she said, anticipating where Frankie was going. "We had sex. Many times. And he was never rough. Really sweet, just like the rest of him. Honest to God, he wasn't the guy who hurt me. I knew Kenny. I knew every part of him, if I can be so frank."

Tammy blushed, but Frankie understood. They had been lovers. Yet, it seemed certain that a connection existed between him and Tammy's rape. The woman had mentioned how young her violator had been, lanky and hairless, possibly a fellow student. Frankie wondered if Dr. Whitman had known Tammy's attacker or if he'd suspected a friend. Something of that nature could cause great anger. Watching what his girlfriend had endured, then losing her, suffering yet another loss in his life—at the hands of a friend who'd betrayed him, no less—could've easily created a dark psychological need, either a lust for revenge or a longing for unfulfilled love.

Yet why the mastectomy? Why remove his victims' breasts? No matter what Frankie learned, nothing seemed to explain it. It was the elephant in the room, the big gaping hole in the unsub's modus operandi, and it frustrated her.

Frankie stood to leave—anxiety, excitement, and confusion fueling her drive to dig deeper into this new information. But she didn't want to leave Tammy without her knowing her case mattered. "You don't know how helpful this has been. I want you to know I'm going to find him, your rapist."

Tammy brushed away a tear.

Frankie stopped at the doorway. "Tammy? You can have a life. You deserve one. Counsel other women. Adopt kids. Even fall in love again. You don't have to keep letting him win. Promise me you'll think about it?"

"Yeah, maybe." And with that Tammy Kay returned to her window, her little spot on the world.

CHAPTER 23

He sat in his car in the middle of the quiet little neighborhood of bungalows and ranch homes watching the clouds boil over the western skies. It was going to be another blistering day of heat, followed by intense storms. The air had that familiar weight he'd learned meant trouble, even as a kid. Tornado weather, his mom used to say. On those days, the afternoon sky would turn an odd combination of gray and green and an eerie quietness would spread over the land, as if all the animals, birds, and insects knew the devil was going to have his day and they'd taken leave.

Agent Johnson had pulled out early from her home as usual, presumably headed for the office. Now he was just waiting for the neighbors. He'd seen most of them stirring—going for an early-morning jog, walking the dog, or just opening the blinds to greet the new day. It wouldn't be long before most exited their cute little homes to go to work. At least he hoped it wouldn't.

Thirty minutes later, the exodus began. The young couple who lived across the street loaded their toddler in the back seat of their sedan and headed out. The older woman next door pulled away five minutes after that. Over the next half hour, several others followed suit. Now the street was largely his, with just a few stragglers remaining.

He waited until it started to sprinkle before he exited the car, knowing the umbrella would add an extra layer of protection to hide his face. He'd walk around the block a couple of times, then make his move. To anyone looking out the windows of their charming little homes, he would just be another neighbor out for a morning walk or headed to the corner deli. Even if they saw him walk up the steps to her house, they'd think he was just hanging flyers or selling the latest home improvement.

The rain intensified during his walk, and his shoes squished against the pavement, reminding him of the roaches he used to crush underfoot as a kid. He took a couple of different paths around the block for good measure, but after seeing that one of the homes adjacent to Agent Johnson's backyard was vacant and for sale, he decided to take advantage of the opportunity and cut through the house's yard to get to hers. He smiled at his good fortune—a sure sign he was meant to be here.

At the window to her guest bedroom, he quickly inserted a flat metal file in the space where the window didn't sit properly in the sill beneath it and, using it as a lever, he thrust it down a few times until he could run the wire hook up inside to the lock and pull it open. From the last time he'd come here to visit and observe, he knew this window was problematic, and her alarm system had sensors on the doors but not the windows. The alarm wouldn't be activated by his entry.

After sliding open the window, he hoisted himself through and shut it behind him. Then he stood there a moment, letting the water drip, and it quickly pooled on the hardwood floor. He shook the folded umbrella and propped it against the wall. So much water. He would have to wipe himself dry before he proceeded to inspect the house and clean up before he left.

He stepped cautiously around the end of the iron bed, which was covered with a yellow-and-white patched quilt, to the guest bathroom on the other side, where he grabbed a towel from the linen closet and used it to dry off. He removed his shoes and left them and the wet towel beneath the window for later use.

Entering the hallway, he saw a small furry shadow race into the living room. The cat. He knew Agent Johnson had a cat from his previous visits; he'd seen it perched on the back of the couch one night with the hair up on its back and its tail twitching as he'd stared through the front picture window.

"Here, kitty kitty," he said.

An unpleasant mewl came from the adjoining room. He slid around the arched entry and saw it, a black-and-gray tabby with green eyes, staring at him from a safe spot beneath the front window. It didn't seem to like him. He couldn't say he blamed it. It probably knew what he'd done to other small animals when he'd been young and furious at his parents.

"No worries, kitty. I'm not here to hurt you. I just want to look around."

He first went into the kitchen, which was separated from the living area by a breakfast bar. There, he traced his hands across the fresh, white cabinets and opened each one to look inside. Her dishes appeared new—a French provincial set rimmed in orange with an olive pattern—but it was obvious she also favored vintage. In one cabinet, she had Pyrex and Fire-King bowls, and in another, an orange juice pitcher and matching glasses he was certain dated to the 1950s. A set of Betty Boop salt and pepper shakers sat on the stove, and an old Pillsbury Doughboy cookie jar decorated a corner.

Most of the other cabinets contained more food than kitchen essentials. One held wine of various kinds—mostly reds—and spices filled another. In the refrigerator, he found fresh vegetables from the farmers' market, chai tea and almond milk, and assorted gourmet cheeses. A sun tea jar sat on the top right shelf, and he poured himself a glass. Took a sip and spit it out. It was unsweetened and bitter, a terrible brew. He removed the jar, added some sugar, and stirred it before placing it back in the refrigerator. He smiled. She would thank him for fixing it.

He opened some leftovers wrapped in foil. One was a deli sandwich of some kind and he tore off a bite-sized piece to taste it. Italian. Salami and provolone cheese. He grabbed a plastic bowl, lifted the lid, and sniffed what appeared to be pasta and possibly crab. Slid it back on the shelf.

Agent Johnson stocked her kitchen very differently than his mother. His mother had been all eggs, bread, and potatoes, with meat straight from the butcher. Except for some halibut and flank stank, there was very little meat in Agent Johnson's refrigerator or freezer at all.

Done with the kitchen, he moved on to the living room. He sat on the couch and flipped through the magazines on her coffee table: *Ebony, Southern Living, O*. He removed photo albums from a built-in bookshelf to the side of the fireplace and thumbed through vinyl pages containing photographs of her as a child. There were pictures of her with her African American mother, a dark beauty with almond eyes and high cheekbones, and separately with her dad, who was white as the sun was bright. The pictures seemed to convey a mostly happy childhood—birthday parties in a cramped apartment, dress-up days in her mom's clothes, ice skating at Rockefeller Plaza—although her mood and manner of clothing appeared to have changed frequently as she'd grown up.

He chuckled. Something else they had in common.

Yet what fascinated him most in the living room was two white posterboards tacked to the wall in place of the lithograph that typically hung there. In that space, she'd written out her ideas about Anna's killer—her *profiles*, as she called them—and what she thought about the suspect everyone was searching for. Words like *anger, abandonment*, and *abuse* jumped out at him, and although he didn't like them, he understood why she'd had to write them. It was a message—just like when she'd looked at him through the television the other day. She was telling him how much she wanted to understand. Unlike the others, she truly wanted to know him—mind, body, and soul.

He ran his hand across the words, felt them pulse beneath his fingertips. *I'm all these things and so much more. Soon you will get to experience me fully, and I, you, and you will understand everything.*

Feeling like he'd gotten a good sense of the things she liked, he realized it was now time to understand her more intimate side. He always saved the best for last, letting the anticipation grow until he couldn't stand it anymore.

As he stepped down the hallway to her bedroom, his heart pounded wildly. This was it, her most private world. The door was shut, but when he opened it, he gasped. Here, then, was her refuge: the pink lampshades, the leopard print duvet cover, the rose satin sheets. An oil painting of an African American nude hung above the headboard. A light sway of ivory curtains covered the front window.

He inhaled deeply, letting the aroma infiltrate his nostrils. Just the smell of her excited him. He walked the perimeter of the room and inspected the finer details. He picked up a music box topped with a ballerina and wound it to let it play. Opened her jewelry box and tried on each of her rings. Spritzed a bit of her perfume, the classic Chanel No 5. He opened each drawer of her dresser and examined the items within, T-shirts and shorts, all folded neatly, and bras and panties, which he fondled and sniffed. In the closet, he caressed the folds of her dresses and slid his hand beneath the hems of the skirts, imagining her wearing them and feeling that moist place between her legs.

Through it all, his excitement grew.

He sat on the edge of the bed and ran his hands across the duvet then slid them underneath to pull it back. He lay face down on the sheets and buried his face in her pillows to breathe in her scent, then turned over and stared at himself in a corner mirror. *She slept here, right here.* He imagined her lying there naked, her dark hair cascading across her shoulders, and groaned involuntarily. He began to rub himself and couldn't stop.

Once satisfied, he rose and remade the bed, then went back to the closet. He selected a red knit dress that he thought perfect for her along with a pair of black high heels. From her dresser he took two pairs of panties and a pink lace bra. He didn't want to take too much too soon, just enough to let her know that he'd received her message and was preparing for her.

He stopped before leaving, wondered if he should leave a note expressing his love. In hindsight, giving the same poems to his girls might've been an error, but then, was it ever a mistake to love someone so deeply? He didn't believe so. And Agent Johnson, he loved her more than anyone he'd ever known. Her beauty was so rich, how could he not express his admiration?

He knew immediately which poem he wanted to leave her.

He'd have to come back a bit later.

Back in the guest bedroom, he dried the floor, slipped into his shoes, and wrapped his new souvenirs in the towel to take with him. The window came back down and the latch relocked. The umbrella opened and he was on his way.

Soon, my love, very soon, we will be together.

CHAPTER 24

rankie arrived home just as a second round of intense thunderstorms lit up the night. After parking her car out front, she ran to the mailbox to retrieve the mail and up the steps, hoping to beat the downpour she knew was coming. Bones seemed happier than usual to see her, greeting her at the front door with a leg rub and loud purring. After throwing the mail on top of the breakfast bar and entering the code for the alarm, she reached down to pick him up. "Did you have a good day, buddy? Did you hide under the desk when it stormed?"

He answered with meows that she assumed meant yes, he'd done exactly that. She rubbed his head and set him on the breakfast bar, where he liked to watch her cook and eat his dinner. Her mother had repeatedly told her it wasn't healthy to allow him on the counter, but Frankie had learned one thing about Bones—Bones was going to do what Bones wanted to do, regardless of what Frankie said. The only place she enforced the rules and disallowed him to roam freely was her bedroom, because he loved to claw the pillows.

She opened the refrigerator to pour herself a glass of tea and retrieved the previous night's pasta leftovers. As they warmed in the microwave, she opened a can of cat food, spooned it into a small dish, and set it in front of Bones. While he ate, she started to check the mail. She took a sip of her tea—and nearly spit it halfway across the room.

What the hell?

She looked at the glass, sniffed inside. The tea tasted funny. She never put sugar in her tea and yet could have sworn this batch was sweetened. She tried another sip. Got the same result.

Maybe I left soap residue in the glass?

She rinsed the glass and refilled it. Still a no-go. She shook her head. "I don't know what I did, but this is terrible," she said to Bones. She removed the sun tea jar from the fridge and poured out what remained of it. She'd have to make more tomorrow.

After taking the heated leftovers from the microwave and stirring them, she topped them with some fresh Parmesan and a squeeze of lemon, then turned on the television in the living room. As she watched the evening news, Bones weaved between her legs and rubbed against her calves, begging for a bite. The downpour she'd expected earlier finally arrived, and large raindrops the size of dimes and pea-size hail began pelting the house. The power flashed as a bolt of lightning hit somewhere close, and the subsequent boom sent Bones running back beneath the desk in her office, crab be damned. It was then that Frankie sensed something was amiss, as the smell of rain overpowered the room and she heard heavy dripping coming from the hallway. A strong draft confirmed her worry.

"Oh no. Not that damn window again," she muttered.

Shoving the food aside, she raced down the hall and flicked on the guest bedroom light. Sure enough, the window had popped open. It always did this if she didn't fully engage the lock, which was hard to do because the window had swollen over time and no longer properly aligned with the sill. Even forcing it closed didn't always work. Sometimes the pressure built to the point it simply sprung open.

She grabbed both sides and jiggled it until it slid back into the sill, then turned the lock as tight as she could. She rounded the bed and grabbed a towel from the guest bathroom to wipe up the floor. Unfortunately, the quilt on the bed had also gotten wet, so she stripped it and threw it in the dryer. When she came back into the hall, she noted that her bedroom door—which she always kept shut when she was away—was also ajar.

Had the wind from the open window caused it to pressurize and push open? Possibly. It had happened before. Yet Frankie had a bad feeling. A musky fragrance she didn't recognize infiltrated her senses.

Frankie retrieved her Glock. Bones joined her, tail twitching. She pushed the bedroom door open with her foot. Normally Bones would bolt right in when granted access to the plush bed, but not so this time. A low mew escaped his throat. He sensed the same trouble she did.

A bolt of lightning flashed outside and briefly lit up the room. A low, steady rumble followed, shaking the walls of the tiny house. Frankie reached around the doorjamb and flicked on the light.

Thankfully, no one was there, but that musky scent remained.

She scouted the room. At first glance, everything seemed okay, until she looked at the bed. One thing her military father had instilled in her at a young age was the habit of making her bed, and to his strict standards. "Make sure you can bounce a quarter off it," he would say. She wasn't quite that strict with herself now, but she still made her bed and did it properly.

But the bed was rumpled. She never would've left it like that.

Had Bones taken advantage of the open door and slept on the bed? It was entirely possible, but it didn't explain two of the pillows, which lay flat. Frankie always propped the pillows against the headboard, with the large ones in back and the smaller decorative ones in front. Unless Bones had rubbed against them and knocked them over, they too seemed out of place.

She edged around the bed, moving toward the closet on the other side of the room. It was a small walk-in with no door, just enough space for three racks and a shelf for shoes and handbags. She quickly rounded the corner.

Thankfully, it also was empty.

She holstered the gun but remained in the closet, listening to the rain coming down outside and staring at the clothes hanging there. Or, more appropriately, gazing at those that weren't hanging there.

"I wish you could tell me what happened here," she said to Bones, "because I'm starting to freak out a little bit right now."

There were many things Frankie wasn't picky about in life, but her bed was one, and her clothes were another. She wasn't a woman who had an abundance of garments, but what she did have she kept systematically organized. Her workout wear, T-shirts, shorts, underwear, and bras, she kept folded in the dresser, while her professional attire—blouses, pants, blazers, and suits—hung in the closet, along with casual dresses and cocktail attire. And when she selected something to wear, the empty hanger went to the bottom rack so it didn't clutter the closet.

There were three empty hangers on the top rail right now: one among the pants, another with the blouses, and a third in the dresses. She wanted to tell herself that she'd taken some items to the cleaners, but then why hadn't she moved the hangers?

A prickly feeling needled its way down the back of her neck.

Something was very wrong here. From the tea to the window to the bed, and now the closet. What had happened? *Did somebody break into my house? Did somebody take my clothes?*

She thought about the personal effects discovered in the farmhouse where Anna Jamison had been murdered, swallowed the hard lump that had formed in her throat. Was someone trying to scare her? Or worse, was the unsub targeting her as his next victim?

She didn't like the thought of either.

Anxiety mixed with fury as she wheeled toward the bed. She ripped the pillows from their cases, then stripped the bed bare. She couldn't crawl in those covers thinking someone else might've been there between the sheets.

She stuffed them in the washer, added soap, hit start.

As a precaution, she immediately checked the rest of the house, including all the doors and windows. Nothing else seemed out of place, but she drew the blinds and curtains anyway, feeling like somebody was watching her. She paced the living room and kitchen, thinking about Dr. Whitman. *Was it him? Did Dr. Whitman break into my home while I was visiting with his former foster mother and girlfriend?*

She couldn't imagine him doing it … and yet, the evidence seemed to indicate otherwise. She turned to look at the posterboards on the wall where she'd written her profiles. Had he seen and read these? Had he understood that the individual she was exploring was him? And what had he thought about that? Was he angry, hurt?

Is that why he decided to target me? To make me pay?

While she was trying to figure these things out, the cell phone in her pocket buzzed. She took it out and read a text message from the woman next door who watched Bones whenever she was away. *Hi Frances. Wanted to let you know you had a friend stop by earlier. She left something in your mailbox.*

Frankie bit a nail. *A friend? What friend?* She glanced at the mail she'd thrown on the breakfast bar. The gnawing in her stomach grew fierce.

She stood over it with a sense of dread. First the clothes and now … what? She sorted through the random pile of bills and junk mail until she saw it—a distinctive pink envelope with her name scrawled across the front. *Frankie.*

She'd started to open it with her bare hands when she thought better of it. If it was from Dr. Whitman—or whoever had violated her domain—there could be fingerprints on the envelope or paper inside. From beneath the kitchen sink, she retrieved a pair of latex gloves and grabbed a pair of tweezers from the bathroom. She used a pair of scissors to slice the top of the envelope and the tweezers to pull out the single piece of stationery inside.

It was printed from a computer. A poem. Lord Byron's "She Walks in Beauty."

> *My lovely Frankie,*
> *This poem reminds me of you.*
> *Me*
>
> *She walks in beauty, like the night*
> *Of cloudless climes and starry skies;*
> *And all that's best of dark and bright*
> *Meet in her aspect and her eyes;*
> *Thus mellowed to that tender light*
> *Which heaven to gaudy day denies.*
>
> *One shade the more, one ray the less,*
> *Had half impaired the nameless grace*
> *Which waves in every raven tress,*
> *Or softly lightens o'er her face;*
> *Where thoughts serenely sweet express,*
> *How pure, how dear their dwelling-place.*

And on that cheek, and o'er that brow,
So soft, so calm, yet eloquent,
The smiles that win, the tints that glow,
But tell of days in goodness spent,
A mind at peace with all below,
A heart whose love is innocent!

She didn't recall this poem being one the unsub had shared with any of the missing women or Tammy Kay, but that didn't mean Dr. Whitman wasn't the one who'd put in her mailbox.

She turned the paper over to see if there was anything on the reverse side, flipped it back. Did the same with the envelope. Nothing. She slightly parted the curtains to glance up and down the now darkened street. She didn't see anybody, but that didn't mean they weren't there. Her paranoia grew.

A poem. Just like those Anna's friends and coworkers had told Sheriff Brenner she'd received at work and at home. Anna had even found one inside her car, as had Emily and Melanie. The poems and letters were always dropped off and never mailed, and no one had ever seen who left them.

And now Frankie had one in her mailbox.

What was Frankie to make of this along with the disappearance of her clothes? Should she take this seriously and assume she was to be the unsub's next target, or was the unsub—whom she believed was Dr. Whitman—playing with her?

Then again, maybe it was just her imagination running wild. It was just one poem, and different from those sent to Anna and the others, so it was possible it wasn't even related. Right? Heck, maybe even in her great distraction during the past two weeks, she had sweetened her tea and taken her clothing to the cleaners. And the window, it was known to become disengaged, and that could have opened her bedroom door, and Bones could've fluffed and slept on the bed. It was all explainable.

She feared, however, that Vicks and Ben would think otherwise and worry that the unsub was targeting Frankie when more than likely he was simply trying to scare her, just as someone had done to race car driver Bobby B. Vicks would likely remove her from the case and put Ben in charge. She couldn't have that. She needed this.

Frankie decided then and there that it was too early to sound an alarm. Ben had made a point recently that she needed to be prepared to act independently, and independently was how she would do this. She needed to learn to stand on her own. She didn't need him, the Bureau, or the BAU protecting her at every turn. She was going to nail this one all by herself, even if it killed her.

CHAPTER 25

The next day, Frankie decided an afternoon out would do her good, not only so she could think about the poem left for her and exactly what it meant but also so she could decide her next steps. Shortly before noon, she left the field office and drove uptown to join the hoard of city workers for lunch. Ben thought it odd that she often headed to the busiest and noisiest place to get away from it all, but Frankie found the traffic, lights, and swarms of people comforting. It was a remnant of her growing up in Queens, where it wasn't the noise that disturbed her but the echo of silence.

As she exited the dark parking garage into the bright sun, the heat enveloped her and ripened the nearby odors of hot dogs, diesel, and newly paved asphalt. Horns honked, engines roared, and somewhere a truck backed up, adding its constant *beep beep beep* to the city blend. After stopping at a café for a turkey wrap and veggies, she found her favorite bench outside the Blumenthal theatre and sat. It was yet another record hot day in what had so far proved to be a record hot week, and she wondered how long it would be before they saw normal temperatures again. Across the busy street, a fellow bench occupant seemed to agree, wrapping her blond hair up in a high ponytail before fanning herself with a brochure. Frankie thought her large round sunglasses made her look like a bumblebee.

With her own eyes hidden behind glasses as well, she caught herself people-watching, focusing on a veteran who sped down the street in his wheelchair with a small American flag attached, then a man arguing with his wife. The small Yorkie the woman held in her arms cast his brown eyes sadly at passersby, as if asking them to intervene.

As Frankie's gaze drifted west, her eyes came to rest on a tall, handsome man in slacks and a light-green polo shirt striding confidently toward her. When he reached her bench, he offered up a charming grin. "Special Agent Johnson, looking beautiful like always. May I join you?"

Frankie stared for a moment, couldn't help but wonder if this was a planned encounter. After yesterday, she was suspicious of everything—and everyone. "Dr. Lawrence Banks. You just happened to be strolling uptown at this time of day?"

He looked up at the bright blue sky. "It was such a nice day. I thought a long walk would do me good."

"You're two miles from the hospital, and it's ninety-eight degrees."

"A long walk. A very long walk. And you know I like it hot, very hot."

Even with the excessive temperatures outside, she felt a pulse of additional warmth course through her body. *Damn.* She cleared her throat, hoping the hot flash didn't show. Maybe he'd been the one who'd sent the poem yesterday? She wanted to ask him but decided to wait.

He saved her as his grin faded. "How have you been?"

"Busy. Very busy."

"Still trying to get the bad guy?"

"Yep."

"Still angry at me?"

"Yep."

He looked at her like a wounded puppy. Frankie shook her head, knowing he was playing her soft side, but told him to sit. He did as she commanded. For the next few minutes, they stared at each other between a gap they wanted to close but felt off-limits, in quiet acknowledgment that he couldn't ask about the case and she couldn't answer.

"People are talking at the hospital," he said.

She slid the cellophane off her wrap and took a bite. "Oh?"

He stared up at the sun. "Do you want to hear?"

She studied the passing midday crowd, businessmen and women in suits and skirts, and thought offhand how the hems were getting shorter and the heels were getting higher. "I can't stop you from talking, so if you happen to speak and I overhear, I mean, there isn't really anything I can do about it."

He nodded and unwrapped a sandwich of his own. He'd come prepared.

Definitely a setup.

"You probably know this, but during Dr. Whitman's residency at Johns Hopkins, he went AWOL for a year. He got permission from the American Board of Surgery and did a six-year residency."

As she chewed, she furrowed her brow.

"Yes, it is unusual," he continued. "Highly. Except for residents taking maternity leave, I can only think of two others who took extended time off during a residency."

She felt the creases in her forehead deepen. She tilted her head.

"What was his reason? I'm glad you asked," he said. "It was a family emergency. That was the official version. You want the unofficial version?"

She raised an eyebrow above her sunglasses.

"There was a woman, a fellow resident at Johns Hopkins by the name of Sara Phillips. She was first-year, Whitman third. Sara evidently grew up with Whitman near Spartanburg when his parents were still alive. Her parents and his parents were good friends, so little Sara and Kenny often played together. But Sara apparently took issue with the older Kenny. She said he was different, not the same kid she remembered."

"Well sure, I imagine he was different," Frankie said, breaking her silence. "His parents died and he spent the rest of his formative years living as an orphan in a foster home. That has to change a person. And if he's the killer we think he is now, that period in his life likely played a critical role in how he became that killer. It's cause and effect. Right now, we know the effect, but we're still searching for the cause."

"Yes, well, it seems this Sara recognized the difference. So much so that she went to the chief resident expressing her fear of him. The point is, when the higher-ups started to pay attention to her, that's when Whitman took his leave."

Frankie stared at the overflowing trash can across Fourth Street. It made sense that Sara might have recognized Whitman was disturbed. In childhood, defenses weren't yet developed, so friendships and their underlying bonds were pure. As adults, people carted around baggage like bellboys at a hotel, but as kids, they had yet to fill the suitcase. "And Sara?"

Dr. Banks chewed on his sandwich for longer than necessary before he swallowed. He seemed on edge, like he'd been at the diner. "Sara never completed her residency. She was murdered the following winter. A jogger discovered her in a park propped up against a park bench with her throat slit. They said it was so cold that night her blood froze in an icicle from the corner of her mouth to the pavement."

Frankie stopped chewing and slowly turned her head to look at him. There were no words to equal the turmoil she was feeling. "Slitting the throat doesn't match the perpetrator's MO," she said. "That kind of anger. It's very personal."

"Right. I just thought you should know."

Frankie stared across the lanes of noontime traffic, wondering how this latest bit of news might blend with the rest of what she knew about Dr. Whitman. Every time she thought she had a pulse on him, something changed course. The man was an enigma.

"Also." Dr. Banks reached inside his pocket and removed a sheet of paper. "I couldn't get it out of my head what you said about Anna, that if her surgery, her disappearance—whatever it was—hadn't gone wrong, she might've never been found or even reported as missing. It bothered me that there might be others. So I asked around."

He handed her the sheet of paper. On it were three names: Rory Spencer, Cheryl Connelly, and Brianna Thomas.

"Who are they?" she asked.

"Other potential victims to check out. Ones that worked at or near hospitals before quitting to move elsewhere with a new man. Rory was a student at Clemson and a barista at a coffee shop outside the regional hospital there. Her parents received a note in the mail three months after she went missing saying she'd dropped out of school to travel the world with a new love. No word since. I found her because she has a friend who's been searching for her on social media. Cheryl Connelly was a physician assistant at Atrium Health near the children's hospital here in Charlotte. She was dating, but no one knew anything was serious until she said she was moving out of the country. Brianna Thomas worked in admissions at Carolina Medical. Her parents found poems and a letter from her to them at her residence expressing her gratitude for everything they'd done for her and saying good-bye. They were shocked, but they'd had a rough go of it with their daughter the past few years and had no reason to believe foul play was involved. The latest headlines have them thinking twice."

Frankie stared at him, mouth agape. She didn't know how to take the news. Part of her was angry at him for getting involved and conducting his own side investigation, yet another part of her was sick at what he'd found. She couldn't take it, the possibility of three other victims. It was like adding two altos and a soprano to the already growing chorus inside her head.

She wondered how many others might be out there. As Frankie had done initially in her search with NCIC and ViCAP, Dr. Banks was looking only into potential victims who had worked at or near a hospital or medical facility. He didn't yet know of the link to Dr. Whitman's practice that Frankie had discovered. If six women who'd worked at or near a hospital were potential victims, how many more victims might there be who weren't related to anything medical? The thought alarmed her.

How many families would come forward with stories of their own missing relatives in the next few weeks, and how many victims would they face in the end? Local law enforcement and the FBI would take a beating from the press for not realizing such a killer was at work. The BAU would have to get involved.

She wrapped up the rest of her sandwich and stuffed it back in the bag, no longer hungry. Her stomach turned over, again and again, like the thoughts in her head. "Were any of these women patients of Dr. Whitman's?"

"That I don't know. Why? Were the others?"

She didn't respond. She couldn't tell him anything more. He was already too involved. She took a deep breath and watched a dozen people cross the street, all of them unaware of what Dr. Banks had just revealed to her. They went about their business as if the world held no evil, talking on cell phones and spooning little cups of ice cream into their mouths. Oblivion had its advantages. Only the fellow blond woman sitting on the bench on the opposite side of the street seemed sullen. She hadn't moved from her spot since Frankie had arrived. She just sat there behind those bumblebee glasses, blond hair piled on top of her head, and stared.

Suddenly, she creeped Frankie out. After finding that poem in her mailbox and her neighbor stating it was a woman who'd delivered it, she couldn't help but feel paranoid. Had Dr. Whitman sent an assistant to deliver the poem and spy on her?

Dr. Banks got up to toss what remained of his sandwich into a nearby receptacle, then rejoined her. "What are you thinking?"

"I'm thinking death certainly seems to follow Dr. Whitman around."

"My thoughts too. Listen, I'm leaving today for a surgical conference in Virginia. There will be a good presence of doctors from the mid-Atlantic area there, including Dr. Whitman. You want me to, I'll keep an eye on him and continue to poke around."

Frankie examined her hands. They were trembling. "Yes." She shook her head. "I mean, no." She abruptly stood. "Listen, you shouldn't be getting involved. I don't want you to get involved."

His eyes locked on her. "With you, or the case?"

Tension filled the weighted air between them. She fidgeted. "Neither. Not now. You're too close."

"With you, or the case?"

She sighed, looked away. "Both."

He shook his head. "Why?"

"You know why. You knew Anna. You can't get involved."

"I explained that. I want to find her killer as much as you do."

"No. I can't risk my career and you can't risk yours," she said, more firmly.

They stood toe-to-toe. She felt the blistering blaze between them and wondered why this was happening now. There hadn't been another man in her life to whom she'd felt such an attraction. For a moment, she didn't think she could turn and walk away from him, but that was exactly what she did.

CHAPTER 26

For the next two days, Frankie relaxed little and slept even less. She couldn't stop thinking about the intrusion into her home, the names Lawrence had given her, or the woman who'd supposedly visited her mailbox.

She'd asked her neighbor to describe the woman, but all her neighbor could tell her was she had blond hair, wore blue jeans and a light-pink shirt, and carried a black umbrella. When Frankie inquired as to her certainty that it was a woman, her neighbor had looked at her oddly but finally admitted she'd assumed so because of the color of the shirt and longer hair. She hadn't seen the person's face due to the umbrella and couldn't note anything about her body except that she was tall.

It wasn't likely that her neighbor was wrong, but Frankie felt the need to ask because, more and more, she felt that she and the investigators were missing something. Sheriff Brenner's team still hadn't discovered the identity of the mysterious blonde with Anna at her apartment in Chapel Hill, and although the police in Hickory thought nothing of the fact that Emily had last been seen speaking with a woman, Frankie was starting to question the coincidence. Maybe she was imagining things, but since her neighbor had told her of her visitor, Frankie couldn't stop thinking about the woman she'd seen standing across the street from her house and the woman sitting outside the theater the other day. That, coupled with the news she'd just received from Dr. Birnbaum—who stated that it appeared no unauthorized visitors had been allowed in Miguel's room the day he died but admitted they were having trouble verifying one of the nurse's names written on the police log—was causing Frankie a great deal of anxiety.

Was it possible their unsub was a woman—as profile number five suggested—or that Dr. Whitman might have an accomplice? Frankie hadn't given the scenario any thought, but it was worthy of consideration.

Frankie had reached out to the families of the women Lawrence had given her and asked them to give her a call, but so far had only heard back from the parents of Brianna Thomas. This afternoon, she planned to visit them. She grabbed her blazer from the back of her office chair and was heading out when Ben appeared at her door.

"Whatever you were planning to do, forget it. We've got a girl missing in Charlottesville, Virginia. The police found poems and a handwritten letter to her parents at her apartment similar to the one Anna left. Grab your stuff. Let's go."

Frankie turned back toward her desk to scoop the stack of folders with the information she had on the cases into a briefcase, and threw in her laptop.

Ben continued. "I already contacted the BAU. They're speeding up their review on Anna's case now and will likely send someone down since Charlottesville is only a couple of hours from Quantico. In the meantime, this just became your first multijurisdictional task force so I hope you're ready."

"I'll make a quick pit stop at the house, then head that way. Who's the contact for the Charlottesville PD? I'll need him to fill me in on the drive up."

"I can do that," Ben said. "I'm coming with you."

Frankie frowned, feeling a swell of uncertainty in her gut. Was he joining her to support her or was his sudden interest due to changing priorities? The Charlotte Memorial race had gone on without any more drama and now all the attention would be on her case. She hoped his intentions were pure but ...

At least he was still calling it her task force. For now.

Twenty minutes after arriving home, Frankie returned to Ben's car with a change of clothes and sundries packed in a small suitcase. On the way out, she'd filled Bone's cat dish with his favorite morsels and refreshed his water, hoping it would last him while she was gone. If it proved to be more than a day, she'd call her neighbor to go in and check on him. His unhappy mewling was already giving her a guilt complex.

"Okay, tell me what you know," she said when they were speeding north. She wasn't happy that Ben had taken the call from Charlottesville PD and not passed it on to her, but she couldn't contend with that right now. She needed to get up to speed.

"Name is Jeanne Mapleton. Student at the University of Virginia, graduate nursing program. There are several doctors in town right now for a conference."

Frankie thought about the conference Dr. Banks had mentioned the other day at lunch. She grunted. "Right. Lawrence mentioned there was a conference in Virginia he was planning to attend. So was Dr. Whitman."

Ben frowned. "Lawrence? You mean Dr. Banks? You saw him again?"

"Yes, at lunch a few days ago. He gave me the names of three more possible victims. Three additional women who apparently just left their lives behind for a new love. The parents of one of the women found poems and letters at her residence, but they didn't think much of their daughter's behavior because they'd had a rough go with her. Then they saw the news about Anna. Now they're questioning their daughter's disappearance. That's where I was headed this afternoon.

"Lawrence also said that Dr. Whitman took an odd leave of absence from Johns Hopkins during his residency there. Apparently, there was this woman and—I don't know—she and Whitman had some kind of conflict. Anyhow, she was murdered."

She turned toward Ben in the driver's seat, continuing to ramble. There was so much she'd learned in the past few days that he didn't know. "Did I tell you that Dr. Whitman gave his high school girlfriend poems? The same damn poems." She began rifling through the papers in her folders to read to him. "I visited with his foster mother and former girlfriend, and—"

"Wait a minute," Ben interrupted. "Go back to Lawrence. Or rather, Dr. Banks. How friendly are you with this guy, and why is he involved in the investigation? That may not be a good idea, under the circumstances."

He issued her a look of warning.

She glared back. "What circumstances are those? He provided information on the obsidian scalpel, led us to Whitman, and identified the suture. We also have three more potential victims to look into because of him." Her shoulders rose as if she were a cat with its hackles up.

Ben squealed the tires around a tight corner. They weren't even on the highway yet but he was hitting interstate speeds.

"Look, I'm not trying to break up a good thing here, Frankie. I'm just saying, take it easy. Wait until the case is over to pursue ... whatever ... with Dr. Banks. We're looking for a doctor or surgeon—one who is luring or abducting women. Doctors are suspects. *All* doctors."

His emphasis on the word *all* came through loud and clear. Yet the only person she could think about right now was Dr. Whitman. Whitman was in Charlottesville. There was a conference in town. And a young woman was missing. *Why didn't I listen to Lawrence the other day? I could've been there. I could've stopped this.*

Right now, that was all that mattered. She focused on the task at hand.

She spent the five-hour drive learning everything she could about Jeanne Mapleton and sharing information with Ben. She didn't know why he was newly interested in the case and what his sudden beef was with Lawrence, but she couldn't worry about it right now.

When they arrived at Charlottesville PD, Lieutenant Gordon led Frankie and Ben into a briefing room, where a task force of local and state law enforcement officers had gathered. Outside the station, the media had descended as well and were barking like hunting dogs waiting for the first scent of the chase. Frankie counted twenty-six individuals in the room wearing some variety of blue—officers from the Charlottesville, Albemarle County, Virginia State, and University of Virginia police forces—ready to work the case. She felt the suffocating heat of the day return, this time due to her adrenaline working overtime.

Was she ready to lead a multijurisdictional task force?

She didn't honestly know.

Lieutenant Gordon, a twenty-year veteran with the Charlottesville PD, secured a color photograph of a strawberry blonde with rosy cheeks and a perfect smile on the whiteboard before turning to speak to the crowd.

"I'll tell you what I know, then Special Agents Johnson and Andrews will fill you in on the rest. Our missing subject is Jeanne Mapleton, a graduate nursing student at the university. She's twenty-three, five foot five, one hundred twenty-six pounds. She was last seen yesterday evening at a birthday party held at Oakhurst bar on Main Street. She was wearing a long floral skirt, sandals, and a light-blue T-shirt. We have some video from the party, which we'll view in a minute.

"She has an on-again, off-again boyfriend by the name of Drew Collins. He wasn't at the party and says he hasn't seen her since they went to a concert last week. She was scheduled to meet her father for lunch yesterday but never showed or called. A check at her apartment turned up a letter to her family that led us to call the Bureau because of similarities to a recent case in North Carolina. We currently don't believe that either family or friends are involved in this abduction."

A young officer in his twenties spoke up. "But you do think it's an abduction?"

"Yes, I do," Gordon said. "Agent Johnson or Andrews may have other theories."

At that, he pushed the play button on the remote and let the images from the birthday party roll. The room of uniforms stood quiet as images of the young woman appeared on the screen. She was among a group of thirty to forty people outside, under a string of red umbrellas and patio lights.

Frankie's heart beat out of her chest.

"Except for a brief time, Jeanne wasn't the videographer's main focus, so Jeanne is largely in the background, mingling with the other guests," Gordon said, noting her position. "The videographer was there to gather happy-birthday wishes for his brother John, who is serving overseas. You'll see he speaks to many of the guests."

"Is he a suspect?" the same young officer asked.

"Everyone is a suspect," Gordon said.

As the video played, Frankie ignored those in front of the camera and focused on Jeanne. She watched as Jeanne spoke to a woman with mousy brown hair, laughed when the woman responded. She didn't appear bothered when a man arrived and joined them. Short, with cropped dark hair, the man popped peanuts and drank a beer as the three conversed, all appearing to be cordial.

The videographer moved between guests, but Frankie stayed on the trio. A bearded young man briefly stopped, said a few words, then left. A couple approached the three, and they all hugged. A blond woman interrupted and offered appetizers. By all accounts, it appeared to be a normal gathering. Nothing out of the ordinary.

It wasn't until the young man with the cropped dark hair left the group that Jeanne's demeanor began to change. Suddenly, she seemed distracted. Her gaze darted left, then right, and she abruptly shot a glance behind her, as if spooked by a stranger.

Frankie felt the pull of her image and walked closer to the screen. Although they couldn't hear her speak, Jeanne's body language was communicating plenty. She gripped her beer with both hands, rocked her weight from side to side, and repeatedly bit her lip. That, coupled with the way her eyes darted about, told Frankie she was nervous—as if she was expecting something to happen or someone to come walking in. But who?

Was her abductor coming to the party? Or was it possible he was already there?

The image shifted again. This time the camera was angled to Jeanne's left, providing a more encompassing shot of the entire crowd. Frankie searched the faces among the guests, seeking familiarity.

Was Dr. Whitman present? She didn't see him.

To everyone's surprise, one of the videographer's last interviews was with Jeanne herself. In tandem, the room of officers drew together as the fresh-faced beauty turned toward the camera and smiled. The videographer asked her if she had any words for John. She waved at the camera and wished John a happy birthday by blowing him a kiss.

Then Jeanne did something unexpected. She cast another glance behind her, leaned in close, and mouthed two words. The former smile was gone.

The videographer didn't hear her. "What? Sorry, I didn't get that last part."

Jeanne took a deep breath—frustrated, panicked, or both. She fidgeted, took another look over her shoulder, then uttered the two words again. But this time they were cut off when a man slapped the videographer on the shoulder, and the camera quickly panned right. A group of three guys and two scantily clad brunettes proceeded to sing a rowdy version of "Happy Birthday."

And Jeanne was gone.

A lump the size of a golf ball formed in Frankie's throat as the full weight of Jeanne's disappearance bore down on her. This was on her. Why hadn't she already gathered the evidence on their unsub, the killer she believed to be Dr. Whitman, and arrested him before he acted again? She prayed to God—the God she was often at odds with—that Jeanne Mapleton was still alive.

"What did she say to the camera at the end?" a women officer asked. "Love you?"

Lieutenant Gordon replayed it. Up close, Frankie examined the tape in split seconds, the way she and Ben often studied interrogations. When the words crossed Jeanne's lips again, Frankie paid close attention to the opening and closing of her mouth and the placement of her tongue. By the third replay, Frankie was certain it wasn't "Love you."

It was "Help me."

CHAPTER 27

Frankie felt herself choking, as if she were in a coffin filling with dirt and trying to salvage breath but only inhaling dust. She stared at the screen. She had no words.

There it was—Jeanne had known she was in trouble.

One of the answers Frankie most needed in order to narrow the profile was whether Anna, Melanie, and Emily had left with their new loves voluntarily or not, and Jeanne had just answered that. The letters and poems were a ruse.

Lieutenant Gordon was right. Jeanne Mapleton had been abducted.

He stepped up to the podium. "At this point, I'll have Special Agent Johnson tell you what they have on the North Carolina case."

Frankie, mind reeling, positioned herself behind the mic. She wasn't used to being thrust into the lead. Normally she was able to stand behind Ben, with all his charm and confidence, as he spoke to officers and the media with ease. Now here she was with a roomful of law enforcement hanging on her every word, and she was barely able to utter a single one.

Their faces were anxious, muscles taut, jaws clenched.

She began with an overview of the Jamison case, running through the evidence and reading the poems and letters. For thirty minutes, the officers jotted notes, asked questions, and made general observations. They were attentive and on board. It wasn't until Frankie gave them the timeline regarding Melanie's and Emily's disappearances that the tension in the room truly escalated.

"Two years? Jesus. I thought you said this Jamison woman disappeared just a month ago?" the young rookie of earlier said. "Don't tell me this guy has been at this for two years and we're just hearing about it now."

A low thunder of voices rattled through the room.

Frankie held up her hand. "Until last month, no one had any idea that Melanie's or Emily's disappearances might be anything but their personal choice. As far as law enforcement knew, each of these women left their former lives on their own. We don't know how many victims might be out there or how long this unsub has been active. What we do know is, in each of these cases, letters and poems were found that were similar to those given to Jeanne. Also, all three women worked at or near a major hospital. Although it's entirely possible our unsub has taken victims outside the medical community, that seems to be his circle of contact. That makes Jeanne a potential victim. Also, it's very likely our unsub is escalating, since he was interrupted last time."

"Where did you say you found the last victim?" The question came from a member of the Virginia State Police, a seasoned officer with an elongated face and jowls like those of a bloodhound. The crooks in his nose left no doubt of its many prior fractures.

"At an abandoned farmhouse in Lexington, North Carolina."

Frankie started to say more, then hesitated. *Can I do it? Am I confident enough now to put a full profile out on the table?*

Feeling that the missing piece of *involuntary leaving, imaginary relationship* had been established with Jeanne's two words, she felt she could narrow the profile. "We believe part of his MO is to locate a house he can prepare for himself and his new wife."

She replayed Dr. Whitman's words. *Spent the night remodeling. Trying to be a real do-it-yourself guy.* Had he been using his alibi to let her know what he'd been doing at the farmhouse, and not on his real home, the night Anna died?

His play on words infuriated her.

She continued. "Just as he selects his victim in advance, he also scouts out the location where he will take her. He moves in medical equipment, a generator, food, and clothing. Once he abducts his new love, he takes her to the house. The motive for what he does next is a mystery. On Anna Jamison, he performed a mastectomy. Whether this is what he does to all his victims, or whether he performs other surgical procedures, we don't know. We haven't located the bodies of the other victims. Right now, we need to focus on finding and searching abandoned or unoccupied property in a rural setting."

At that, Gordon snapped his fingers at one of his veteran officers near the back of the room. "Jones, call the county clerk and tell her what we need. And ask admin to prepare a bulletin and email it to every real estate agent in the four-county area. Who knows, they might have an idea of just the property we're looking for."

Frankie was impressed with Gordon. He'd done exactly what she was thinking.

The officer with the boxer's nose continued with his questions. "You got a profile for us?"

Frankie picked up a marker and wrote out profile four on the whiteboard: *White male. Age 30-45. Some college with medical training. Single, renter, within two miles of a major hospital. Average looks. Fantasy obsessive or erotomaniac. In need of deep, abiding love. Believes fantasy is real but punishes them when they don't please. Mother incapable of love or abandoned him. May desire prepubescent girls or be unable to perform sexually. History of stalking in adolescence.*

As Frankie wrote, she again thought of Dr. Whitman. Whitman's mother had abandoned him by death. Tammy Kay had abandoned him by rape. Yes, this was a man in need of deep, abiding love. He'd likely started creating these fantasy relationships because they were safer than reality. In his fantasy, he loved and was loved, but it wasn't real. They didn't love him, and when they tried to leave him—as Anna had tried in her attempted escape—it made him angry enough to kill.

If he couldn't have them, no one could.

"There are two comments I want to make about this profile," she said. "Although the profile says some college, it's very possible this unsub has a medical license. The preciseness of the incisions and knot tying on the sutures indicate he's a professional. Second, if he does have a license, he likely owns a home instead of rents."

"Can you explain this psychology?" Gordon asked. "What is an erotomaniac?"

"Erotomania is a delusional disorder," Frankie explained. "Erotomaniacs are obsessive individuals who believe the objects of their desire, often called idols, love them as much as the erotomaniac loves them. Letters and gifts are some of their favorite methods for communicating with their idols and revealing their love. Even through repeated rejections and outright hostility, erotomaniacs will reason that their idols truly love them and only behave that way to conceal from others their true love.

"You might remember hearing about a young actress gunned down in 1989 at her home in West Hollywood. Rebecca Schaeffer played the younger sister on a television sitcom. Her killer was an erotomaniac who believed he and Rebecca were meant to be together. He thought she sent him signals and messages through the television screen. And more recently, a contestant from a hit singing show was killed by a fan with a similar obsession. That is erotomania at its most dangerous. I believe our unsub expresses similar traits. His letters, his poems, they speak of fate and destiny."

"What about the return letters from the women? They equally speak of their devotion, their love. You think he wrote those too?" Lieutenant Gordon asked.

"No, I don't. In each case, the handwriting is different and matches samples from each of the women. But analysis completed by our experts indicates the letters exhibit signs of stress, as if they were written under duress. Before today, I wasn't certain whether that stress was due to them leaving their life and loved ones for a new adventure, or because the letters were written in a hurry. Now, I feel certain our unsub forces his victims to write the letters after he gains control of them."

Frankie gripped the podium. She felt herself formulating new insights about the unsub—the man she felt was Dr. Whitman—as quickly as the officers in the room were first learning about him. And what surprised her most was just how strongly she now believed in those insights.

"Do you have any suspects in your case?" asked a clean-shaven sergeant with a military buzz cut on loan from the University of Virginia Police.

"We recently interviewed a person of interest, and I can tell you that individual is in town at this surgical conference. I plan on bringing him in, but right now, our most important task is to find Jeanne Mapleton."

Gordon stepped forward. "All right, people, we've got a job to do. Let's get organized and hit the streets. I don't care if we have to knock on every door in the four-county area."

Jones reentered the room with maps in hand, and they divided territories and responsibilities across Albemarle, Fluvanna, Nelson, and Greene Counties.

As the troops gathered, Ben pulled Frankie into a private huddle. "MO? You really put yourself out there," he whispered. "What makes you so certain suddenly that profile four is the right one? We don't even have a complete crime scene. You're filling in holes with theories."

Frankie shook her head. "I don't think so. Jeanne filled in the missing piece of the profile for us. She was already under his control at that party. 'Help me.' She mouthed the words 'Help me.' Remember how Ryan said Emily cried the night before she left? Why? Because Emily knew what was going to happen. She knew she was going to take her family on a picnic, drive to the store, and never come back. Yet she didn't feel like she could tell her husband. Why? This unsub, he's threatening them somehow. I can feel it. They don't go voluntarily. These women are abducted."

Ben shook his head. "Listen, theorizing is great for the whiteboard, but not while running a task force. You don't know for certain 'Help me' is what Jeanne said. And even if it was, you certainly don't know this man is an erotomaniac. He could just as easily be a psychopath who lures these women into his presence and then exerts control. You've got to stick to the facts."

"He doesn't hate these women. He loves these women."

"He's cutting off their breasts. Does that sound like love?"

"I think he may want them prepubescent, virginal. Look, I can't fully explain that yet, but he loves them, trust me. I can feel it in my gut."

Ben cocked his head and issued her a stern gaze. "That's what I'm saying. That's instinct. You know how I feel about ..."

Lieutenant Gordon interrupted. "Everything okay here?"

Frankie gave a firm nod. "We're good. Let's go."

She turned to face Ben and pointed a rigid finger deep in his chest. "Ben, instinct is what your mind connects when the facts haven't yet presented all the details. It's the evolution from millions of ancestors and the shared human experience. It's when you know to cross the street because the person two blocks down means you harm.

It's when an animal senses that it's being hunted before the lion appears through the brush."

His lips tightened. He shook his head. "It isn't protocol, and the top dogs are watching. Don't forget that."

Protocol. The word tasted sour to her, like biting into a lemon and sucking it whole. To date, Ben had been her biggest supporter and champion in the Bureau, even defending her with Vicks when she'd made mistakes or gone rogue. Yet it seemed that when the stakes got higher or the cases got bigger, Ben became more Bureau brass than mentor and teacher. She knew he wanted to rise to supervisory special agent and eventually special agent in charge, so she tried to understand, but when career and politics outranked friendship and loyalty, it left a bad taste in her mouth.

In fact, she was certain his career aspirations were the main reason he was here now and not with Tommy pursuing the New Patriots. The race was over, and the news surrounding Bobby B had moved on. Here there was media and national attention. The Behavioral Analysis Unit had taken notice. They might even send someone down. He wanted to be part of the action, even though officially it wasn't his case to lead. It was part of his *we* to *me* mentality shift, his belief only he could solve the problem when others—including Frankie—failed in their mission.

"I get it," she said. "And I get you. Don't forget that either."

CHAPTER 28

Frankie sipped her second latte of the morning, having not slept, and phoned Dr. Kenneth Whitman. Given the ending of the last interview, she knew he might tell her to call his lawyer or to go fuck herself, but to her surprise, he answered. She briefly told him of the newly missing woman and asked if he would come in and help the investigation. After she assured him that it would only be her asking the questions—which he once again insisted upon—he agreed.

She wasn't sure if he had an ulterior motive, but she'd find out soon enough.

Dr. Whitman arrived that afternoon, dressed nicely as usual and smelling of fresh soap, in sharp contrast to Frankie, who wore the same clothes she'd been in the past two days and had her hair pulled back in a ponytail. The war room at the Charlottesville PD was also in disarray, with leftover coffee cups and soda cans littering the tables and trash cans running over with takeout food containers.

Frankie took him to the interrogation room, where she'd stationed a mobile whiteboard filled with information on the case: a collage of letters, poems, photos, and evidence. At the first interrogation, she'd purposefully cleared the room of anything incriminating, but now she wanted to turn up the heat. She made certain to display enlarged photos of the green-braided sutures and the obsidian scalpel and had circled the title of the poem "Go, Lovely Rose." A black-and-white photo of Anna Jamison's charred, dead face rested next to a striking full-color photo of Jeanne Mapleton and, beneath that, a snapshot of Melanie Higby along with the newspaper headline *Missing Person Case Reopened*. To the right of that was a family photo of Ryan and Emily Dearborn with their two young daughters. Frankie had also taped up newly acquired photos of the women Dr. Banks had given her and filled in the blank spaces with random pictures of shoe and tire tracks and various fibers, none of which actually applied to the case but could serve to make Dr. Whitman believe they had additional evidence.

As soon as Dr. Whitman entered, she noted his interest in the whiteboard. His head turned up and eyes focused as he slid into the only available chair at the table, positioned so he would have no choice but to look at the mounting evidence before him. She watched as the whites of his eyes slightly expanded and his lips thinned.

He stroked his tie several times.

Frankie sat on the edge of the table to the side of him and regarded the whiteboard with him. She was fully aware of the four tense faces that observed from an adjoining room: Lieutenant Gordon and his lead detective, Jones, along with Ben and ASAC Vicks, who'd arrived an hour before to watch the big show.

She could not screw this up.

"So," she said, louder than usual. "We meet again."

Dr. Whitman's wintry blue gaze moved from her thigh, inches away, up her torso to her face. "You seem angry, Agent Johnson."

"I am. I am angry. Another woman is missing."

"There's a surgical conference in town. Hundreds of surgeons."

"That's why I called. With the conference ending today, we have no time to lose."

"How do you expect to find one out of so many?"

"Well, I'm not looking for just any surgeon. I'm looking for a special one, one who likes to lure young women and play house. See," she swept her hand across the whiteboard, "we now know it wasn't only Anna, Melanie, and Emily our perpetrator attracted. We found three more, all connected."

He checked out the board again. "These women are all related to Anna's case? You've discovered their bodies?" He tilted his head and elevated the pitch of his voice in a way that indicated he was challenging her.

"Not yet, but we're getting closer, and we won't stop until we do."

They exchanged a silent moment.

She pointed at the three new additions. "Do you recognize these women? Clients of yours, perhaps? Or ladies you've met while consulting on cases at other local hospitals?" She hadn't had time to dig into the women's backgrounds or even speak to relatives, so she didn't have anything yet to level at him, but she still wanted to see if he would offer a response.

"Hmm. I couldn't really say. I have many clients. Meet lots of people. How did you find them, and what makes you think they're related?"

She thought of Lawrence. "Some good detective work and similarity of evidence."

He smirked. "I see." He paused. "Well, if true, that's tragic. Now, about this local girl you needed help with?"

He didn't want to talk about the other three women. Which was fine—for now.

"Yes." She got up and to remove the smiling photo of Jeanne from the whiteboard and placed it in front of him. "Take a look. Do you recognize this young woman?"

Dr. Whitman hovered over the photograph. "Yes. She was at the conference this week. I saw her in a session I also attended. The one Dr. Banks gave on trauma and stories of the ER."

His gaze moved up while his head stayed lowered, slightly creeping Frankie out. "You remember Dr. Banks? The one who told you I used obsidian scalpels?"

Frankie narrowed her eyes. The scorn in his voice was obvious. "Yes, I remember. Did you speak to the young woman at the conference?" she asked, shifting the focus back to Jeanne.

"No, not so much as an introduction. Dr. Banks did, however. I saw him talk with her after his session Tuesday afternoon. She seemed smitten with him, as so many women are."

Frankie felt a sting, though whether it was from him bringing up Lawrence's name again or from Jeanne's supposed interest, she wasn't sure. Still, she wasn't going to let him bait her. "When did you arrive in town for this conference?"

"Monday afternoon. I checked into the hotel, prepared for my Tuesday sessions, showered, met colleagues—including Dr. Banks—for dinner at seven p.m. He seemed eager to be by my side that night. Talked to me for hours. Asked me some interesting questions." He chuckled as if that were funny. "You probably don't know anything about that."

She cocked her head. It was obvious he was trying to goad her. Either he knew about Frankie and Lawrence's interest in each other, or he was aware that Lawrence had been helping her—researching the suture, checking into Whitman's background in Baltimore, and collecting the names of additional potential victims.

"Where did you eat?" she asked, showing no emotion.

"Hamilton's, on First and Main. There were five of us. Some went out for drinks afterward, but I was back at the hotel by ten p.m. Never left afterward."

"Did you see this young woman at any point that night?"

"No. It wasn't until Tuesday that I saw her, first in Dr. Banks's session, then later in the lobby."

"What time was that?"

"Around four p.m., I guess. I was there talking with a doctor from Johns Hopkins about an interesting case of his. Your girl Jeanne was still there when I returned to my room at four thirty p.m."

Frankie rose from the edge of the table, paced the small room.

He'd led her right to the critical time surrounding Jeanne's disappearance. Jeanne had last been seen at the party on Main Street at six thirty p.m., so whatever had happened between the time she'd been at the hotel and the time she'd gone to the bar was essential. Maybe he knew that, maybe he didn't. "Tell me about your Tuesday evening. What did you do between the hours of four thirty and six thirty p.m.?"

He paused as if recollecting. "I went to the hotel gym for a brief run on the treadmill, took a shower, and left at five thirty p.m. I walked the pedestrian mall. Stopped at a bar and ordered a glass of wine. I met colleagues for dinner at C & O later, near seven thirty p.m. Dr. Banks canceled on us that evening. Apparently, he had other plans."

Frankie studied Dr. Whitman. She knew this constant mentioning of Lawrence was intentional, but the question was, why? He seemed to be trying to get a little payback and make Lawrence appear suspicious in some manner.

But it didn't matter. She wouldn't play along. She didn't want to make this interrogation about Dr. Banks.

Frankie looked at the map on her phone. C & O was just a mile from the Oakhurst bar, but on the opposite end of the pedestrian mall. She thought the dinner time interesting, however. With Jeanne last seen at six thirty and Dr. Whitman on his own from five thirty to seven thirty, he clearly had time enough to abduct her from the bar, take her somewhere, and return to meet his colleagues for dinner. But it would have had to be somewhere close, within a twenty- to thirty-minute drive.

She glanced into the camera, hoping Ben and Lieutenant Gordon were reading her mind. They needed to gather video of various locations along the pedestrian mall to see if Dr. Whitman was telling the truth, and they needed to narrow the search range for Jeanne within a short drive.

"My car never left the hotel. You can check with the valet," Whitman said, as if was the one reading her mind. "And once again, I was back at the hotel at ten p.m."

He took a deep breath. "I know you're going to ask about Wednesday too, so I'll just get it out there. No, I didn't see your girl, but I mainly stayed in my room that day, as I was feeling under the weather. I had a session scheduled that morning and needed to find a replacement, so I tried to ring Dr. Banks, but the front desk informed me he wasn't staying at the conference hotel. I called his cell phone instead, and after repeated attempts, he finally answered. He was annoyed that I asked him to cover for me. When he arrived at the hotel, we got into a bit of an argument. I simply asked him why it took him so long to answer and asked where he'd been, but he said his whereabouts were none of my business. Quite funny given the inquisition he put me through Monday night, but there you have it."

Dr. Whitman raised his palms at that, as if giving Frankie and the others in the next room a Sunday offering.

Frankie remained silent for a minute. The air conditioning hummed above, blowing the edges of a stack of nearby papers. Outside the room, faint voices murmured, phones rang, and the odor of a microwave dinner wafted in.

Dr. Whitman was playing things very differently this time. Despite his initial interest in the whiteboard, he hadn't displayed any pen twirling or grooming gestures that indicated he was nervous as he had during the prior interview. This time he was controlled, even defiant.

He *wanted* her to have this information. And why? To throw Dr. Banks under the bus. *That* was his motive for this interview, why he'd agreed to talk.

She grabbed a chair from the corner and placed it in front of Dr. Whitman. She sat, leaning close enough to Dr. Whitman's face to inhale his cologne and observe the tiny flecks of royal blue in his irises. In return, she gave him the stink of her two days chasing bad guys without showering.

"Why do you keep bringing up Dr. Banks?"

"You asked for my help. I'm giving it to you."

"You mean you're giving *him* to me."

"Dr. Banks knew Anna Jamison. Are you aware of that?"

"Yes, I am. He told me all about her."

He tilted his head. "Did he now? Everything?"

A fire flared in her gut. She had a momentary visual of pounding Whitman's head into the wall. He just wouldn't let it alone. "Is there something you would like to add?"

"Perhaps you should bring him in and give him the same inquisition that you've given me, discover it for yourself." He glanced at the camera with a raised eyebrow, as if indicating to the old boys' club how easily manipulated a woman could be.

Frankie wanted to light him up like a bonfire but held her tongue.

"I see. You think Dr. Banks is a suspect? Unfortunately, there's a little problem with your theory." She waved her hand toward the whiteboard. "It's all these other women. You know, the ones you don't want to talk about? See, from everything we've gathered, these five women don't have a connection to Dr. Banks. But you, they're either your clients or you consulted on cases near their workplaces mere months before they disappeared."

That wasn't exactly true with the three new women Lawrence had given her, but she suspected it nonetheless.

"Actually," he shot back, "I think it would be very difficult to prove that these other women are connected to Anna. Nothing truly ties them together."

"What about the poems and letters found at several of the women's residences?"

He shrugged. "The poems are available to anyone," he said. "I didn't write them. The majority are well-known works—Marlowe, Byron."

Byron, yes. Byron as in "She Walks in Beauty," the poem left in her mailbox. She desperately wanted to ask Whitman about it and whether he'd broken into her house, but she couldn't. Vicks and Ben were listening and she hadn't mentioned the incident to them—and wouldn't.

"Well, you would know. You're a big fan of poetry. You always have been. Take 'Go, Lovely Rose.' Our perpetrator gave this poem to Anna and Melanie, just like you gave it to Tammy Kay when you were a teenager." She grabbed another. "And this one, 'Whoever Loved That Loved Not at First Sight?' This was found at Melanie Higby's and Emily Dearborn's residences, and as it turns out, you also gave this one to your high school girlfriend. So, coincidence?"

At the mention of Tammy Kay, Dr. Whitman's entire body froze. The delicate curve of his cheekbone and the angle of his jaw set like an ice sculpture, and the blood beneath his skin fled, leaving it glacier white. A single word quivered from his lips. "Tammy?"

"Oh, I'm sorry. Didn't I tell you? I had the occasion to visit with your foster mother, Betty Sue Taylor, this past week." She leaned closer to whisper. "Betty told me about you and Tammy. Sounds like the two of you were deeply in love once upon a time. I'm sorry it didn't work out."

At that, Dr. Whitman curled into himself. He folded his hands and let the tips of his fingers graze one another, as if searching for the memory of his lost love. His lips parted, but no words came out.

Frankie sat quietly, watching him battle with his emotions, wishing she could fold back his skin and experience them to understand what he was feeling. Because she could see them all there—anger, hurt, love, betrayal—bundled in a fiery ball of micro expressions on his face.

A pulsing vein appeared on his forehead.

"Once upon a time is right," he said. "A fairy tale."

She let him continue to battle. Knuckles clenched and joints popped. His face flushed. Tears surfaced only to be brushed away.

"Betty Sue says you send cards but never come to visit. Why is that? Why don't you visit her? Don't you love her? She clearly still loves you," Frankie said.

Dr. Whitman slumped even more. It was clear he didn't want to talk about it.

When he didn't answer, she tried a different angle. "You were quite the poet. I read some of your original works as well."

He glanced up. The brims of his eyes were red. "I was a lot of things then, Agent Johnson. It was a different life." His voice cracked.

He rubbed his face. "Look, I thought you wanted to talk to me about this latest missing girl. These other women and the poems you keep bringing up, I don't know what to say. What you're telling me, it's disturbing. I mean, this is crazy. I feel like I'm being set up," Dr. Whitman said. His eyes pleaded. "Seriously. I do."

Frankie felt the corners of her eyes pull. Finally, she was getting somewhere. Bringing up Tammy Kay had done it. He could no longer deny the growing evidence.

She considered Dr. Whitman the primary suspect, but if it wasn't him, it had to be someone connected to him. Only recently had she given any thought to the possibility of an accomplice or another unsub entirely. It wasn't out of the realm of possibility that someone who knew Whitman could be playing doctor with his patients.

She settled back in the chair. Nodded to silently let him know that she was glad he was opening up. Grabbed her notepad. "Okay. Let's explore that, Dr. Whitman. Who might have access to your patient list as well as know about your past relationship with Tammy Kay and your love of poetry? Is there someone from your office or your past who you've hurt in some manner where they'd want to get revenge? Or perhaps someone who idolizes you?"

He looked confused. "Idolizes me?"

"Yes," Frankie said. "Maybe they've stalked you in the past? A man, or even a woman, who seemed overenthusiastic about you or your work? Maybe someone like your old girlfriend, Mary?"

In her brief exploration of an accomplice or separate unsub, Frankie had repeatedly come back to the question of a woman's involvement. Dr. Whitman had acted deceptively when Frankie had asked about Mary Campbell before, and she still wanted to explore his relationship with the woman he considered a nobody.

Dr. Whitman stared at her oddly, as if he didn't know what to say.

She had started to gently nudge him when the door to the interrogation room flew open and Lieutenant Gordon's lead detective, Jones, burst into the room.

"I can't believe you're buying the shit this guy is shoveling," he shouted at Frankie. "This piece of shit is a murderer."

He yanked Dr. Whitman's chair back from the table, with Whitman still in it, and shoved his face within an inch of his own. "So much coincidence. You know what coincidence is, Dr. Whitman? It's the shit that piles up when you forget to flush."

Jones unfolded a piece of paper in his hand. On it was an artist's depiction of a man who resembled Dr. Whitman. "This is a sketch of the man last seen with Jeanne Mapleton. Recognize this guy? This is the last turd on the stack, and that turd is you."

Frankie abruptly stood, stunned at Jones's outburst, wondering who the hell had ordered this good cop, bad cop routine. Interrogations were a slow, dutiful, diligent process, taking suspects through detailed stages of behavior, and she'd barely moved Whitman into a new stage before this interruption. No eyewitness existed, as far as she knew, and this seemed like a wasted attempt to scare him into confessing.

"Where is Jeanne Mapleton?" Jones demanded. "She'd better be alive, sucker, or you're as good as dead. Alive, you might be able to bargain your way out of this, make a deal with the DA. But dead? You're dead. So tell us, where is she?"

Frankie shot a glance at the camera, imagining the man-pack huddled in the other room, wondering if any of them understood that treating a surgeon, a well-educated professional, as equivalent to the basic everyday scum they scraped off the streets wasn't going to yield the same results. Dr. Whitman wasn't someone they could scare into a confession. He was organized and methodical and would see this intrusion as illogical—even comical—a desperate grasping of straws. Also, killer though Dr.

Whitman might be, he was a man of some taste, and he wouldn't respond to Jones's crude tactics.

As Jones yelled, Dr. Whitman sat motionless as glass, staring at the man with an expression somewhere between bewilderment and hostility.

"Where is she?" Jones demanded again, spittle flying.

Frankie sighed and reached for Jones's arm. "Listen ..."

He shouldered Frankie out of the way. "You've had your time."

To her dismay, Frankie stumbled, wobbling like a drunk at a bar, and Dr. Whitman rose to catch her. A glare appeared in Dr. Whitman's eyes, a veil of hatred unmasked that dared Jones to touch her, and it caught Frankie by surprise.

Why would Whitman be so protective of her?

The door again flew open, and Ben appeared, concern etched on his brow. He demanded that Dr. Whitman release Frankie, then ordered Jones out of the room. After a minute of grumbling, Jones acquiesced, slamming the door behind him.

Ben tried to touch her, but Frankie yanked away, barely able to contain her fury. Had this bad cop, good cop routine been planned? Was this their way of getting Ben in the room without losing Frankie's credibility with Dr. Whitman? If so, they'd failed, and miserably. They had ruined every ounce of progress she'd made with Dr. Whitman.

She couldn't believe they had violated her like this.

As the three of them cooled, Ben apologized. "I'm sorry, Dr. Whitman. As you can imagine, this woman's disappearance has many people on edge. Please ignore—"

"First the ape and now the monkey. Add in some peanuts and we'll have a full circus," Dr. Whitman said. The skin glowed red on his face and neck. He brushed at the arms and chest of his shirt, as if ridding himself of the filth that had just sullied his person.

Frankie saw Ben's jaw clench, but to his credit, he filed his counterattack in its proper folder. "Please ignore Detective Jones's intrusion," he finished. He waited a moment for the energy in the room to clear before speaking again. "Look, you've been kind enough to answer Agent Johnson's questions about Jeanne. I wondered if you would answer some of mine."

"I will not," Whitman said. He straightened his tie.

Ben looked to Frankie to ease the tension, to support him in his effort. But Frankie wouldn't have it. Ben wasn't going to disrespect her like this. "As you said, he answered my questions." She started to gather her things.

"That's correct. I have. So, unless either of you plan to arrest me, I am now leaving. I will not speak to either of you again without a lawyer, even as a favor."

He walked to the door and started to open it when he turned back. "If you want to get your man, Agent Johnson, then you should listen to what I've told you. If you don't believe me, then maybe the monkey can convince you otherwise."

CHAPTER 29

Back in the war room, Frankie slammed her fists on the table. "What the hell was that? I had him. He wasn't in the depression stage for even two minutes." She threw the folders on the desk, kicked a chair across the room. "You know how long the process takes."

Ben started to object, but she shut him down. "Don't even. No excuses. And you," she yelled at Jones, "you think treating a highly intelligent surgeon like some thug is going to make him piss his pants and tell all?"

Jones rocked on his heels, hands in his pockets. Lieutenant Gordon placed a hand on his shoulder. "Detective Jones just did what we asked of him."

"We didn't mean to infringe on your interrogation," Ben said. "We just felt he was playing you. He clearly knows Dr. Banks has been feeding you information and has a nonprofessional interest in you. He had no intention of giving you anything of value."

"You don't know that. I just had him on the verge of accepting that he's the connection between these cases and talking about the one person he hasn't wanted to discuss this entire time—"

"We're running out of time to find Jeanne," Ben interrupted.

"Who's this *we*? Don't you mean *you*?" Despite being several inches shorter than Ben, she stood toe-to-toe with him, violating his personal space. "Was this *your* call?"

To her surprise, he backed up.

A voice came from behind her. "It was mine," ASAC Vicks said, his trademark V etched into his brow. "Look, we needed to try to get him to give up Jeanne's locale. It didn't work. Forget it, let's move on. We've got work to do."

Frankie spun, watching grown men scatter like rodents from a snake. A bunch of old boys who'd felt like they could intimidate the suspect into confessing because the little lady wasn't getting results fast enough for their liking.

She silently called them names she couldn't say aloud.

A member of the task force approached Lieutenant Gordon and whispered in his ear. Gordon snapped his fingers, gaining everyone's attention. "They found Jeanne's car. We need to go."

They grabbed their things and headed for the door. All except Frankie.

"Aren't you coming?" Ben asked, hesitating before he ran out.

"No, you go. I want to look at the conference hotel video." She passed by, bumping him as she did. "I'm sure you can provide your expert opinion later."

She grabbed a day-old chicken wrap from a tray of catered-in deli sandwiches and a can of warm soda and went to one of the PD's empty offices. She needed her space to calm down and compose herself. Videos from the conference hotel's security had arrived in her in-box that morning, and she'd been anxious to review them all day, so this would give her a necessary reprieve.

The hotel had agreed to turn over footage from the entire conference and lobby area as well as the three public entries and exits but not from the individual floors or elevators, noting the lack of a warrant targeting specific persons. Originally interested in identifying Jeanne and the company she kept, Frankie also wanted to observe Dr. Whitman's movements and see if he really had departed and returned to the hotel at the times he'd stated.

She started with Tuesday in the lobby and watched as a blur of men and women sped through the atrium leading to the pedestrian mall while others arrived and departed via the motor court. By four p.m., the lobby and bar were full of conference attendees, just as Dr. Whitman had stated. Whitman himself stood speaking with a man Frankie presumed was the doctor from Johns Hopkins. As they spoke, Jeanne Mapleton appeared and joined a small group nearby, where she remained for the next half hour. At no time in the next thirty minutes did Frankie see Dr. Whitman veer his movement toward or glance at Jeanne across the room, nor did Jeanne do so with Dr. Whitman.

The only odd thing Frankie noticed during that time was that, just like at Oakhurst bar later that evening, while so many others spoke and texted on various devices, Jeanne Mapleton did not. It appeared Jeanne hadn't had her phone with her at the bar or at the hotel earlier in the day. So where was it?

Frankie texted Ben. Asked him to look for Jeanne's phone in or near her vehicle. *Make yourself useful, asshole.*

She still couldn't believe they'd disrupted her interrogation like that.

At four thirty p.m. on the tape, Dr. Whitman disappeared in the direction of the elevators, and fifteen minutes later Jeanne exited the door to the motor court. Frankie switched to the outdoor view and observed Jeanne walk up the street for another few seconds, then vanish.

Twenty minutes later, she would arrive at Oakhurst bar for the party.

What had happened in those twenty minutes that suddenly made Jeanne fear for her life? Or had it occurred before or after, either at the hotel or at the bar?

Frankie fast-forwarded the tape another forty-five minutes. True to his word, Dr. Whitman walked directly through the lobby and out the revolving doors to the pedestrian mall. She played through the rest of the evening as couples and individuals exited and entered. Dr. Whitman wasn't on the video again until he arrived shortly after ten p.m. Out at five thirty p.m. and back in the doors by ten p.m., then straight up the elevator to his room, just as he'd stated.

She sat back in the chair, shook her head. "Damn."

Her gut twisted and squirmed. *So maybe the unsub isn't Whitman?*

She thought about the possibility of an accomplice again, or another unsub entirely—perhaps a woman. Her disappointment at not being able to complete her conversation with Dr. Whitman overwhelmed her.

No telling what I might've learned. Maybe I could've stopped a killer.

But Ben had stopped her cold. She huffed. Ben, the one who was always pushing her to explore all the options had cut her off when he thought she was traveling down a useless path. She shook her head.

She continued to scan the tapes as they progressed through the late-evening and early-morning hours. Dr. Whitman was never seen exiting the hotel but there was a woman who departed the elevators wearing a baseball cap and sunglasses shortly after midnight. She rounded the corner and disappeared down the stairs to the parking garage. It wasn't much; still, it could be something.

I mean, who the hell wears sunglasses at midnight?

Frankie slowed the video and replayed the woman's exit. Then played it again. And again. She shook her head. There was no way she could get any facial recognition from the video stream. If she had the hallway footage, she could determine what room the woman had come from, but she didn't.

She moved on to Wednesday morning. Dr. Whitman appeared in the lobby at nine a.m. He spoke to the front desk clerk while at times holding his phone to his ear, presumably calling Dr. Banks. At ten a.m. he was again talking on the phone, this time flailing his arms and pacing in a circle. His stern posture spoke of his frustration. As he waited, he constantly checked his watch. Forty-five minutes later, Dr. Banks arrived. The two appeared to exchange harsh words before Dr. Whitman departed for the elevators and Lawrence toward the conference ballrooms. Out of curiosity, Frankie watched Lawrence for the remainder of the day. He covered Dr. Whitman's session that morning, ate lunch with his colleagues at the hotel, then presented one more session at one p.m. After that, he abruptly left. As Dr. Whitman had mentioned, it appeared Lawrence was not staying at the hotel.

Her stomach twisted again, a little rupture of annoyance.

Frankie thought about calling him to see if he was still in town.

Outside the room, she heard the rumble of officers arriving—Lieutenant Gordon, Ben, and the others returning to the station. Gordon was giving orders and discussing new directions in the search for Jeanne Mapleton. A few minutes later, Ben knocked on the office door and gave her a once-over, no doubt wondering if she was still angry at him.

"The answer is yes," she said, continuing to scroll through the video, "but I need to know what you found, so I'll have to wait for a more opportune time to chew your ass out."

"I can hardly wait." He entered, grabbed a chair. "Car was located at a strip mall northwest of the city. Nothing inside but fast-food wrappers, knitting materials, cat hair, and this." He waved a plastic bag. Jeanne's phone.

Frankie frowned. "So it was there. Damn. That's not a good sign. Do they know how long the car had been there?"

"Looks like she bought a bagel and coffee at a shop in the strip mall just after eight a.m. Tuesday morning. Which makes me believe she didn't drive to the conference but had someone meet her at the café that morning, or—"

"Or she was abducted that morning, just like Emily Dearborn at the convenience store. Shit." Frankie sat back in the chair, chewed a nail. It seemed certain now that Jeanne had not been in possession of her phone Tuesday, and while it could've been accidental, that didn't seem likely. If the unsub had abducted her that morning, it would explain the phone, but not why she'd be at the conference all day appearing as if nothing was out of the ordinary. Yet two hours after the conference ended for the day, she was whispering "Help me" into a video camera less than a mile away.

Frankie couldn't explain it.

She updated Ben on her review of the tapes. "No one suspicious except a woman leaving in the middle of the night under the cover of a baseball cap and sunglasses."

"Hardly newsworthy. A woman hiding her identity leaving a conference full of men early in the morning? Keep watching. You're bound to see at least three or four others in the wee hours and another half-dozen after breakfast."

Frankie sighed. "Touché."

"The question is, when do you see Dr. Whitman leaving and returning?"

"All of his times check out, and his car never leaves the hotel until Wednesday."

Ben grunted. "Not helping your case. How about Dr. Banks?"

Frankie eye-fucked him for the second time that day.

"Can't rule it out," he said, coming to his own defense.

"Can't rule out an accomplice or a woman's involvement either. What the hell do you think I was trying to explore with today's interrogation?"

"I'm sorry. I am. It's just that ASAC Vicks—"

"Right. And you jumped at his command." She sighed. Shut her laptop. "Are you starting to have doubts Dr. Whitman is our unsub? With all the evidence that points to him—the scalpel, the suture, the poetry? Despite my probing into accomplices, I still believe he's either our guy or connected."

"He's slippery, I'll give you that," Ben said. "Like a wet fish on a recently mopped deck. But you have to admit, his alibis are tough to break this time. At this point, I think we have to keep our minds open to other possibilities, at least concerning Jeanne. Maybe it is a different unsub. Maybe it's an old beau who saw the information about Anna in the news and copied the poems."

"Or maybe Dr. Whitman is being set up, or maybe he's playing a game with us that we don't understand," Frankie said, rubbing her hands through her hair. "I don't know anymore."

"I know," Ben said. "And I know another thing. You're tired. Go to the hotel and take a shower and get a few hours' sleep. I will call you the minute anything breaks."

He didn't have to say it twice. She packed up her paperwork and laptop and made for the exit. It was the first time she'd agreed with anything Ben had said all day.

CHAPTER 30

Frankie was headed toward the front doors when Lieutenant Gordon rounded the corner with a petite blond woman in tow. "Agent Johnson, wait up." The woman, dressed in a light-yellow suit and sensible shoes, kept up a brisk pace beside him. Frankie's impression that she was a real estate agent was confirmed when she handed Frankie her card. "This is Ms. Sommers. She might have a lead."

Ms. Sommers's eyes flashed a brilliant green. "I have a listing in the county, about fifteen minutes from here, a very nice colonial on three acres. The owners vacated the house two months ago, but we kept the place furnished and put a timer on the lights so anyone watching would believe it's occupied. I check my properties every week, and yesterday, as I pulled up in the drive, I saw movement behind the curtains in the front window. I peeked inside the window and saw matches, candles, and food in the kitchen. I called the police, figuring I had some squatters on the property, and they informed me of your situation. I had no idea it could be something more dangerous."

Frankie felt her brow furrow. "This house, how secluded is it?"

"Trees border one full side and the back, but the front and east are open. Rolling hills like most of this area. You can see other homes from a distance, but none are close in proximity."

"What about a basement?"

Ms. Sommers nodded. "Full finished basement, invisible from the road, but walkout access from the back."

Frankie glanced at Ben, who had joined them from the war room. "The candles, food, and location make sense, but the house is actively on the market," she said. "He'd have to know there might be showings. That's one hell of a risk, and risk isn't in this unsub's nature. He's much too planned and organized to take such a chance."

Ben shrugged. "If it is him and he's escalating, then it's likely his desperation is increasing. We know he didn't have time to plan this one out as carefully as the last. This may have been a crime of opportunity, so it's not improbable he took up residence in the first house he found acceptable. Also, this could be a different unsub entirely. Someone trying to make this look like it's related to Anna's case. We have to remember that."

Oh yes, I remember. Frankie wanted to comment, but she kept her mouth shut.

She paced, feeling the pulse of optimism course through her veins. What if Dr. Whitman had left the police station and was now at the property where he'd taken Jeanne?

The nap would have to wait.

"Okay, we should go, but let's not notify the cavalry. Lieutenant Gordon, you have a few men available? Ms. Sommers, we'll need the combination to the lockbox and a diagram of the house."

Thirty minutes later a small subgroup of the task force huddled in the war room. After clearing a space on the table, they reviewed the layout of the house and surrounding landscape and devised a plan. Lieutenant Gordon and members of his SWAT team would go in first and secure the grounds while Ben and Frankie followed close behind.

Gordon recruited an officer to drive, and the six of them—three SWAT, Gordon, and Frankie and Ben—piled into the van. Twenty minutes later the lights went dark as they turned onto a narrow drive and ambled their way down a quiet, tree-lined country lane. Five hundred feet from the house, the driver parked off the side of the road, the van doors opened, and they all spilled into the night.

As their feet hit the ground, all conversation transformed into sign language. Around them the night came alive, bullfrogs and crickets chanting in harmony. Heat lightning danced across the rolling hills in shades of violet and blue, followed by the low rumble of thunder. They hiked the distance to the house in formation, gravel and dirt crunching under the weight of their boots.

The SWAT commander motioned for two of his team to circle around back. Meanwhile, he stayed with Lieutenant Gordon, aiming his assault weapon at the front door while Gordon held a small flashlight between his teeth and entered the combination on the lockbox. Frankie and Ben kept to the side with their backs to the house. When the lockbox opened, Gordon removed the single key, inserted it into the keyhole, and turned it gently before quietly popping the door open. Then he let the SWAT commander take the lead.

The commander examined the entire room through his night-vision scope before entering to the left. Lieutenant Gordon moved in behind him and maneuvered right. Frankie and Ben followed: Frankie behind the commander, Ben with Gordon. The two SWAT members who'd entered from the back quickly met the party of four in the front and gave the all-clear sign. The commander pointed at the stairs. Two of the SWAT members took position on each side of the banisters as the commander and Gordon climbed. When they reached the top, they stood guard as the next two ascended.

Frankie and Ben stayed at the base of the stairs in case their uninvited guest planned an ambush or tried to make a run for it.

As Lieutenant Gordon and the SWAT team cleared each room upstairs, Frankie eyed the basement door. She felt certain that if Whitman was in the house, he would have settled in the basement, with easy escape access through the walkout below the back deck. When the team reappeared at the top of the stairs with the all-clear sign, she motioned for them to follow her. They maneuvered back down, and soon all six of them stood outside the basement. Ben and the SWAT members stayed to the side as Frankie turned the knob and Gordon pushed the door open with the slightest touch of his fingers. Instantly the aroma of gardenia wafted from below.

Somebody was burning a candle.

Frankie felt her adrenaline flow. At least the basement didn't smell like death. That was a good sign. Was Dr. Whitman in the basement with their missing girl? She gritted her teeth.

The SWAT commander took a quick glance around the doorjamb before fully entering the doorway. Two seconds later the six of them began to inch their way down the steps. When the commander reached the bottom, he held up a hand and put a finger to his lips.

The six of them halted and listened.

There were voices coming from below.

The team continued until one of the stairs cracked beneath their weight. Now the voices were louder. A few more steps, another loud pop, and the voices stopped.

The commander held his weapon steady, expecting the unsub to burst into view at any moment. When nothing happened, he swung himself free of the rest of the stairs and landed with the lightest step. He scoped the basement, then nodded once toward a door off to the right. The rest of the team treaded lightly behind him.

Frankie examined the surroundings when she reached the ground floor. Like the rest of the house, the basement was empty of furnishings, but she noted canned goods stocked in a corner and two piles of folded clothes. She didn't see any signs of a generator in use or any type of medical equipment, however.

Was it possible Dr. Whitman had abducted Jeanne but hadn't yet begun any type of surgical procedure? Was Jeanne Mapleton still alive and waiting for them to rescue her on the other side of this door? She thought of the young woman whispering into the video camera. "Help me."

Her gut lurched.

Suddenly breaking the silence, Lieutenant Gordon rapped on the door and shouted, "We know you're in there. Put down any weapons and come out with your hands up."

A stifled scream preceded scurrying footsteps and hushed voices, then a crash and the sound of breaking glass. Gordon continued his verbal assault. "I'm going to count to three. One, two—"

When the team broke down the door, words began to fly. SWAT rushed in to take control, and within seconds a partially undressed African American couple emerged with their hands cuffed behind their backs.

"We're sorry. It was my idea," a man said in a heavy Nigerian accent. "We needed a temporary place to stay. I could not afford a hotel." The woman was crying.

Frankie sighed, holstered her Glock. "Damn it. False alarm."

The two squatters huddled with their limited possessions surrounding them. Frankie retrieved a blanket and wrapped it around their shoulders.

Lieutenant Gordon spoke to the SWAT commander. "Let's help them gather their things and we'll take them to a local shelter. Then it looks like we're back on the hunt."

CHAPTER 31

After a quick shower at the hotel and an unexpected call, Frankie found herself knocking on the door of Dr. Banks's rented condo. "I shouldn't be here," she said, leaning against the doorway.

"I know, but you sounded exhausted on the phone. A break will do you good."

She hung her head. It was true, but it didn't ease her guilt. The reality was, even with the latest setback, she had no right to stop searching for Jeanne. Jeanne was still out there, at the mercy of a killer. An hour, a single minute, could mean the difference between life and death. And yet, she was so tired.

Lawrence took her hand. "Come on, get out of this heat."

Frankie stepped into the air-conditioned room and mopped her face with the edge of her T-shirt. Though the sun had gone down, it was still eighty-three degrees out. To her surprise, Lawrence pecked her lightly on the cheek before retreating to the kitchen. He didn't look back to see her glance of professional warning, even if it was false. The kiss had been nice.

While he removed two cold beers from the fridge, Frankie pulled her hair into a ponytail and fell into the sofa. "Somewhere Al Gore is wearing a T-shirt that says *I told you so*," she said.

The doctor's mellow laugh filled the room. "Here, this will make you feel better."

"I shouldn't. They could call. I need to be ready."

"Stop saying you shouldn't. One won't hurt you. I have some leftover wings and salad, too, in case you're hungry."

Frankie took a long pull on the beer. She wasn't much of a beer girl, but she had to admit, it tasted good. She felt the stress in her neck ease, if only for a moment.

Lawrence slid onto the cushion beside her, but they said little, speaking only with the occasional glance. Finally, he broke the silence. "I tried to keep an eye on him, but he sensed what I was up to. He even confronted me about it. I can't believe he'd be so bold as to still go through with it—abduct another victim?" He shook his head. "Do you think he's crazy? I mean, he must be."

Frankie thought about telling him how Dr. Whitman had implied it was Lawrence who'd taken Jeanne, but she decided to hear his version of events first. "How often did you see him at the conference?"

"A couple of times. I made sure he was part of our dinner plans Monday, because, like I said, I wanted to keep an eye on him, but I guess I asked too many questions, because he lit me up like a firecracker afterward."

"How about Tuesday?"

"Only in passing. We both had sessions to present that day."

"What was yours?"

"'Stories of the ER: Options for Trauma Management.' I had a good turnout. Everyone likes the lowdown on the ER. The crazier the stories, the better."

Frankie raised an eyebrow. "Compelling."

"Far better than 'Options in Transanal Wound Care' or 'Debates and Updates in Inflammatory Bowel Disease.'"

She cringed. "You really know how to turn a girl on."

He laughed. "That's what they tell me."

She took a sip of the beer, thought about how best to approach the subject of Jeanne. "I don't know if you're aware, but the missing woman was in your Tuesday session."

Frankie pulled out Jeanne's headshot from the file she'd brought containing all the information she had on the missing woman. "Do you remember her? Recall speaking to her? Dr. Whitman mentioned that she asked you a question after the lecture."

He huffed. "Oh, he did, did he?"

He studied the picture, wrinkled his brow. "This is her? Damn. He's right, I did talk with her." He handed the photo back. "She was nice. A student at the university, right?"

Frankie nodded. "Did you see her or Dr. Whitman anytime later that evening?"

"Tuesday? No. I was planning to join him and others for dinner, but after our exchange the previous night, I decided to make other arrangements."

Frankie studied him. "Hot date?"

He laughed. "Yes. Very. Very hot date. With a one-hundred-twenty-pound Asian man by the name of Kawaguchi. He looks sixteen, but he's one of the top trauma surgeons in the region. We got to talking shop after my session Tuesday, and he invited me to dinner."

"You were with him the entire time after your lecture until dinner?"

Lawrence thought. "No. I came back here to take a run, shower, and make some calls. I met him for dinner later."

"Where did you go?"

"Some fish-and-oyster place. He likes seafood."

"You didn't go anywhere else before dinner? Happy hour at another bar?"

"No." He shifted sideways and cocked his head. "Okay, what's going on? What's with all the questions?"

"Is there anyone that can vouch for you between six and eight p.m. Tuesday?"

His eyebrows shot up. "Do they need to?"

She sighed. "It would be best. That seems to be the time Jeanne went missing. And, as Dr. Whitman pointed out several times during our talk today, you knew Anna too, and you are also here in Charlottesville."

His lips thinned. He shook his head. It was the same look she'd seen on the hotel video when he and Dr. Whitman were arguing in the lobby. Annoyed. "I see. So that's how he wants to play it? Yes, okay, I knew Anna and I'm here in town, but I don't have a connection with the other women you believe are victims."

Frankie raised an eyebrow. "True, but you are the one who led me to Dr. Whitman's use of the obsidian scalpel. You're also the one who found the suture, who told me about his missing year in Baltimore, and who gathered and gave me other names to look into."

"Which makes no sense if I was your killer. Why would I help you get evidence? Why would I give you leads to my own victims?" His clipped tone confirmed his aggravation. He finished off the beer, rose to get another. "That guy. I'll tell you what it is—he's pissed off that I'm helping you."

He tossed the empty beer bottle in the trash and retrieved another.

"I understand you two had some words in the lobby yesterday morning. What did you say to him?"

"I told him the same thing he told me—to stop meddling in my business. I don't even think he was sick. I think he just wanted to screw up my day. He wanted to know why I didn't pick up my phone right away and why I wasn't staying at the hotel."

Frankie took a glance at the condo's furnishings, the plush, cream-colored couch and loveseat, the built-in shelving lined with books and animal statues. "It's a fair question. Why are you staying out here in the burbs and not downtown?"

He sighed. "I like the privacy, and it's next to the country club and golf course where a charity event is taking place this weekend—which is why I'm still in town, to answer your next question."

"Is that so?" She took a drink of the beer and gave him a hard stare, as if she didn't believe him. She examined his defenses: the set jaw, rigid chest, and tightened fingers around his beer. He'd started to plead his case when she released the tautness at the corner of her mouth.

He fell back onto the couch. "Damn, woman. You scared me." He pulled her to him and nuzzled the base of her neck. "Busted. I admit it. I'm only here because I'm stalking you."

They wrestled playfully on the couch before Frankie pulled back. She felt guilty for having a moment of fun with Jeanne still missing. Her smile faded. "On a serious note, if our killer is Dr. Whitman, I fear Jeanne is already dead. Word is Whitman arrived home in Charlotte a few hours ago, so unless he took Jeanne to North Carolina with him, it's likely she's gone. And I'm responsible."

She felt her throat constrict and her eyes sting, but she quickly pushed her feelings away. She didn't want to be emotional in front of Lawrence. She leaned forward and rubbed her hands together. "I need to find physical evidence to link him to all these women, and I need to fully understand his motive."

Lawrence sat up. "What else can I do to help? Do you have other evidence I can check into? What are these?" He pulled out additional papers from the folder she'd brought containing Jeanne's photograph.

She took them away. "Stop. No, you've already gotten me in trouble."

"Come on. Let me see. Please?"

"They're nothing you would be interested in, just poems they found at Jeanne's apartment."

He tilted his head. "You know ... I'm pretty-well versed in poetry. I did slams in college. I was actually pretty good. Stanzas and verses and rhythms and all that."

"Is that so?" She made an amused face. "Aren't you impressive?"

He chuckled. "I know. Not your typical black man's hobby. But I like rap, and to me, rap is poetry. It's a message of the times, right? I study it. The old stuff and the new."

Frankie considered this. Ben would tell her this knowledge made Lawrence more of a suspect, but it simply made her curious. She handed them over.

Lawrence sorted through them, reading. "I know this one—'Go, Lovely Rose.'"

"Yeah?"

"Yeah. It's an envoy."

"A what?"

"An envoy. A letter sent through a third party to a love someone idolizes from a distance or cannot have."

Frankie sat up. "Idolizes but can't have? Interesting. Go on."

"It's about sending a rose to a young lady the poet admires and desires. Like the rose, her beauty is brief and will soon wither and die. He's telling her to seize the day, carpe diem. They should be together before it's too late."

Frankie stared at him, her mind racing, one side wrestling with his unexpected knowledge, the other realizing how well this analysis fit with her profile of a fantasy obsessive or erotomaniac—someone who believed they were in love with another but couldn't be with that person because of circumstance or distance.

"It's the same theme expressed in 'To His Coy Mistress' and 'To the Virgins to Make Much of Time,' which I see he liked as well," Lawrence added. "Time is fleeting.

We could spend eternity in courtship, but we must enjoy the pleasure of each other now. Stop playing hard to get. This is your opportunity to win a husband, which in those days was very important for a young woman."

Frankie's chest buzzed, as if someone had wound a child's top and placed it there to spin. These poems reflected the unsub's motive. The poems and letters spoke of his courtship, the farmhouse of finding his bride a home, and the surgery of molding her into his perfect wife—most likely removing her breasts to make her young and virginal.

That had to be the motive.

"What?" Lawrence asked. "Doesn't fit?"

"No, on the contrary, it fits perfectly." She sighed. "Now if only I could prove it."

She fixed her gaze across the room, trying to process this new information. But her mind was muddled with cobwebs, thick, sticky strings she couldn't think past. The lids of her eyes and the folds beneath them felt waxy, like the face of a mannequin.

She was tired.

Lawrence put the poems back in the folder, then reached behind her to massage her shoulders. His fingers kneaded into muscles as hard as bricks. Frankie leaned into his thumbs as they rolled beneath her shoulder blades, erupting small fires of nerves that both pained and pleasured. He was showing off his knowledge of anatomy, and she wasn't about to object.

"Why didn't I listen to you when you said there was a conference?" she said. "I should've known he was going to escalate after he didn't get to finish with Anna. I should've been here. I could've stopped him."

Lawrence pulled her back into his arms and rested his chin on her shoulder. His words graced her ear. "Don't do that to yourself. How could you know he would be so brazen? How could you know who he would target?"

"That's easy for you to say. You won't be the one responsible for her death if I don't find her in time."

"Maybe not, but I've had patients die under my care, so I know what it feels like to believe you should've seen it coming and done something differently. Believe me, you can't, and the times that you do often involve more luck than skill."

Frankie sighed. "Well, I could use some luck then, because Dr. Whitman—or whoever the perpetrator is—is either the luckiest or the smartest killer I have ever met."

They sat for a few moments not speaking, listening to the cicadas fill the night outside and the television from the next condo infiltrate the walls. Late-night lineup.

She wondered what Ben would say if he knew she was here instead of at the hotel getting some much-needed sleep. She was treading dangerous territory, yet for the first time in weeks, she felt safe and comforted. *Just ten more minutes. Fifteen tops.*

Moving back to her side, Lawrence directed those soft chocolate eyes at her, leaned in, and kissed her. Mingling beer mustaches. His breath, his tongue, his mouth, warm and wet. She felt a heat rise that had been missing far too long.

"Stop," Frankie mumbled. "We have to ..."

But he didn't. And when it was clear her resistance was futile, she found herself leaning into him, passion getting the best of her. Sure, it was easy to say she was all about the job, but life's wants and desires didn't always behave in such a professional manner. She wanted a relationship, but the timing was rotten. Later, maybe, after the case was closed, but right now, he was the temptation of forbidden fruit. The bad guy. The married man. Since the snake fooled Eve, women had been drawn to them like they held the secret of the world.

He stopped momentarily to gaze at her. He ran a finger down her arm and across her thigh. "I missed you." Then he was back, pulling her closer, their kisses deeper.

Until the cold, hard wraith of guilt rained down on her like a hailstorm.

She pulled away. "I can't do this. No, I can't do this, Lawrence. I have to go."

She slid from his grasp and stood, brushing the hair from her face. *What the hell am I doing?* She started to grab her things.

He hugged her from behind. "One dance before you leave?"

She regarded the door, then him, now standing in front of her. He touched a few buttons on his phone and some smooth R & B began to play. She sighed. "One."

He slid his arms around the small of her waist. For a few minutes they swayed, until she leaned in and rested her head on his shoulder. They danced in rhythm, his lead slow and steady, her face coupled with his neck taking in his scent with every step. One song turned into two, then three, then she lost count. He had, if only for a short time, allowed her mind to think about something other than death. She closed her eyes and rocked.

She never felt the sleep come upon her.

CHAPTER 32

I n her dream, Frankie was approached by a most odd being. The creature's limbs were long, her body nimble, yet her face was chiseled, with a strong jaw, high cheekbones, and angular nose. Blond hair fanned out behind her, surrounded by a strange bluish-gray light, taking on the appearance of water. But in place of her eyes, there was fire, flames licking upward from their sockets. She was both mermaid and dragon, enticing and fearful, and when her hand reached out with fingers splayed, she held in it an object of love. Perfume, perhaps, or an aphrodisiac. Frankie had started to take it when she realized the object could be a bottle of poison. Such beautiful packages often turned out to be the most dangerous, their allure so enticing one scarcely noticed their toxicity until it was too late. And true to its nature, when Frankie pulled her hand back and refused the being's gift, it transformed into a beast.

Frankie woke with a start, an incessant buzzing in her ears. In the haziness between sleep and reality, she attempted to understand where she was and why. Except for her shoes, she was fully clothed, with a blanket tossed over her for comfort. The radio and television were off. The open suitcase reminded her she wasn't at home, but something else felt amiss. Rising from the bed, she was alarmed to see a sliver of light shining behind the blinds. It wasn't night any longer, but day, with fog blanketing the outside.

And she was not in her hotel.

She frantically searched for her gun and cell phone, and found each on the nightstand. She grabbed her phone and couldn't comprehend the number of messages in front of her—nineteen. She shook her head, trying to rid herself of the nightmare, of the potential consequences of missing so many voice mails. She hit play and listened to the first one. It was Lieutenant Gordon, telling of a fire at an old house on Pine Bluff Road.

The second message, Ben. "Where the hell are you? I'm knocking on your door." She heard banging, presumably Ben pounding on her hotel door. "Frankie, are you in there?"

Ten minutes later, Ben again. "Frankie, the car isn't in the lot. Did you leave without me? Pick up your phone, there's a fire." Click.

A third. "I just had the hotel manager open your door. The bed hasn't been slept in. Did you keep searching for Jeanne? Did you lose your phone? Are you hurt? Shit." Click.

Another. "Listen, I don't know whether to be really pissed off right now or worried sick. I've talked to Gordon, to Vicks, even your father. Nobody has seen or heard from you since we left HQ last night. Everyone is worried. Damn it, call me."

And on and on. Every five, ten minutes. Ben, Lieutenant Gordon, then ASAC Vicks. *Shit* was right. *How could I have slept through so many phone calls?*

The phone began to vibrate in her hand. *Vicks.* She studied the device, confused. She never turned the ringer off in such circumstances. Never. Had Lawrence turned it off so as not to disturb her? But why? *Shit. Lawrence. Where in the hell is he?*

Never mind. It didn't matter. She was an hour late to the scene of a crime on her own task force, and there wasn't an excuse big enough in the world to save her from the fallout. She slipped into her shoes, grabbed her gun, and barreled through the door.

She called Ben as soon as she was in the car. "I just got your messages. Are you still at the hotel? I'm on my way." She didn't give him a chance to ask any questions.

The engine roared as she snaked among minimal traffic, lights flashing. Ben was waiting outside the front doors at the hotel. She skidded to a stop. "Get in!"

Cursing, Ben slid into the passenger seat. He shot her a glare that spoke volumes. "What the hell? Where have you been?"

"Not now. Where to?"

She could see the fury burning in the pit of his stomach, but he concentrated on the business at hand. They'd have plenty of time to discuss her behavior later—and there would be a discussion, no doubt about it.

Five minutes later they were peeling up and down a rollercoaster of a road—first high, where they could see across rolling green hills and country farmhouses, then low, where the fog remained settled among haystacks and grazing cattle. Up over the next rise, she saw it, a single trail of smoke billowing into the morning sky, now thick with the scent of disaster. Ben shot another look at her, and she wondered if she appeared as sick as she felt. If they discovered Jeanne Mapleton's charred remains in that house, she believed the guilt might be too much to bear, that it would manifest beneath her skin like maggots and consume her flesh until nothing was left. Not that oversleeping at her hotel would have done any more good than oversleeping at Lawrence's condo, but that wasn't how the mind worked. It told you that you were guilty not because of where you'd been, but because of where you hadn't—not because of where you'd slept, but because you'd slept at all.

Ben pounded the dashboard and screamed at a tractor to get out of their way. Frankie floored the accelerator and passed on the double yellow against all common sense.

She imagined Ben's thoughts as they raced to the scene. *Where in the hell has she been? Surely not with Dr. Banks. I can't believe her irresponsibility. While we're out chasing one of the biggest cases of our lives, she's busy playing doctor? No. It isn't possible. My trainee wouldn't jeopardize her career this way.*

Nor mine. Especially mine.

She saw his face flush.

I think I just read his mind.

"Let's hope Vicks isn't on the warpath," Ben said.

No such luck. As soon as they pulled up, he charged toward the car like a three-hundred-pound bull in a silk suit. "What the hell, Agent Johnson? You want to explain this situation?"

Ben tried to intervene. "Sir, we've been following every lead and searching every known unoccupied property for the last three days. This house was not on the list."

But Vicks wasn't having it. He went straight for Frankie's jugular. "I've been calling you for over an hour. Where the hell have you been? Andrews said you weren't at the hotel. You weren't in the war room, and you damn sure weren't here. Explain."

Frankie took a step back. "I'm sorry. I fell asleep. I admit it. I've barely slept three hours since I arrived here three days ago. Last night I was too tired to drive. I didn't trust myself behind the wheel. I thought if I just shut my eyes for a few minutes, I would be okay. My phone was on vibrate. I don't know why. I don't remember putting it on vibrate. I wouldn't do that."

He leaned in, snorting breaths an inch from her face. "Well, while you were shutting your eyes for a few minutes, Jeanne Mapleton was shutting hers forever. So I guess you'd better get in there and clean up this mess."

He marched off, shouting orders to officers who weren't even under his command.

Frankie stilled, speechless, his words crushing her like a pop can underfoot. She wanted to throw up, to hit something, to scream, but since she couldn't do any of those things, she did the only thing she could—swallowed every ounce of her pride and charged in.

Lieutenant Gordon, kneeling over an item on the floor, stood when he saw her. "Agent Johnson, are you all right? We were getting damn worried."

She held up a hand, palm out. "I'm fine. Long story. Tell me what we've got."

"She was found there," he said, nodding at what remained of a gurney. "But on first impression, it looks like the fire started over there, in a pile of clothes." The odor of gas continued to permeate the air, as if the place might reignite at any moment.

"We found a matchbook outside from the bar where she was last seen. Not sure if those were the matches that started the fire, but you have to believe so."

Frankie nodded at a piece of silver metal with a partial etching of an O remaining. "What is that? An oxygen tank?"

Lieutenant Gordon glanced behind him, nodded. "I think so. Probably what ignited and blew this place apart. I don't think he intended to leave much behind."

Frankie scanned the area. He was right. It looked like a bomb had gone off. Nothing of the house remained, including the stone chimney. Officers and firefighters examined items a hundred yards away.

"You can look but don't touch," Gordon said. "You know the drill."

They walked the perimeter of what used to be the main floor, Frankie sifting through the debris with a stick, careful not to move items from their original location. She lifted a scrap of wood to reveal a family photo, now covered in soot. The remains of several others lay nearby, along with charred debris.

"How come this place didn't pop up on our list of properties?" Ben asked.

"Because it's not unoccupied," Gordon said. "A family lives here, but they're on vacation. Three weeks in Europe. Somehow he must've known."

Frankie stopped at the gurney where Jeanne Mapleton had died. A piece of the floral skirt she'd worn in the video still stuck to the side rail. Suddenly it felt like someone had shoved a fist down her throat and left it there.

She choked back her emotions. "Do we know time of death yet? If she died before the fire?" She wanted—no, needed—to know that Jeanne had died with an injection of ketamine as Anna had. She didn't think she could handle the alternative. Right now, she wasn't sure she could handle this one.

"Only the autopsy can determine that." Gordon glanced up, only to return his attention to the floor. "If they can determine that. There wasn't much left of her to be honest."

He could've stabbed her with a knife. It would've hurt less.

"We'll leave you and your team to do your job," Ben said. He tapped Frankie on the shoulder and motioned her outside.

Away from the scene, Frankie took several deep breaths, trying to clear her mind. She began to pace, intuition nagging at her conscience. Was it true the unsub hadn't wanted to leave anything behind, as Lieutenant Gordon had suggested? For some reason, she felt the opposite. *He may not have wanted to leave behind much evidence, but he wanted an explosion large enough for us to find her.* He wanted their attention; she was sure of it.

"This is all wrong, Ben," she said. "Our unsub went to great lengths to make sure his prior victims weren't discovered. Anna was a mistake. If the two teens hadn't interrupted him, we never would've found her. He wouldn't repeat a mistake."

"Maybe we just know what to look for now. You said yourself most of the ViCAP reports that matched were seeking an arsonist and not a murderer."

"That's just the point. There weren't any bodies in any of the other matches. We don't know how long he kept his prior victims playing house before he tired of them, but when he did, he disposed of them. They were likely buried, not left in the house to die, and he certainly didn't leave a book of matches and an oxygen tank nearby."

Vicks approached with another man in a shiny blue suit. As soon as Frankie saw him, she knew she was likely no longer in charge of the task force.

"This is Special Agent Elliot Rader from the BAU," Vicks announced. "He's reviewed the evidence and has been brought up to date."

Frankie knew the name—and the reputation. Elliot Rader was known as *Radar* in Bureau circles because his profiles were spot-on. One of the best, he had instincts and cunning just this side of criminal. Frankie and Ben introduced themselves.

"What's the verdict?" Vicks asked.

"Sir, Agent Johnson believes this may not be the same unsub. Or that the unsub had a different motive with this victim," Ben said.

Frankie wheeled, casting Ben an icy stare. She didn't need him to speak for her.

"Oh, why's that?" Vicks asked.

"Anna was discovered because a couple of teens wandered into the wrong part of the woods," Frankie said. "Our unsub was busted. He set that fire out of desperation and necessity, to get rid of the evidence."

"This one too," Vicks said.

"No, not this one. This one was meant to look the same, but we're less than a football field away from the highway and an oxygen tank was added so it would explode. He wanted us to see the fire and find the victim this time. In no other circumstances has a body been left at the scene."

"You think this is a copycat?" Vicks asked.

Frankie placed her hands on her hips. "Actually, no."

"Well then, what is it Agent Johnson? It's the same. It's not the same. You're really not making sense to me. Do you believe this is the same unsub, and do you still believe Dr. Whitman is your main suspect?"

Vicks was clearly losing patience, but she needed him to listen to her. "Yes sir, I am. Look, last night I learned additional details about the poems sent to Dr. Whitman's love interests. Their meaning ties directly to Whitman's desire to have a wife, to some type of obsessive or erotomaniac behavior."

"What details?"

"I showed the poems to Dr. Banks last night. He knows a bit about poetry."

Vicks's eyes cast stones. "You saw Dr. Banks last evening? I thought you were too tired to drive home. I thought you shut your eyes for a while and fell asleep, presumably by the side of the road."

She turned to Ben, only to see him flush and turn away. Rader smirked.

"Yes, the road. I did, once I left there." *Shit.*

"Agent Johnson, even if what you say is true, the fire started this morning and Dr. Whitman arrived home yesterday. How do you explain that?" Agent Rader asked.

"I don't know. Maybe he set an incendiary device and used the oxygen to ignite it. If you give me a chance to investigate—"

Vicks loomed over her, arms crossed. "Do you have one ounce of tangible physical evidence we can use to charge and convict Dr. Whitman?"

"The scalpel, the sutures—"

"Not without prints," he interrupted. "Coincidental at best."

"The poems."

"Like the doctor said, the poems are well-known works. High school lit class material. Lots of people read poetry, Agent Johnson, including apparently your good friend Dr. Banks."

He grunted and took off, the strides of his steps twice as wide and twice as fast as her own. Frankie caught up to him, determined to make him hear her out. Ben and Rader trailed behind. As usual when Vicks exploded, Ben kept his mouth shut.

"Sir, you know the women were his clients and he consulted on cases at hospitals near their workplaces mere months before those women disappeared. He had lunch with Melanie Higby. He admitted his infatuation with Anna Jamison. Sir, he knew about the girl."

Vicks stopped and spun toward her. His hands were on his hips, his substantial chest pushed out. "He explained that, didn't he? In fact, he's explained just about every single thing you've thrown at him. Maybe it's time you looked at other options."

As she was about to object, one of Lieutenant Gordon's officers approached, a flash drive in his hand. "Sir, I think you'll want to see this. Come with me."

CHAPTER 33

They huddled around the officer's patrol car as he popped the flash drive in his laptop, downloaded a video file, and hit play. "The conference recorded each of the sessions so attendees could buy copies. This one is from Tuesday, and it's interesting."

Frankie's heart raced, thumping hard enough for her to see the rise in her chest. She waited anxiously, expecting to see Dr. Whitman appear on the screen. But when the images began to unfold, it was a different doctor behind the podium.

Lawrence.

Her heart took a deep dive into shallow water.

The minute she saw Jeanne Mapleton standing in line before the podium, Frankie knew what was coming. This was video from Lawrence's session on trauma and the ER. Jeanne was waiting her turn to ask him a question after his Tuesday lecture. Dr. Whitman had mentioned Jeanne had spoken to Lawrence, and now they were going to watch it unfold.

The six of them huddled around the laptop to watch as Jeanne stepped up to the podium. She smiled and flipped her hair, then leaned forward, just enough to show a bit of cleavage. As she asked her question, Lawrence smiled and nodded, looking every bit the interested doctor. He spent the next five minutes answering her while being his usual charming self, which she appeared to appreciate. *Smitten*, Dr. Whitman had said.

The officer stopped the tape when Lawrence handed Jeanne his business card, and she brushed his arm to say good-bye. The time stamp read Tuesday, 3:47 p.m. A few minutes later, Jeanne would appear in the lobby and join a group of strangers to converse, then leave and walk to Oakhurst bar, where she would utter "Help me" at six thirty p.m.

ASAC Vicks turned to Frankie. "Your good friend Dr. Banks. He was still in town last night. You said so yourself. You saw him."

"Yes, late. Around midnight."

But not this morning. *Where did he go this morning?*

Her head was swimming. Her throat hot. She wanted to vomit. She could see Ben examining her, dying to ask her a thousand questions, especially if she'd stayed the night. Rader seemed to have picked up on the circumstances too and was boring holes in her direction. She felt surrounded, an adulteress waiting to be stoned.

"He wasn't the only surgeon still in town. There's a charity golf tournament this weekend. He stayed for the tournament. This video doesn't mean anything," she said.

But silently she wondered if Lawrence would've had time to stop here before going to the golf tournament. What time had he left? She had no idea.

Vicks clicked his fingers at the officer with the flash drive. "Find Dr. Banks. Bring him in for a chat." He walked away, shouting orders and making a fuss, clearly no longer interested in anything Frankie had to say.

Ben seized the opportunity, grabbing her arm and leading her away from Vicks and, thankfully, Rader. *Of all the times for the BAU to arrive.* Frankie bet she was making one hell of an impression.

"What the hell? Do not tell me you were with Dr. Banks the entire night."

"It's none of your business." She yanked her arm free, turned away.

"Shit," Ben muttered. "You can't even look me in the eye, Johnson. I can't believe you. Playing doctor instead of working. Jesus."

He always did this, referring to her as Johnson when he needed to distance himself. "I fell asleep, like you told me to. What does it matter where it was?"

"Was he there this morning when you woke up?"

"Why?"

"Why? You damn well know why. Was he there?"

Frankie felt her throat seize, her legs tremble.

"Oh my God," Ben said.

"The tournament started early this morning. It's not him, I'm telling you."

Ben paced, hands on hips. "He could've been using you this entire time. To find out information. Lead you toward Dr. Whitman and away from him. I should've seen this sooner."

From *we* to *me*. Typical Ben.

"Wait a minute. You're telling me the doctor you teased me relentlessly about when I was in the hospital is now considered a suspect because a girl flirted with him before she died? I thought you were with me on this case. You know the gaps in Whitman's story and his links to the poetry. Are you telling me one video overrides every other factor? I don't buy that. Lawrence doesn't fit any of the profiles."

Ben stopped pacing. He leaned over her, like a true big brother. "No? Did you look? How about number one, the charming seducer who secretly hates women? Do you know anything about his background, his childhood, his parents? All this time you've focused on Dr. Whitman. I warned you about focusing on one suspect, that once you have a subject in mind, you are no longer doing a profile but a personality assessment."

"I am focused on one suspect because all the evidence points to one suspect, either as the unsub or as a connection to the unsub. Who was the one trying to explore the possibility that he was being set up, or that a woman from his past was involved, when I was so rudely interrupted?"

Ben shook his head violently. He didn't want to acknowledge it. "That's not what I meant. There was nothing to that. The women in the cases are simply coincidental."

"Well, I guess we'll never know now, will we? Thanks to you and Vicks."

"What I'm saying is maybe there have been other clues all along and you haven't seen them because you're biased. Did you ever think of that?"

Biased. As in, she had feelings for Dr. Banks.

A pattering she'd never felt before rose in her chest, like hundreds of blackbirds flapping their wings at once. "Did you ever think you're letting Bureau politics cloud your judgment—not for the first time, and probably not for the last?"

Ben's face turned a shade of violet. "Don't go there. Just because you're choosing to lose your perspective on this case doesn't mean I need to. Not to mention your professional demeanor in sleeping with a suspect," he whispered in harsh tones.

There it was. Frankie started to defend herself, then choked it back, swallowing the raw pain she felt. She hated it when her emotions took her logic hostage, when fear or betrayal or hurt hijacked her words. Why was it she could defend others with such force and yet face such difficulty in standing up for herself?

Her eyelids fluttered in the morning wind.

Ben's mouth opened to reply, then promptly shut. He slid his hands into his pockets. Vicks charged between them, updating Agent Rader on their new suspect.

Frankie issued Ben one last glare, then turned to follow Vicks. She knew she shouldn't say it—she was in enough deep shit as it was, and it wouldn't make a good first impression with the BAU—but the words spewed from her mouth before she could snatch them back. "Sir, I think you're making a mistake."

Vicks halted so suddenly that Frankie practically ran halfway up his ass.

He wheeled. "What did you say?"

"Listen, if you want me to interrogate Dr. Banks, that's fine, but—"

"Jesus Christ, Johnson, I don't want you anywhere near him, in an interrogation room or otherwise. You're practically shagging the guy. You've crossed the boundary of professionalism enough already, don't you think?"

"If you would just listen—about the poems."

"Johnson, you're the one not listening. So hear me now, because I'm not going to repeat myself. This isn't a request. Take a vacation. You're off the case."

CHAPTER 34

Frankie sat on a barstool late in the afternoon, staring at a second glass of wine and wondering how in a single day she'd thrown away her entire career. Just a day ago, she'd interrogated Dr. Whitman and had him admitting how bad things looked for him. Then this morning, with a single video, everything had changed. The hunt was now on for Dr. Lawrence Banks, and no one cared any longer about the inconsistent and consequential nature of Dr. Whitman's connection to the evidence and the victims. The look on Vicks's face had said it all.

Jesus, Johnson, you're practically shagging the guy.

Disgusted. Disgraced. How could she have fallen for such a ruse? The killer had been right in front of her, playing her from day one. Now she had to ask herself, was it true?

She thought back through her meetings with Lawrence. His disturbance over the photographs of Anna. Showing up at the hospital right after Miguel Herrera's passing. His knowledge of poetry. His statements—charming, apologetic, or defiant.

And possibly entirely dishonest.

He'd led Frankie down the yellow brick road to the land of Oz, to the great and mighty killer Dr. Kenneth Whitman. Yet now it appeared that, like Oz, the great and mighty killer was just a man with a loud voice and a large presence, a total ruse.

But was it? All the things she'd learned about Dr. Whitman—his longing for a wife, his abandonment as a child, Tammy's rejection of him, his use of the obsidian scalpel and green-braided sutures, the poetry, the timing of the cases he'd consulted—said he was the unsub or knew who was, so perfectly wrapped that they could have made the shiniest Christmas package all tied up with a beautiful bow.

Now another girl was dead. No, not just another girl—Jeanne Mapleton. The image of her permanently rested on Frankie's memory: the strawberry-blond hair, brown eyes, and pink lips smiling at her for all eternity.

I had a life, damn it. I had a life and now I don't, and it's all because of you.

Frankie threw back the remaining wine and set the glass on the table. Maybe she was in the wrong occupation. Maybe, after all this time, her belief in her ability to analyze people and their behavior was greater than the reality. And Ben, he'd turned his back on her. He'd never done that before. He'd been her support, her biggest champion. There had been times before when he'd refused to stand up for teammates when things went bad. She'd just never thought it would happen to her.

Apparently, for him, loyalty only went as far as the person with the more impressive title. Especially when the BAU was present.

Frankie motioned the bartender for another. He reached for a new bottle, uncorked it, poured her glass full. "Maybe you should just leave it," she said.

"Bad day, huh? Join the club." With his bar rag, he motioned toward the rest of the patrons. Randomly seated, they all displayed the same posture—elbows on the table, head down, staring into their choice of magic liquid, waiting for the oracle to appear and read their future. Tell them how things had ended up this bad and how they could fix it.

She imagined the stories of the bar's other inhabitants, like the fading blonde who sat in the corner, lapping what looked to be vodka on the rocks. Maybe she'd just been served divorce papers or realized the handsome young stud she'd been screwing had played her for a couple hundred thousand. Or take the bespectacled banker nearby, his suit looking like he'd slept in it two days straight, gazing into his amber cocktail like he'd bankrupted the company and was wondering how his boss would take the news. Or the young father, T-shirt and three days unshaven, figuring out how he was going to pay off the gambling debt he'd incurred the night before without losing his house, wife, and kids.

She wondered too what they thought of her, the young professional with a holster devoid of a gun. Stripped of her honor? *Worse, much worse*, she wanted to tell them. *Me, I let a killer charm me and allowed a young woman to die.*

Welcome to the very awful, terribly bad day club.

Frankie felt the vibration of her cell phone in her pocket, this time turned off for a reason. She had started to select ignore when she saw that the caller was the mother of Rory Spencer, one of the women that Lawrence had given her as a possible victim. With the hunt for Jeanne taking precedence the past few days, Frankie hadn't been able to connect or follow up with the families. Now that she was off the case, she had all the time in the world.

Frankie answered, hoping the wine didn't slur her words too badly.

After she briefly told the woman why she was interested in hearing about Rory's disappearance, the woman filled her in. Rory had been a college student at Clemson, studying botany and hoping to find work improving the environment. She was employed at a coffee shop near one of the major hospitals in Spartanburg. A girl who wanted a life of adventure, she'd left them a note stating that she'd met someone and was dropping out of school to travel the world, and they hadn't heard from her since.

Her mother went on to say that Rory had a friend who'd been searching for her online for over two years and suggested that Frankie learn more about it on her social media. After looking at Rory's friend's page, and reading about her plea that anyone with information come forward, Frankie decided to call her. They'd spoken for a few minutes when the friend made a bombshell announcement.

"No, you don't understand. Rory wasn't in love with a man. Rory was a lesbian. Her mother couldn't accept it, but the person she was in love with was a woman. Her name was Mary."

Frankie accidently knocked her glass of wine over on the bar. She mumbled an apology to the bartender, who wiped it up and gave her a fresh cocktail napkin.

"Mary? Are you certain?" Frankie asked. "Do you remember her last name?"

"No, I'm afraid not. But she was tall, with shoulder-length blond hair. Rory told me she would drop by the café and they would go out to lunch. I met her once and I didn't like her at all. I don't know how to explain it, but I got a bad vibe. I think she might've hurt Rory. That's why I've been searching, because I know Rory would check in with her family and friends if she was traveling. She'd post pictures from everywhere she went. But this Mary, she's like a ghost. No one knows her."

Frankie thanked her and ended the call. A woman. Tall, with blond hair. Like the mysterious blonde who'd escorted Anna to her apartment in Chapel Hill to pack her suitcase. Like the patron who'd last spoken to Emily Dearborn at the convenience store. Like the woman who'd visited her mailbox and left a poem for Frankie. A woman named Mary.

Theories be damned, Ben Andrews.

Maybe Frankie was on the right path after all.

A half minute later she called Brianna Thomas's parents, the people she was supposed to have met the day everything blew up with Jeanne. Brianna's father wasn't available, but her mother filled Frankie in on all the details.

"We'd had our struggles with Brianna since high school, but a year after working at the hospital, she seemed to be doing well. She loved her job, and she was dating again. After the surgery, she was like a new woman."

The word prompted a spike of adrenaline. "Surgery?"

"Yes, a nose job and chin reduction. Brianna had always been insecure about her looks until a plastic surgeon she'd met suggested the changes."

The surgeon: Dr. Kenneth Whitman.

Frankie closed her eyes, silently uttering a string of curse words. She wasn't wrong about Dr. Whitman. The coincidence simply defied logic. But then how in the hell did Mary fit in? Was she an accomplice or what?

Frankie sat on the stool, rapping her fingers on the bar. What was she missing?

She pulled up the numbers of Dr. Whitman's supposed former girlfriends, the two women whose numbers he'd written down in haste and given to her during her first interview with him. Frankie hadn't been able to connect with the first woman, Dr. Ariana Ajwandahi, because she'd been in Africa, working with Doctors without Borders, or the second, Hannah Franklin, because she'd been on her honeymoon. But both should be back in the States now.

"We went out to dinner and movie a few times, but that was it," Ariana said in broken English. "I found him polite. What do you say in America—a gentleman? But he was like a wall. I could never get to know him."

"I know this is terribly personal, but did you ever have sex with him?" Frankie asked. She felt the eyes of the bartender and the unshaven young man turn her way.

"No, we kissed a few times. He seemed uncomfortable. Pushed me away. But nice about it. I asked why he hadn't married. He said he was waiting for the perfect wife."

The perfect wife. Chills prickled Frankie's spine.

Frankie thanked Dr. Ajwandahi. Her curiosity piqued, she followed up with a call to Hannah Franklin-Myers. She congratulated the woman on her recent marriage, then explained what she needed.

"To be honest, I thought Dr. Whitman was gay," Hannah said, her voice a sugary concoction of cotton candy and caramel. "I just figured he hadn't come out of the closet yet, or like he was still trying to decide. I can't imagine a man being a virgin at his age."

"He said he was a virgin?"

"Yes, he said he was waiting for the perfect woman."

Frankie hung up and shook her head. Maybe it was the wine, but she didn't get it. Not about the connections to Dr. Whitman, not about the blond woman present in some of the cases, and not about the sex. Tammy Kay had said they'd had sex. These women said they didn't. It was contradictory. But then again, everything she'd learned about Dr. Whitman was contradictory.

Frankie set her phone on the bar, more confused than ever.

Just as the young unshaven man was sidling up to her—likely engaged by all her talk of virginity and sex—her cell vibrated again. She frowned at the faceplate. It was Ben. *Should I answer?*

She stared at the man now next to her, who raised a hopeful eyebrow. Frankie regarded the brown patches on the elbows of his sport coat, a relic from the nineties. Suddenly the call seemed enticing. "Johnson."

"Where are you?"

She glanced at the fake palm tree, the neon Corona sign, posters of girls in bikinis. "A tiki bar on the beach." She was surprised to hear the slur in her words this time.

He sighed. "Drinking isn't going to help."

"Another of Ben's wise sayings. I bow to the king."

163

"I didn't call to argue with you. I wanted to let you know I'm bringing in Dr. Banks for questioning tomorrow and I've cleared it for you to be there ... if you want."

The images before her swayed under the influence, including the guy next to her folding a napkin into some odd original creation. She didn't know what to make of Ben's offer. "Why? Why would you do that?"

"Consider it a favor. Sober up. I'll see you at nine a.m."

CHAPTER 35

Ben allowed Dr. Banks to wait in the small, gray, windowless room for more than forty minutes. In interrogations, waiting created fear, and Ben wanted Dr. Banks to worry about the type of evidence the police might have against him. For added effect, he whisked back and forth in front of the open door, grabbing paper work and stopping to discourse with two bulky officers, each of whom eyeballed the doctor as Ben spoke.

Frankie, who sat in the same room with Vicks, Lieutenant Gordon, and Agent Rader but kept her distance, would watch the interrogation via live camera from the war room. Vicks had made it clear he was no fan of having her present, and Ben knew the interrogation would be tough, but he felt it his responsibility to place things in perspective for her. He'd hated the altercation that had occurred outside Jeanne's crime scene, and knew that Frankie thought he was being a bureaucratic dick, but there were times rules and basic sense prevailed. If Frankie had a weakness, it was that she acted too much on instinct or emotion and not procedure, and this time it had left her ass exposed, potentially for good.

Upon entering the room, Ben was happy to see that his preparatory tactics had worked. Dr. Banks was irritated, pacing and loosening his tie. He cast an intimidating glare at Ben. "What the hell is this about? Do you know how long I've been waiting?"

He strained to make eye contact, but Ben refused, coolly removing his suit jacket, and sliding it over the back of a chair. He unbuttoned his cuffs and rolled up his sleeves—body language that communicated his preparation for a fight. Through it all, he said nothing.

"Look," Dr. Banks said, "my time is valuable, Agent Andrews. Maybe you don't think so, but I'm due back at the hospital tomorrow morning. I have surgeries scheduled. I need to get on the road this afternoon."

Ben slid out a chair. "Have a seat. We could be here awhile. I don't want you to wear yourself out pacing the back wall."

Dr. Banks ignored his command. He leaned across the table and whispered. "If this is about the other night, it's none of your business. Agent Johnson ..."

"This is about the other night, but not Agent Johnson," Ben snapped. "The Office of Professional Responsibility can take up that cause." As soon as the words cleared his mouth, a fire erupted in his gut; Frankie was in the other room. But he couldn't be concerned about that now. He pointed to the chair again and this time made sure his message was clear. "Take a seat."

The doctor's gaze shifted toward the video camera in the corner. "Is Agent Johnson here? I want to speak with her."

"No, she is not." Ben lied. "Now, sit."

Reluctantly, Banks obliged, throwing himself down and growling.

Ben cleared his throat. He needed to make it crystal clear that this was no friendly chat. Frankie had questioned him before, but the interview—if you could even call it that—hadn't been official. It had been a conversation over dinner, worse, a dinner that could easily be construed as a date, and let's face it, she'd been biased the minute she'd set eyes on him. She'd never adequately established his baseline behavior, let alone questioned his answers and committed to an interrogation.

Ben began with the routine questions: name, address, birth date, marital status. With each question, the doctor grew more agitated.

"What schools did you attend?"

"University of North Carolina, undergraduate and medical school."

"You skipped high school?"

Dr. Banks sighed. "West Charlotte High."

"Parents?" Ben asked.

"I have two. Wilma Brown and Billy Thompson, if you believe the birth records."

Ben noted the contempt. "Siblings?"

"Antonne. He's in prison for armed robbery, which I'm sure you'll make some judgment or comment about."

"What about you? Have you ever been arrested?"

A pause, then, "No. Come on, you know all of this. It's all right there in your little notebook," Dr. Banks said.

Of course, he was right. Ben knew all this information already, but that wasn't the point. The point was to establish Dr. Banks's baseline behavior and personality and see if his normal behavior included deceptive acts. So far he was firing truthfully, and aggressively so.

Ben continued. "Military?"

"No."

"Ever been hospitalized in the past five years?"

"Excuse me? That's none of your business."

"Are you currently under the care of a physician or psychologist?"

"I know you can't be serious."

"Taking any medication?"

"Not answering that either."

Ben put his pen down, feeling like he had a good baseline established. Dr. Banks was clearly an active extrovert, a straightforward, talk-his-way-through-anything individual. Charming, manipulative, and intelligent. And if he was the perpetrator of these crimes, also likely a sociopath. Which was just fine with Ben. He'd dealt with his share of men without a conscience before.

He held the doctor's gaze. "Do you know why we asked you here today?"

"You're finally going to tell me? It's been well over an hour, and I'm still waiting for an answer. I guess you enjoy violating my rights."

Ben ignored the remark. "Yesterday morning the body of a University of Virginia nursing student was discovered mutilated and burned in a house west of Charlottesville." Ben removed two photographs of her. He laid the first one, of a smiling, strawberry-blond Jeanne Mapleton, facing Dr. Banks. "This is that student. Do you recognize her?"

Without waiting for him to answer, he laid the second photo—of her charred, burned body—next to the first. "Or maybe she looks more familiar to you this way."

Dr. Banks violently shoved his chair back from the table and stood. "What the hell is this about? I didn't do this. Why are you accusing me?"

"Are you saying you don't recognize her?"

Dr. Banks glanced down at the photograph again before turning away just as quickly, as if the photo smelled as bad as it looked. He didn't answer.

"Maybe I can refresh your memory. Do you like movies? I'd like to watch a movie." Ben grabbed his laptop and set the video in motion. The minute Dr. Banks saw his image grace the screen, he bristled. When the doctor's gaze found Jeanne's cleavage, Ben stopped the tape.

"Less than three hours after this little encounter, Jeanne was last seen at a birthday party at Oakhurst bar. That makes you one of the last people who saw her alive."

"I didn't attend any party. I don't know her. She just asked me a question."

Ben motioned back to the chair. "Sit," he said.

Dr. Banks reluctantly returned to the table.

"When did you arrive in town for this conference?"

"Monday afternoon. I settled in and met colleagues for dinner that night. I can give you their names."

"No need. I have them. Tell me about this Tuesday. What did you do?"

The doctor jerked his head around like a chicken. "What? The whole day? You want to know what I ate for breakfast? For lunch? Want to know when I took a shit?"

"If you did it in the presence of Jeanne Mapleton, then yes, I do."

He slammed a fist on the table. "I don't know this girl!"

"Tuesday," Ben shouted. "Now!"

Dr. Banks muttered words under his breath. He went through the normality of his day—waking, showering, and grabbing a coffee from a nearby café.

"Would that café happen to be Joe's on Ivy Road?"

"I don't recall. It was in a strip mall and on my way."

Ben tilted his head, chin up. This would be the first of many revelations for Dr. Banks to process, not to mention Frankie. "It was Joe's. Here's a copy of your receipt to refresh your memory. You purchased a blueberry bagel and coffee at seven fifty-four a.m."

"Then why are you asking me about it?"

Ben was surprised that the doctor didn't seem concerned about the location. But then again, if he was a sociopath, he would be well practiced in acting unaffected.

"Would it surprise you to know Jeanne Mapleton also stopped at Joe's that same morning, just after you, at eight-fifteen a.m.? And that we found her car in the parking lot of that strip mall?"

Dr. Banks's eyes widened, clearly reading through the implication of Ben's accusations. He vehemently shook his head. "No, no, no, no. I did not meet that girl there. I only spoke with her at my session, that was it. No time earlier, no time later."

"Are you sure? Maybe she had car trouble and you offered her a ride?"

"No, absolutely not. I didn't see her at the café. Just Tuesday at my session."

"What time was that?"

"From two fifteen p.m. until three thirty p.m. I stayed another hour to answer questions and left the hotel around four thirty p.m."

Ben chuckled. "Convenient. That's the same time Jeanne left, on foot."

"Well, I was driving, and she wasn't with me," Dr. Banks snapped.

"What were you driving? Make and model?"

"My own car. I drove here. A 2016 silver Lexus GS."

Ben wrote the type of car in large letters, then the words *check video* in even larger letters. He noticed the doctor's annoyance as he twisted the corner of his mouth and huffed. His head hadn't stopped shaking for ten minutes.

"What did you do Tuesday night?"

"I had dinner with a colleague, Akem Kawaguchi, at eight p.m. It was late when I returned to the condo, around eleven p.m., in time for the news."

"Wait, what happened between four thirty p.m. and dinner? That's quite a gap."

Dr. Banks threw his hands in the air. "I was at the condo. I took a run, checked email, made phone calls, nothing special. I don't know what to tell you."

Ben leaned in. "So let me get this right. You were at the coffee shop within minutes of Jeanne Tuesday morning. Then she attends your afternoon session and you're caught on camera flirting with her. Later, you both leave the hotel at the same time, and according to you, you were basically doing *nothing* for the two hours between the time you both left the hotel and the time she was last seen at the party just blocks away."

"Come on, that's not fair," Dr. Banks shot back. "I don't know what time she left." He viciously rubbed his head. "This is ridiculous."

Ben took note of how Dr. Banks would not say Jeanne's name. Distancing from a victim was a common tactic of a guilty perp. "You were at your condo alone for three-plus hours, is that what we're supposed to believe? Not that you left the hotel and stalked Jeanne Mapleton? Watched and waited outside the bar as she attended the party, then intercepted her when she left?"

"Yes, because it's true." He started to say more but sat back and crossed his arms. Ben took note of his heavy breathing and the sweat forming on his brow.

He was starting to get to him.

"Where were you Wednesday morning?" Ben asked.

"Why is everyone so interested in Wednesday morning?"

"Why not Wednesday morning?"

More sighing. "I had planned to play golf, but I got a phone call from a colleague who said he needed me to cover his session, as he was feeling under the weather. So I covered his session in the morning, presented my own after lunch, then played golf later that afternoon."

"What is it with you doctors and golf? Is that all you do?" Ben needled.

"It's a time to talk shop and relax. Being a surgeon is kind of a high-stress job, in case you weren't aware. You're responsible for people's lives."

"Interesting choice of words. That makes us sort of brothers, doesn't it? Brothers in saving lives. I wish I could've saved Jeanne Mapleton's life. I wish I could've saved Anna Jamison's life."

Dr. Banks flinched at the mention of Anna.

"That makes two of us," he said. He crossed his arms tighter and the muscles in his arms stood out like basketballs that couldn't be filled with another drop of air before bursting. "Look, I did nothing remotely interesting this week. I attended lectures. I played golf. I talked shop—"

"You abducted a young woman and burned her body," Ben said.

"I had nothing to do with what happened to her!" he shouted.

"So you claim," Ben said, remaining calm. "Tell me, Dr. Banks, why didn't you stay at the conference hotel downtown? And why are you still here? The conference ended two days ago."

"The condo was private and near the golf course. There's a charity golf tournament in town this weekend for the Make-a-Wish Foundation."

"Not because you didn't want anyone else to see your comings and goings?"

"I hope they did. Then you'll know I'm not responsible for this terrible act."

Dr. Banks suddenly glared at Ben. "You know, I already explained all of this to Agent Johnson. Don't the two of you talk to each other? I thought you two were tight. When she was in the hospital, you stayed by her side all night, worrying about her recovery. It was you who suggested—"

Ben frowned. He didn't want to get into it, especially the part about his own role in bringing the doctor and Frankie together. "Agent Johnson asked you these questions?" he interrupted. "When was that?"

The doctor gave him a disapproving look, both for cutting him off and for throwing Frankie under the bus. He could tell. "Yes. She did. She's a good agent. Two nights ago."

Ben's stomach burned. He hated bringing Frankie deeper into this, especially when Dr. Banks was looking at him as if he were Judas. "Agent Johnson visited you the night before Jeanne Mapleton's burned body was discovered. Can Agent Johnson vouch for your whereabouts the entire night? Can she—or anyone else—prove you were not in that house that burned early Wednesday morning with Jeanne Mapleton in it?"

Ben stayed silent. The moment of truth. Would he use Frankie as a cover?

Dr. Banks ground his teeth. He glanced at the video camera once, then twice, seeming to think about his options. "No."

Ben raised an eyebrow. "No?"

Dr. Banks broke eye contact and looked away. "No. She wasn't there. She just stopped by to ask me some questions. Then she left." He bit his bottom lip. "Look, everything I'm telling you is the truth. I have nothing to hide."

Ben smiled. *I'm going to make you eat those words.*

CHAPTER 36

Frankie watched Ben pace along the wall, slapping one fist into the palm of his other hand, initiating a subtle threat, the implied act of fighting. She'd had just about enough of this charade. Ben was being nothing but a bully, putting on a show for the powers-that-be, and so far, he had produced little. Yes, that Lawrence and Jeanne had both stopped for coffee at the same café was strange, as was the fact that Jeanne's car had been found parked there later, but they had no video of Dr. Banks and Jeanne arriving or leaving together at the hotel or at Oakhurst bar. Yet Vicks kept smiling, as if he knew more was coming.

"Nothing to hide," Ben said. "I'm glad you feel that way. Let me ask you a question. Do you know how often the perpetrators of crimes insert themselves into their own investigations?"

"Agent Johnson came to me, not the other way around," Lawrence said, clearly understanding where Ben was going with his question.

"Yes, initially, but since then, you've taken an active role in this investigation, haven't you? Done some research? Even given her names of other potential victims?"

"I just wanted to help. Anna Jamison was a friend."

Ben chuckled. Laughing while another person spoke was a known tactic to undermine someone's credibility, and Frankie despised it. It was, however, one of Ben's favorites.

"Ah yes, a friend. Let's talk about your friend, shall we?" He thumbed through some papers. "You don't mind if we revisit some of the conversations you and Agent Johnson had previously, since they weren't recorded?"

"Do I have a choice?"

Ben ignored his question. "During your first conversation with Agent Johnson, you didn't reveal that you knew Anna Jamison, is that correct?"

Lawrence squirmed. "I didn't think it was relevant at the time."

"She allowed you to review some key evidence in the case—photographs of surgical instruments and equipment discovered at the scene. Did you know when you viewed those items that the victim was Anna Jamison?"

"No, not really. I'd heard about Anna's death, but not the details."

"What details?"

"The mastectomy. The fire."

"And when you learned of the details, only then you knew?"

"Yes, and I really wanted to help. I found information about the suture in development. I intercepted Agent Johnson at the hospital after I heard about Miguel Herrera's death and gave her what I'd discovered."

Ben glanced up. "You were at the hospital when Herrera died? Convenient."

"It wasn't convenient. I'm often at the hospital late, making rounds."

"And it was that same night you finally revealed that you knew Anna Jamison? Did Agent Johnson question you after your revelation?"

He cleared his throat. "Very much so. She wasn't happy."

Frankie felt more than saw the sideways glances from Vicks and Agent Rader across the room.

"I bet. What exactly did you tell her about your relationship with Anna?"

"That I knew her. That we had gone to a basketball game once, UNC versus Duke. That I had met her at an alumni event for UNC."

"And how about the last time you saw Anna? What was your response when she questioned you about that?"

Lawrence hesitated. "I believe I said I hadn't seen her since February." He quickly did a double-take at the video camera, then cast his gaze back down at the table.

Frankie sensed trouble and her stomach did a slow roll. She could feel Vicks and Rader staring at her again.

"And was that true?" Ben asked.

When Lawrence grabbed at the collar of his shirt and he pulled it away from his neck, Frankie knew he'd lied to her. "No, not exactly. I saw her after that. She called and asked to meet for drinks."

Ben shrugged, smug. "Oh, well, that was probably months ago and you forgot. I mean, right? It was months ago, the last time you spoke to her or saw her?" He leaned on the edge of the interrogation table and awaited the doctor's answer.

Frankie held her breath. She didn't know if she wanted to hear this.

Lawrence writhed. There was no doubt he didn't want to answer this question.

He finally spit it out like a bad-tasting vegetable. "It was the last Friday she was in town. I met her and several others at the restaurant where she'd just had dinner with her parents. But it was a large group, twelve people. I wasn't with her specifically."

Silently, Frankie cursed. She heard Vicks sigh. She didn't look at him.

For the next two minutes, Ben let the sounds of Lawrence's breathing fill the room. Frankie knew what he was doing. Ben wanted his words to sink in, to weight the air with them as if they were physically hanging in the space between him and Lawrence before he dropped his bombshell.

"You're telling me that you spoke to Anna on the last Friday she was in town, one day before she met her friend at a bar and told her she was leaving her fiancé for another man? Two days before she was seen at her apartment packing up a suitcase? Five days before she died in a barn in Lexington, cut up and burned at the hands of a surgeon? Is that what you're saying?"

Dr. Banks lowered his head. "It's not what it looks like."

"I think it's exactly what it looks like. Otherwise why not mention it?" Ben hovered over him. "Tell me, what else did you fail to mention to Agent Johnson about your relationship with Anna Jamison?"

Lawrence shut his eyes and wiped the sweat from his face. The control he'd exuded so far was being replaced by a deep, brewing anger, Frankie could tell. She understood how Ben would work to bring that out—his anger—and wished she could tell him to refrain.

"Please, don't do this," Lawrence said.

"Don't do what?" Ben asked.

"It isn't relevant. None of it matters."

"It doesn't? Then why not let it be known?"

Ben left the table and once again paced like a tiger along the back wall. He briefly glanced into the video camera, as if letting Frankie know what he was about to do. He would tell her he was only doing it to show her what bias could do to wreck a case, but the truth was, if he pursued it, it would further stress the delicate thread of friendship that remained between them. And yet, he continued.

"When Agent Johnson questioned you in the diner, she didn't really get too detailed about your former relationship with Anna, did she? Maybe she didn't want to know, so she didn't ask. But I will. Dr. Banks, did you ever have sex with Anna Jamison?"

Lawrence groaned. Uttered an inaudible response.

"Could you speak up? For the recording?"

"Yes." His voice was sharp. "But not that Friday. We were just friends."

Ben didn't listen. "You had sex with Anna Jamison. You went back to her place after that basketball game and you stayed the night. Then you kept in contact and periodically saw each other, including the very night before she told her friend she was leaving her fiancé for another man."

He turned. "That man was you."

Lawrence had heard enough. Ben had finally managed to push the right button. Frankie could see it in his body language. He jumped from the chair and charged forward.

He pointed a finger in Ben's face. "I did not do this. The only reason I didn't tell Agent Johnson about my past with Anna is because I knew she would no longer let me help with the case."

He swiveled toward the camera. "Frankie, I swear. I did not hurt Anna."

He wagged his finger at both Ben and the video camera. "I know how you police operate. How you like to twist things and make people look guilty when they're not. This is all circumstantial evidence, and you know it."

Ben circled him. "You know how we operate? How would you know? Dr. Banks, have you been through this before?"

Lawrence moved within an inch of Ben's face, so close his spittle landed on Ben's chin. "I am not going to confess to something I did not do."

Ben laughed. "You do know how this is done, don't you? You know how it's done because you've been here before. When you were fourteen, you sat in a room just like this one. Except you weren't Lawrence Banks then. You weren't doctor somebody. No, you were just little KJ from the hood."

A shadow passed over Lawrence's face then—a knowledge, a realization, that Ben knew more than he was letting on. He abruptly pivoted to face the opposite wall. His back rose and fell with heavy breaths. No doubt he was trying to calm himself before he did something irrational.

Frankie couldn't breathe. *What the hell is Ben talking about? Who is KJ?* She watched in horror as Ben grabbed his notebook off the table and flipped a page.

"You said your father's name was Billy Thompson, and your brother, Antonne, his last name is Thompson. Your last name used to be Thompson too, didn't it? Kendall Jamal Thompson."

"It's not a crime to change your name," Lawrence said.

Frankie could hear the pain and agony in his voice.

"It is if you're running away from something."

Lawrence remained silent, his breaths still deep. He kept his back turned to the camera and Ben.

"It doesn't have anything to do with this juvie record, right?" Ben slapped a file folder against the wall in front of him, forcing him to look. "Rape and attempted murder? Pretty serious allegations."

Lawrence wheeled. "I was never charged in that case. Just like now, I was falsely accused and questioned even though I never did a damn thing. I wasn't guilty then, and I'm not guilty now. You've got the wrong man."

His eyes raged with an intensity Frankie had never seen. The pulsing muscles in his face spoke of the outrage of injustice and a time better left forgotten. He looked to the camera and pleaded with her. "Frankie, I swear, he's got it all wrong."

But Frankie had heard enough. Her heart hurt with the weight of betrayal and humiliation from not just one but two of the men she'd most trusted in her life. She slipped past Vicks, Lieutenant Gordon, and Rader out the door of the war room and ran down the hall of the Charlottesville PD. Behind her she heard chaos erupting and Lawrence's voice calling for her. But it was too late.

She was done.

CHAPTER 37

It was time. He pulled down the long-overgrown dirt road, feeling the tires rise and fall over ruts and bumps twenty-five years in the making. He'd spent hours thinking about the right place for her, had searched farmhouses from Virginia to South Carolina, but none had felt right for his bride-to-be. There was only one place that would be suitable for her—the one and final—and that place was home.

This was where it had all begun: his birth, his death, and his rebirth.

His pulse quickened as he pulled up to the ruins of the four-bedroom house that had once stood proudly facing the highway from afar. All that remained now was a portion of the brick chimney and the cement stairs that descended into the crawl space, the place where he'd started the fire as a child that had killed his family. He remembered how he'd cried to the police later, apologizing for smoking, for being so careless with the matches.

He knew others would be horrified by what he'd done, but killing his parents had not been a bad act. When he'd blocked those doors and locked those windows, he'd done a good deed, as good as helping a blind man cross the street or saving a child from the path of a speeding car. He had rid the world of two evil adults. Had he not done so, they would've killed him, continuing to inflict their choices upon him without cause. It had come down to a battle for survival. Nothing more, nothing less.

Outside, the heat broiled his skin and the cicadas screamed as he walked through the remains of the house and property. Although the place cast many a dark memory over him, he could still sense the good too: the smell of pie cooling in the window, the fresh-cut hay in the field, the honeysuckle on the vine. The tire swing beneath the old oak brought a familiar sense of freedom, of twirling as fast as he could with his legs straight out and his head back. Even the spider-infested crawl space, where they'd forced him to go after his particularly bad deeds, had eventually become a place of comfort. A source of solace where he could be his true self, out of the way of both the mental and physical abuse. So in some ways his return was not all bad. It was redemptive. He'd always wanted to come home and make things right.

He continued past the house and across the long-forgotten farmland until he came upon a run of pine trees that partially divided his land from his neighbor's. Like the open fields, the pines had grown unfettered for twenty-five years, leaving their branches entwined with heavy brambles and brush twenty feet high. This provided welcome shade, but even better, a barrier, a high wall to keep trespassers out.

He walked along the tree line until he came to an opening, a hole in the thicket big enough to step through. As he emerged on the other side, where his family's land continued, he expected to see a pile of rubble, but he was delighted to see the old barn still stood. It was weathered—in need of patching, paint, and reinforcement—but it was standing nonetheless. He felt like a kid of thirteen again.

It was a sure sign, a gift from God. He had selected the right place.

Unlatching the wooden lock, he released the darkness from within it like a prisoner from solitary confinement. He took stock of the surroundings, the throngs of bats hanging from the rafters, the rodent nests overrunning the old tractor, the loft windows covered with a thick, dark grime, as if someone had painted them over. But these were minor things. He could clean the place out, repair it, and make it a lovely home.

An altar for his bride-to-be.

He surveyed the area, sketching out the arrangement he had in mind. They would need a bedroom with a king-size mattress, a kitchen with a table, and a study, a place to engage their minds in books and conversation. And of course, he would need the modification room, a place to make his bride as perfect as she could be.

He couldn't wait to see them stand before the mirror—as one form.

He scouted the stall nearest the door. Here was the perfect place for the kitchen. He could easily run a generator from outside to operate a small portable stove and refrigerator. A table for two would make a nice addition to the corner, and he would build shelving on the far wall as a pantry for her favorite foods. He would line the top shelf with select bottles of her wines prior to her arrival and show his bride just how much he paid attention.

The tour of her home in her absence had taught him much about her preferences.

In a separate stall, he would create a special room for her, a place where she could bathe and properly prepare herself for him. He would bring in a tub—he knew how she loved her baths—and make available handmade soaps. He would hang a plush, pink robe on a hook for her to use and provide a vanity for her with all the amenities. He would overlay the dirt floor with a large, soft rug and have her favorite perfume on hand, Chanel No 5, and lingerie too. Then she would see how caring he was and how much thought he had put into preparing this place just for her.

Next to the bath would be the bedroom—their bedroom—with a king-size mattress surrounded by candles. The beams above would serve well as a closet, where he could hang clothing, starting with the pieces he had taken from her house. He would position the full-length mirror in the corner so they could watch each other.

He closed his eyes and imagined them there, embraced in passion.

The two stalls on the far side of the barn would be the best setting for the modification room. His father used to slaughter and prepare their animals in the same corner. He would knock out the adjoining wall and roll in the needed equipment: lights, gurney, monitor. A rolling tray would hold his surgical tools and instruments.

He stood in their future house, feeling a growing excitement that he hadn't felt since his preparations for Anna. *It's perfect.* They had worked so hard the past several weeks to be together; he knew his bride would love it the moment she arrived and would want to stay with him forever. Still, he knew how women loved the chase, and she might try to flee in anticipation of him following and proving his love. Anna, like the others, had taught him a valuable lesson. Though he had been a bit lax about security in the past, he would not let that happen with his new bride. Once he brought her in, he'd make certain she remained. This one was his last, his ultimate love.

And by the time anyone figured out who he was—if they ever did—the two of them would be together in eternity. He turned to view the barn one last time before he slid the door shut.

There was no place like home.

CHAPTER 38

Frankie sped west across the two-lane country roads of Virginia, knowing automatically where she was headed. She would've liked to say things had changed since her childhood, but there was only one place Frankie wanted to be when she felt hurt and alone, and that was in the company of her father.

She punched the accelerator, driving over hills and passing through the towns of Ruckersville, Madison, and Culpeper without so much as a glance. For a night, she wanted to push all the thoughts of the last month out of her mind.

A bit after four that afternoon, she pulled into the drive of the little white house off the county road near Manassas, Virginia, and parked behind her father's aging Buick. Stepping out, she breathed the hot country air. A breeze swept over the field from the west, but the trees flanking the road simply stood there, limbs drooped, surrendering to their misery.

The tattered screen door on the porch opened and her father appeared, closely followed by Lexie, his nine-year-old golden retriever. Her father broke into a big smile and reached out his arms. Lexie's tail wagged and she barked.

"To what do I owe this honor?" her father asked as he gave her his typical bear hug. She inhaled the familiar scent of his soap and aftershave and instantly felt relief. It was like being sixteen again after she'd experienced her first heartbreak—thinking life was over, then getting that hug and knowing everything would be okay again.

Inside, he put on a pot of coffee, despite the heat, and Frankie took a seat at the old chrome kitchen table. Pretty much everything in the house remained as it had been decades ago, from the white kitchen cabinets and checkered curtains to the black-and-white-tiled floor. Her father prided himself on being a relic, just like the possessions that surrounded him.

As the two of them, father and dog, lumbered around the kitchen, she realized both had aged since her last visit. Her father's final patch of brown hair had faded into the same mottled gray as Lexie's muzzle, and Lexie limped on a bad left hip just like her owner.

He set a steaming cup of coffee on the table. "There you go, kiddo. You'd probably like it with some of those crazy new flavorings or whips or whatever the hell it is that they do, but I don't have any of that fancy schmancy stuff."

Frankie smiled. "Thanks, Dad. This is fine."

"So what's the occasion? I thought you were on a big case." He brushed the hair from her face. "You look tired. Why so tired? You have to sleep, even on a big case."

"This is advice coming from you? The man who counts his sleep in winks?"

He chuckled. "Always keep one eye open. You never know when the enemy will sneak up on you."

She huffed. *Never truer words.* "Actually, I was in the area."

"I know. Charlottesville, right? Girl missing. You find her?"

She sighed. She didn't want to talk about it, not yet. She put an elbow on the table and cupped her chin. "How are you, Dad? How's your health? How are all your lady friends? Tell me something good."

To her relief, her father accommodated her wishes and for the next forty minutes regaled her with stories of women named Susie, Lucy, and Birdie. Having never married, he was still considered a catch, and there was never any shortage of retired and widowed ladies determined to land the elusive Frank Johnson. His refrigerator was full of pies, casseroles, and other assorted eats that were each supposed to remind him of the lady who cooked it, or even better, get him to invite said lady over to share it with him.

Their second cup of coffee was greeted by five minutes of silence before her father spoke. "Okay, your turn. Why are you really here? No more avoidance, kiddo."

Damn. He hadn't forgotten her old habits any more than she'd changed them.

Frankie proceeded to update him on the case—the victims, Lawrence, Dr. Whitman, and Ben—and all the mistakes she might've made. To his credit, he listened to it all as only a father could do, with an empathetic ear and sympathetic heart. "In short, I'm off the case. It's entirely possible I've seriously damaged my career with the Bureau."

Her father sat back and squinted his clouding blue eyes. "You remember that time, I think you were twelve, you were sitting in my car while we surveilled a threat that had come in that week? The entire Secret Service was focused on one building, a row house that looked like every other row house in the damn area. We'd verified the address that had come in with the threat, but as my men approached, you said, 'Dad, I think you've got the wrong house.'"

He laughed, a deep-throated chuckle that always made Frankie smile.

"You said, 'Look, the curtain keeps moving over there in that house. I think that's your man. He's watching you.' And sure enough, as my men went into the other house, the man we were looking for slipped out next door."

Frankie smiled. She remembered it well.

"The point is, you've always had good instincts. I'm saying this because I think you're on the right track with this Dr. Whitman. I don't know what to make of the Charlottesville girl's disappearance, but I agree it doesn't smell right. Your unsub, whoever he is, didn't get this far without being caught because he placed an oxygen tank next to a pack of matches, know what I'm saying?"

Frankie nodded. "My thought too."

"And this theory of a woman's involvement ... well, it's damn strange. But it wouldn't be the first time I've heard of a woman helping to abduct other women for a man. That could be what you're looking at. If I were you, I'd focus on finding this Mary Campbell."

"But I'm off the case," she said wearily.

He raised an eyebrow. "Never would've stopped your old man." He winked.

Frankie perked up. "You think I should continue? On my own?" Her thoughts went back to Ben's words, how sometimes you had to be prepared to finish the job alone.

We to *me*. Maybe this was one of those times.

"Never hurts to keep poking around, just as long as you don't jab your stick in the snake pit."

Lexie groaned from the floor as she rolled over, seeming to agree.

Her father's hand trembled as he drank the last of his coffee. He'd had the tremor for as long as she could remember. He attributed it to an old football injury, but her mom claimed it had started after he'd shot a mentally ill man who'd threatened President Reagan.

They continued their talk through dinner and afterward, when they exchanged the cups of coffee for shots of bourbon. Then they both went to bed. Her father still had her room decorated from the times she'd stayed there on weekends home from Georgetown, and it made her both nostalgic and sad. Her parents had worked so hard to see her succeed. She didn't want to disappoint them.

After a mostly sleepless night, she rose early to clean her father's house and do the laundry. It wasn't much, but it felt good to help in whatever way she could. It also allowed her mind to relax and think about next steps. For much of the night, she'd wrestled with whether she should step away and let Ben and Rader handle the case, but she couldn't do it. She didn't have all the answers, but she had to go on with the investigation, even if she was no longer officially on the case. Whether Lawrence was truly involved somehow or whether he was being used as a pawn in a bigger game, Frankie owed it to him to discover the truth. He'd saved her life nearly a year ago and, regardless of the lies and mistruths Ben had exposed, she didn't believe he was a killer.

Her theory was right. She felt it in her gut. All the clues led to Dr. Kenneth Whitman—and possibly Mary Campbell.

On a sheet of paper torn from a memo pad, she wrote her father a note with her signature, *xoxo*, and a promise to return soon. She knew he would smile at her decision to continue, to be a bit of the rebel he'd always been with the Secret Service. She picked two daisies from the garden, placed them in a vase, and set them on the kitchen table. She tucked the corner of the note beneath the vase so he'd see it when he came down the stairs. It was one of the images she would always recall when remembering her dad—a man in his shorts, T-shirt, and reading glasses, sauntering down the stairs for his morning politics and cup of coffee.

It was a good image.

Frankie threw her suitcase in her trunk, then removed a file folder from her laptop bag and slapped it onto the passenger seat. In it was the information Lawrence had given her regarding Sara Phillips, the woman murdered in Baltimore. Maybe it would be a wild-goose chase, but she felt that if Dr. Whitman was the unsub, his time in Maryland might help explain things. He'd spent some time off the grid there, and it seemed a good place to start.

Plus, neither Ben or Rader would be poking around there, so she'd avoid the snake pit.

She turned on her cell phone and saw that several calls had come in overnight from Ben and Lawrence, but she didn't have time to address them now. Instead, she rang her favorite analyst, Allison, back in the field office. Allison, having heard what had happened, was surprised to hear from her and asked her what the hell was going on.

"I don't have time to explain, but I need you to do me a favor. Expand the original NCIC and ViCAP searches I requested to include Maryland and anything within a one-hundred-mile radius of Baltimore. I need it on the q.t., though, if anyone asks."

"What about Agent Andrews?"

"Especially him. Don't mention me to anyone. I'm on my own."

CHAPTER 39

ursing the morning DC traffic, Frankie crawled along the George Washington Parkway at twenty miles an hour. The dull, gray buildings cut from the same mold on each side of the highway reminded her of the bureaucracy of government, of men in white shirts with jutted ties pushing paper, smoking cigarettes, and talking on phones. It was the imprint of all the time spent in her father's office as a youth, when a few ashtrays still graced the desks, phones were corded, and fingers rattled electric typewriters or keyboards hooked to computers the size of console televisions.

She smiled at the realization of how little her dad had changed over the years. He still preferred the occasional cigarette, the old phones, the typewriters, the cold war.

As she spent the next ninety minutes creeping along the Beltway, she phoned Johns Hopkins and proceeded to be transferred from one administrative person to the next until they found someone who remembered Kenneth Whitman. Frankie made an appointment with the woman, a Dr. Kristin Conti, who had been chief resident during Whitman's stay and was now a professor of plastic and reconstructive surgery.

Dr. Conti, a brunette wearing a white lab coat and square glasses, greeted Frankie in the designated courtyard and led her through the sprawling campus to her office. There they were joined by another woman, Dr. Lynn Armstrong, a professor and director of gynecology and obstetrics. "I asked Dr. Armstrong to join us, since she also remembers Dr. Whitman," Dr. Conti said.

"What do the two of you remember about him?" Frankie began.

Dr. Conti answered. "He was a good doctor from what I recall. Nothing really out of the ordinary." She frowned. "He did take a leave of absence during his residency."

Frankie nodded. "Yes, that's what I was told. Do you know what happened?"

"The official version was that he left to take care of an ailing family member."

"And the unofficial version?"

"He was having problems with a woman here. Her name was Sara Phillips. She was another resident and apparently knew Kenneth as a child. She wanted to rekindle their friendship but he wanted nothing to do with her. He told her she reminded him of a time he no longer wanted to recall, before his parents died. That seemed reasonable to me and everyone else, but it didn't set too well with her. She became so obsessed, she started stalking him. Off campus or on breaks, always trying to be at the same place at the same time, even though they were two years apart in residency and on very different schedules. We told him to lodge an official complaint or even get a restraining order, but for some reason, he wouldn't. Anyhow, he took leave after his third year and didn't return until after ..." Dr. Conti's skin paled.

"Sara was murdered," Frankie finished for her.

Dr. Armstrong gasped. "Is that what you're here about? You don't think ...?"

"I'm not sure. Do you remember anything about the investigation, Dr. Conti? Did Kenneth Whitman's name ever come up as a suspect?"

"I don't believe so," she said. "He'd taken leave several months earlier and didn't return until the following summer, so I can't believe it could be him. I mean, other than his brief altercation with Dr. Armstrong, he never seemed to be a violent man. Like I said, he wouldn't even lodge a complaint against Sara."

Frankie turned her attention to Dr. Armstrong, a petite older woman with gray eyes. "You had an altercation with him? Tell me about that."

"I didn't really know him," she said. "Over the years, all the residents begin to look alike. Mainly what I can tell you about is an argument we had over a patient during his time here. There was a child born with unclear genitalia, or UG, not male exactly, nor female. It happens in about one out of two thousand births. Typically we make these children female, and in this case, we explained the issue to the parents and recommended the child become female. Though the child would never be able to have children of her own, she would live a happy and productive life. Kenneth Whitman learned of the case and came to see me, but it ended up being far more than a discussion. He said we should not decide the child's sex but let the child decide when he or she was ready. I tried to explain to him that the child would likely suffer psychological damage growing up with parts of two genitalia, being neither integrated into society as a female or male, and would suffer ridicule throughout childhood and at school. It's the ongoing argument in UG circles, you see. Doctors and parents making an informed decision for what we see as the good of the child versus intersex individuals who argue that until a child knows what sex it belongs to or feels inside, nothing should be done. Society should accept them as is. Easy to say, far more difficult to make that acceptance a reality."

Frankie listened, taking all of it in, unclear about what, if anything, this had to do with her case but interested nonetheless. She recalled Dr. Whitman mentioning his sex reassignment surgery patients. She supposed that included patients designated as UG. "I take it Dr. Whitman was on the side of the intersex individuals?"

"Adamantly so. When I tried to explain the position of Johns Hopkins—the very pioneers in this field, by the way—he boiled over. He pushed me against the wall and threatened me. I ended up filing an official complaint."

Frankie thought a moment. "Interesting. Do you have any idea what made him so passionate about this particular topic?"

Dr. Armstrong was shaking her head before Frankie even finished the question. "No idea. Sometimes doctors are passionate about a particular field because they've had a personal experience with a family member or close friend who's had the condition. So that might be the case with him. But I never asked."

After a few more minutes of discussion, Frankie stood to leave. "One more question—do either of you ever remember Kenneth Whitman having a girlfriend, a woman by the name of Mary Campbell?"

Dr. Conti shook her head. "No, in fact, I don't ever remember Kenneth having a girlfriend at all. Or a boyfriend. He seemed pretty dedicated to his career."

After thanking them for their time, Frankie decided to make a spontaneous visit to the Baltimore PD's Southeastern District. In addition to Patterson Park, it covered Sara Phillips's former neighborhood in Butcher Hill. Frankie wasn't sure Sara's murder was related, but she was curious to know if Dr. Whitman's name had ever surfaced in the investigation. After finding a place to park, she elbowed her way through a small crowd of people arguing outside the front doors. Inside, she showed her creds to the desk sergeant and asked to speak with an available detective. To her surprise, not only was one available, he had been the original investigating officer in Sara's death.

"What? No courtesy call, Agent Johnson? Feebies just dropping by these days?"

Detective John Sulley was a mass of a man, with rolling flesh under his jaw and acne pits the size of moon craters. He downed the rest of a diet cola, one of six empty cans littering his desk. He was about the closest stereotype to a grade A blowhard she'd ever seen, but the last thing she needed was to rattle his cage and have him make an inquiry about her with the Bureau.

"I'm not on official business. More like a personal quest. I'm hoping for some information about a cold case of yours. Twelve years ago a young medical resident, name of Sara Phillips, died in Patterson Park. Remember her?"

The detective shrugged. "Lots of cases go through here. I can't recall them all." His indifference didn't surprise her. It was as if he regarded any attempt at thinking a waste of time.

"Well, this girl was murdered—do you remember that?"

Her abrupt tone finally got his attention. He tapped a pencil on his desk, coming to some conclusion about her. She didn't much care what the conclusion was as long as he made the right decision. "What was her name again?"

"Sara Phillips."

Detective Sulley lumbered off for fifteen minutes. He returned with not only the murder book but a cup of coffee and a stale doughnut as a peace offering.

"Here we go." He opened the book. "Okay," he said. "Yes, I remember her. Light-brown hair, ponytail, pug nose. She went out for a run on a cold winter morning in January and never made it home. She was found propped against a park bench with her throat slit. Autopsy indicated she'd been raped with a foreign object, likely a branch or stick of some kind, before she died. They found all kinds of debris in her vagina."

"Wait, she'd been raped?" Frankie's heart thudded wildly in her chest. Images of Tammy Kay passed through her mind. "Could I see that?"

He handed her the murder book. "Be my guest."

She thumbed through the photos and the reports, seeking anything else that could link the two women. As in Tammy Kay's case, the photos of Sara indicated a very personal attack, although in Sara's case it had been final, with the slashing of her throat. "Did the name Kenneth Whitman ever come up as a suspect?"

He slid the book back in his direction. "His name is on the call list." He pointed. "Looks like we tried to reach him several times, but the phone was out of service. Ditto the old address. No one lived there. I noted there that he'd left the Baltimore area. Never found him."

"Did you know he returned to Baltimore and Johns Hopkins later that year?"

Her question seemed to agitate him. He fidgeted, suddenly unable to get comfortable in his much-too-small chair. "Guess not. Nobody called to check in on the status of the case except her parents once in a while. Wanted to know if there were any new leads."

"They ever mention Kenneth Whitman? Ever mention Sara's conflict with him?" She explained Sara's obsession with Whitman, how they'd grown up together as kids.

"Never heard that one. I really don't recall any mention of him as a possible suspect. He didn't live here at the time, and eyewitnesses reported seeing a suspect with blond hair wearing a gray hoodie standing over the body. There was a big homeless and drug problem in the park at the time. That's where the focus of the investigation led."

"Blond hair?" Frankie could only think of one name: Mary Campbell. "Was it possible her perp was a woman? Did the name Mary Campbell ever come up in the investigation?"

Detective Sully huffed. "A woman trying to rape another woman? I don't think so. Also, Sara looked pretty fit. She would've been able to take on a woman."

Frankie flipped through pages of the autopsy report. "Autopsy indicates an abundance of defensive wounds, so she definitely fought her attacker." She saw no mention of Mary Campbell. "And you never tried to locate Kenneth Whitman or contact him again upon his return to the hospital?"

He sighed. "Evidently not. Look, Agent Johnson, do you know something about this guy we don't? I'm guessing you do, or you wouldn't be here."

Frankie slapped the book closed. "I'm not sure how it all ties together yet, but I plan on finding out." She pulled out a business card, wrote on the back. "Can you have someone send me copies of all this?"

He took a glance. "You want it sent to your home address?" he asked, suspicion now underlying his gaze. "Why not the field office?"

"It's complicated. Do me a favor, and I'll let you know who Sara's killer is as soon as I do."

CHAPTER 40

After spending the night in a hotel and poring over the day's news, Frankie got a call from Allison the next morning that changed her course for the day.

When Rhonda Stewart had disappeared on a spring day twelve years ago, she'd been an admissions clerk at Waynesboro Hospital in Pennsylvania. Her car, a white Oldsmobile Alero, had been found at a mall in Maryland a few miles from the state border. The same year, Dr. Whitman had taken leave from Johns Hopkins a mere hour away. No poems or letters indicating that she'd left on her own were found, but given that she was a hospital employee and her car was found elsewhere—as Anna's and Jeanne's had been—Frankie couldn't help but think there could be a connection. Frankie wanted to talk to the family and learn more about the case, discover if Rhonda had been seeing anyone new at the time she disappeared.

Once out of the city, the traffic thinned, and soon she was cruising on I-270. A thunderstorm dealt a brief but heavy rain, cleansing the air. She rolled down the window to breathe it in, the scent of wet hay and countryside. She wanted to fill her lungs and her head with everything good before facing all that was bad, a young woman who'd been missing for more than a decade.

By the time she reached exit five across the Pennsylvania state line, fog had settled in like apparitions between the valleys. Main Street was a ghost town, Waynesboro yet another city still haunted by the last recession. Historic storefronts sat empty with FOR LEASE signs in the windows, covered with random graffiti and old tape. Only a hardware store and two consignment shops were open for business.

Frankie continued to the east side where Waynesboro Hospital stood, a modest brick structure that at capacity could care for seventy patients. Studying the place from a distance, she wondered if Dr. Whitman might have begun his consulting practice here, during his year of absence. Deep down she still believed he was their unsub, despite the lack of concrete evidence and the Bureau's take on Dr. Banks.

She followed the directions provided to her by Detective Norton, now retired, who'd led the investigation into Rhonda Stewart's disappearance. He'd been captivated by Frankie's call that morning, even volunteering to drive the parents down to Baltimore if necessary. He told her the parents would have no problem providing any details she thought important. They, like he, had been haunted by the disappearance of their daughter for twelve long years.

Five minutes later she pulled up to the curb of a small brick ranch, long overdue for yard care and in need of a new roof. The street was split in more than a few places and lined with oaks twenty feet high, speaking of the age of the neighborhood and the lack of a city budget. After ringing the doorbell, she was greeted by a short man with ruddy cheeks. He introduced himself as Norton and nodded toward the couple behind him on the couch. Mr. Stewart, a burly lumberjack of a man, stood to shake Frankie's hand. Mrs. Stewart, petite with mousy brown hair lined with gray, remained seated.

Frankie sat in a soft, brown chair decorated with a quilted throw that appeared homemade. Mrs. Stewart watched her intently, her eyes shifting back and forth, either very suspicious or very frightened. She shivered, as if the four of them were meeting in the dead of winter rather than late June.

"Mr. and Mrs. Stewart, thank you for taking the time to meet with me," Frankie said. "As Detective Norton has informed you, I am interested in the disappearance of your daughter twelve years ago. Any information you can provide would be beneficial."

The Stewarts shared a glance, as if her introduction alone were reawakening memories they had long put away. "We want to help in any way we can," Mr. Stewart said. "We just want to know what happened to our daughter."

Frankie nodded. She couldn't recount how many times she'd heard those words in her short career, but they were starting to sound much too familiar.

"Detective Norton says you think our daughter might have been abducted by a serial killer," he continued. "That she might've been one of his first victims. Is that true?"

Frankie bristled at Mr. Stewart's question. She wanted to scold Detective Norton for spilling such information, but she also understood; it was a new development in a long-cold case. Still, she had hoped for a bit more discretion.

She chose her words carefully. "I am investigating the death of a woman right now that has similarities to your daughter's case. For instance, the police report mentioned that they located your daughter's car in a mall parking lot. In my case, we found the victim's car at a rest area, but she had frequented the mall the day before."

"But there's more than that, isn't there?" Mr. Stewart said. "I mean, you wouldn't have traveled all the way up here just for a car in a parking lot."

Mr. Stewart was a no-bullshit kind of man, like Frankie's father. She liked him.

"There is also the fact that your daughter was a hospital employee. In my case, as well as other cases we're investigating, the victims were either medical personnel or worked near a hospital. There is also the proximity of a suspect to your area around the time of your daughter's disappearance."

Mrs. Stewart released a muffled cry, like that of a small wounded animal.

Frankie leaned forward in the chair. "Look, I know this is extremely difficult. To think about the possibility that your daughter is no longer alive—I can't put words to that kind of pain. But you need to know, whatever we can do to solve your daughter's case may save other lives. The man who is responsible, he is escalating, meaning that his desire to do harm is increasing. Anything you can tell me could prove helpful."

His arm secured around his trembling wife, Mr. Stewart told their story: Rhonda's day trip to the mall Saturday alone with no return trip home, two days spent calling friends, locating her car the following Tuesday, a police bulletin Wednesday. "It went from bad to worse."

As he recounted their nightmare—the organized searches, the false sightings, the hope-inducing but eventually useless tips—Mrs. Stewart gripped the fabric belt of her cardigan with nervous fingers and tightened it repeatedly around her waist. The beige fabric was worn so thin in places Frankie could see through it, like the woman herself.

"What about security tapes from the mall?" Frankie asked.

"They showed her leaving the mall around two p.m.," Detective Norton said. "She got in the car, sat for about ten minutes, then went back inside. She never came out again."

"The car wouldn't start," Mr. Stewart said. "We ended up towing it home."

"To be precise, the car wasn't towed until three days later," Norton added. "We can't say for sure that it wouldn't start for Rhonda."

"There was a loose wire when we got it. It wouldn't start," Mr. Stewart grumbled.

Norton nodded. "Our theory was it wouldn't start and Rhonda went back inside the mall to call for help. But no call was made. She didn't have a cell phone."

"Not then," Mr. Stewart said. "Now everyone's got one of those things." He appeared to choke on his words. "She could've called me. I would've gone to get her."

Now it was Mrs. Stewart's turn to comfort her husband. She patted his leg.

"Did mall security or information report her asking to use a phone?"

"After she went back inside the mall, there was a brief moment you could see Rhonda speaking with a woman, then they took off down a corridor toward another parking garage. That was the last video we have of her," Norton said.

A woman. Again with the woman. Frankie's former theory was starting to look more and more like reality. "Was Rhonda dating? Any new men or friends in her life?"

"Rhonda ran with the same group of friends she had since high school," Mr. Stewart said. "Those that didn't go off to college stayed local and got what jobs they could or attended the local community college. We talked to them all after she disappeared. None of them spoke with her that day or heard from her later."

To Frankie's surprise, Mrs. Stewart finally spoke. Her voice was as tiny as herself. "I thought the woman in the tape looked like one of Rhonda's coworkers. She worked at the hospital for a time, but she moved back to Baltimore a few months before Rhonda disappeared. Her name was Mary Campbell. We tried to track her down after it happened, but we couldn't find her."

Frankie nearly tore the fabric from the arms of the chair. Her fingers dug in, clawing, as her feet cemented to the floor. She opened her mouth to speak, but she couldn't force out the words.

Mr. Stewart continued. "The woman in the video had blond hair like Mary, that's all. She had a hat on, and we couldn't see her face. I mean, maybe, but Mary had moved away months before, and they weren't that good of friends."

Frankie hoped she didn't look as pale as she felt. "Back up. Mary Campbell? Tell me about her. She worked at the hospital? She had blond hair?"

She could almost hear the crack of Mr. Stewart's ribs as his heart exploded, the sudden revelation that he might have met his daughter's killer. Detective Norton cast Frankie a quizzical glance—a *what did I miss* look.

"She was tall for a girl," Mr. Stewart said. "You think she had something to do with Rhonda's disappearance?"

Mrs. Stewart wrapped the cardigan tighter around herself. She was staring into her lap. "I told you I didn't like her," she said, so softly Frankie could barely hear. "I told you something wasn't right with her." A single tear fell.

Mr. Stewart's face contorted into odd shapes. Frankie could tell he wasn't a man of emotion, and he'd incorrectly dismissed his wife's feelings as something weak and insignificant. His view of hunches was the same as Ben's—they had no place in an investigation.

Frankie stood. "Listen, you've been very helpful. Both of you." She turned. "Detective, could I speak with you outside?"

Out on the street, Frankie drew in a deep breath and paced. She didn't know what to make of this revelation. Mary Campbell. Who was she and where had she come from? She was what they'd been missing this entire time, right in front of them and yet invisible.

Various images flashed in Frankie's mind. Mary who'd accompanied Anna to her Chapel Hill apartment. Mary who'd intercepted Emily at the convenience store outside Hickory. Mary, maybe the woman serving appetizers at the party or wearing a baseball cap leaving the hotel in Charlottesville at two a.m. to attend to Jeanne. And last but not least, Mary leaving a note in Frankie's mailbox and breaking into her house.

She shuddered.

Thoughts and theories abounded now. Suspect or accomplice? Friend or foe? Was Mary Campbell helping Dr. Whitman abduct these women, or was she acting on her own? Frankie considered Dr. Whitman's words. *She's nobody, the little sister of a friend. To tell you the truth, I'd forgotten about her.*

Maybe, but Mary hadn't forgotten about him.

She replayed profile number five in her mind: *Woman—Imaginary Relationship/Involuntary Leaving/Love. White female. Age 30-45. Some college with medical training. Single, renter, within two miles of a major hospital. Average looks. Fantasy obsessive or erotomaniac. In need of deep, abiding love. Believes fantasy is real but punishes them when they don't please. Mother incapable of love or abandoned her. No sexual contact, same gender. History of stalking in adolescence.*

An erotomaniac. Mary Campbell was an erotomaniac. Frankie sensed it in her bones. But was her fantasy idol the victims or Dr. Whitman himself? Could that be why she'd abducted and killed the others, out of jealousy? If she couldn't be with him, then maybe nobody else could be either.

And how long had she loved him? Since college, or even further back?

Since high school. Since the days he'd loved Tammy Kay.

Poor Kenny. Everybody he loves dies.

Frankie's mind whirled.

She waited for Detective Norton to join her at the curb. "I didn't want to discuss this in front of the parents, but the two bodies we've located were in unoccupied residences, one in an abandoned farmhouse, one in a family home while they were on vacation. Both burned down." She removed one of the new reports Allison had provided, the arson list expanded to include Maryland and a one-hundred-mile radius of Baltimore. "You had a suspicious fire here about a month after Rhonda disappeared. That property, do you know if it was occupied?"

He looked at the paper. "I don't know. Why?"

"That's where you need to search for Rhonda's body."

CHAPTER 41

Frankie paced the kitchen floor, the events of the last few days continually crashing in her mind like a car wreck. She thought of Rhonda's car at the mall, of Sara's slashed throat, of Mrs. Stewart's dark sunken eye sockets. How many days and nights, how many hours, had that woman prayed for her daughter's safe return, only to learn she was likely the first victim in an erotomaniac's house of horrors? And how did she feel now, knowing the young woman Rhonda had befriended was possibly that killer? Justice needed to happen, and not solely for the victims.

Bones darted between her legs and mewled, unused to his human in such a state of chaos. But it wasn't only Bones feeling disturbed. Since she'd returned home, the entire house had felt unfamiliar, like Frankie had walked into a place that wasn't her own. Her neighbor had been in the house to water the plants and feed Bones, but she hadn't been the only one. Frankie noticed several knickknacks moved, wine bottles lined up with labels facing outward, clothing in the closet once again disturbed. And she'd found a new note—this time left for her in the middle of her bed.

My lovely Frankie,

Just a quick note to let you know I thought about your message and agree one hundred percent. I will do as you suggest and wait until the time is right for us. I'm working hard to make that happen. Just know how much I admire you and look forward to our time together.

To the future,

Me

Message. What message? Mary was clearly reading into something Frankie had said or done, as erotomaniacs tended to do. And what to make of the references to *our time* and *the future*? Frankie no longer wondered if the unsub was trying to scare her. Mary Campbell was coming for her.

But why? Because Dr. Whitman had expressed an interest in her, or because Frankie was threatening to expose Mary, and possibly Dr. Whitman, just as Lawrence had been?

Yes, of course.

The entire abduction of Jeanne and her death had been a planned production, a way to get Lawrence and the Bureau to back off while Mary made additional plans.

Plans for Frankie.

Frankie paced the house, paranoia setting in like a permanent houseguest. She checked the door locks, drew the window shades tight, searched for any listening or video devices. Mary could've planted them in the house and be watching her at this very moment.

She wondered if she should call Ben to inform him of these latest developments, admit to the letters she'd received and the missing items from her closet.

She didn't have to. Her cell phone rang, and she knew by the ringtone—"Traitor" by Daughtry—that it was Ben. She'd changed the ringtone for his number, her little private dig based on her current feelings for him.

She answered, the first time in days that she'd responded to his calls.

"Thank God, you're alive," he said.

"For now," she said.

"What's that mean?"

"I think our unsub is coming for me."

"Coming for you? Why?"

She sighed. Confession time. "A couple of weeks ago, my neighbor told me a woman stopped by. I found a poem in my mailbox—'She Walks in Beauty.' My back window was open and some things were rearranged in my house. Also, some clothes were missing from my closet."

"Maybe you got robbed. Maybe—"

"I came home today and found a note in the middle of my bed."

She read it to him. He let out a string of curse words.

"This is why I called," Ben said. "This unsub is dangerous. You should be safe, for now at least, given today's events. But I'll notify Rader and—"

Frankie cut him off. "Wait, what events? What are you talking about?"

"Surely you've seen the news today?"

Frankie frowned. "No. Television is off."

"Internet? Google? Where are you, the middle of the ocean?"

"I'm thinking. A lot has happened in my ... time off."

"Another woman has gone missing."

Frankie fell against the back of the couch. Her face darkened. *Another woman?* That didn't make sense. "When? Where?"

"Local. Today. Listen, I need to let you know some things."

"Offering Bureau secrets? Why would you do that? I'm not on the case. I'm barely on the payroll." *Thanks to you,* she wanted to add.

"I need to tell you what I've discovered about Dr. Banks."

The dull groan escaped her throat before she could retract it. Was he even listening to her? "So, you're calling to rub additional dirt in my face? The interrogation wasn't enough? You needed even more of an ego boost? Is that it?"

"No. Frankie, I'm worried about you. Truly. Even more so now that you told me about these notes—which you should've done immediately by the way. There are things about Dr. Banks that you aren't aware of."

"Isn't that sweet? Big brother is still protecting weak little me."

He sighed. "Stop it. I don't think you're weak. I've never thought that about you, and you know it. I didn't mean to disrespect. You know me better than that."

I don't know you at all.

"Look, you need to stay away from him, Frankie. He's bad news. His mother and her boyfriend died in a murder/suicide when he was fifteen. His mother was a drug addict her entire adult life, and his real father was an abusive alcoholic, as were the majority of his mom's boyfriends after his father left. I don't have to remind you he's a surgeon and knew Anna Jamison."

"He knew a victim, one victim."

"And Jeanne. You saw the video yourself. That's two."

"Two victims. Not Melanie, not Emily."

"Actually, a witness has come forward. She can place him with Melanie."

Frankie flinched. "What? That doesn't—"

"Frankie, he changed his name."

"It's not a crime to want to put your past behind you. You should know."

She could hear the click of his tongue, the heavy breathing. He was trying to keep his cool. "He was suspected of rape and attempted murder."

"Falsely. He was never charged with a crime. In fact, he was questioned and let go. Did you even read the full report? I did."

Her raised voice rattled the walls. She was surprised at the defensiveness in her tone, how she could be so adamant about Lawrence's innocence. Ben's voice was equal but opposite, conveying his frustration at her not believing him. Bones didn't care much for either of their angry diatribes and contributed his own displeasure.

"I did read the report. He said the rape was a gang initiation and he was only present because his brother was a member. He said he got upset and ran home when a member tried to get him to hold the knife. He refused."

Frankie huffed. "That's right. He refused, and the police believed him. The man worked his ass off to get away from his shitty childhood and do some good in the world, Ben. You thought the world of him when he was taking care of me in the hospital. What happened?"

"He got too involved in this case, and with you. Did you know that he was the one found with the gun in his hand when the police discovered his mom and boyfriend dead? Do you know that some of those officers suspect to this day that he killed them, but because the police found him and his brother so abused and neglected, they felt it better to blame it on the boyfriend and never press KJ for details?"

Frankie felt her blood boil, his absolute refusal to believe anything but the worst about Lawrence. She simply didn't understand it. He'd done nothing but help her.

"By the way, the latest missing woman was seen with Dr. Banks yesterday. Do you remember how you told Dr. Whitman that with all his logic, he couldn't deny the connections to these women? Well, the same is true with Dr. Banks."

Frankie balled her hands into fists. "I understand, but all that logic isn't going to get you anywhere, because you've got it all wrong. Lawrence is not the killer. Our unsub is misdirecting you, just like the Imposter did last year, and you're falling for it all over again. See, I've been doing a little digging myself, and guess who I found? Mary Campbell, our mystery woman. Mary has been following Dr. Whitman around for years, obsessed with him and his love interests. She is our unsub, I'm sure of it. What I don't know yet is the degree to which Dr. Whitman is involved."

Ben sputtered. "What? No. Frankie, what the hell are you talking about?"

"An erotomaniac, Ben. Mary is the erotomaniac. It's profile number five. She was right there in front of us all along. With Anna on Sunday at her apartment, with Emily at the convenience store, even with Jeanne, at the cocktail party, handing her the tray of appetizers. Somehow she interjects herself into these women's lives and controls their movements."

Frankie's words tumbled from her mouth in a rush. She wanted to get it all out to make him understand, but she couldn't prove her case in a single breath. "There's so much more. I can't explain it all in five minutes."

Ben took his own deep breath.

"Look," he said, "I have to search for this missing woman right now, but just ... sit tight. Stay away from both Dr. Banks and Dr. Whitman. Then we can compare notes. Frankie, promise me you won't do anything crazy. Okay?"

She hung up, dropped the phone on the couch cushion. Felt a swell of emotion. He wouldn't listen, and it didn't matter. He'd told her there were times you had to go it alone, and this was clearly one of those times. From *we* to *me*.

He would never approve of what she was about to do. *Crazy?* He had no idea. She picked up her phone and punched in Dr. Whitman's number. It had to go down like this.

CHAPTER 42

D r. Whitman stood on the pier, arms resting on the wooden railing, watching the birds swoop over Lake Norman. He wore a blue linen shirt untucked over khaki slacks, an outfit befitting the water. He and Frankie said little as the hostess seated them on the outdoor deck with a view of the sunset, which was shaping up to be a stunner.

"Looks like we'll have a few clear days before Hurricane Isabel makes landfall and moves inland," Whitman said. "Best take advantage. They're saying this one is going to move slow and dump several inches of rain."

"I heard the same," Frankie said. The server offered wine and poured each of them a glass of a chilled house white. After he departed, Frankie raised her glass. "Thank you for accepting my invitation. To new beginnings?"

They clinked glasses. "My pleasure," he drawled. "I'm still shocked you called."

"Well, recent events changed things," Frankie said.

Whitman studied the water as it lapped against a pylon. "I'm glad you came to your senses. Dr. Banks is no good for you. He's a player and, apparently, a predator."

Frankie didn't object, but she didn't agree either. It amazed her how quickly people turned on each other. Champions for the underdog one minute, beheading the next. It didn't matter the business, sport, or country.

"Naturally, the hospital has been abuzz," he continued. "The administration has even begun conducting their own investigation—quietly, of course." As if on cue, a school of fish gathered to devour the remains of one of their own.

Frankie looked away from the water and the carnage. She knew the Bureau had begun circling Lawrence but had been unaware of the intercession of the hospital administration, an equal group of scavengers. She hoped that when Lawrence was cleared—as she believed he would be—his reputation would rebound.

As for Dr. Whitman, that remained to be seen.

"I know you believe Dr. Banks is a predator, and you might be right, but I wanted to talk to you about another possibility. Someone else I believe who may have had a motive."

He looked at her quizzically. "Someone else? Who?"

"You once felt that you were being set up. Do you still believe that?"

"Yes. That's what I've been trying to tell you. Dr. Banks—"

She cut him off. "Yes, Dr. Banks knew Anna and had a brief connection to Jeanne, but there are no links between him and these other women."

He offered a slight smile. "We really don't know if these women are connected."

"Yes, we do, Dr. Whitman. You know it and I know it. Women don't leave their sick mothers or husbands and children behind. They just don't. The truth is, other than Anna, Dr. Banks doesn't have any links to these women. But you do. You're the common thread. Jeanne Mapleton ..." She shook her head. "Sadly, her death was just a decoy, as is this latest missing woman."

His pale-blue irises bloomed like petals on a flower. He set his wine down. "Do you think so?"

"I know so."

He stared. She finally had his attention.

"You once said that death seems to follow you. And you're right, it really does. From your parents to friends and women you know. Even your old girlfriend, Tammy. Although she didn't die, she almost did."

A sadness infiltrated his eyes.

"Dr. Whitman—"

"Please, call me Kenneth."

She nodded. "Okay. Kenneth, I need you to talk to me. I think you have an idea of who is courting and murdering these women, and I don't know why you're protecting her, but it's time that it comes to a stop."

She reached across the table and grabbed his hand.

"I need you to tell me about Mary Campbell."

Dr. Whitman flinched, and for a moment Frankie thought he was going to bolt from the table. Instead, he underwent a strange metamorphosis, his facial muscles contorting into fun house images until a firm realization came to rest. She wasn't sure what his conscience was telling him, but she sensed she was getting through, so she continued.

"Look, I'm not one hundred percent positive, but I believe Mary Campbell has been following you most of your adult life. Now I don't know where you met her or how she became infatuated with you, but I can tell you, at some point, that obsession took a dangerous turn. To help her, I really need to understand her, and I need your help to do that. Can you?"

She made certain to emphasize that she was only out to help Mary and not harm or accuse her in any way, in case Dr. Whitman was involved with her or aided her in abducting these women.

Whitman fidgeted, obviously troubled. He thought for several moments. He picked at the lint on his shirt. He scrubbed the legs of his slacks. Words surfaced to his lips, only to be brushed away.

"Kenneth?" she pleaded.

"I don't know what to say. This is very ... shocking."

"Was Mary your girlfriend?"

He shook his head. "No. I told you."

"Okay. You said she was the sister of a friend, right? Who is that friend?"

At that, Dr. Whitman turned away, appearing as if he might be sick. Seeing his distress, the waiter paused at the table and asked if he was okay. Frankie considered asking for a paper bag in case he started to hyperventilate.

He removed his hand from Frankie's, grabbed a napkin, and dabbed at his forehead. "Sorry. This just brings back so much." He cleared his throat and took a moment to gather himself. Finally, he continued, "Have you found Mary? Seen her in person?"

Frankie frowned. "I don't know. I can't identify her, not yet. Unfortunately, the only place I know where she once worked—a hospital in Waynesboro, Pennsylvania—had no photo ID of her on file, and other than her brief employment there, I can find no trace of her. It's like she's a ghost."

He nodded, glanced across the serene water. "Yes, well, that's appropriate, since she's dead." He looked up. "I mean, technically, she's dead."

Frankie felt a charge to her heart, like two defib paddles to the chest. *It can't be. It isn't possible.* "She's dead? How? When? What do you mean, technically she's dead? Is she or not?"

Dr. Whitman exhaled. He stared at the sky, as if making a plea to God. "I've never told anyone this before, but I guess I have to now given what's happened. I hope it doesn't cause trouble."

Frankie's heart pounded. What on earth was he getting at? Finding Mary was enough of a blow. Her death would be even worse, destroying Frankie's theory that she was the unsub and, God forbid, possibly proving Ben right.

He downed the last of his wine and motioned the waiter for another. The young man quickly responded and refilled Frankie's glass as well. She must've looked like she needed it.

"When you visited my foster mom, did she mention my foster brother, Perry?"

Frankie hesitated. "Perry? Yes, she did. I saw photos of both of you. Betty Sue said the two of you were close but you parted ways in high school. He dropped out of school and left the house."

"Yes. All of that is true. Did she say anything about Mary?"

Frankie felt a gnawing in her gut, like rats trying to escape an enclosed space. She didn't like where this was going. "No, she didn't mention Mary. She just said Perry's family died in a fire." She narrowed her eyes. "Was Mary part of your family too? Was Mary your foster sister?"

If true, it would explain a great deal. A young girl who grew up with Kenneth could easily have developed an obsessive crush on him. That crush would've made her jealous of his relationship with Tammy. She could've tried to harm her to remove her from the picture. It would explain her rape with an object. It would explain her anger with Sara Phillips. It would explain her desire to learn his craft, understand the tools he used, and pursue other women he showed interest in.

It would explain it all—except her death.

Dr. Whitman didn't move. He bit his lower lip. "Yes. And no. Perry's family—his entire family—died in the fire. On paper, that included Mary." His lips pressed back together, as if he'd broken their seal and needed to heal it. "But what I'm telling you is, in life, she didn't. Perry, her brother, did."

Frankie sat back, stunned. A tingling like electrical current hummed through her nerves. She felt her brow furrow. "I don't understand. I saw pictures of him. I never saw a single photo of Mary. Betty referred to him as Perry."

He was already shaking his head. "Mama Betty didn't know."

He watched her closely. He seemed on edge, awaiting her reaction.

"Didn't know what?"

"That Perry wasn't Perry. That Perry was Mary."

"How is that possible? I mean, physically, the bodies?"

"They were twins, identical twins. Biologically, Mary was male, at least by outward appearance, and she posed as Perry when they came for the bodies. I don't know that the authorities even did an autopsy on the real Perry, or just took Mary at her word, since he was the one alive. And Mama Betty, she never had the need to see him naked."

Frankie felt the blood drain from her face. She was starting to understand.

The argument with Dr. Armstrong over the UG patient. "Mary was born with UG?"

Dr. Whitman wriggled in his chair. He seemed surprised at her knowledge. "Again, yes, and no. Perry and Mary were identical twins, both male. But the doctors botched Mary's circumcision so badly after his birth that they informed his parents he was born with UG and should be made female. His parents agreed, so they altered him. The doctors told his parents nurture would overcome nature, but Mary never felt like a girl, even at a young age. When he found out he was an identical twin and not fraternal, everything made sense. But that didn't help his anger. Not toward the doctors, not toward his parents, not even toward his brother."

Dr. Whitman exhaled a long-held breath, like he'd just let go of a lifelong burden.

"And at some point in your relationship, he told you all this?" Frankie asked.

"No, not exactly." The muscles below Whitman's eyes twitched, making him appear in pain as he spoke. "In school, the guys eventually caught on that Perry never used a urinal. He was a stall guy, always the stall, and after a while, they started to make fun of him. One day, they surrounded him in the bathroom and pinned him down."

She watched as Whitman struggled to convey the rest of the story. A single vein appeared on his forehead. His jaw clenched, released. "It was horrifying. He sat there with his legs spread, exposed, with nothing to show except the labia. No penis. No vagina either. Apparently, that was to come next, when he turned thirteen."

His eyes met hers. "That's why he did it."

Frankie could've poured what was left of her resolve into a spoon. She knew at once what he meant. "The fire wasn't an accident. Mary Campbell killed her family. Mary Campbell posed as Perry so she could have a new life."

"Yes, she did."

It was Frankie's turn to release a great rush of air.

"Jesus. You've never told anyone this?"

Dr. Whitman stared at his lap, shook his head. "No. I couldn't. Perry dropped out of school and the rumors swirled, but it was best forgotten. Soon there were new kids, new rumors, new lives to ruin."

Frankie looked back at the previous carnage in the lake. There was nothing left of the dead fish now. She thought how it could often be like that with kids, the cruelty they unleashed on each other.

She glanced at Dr. Whitman. "This is what brought you to care so deeply about UG? When I spoke to a former colleague of yours at Johns Hopkins, she said you argued about a UG case there. That you were very passionate about it."

He nodded. "Johns Hopkins pioneered UG research. Unfortunately, they were the ones that initially preached the practice of nurture over nature. Don't wait until the child is old enough to decide, just choose for them. I wanted to be a part of the revolution to change that thinking. And it is now. It's changing. Although it's too late for Mary. Much too late for Mary." His voice fell away.

"Didn't you ever suspect that she was following you? That she was obsessed with you enough to want to be you or pursue the same love interests as you? There must've been signs. Didn't you ever consider that it was her who raped Tammy with a stick? Or later, murdered Sara Phillips?" She didn't want to sound accusatory, but she couldn't imagine he didn't have an idea at some point.

And there was still the possibility of his involvement; she couldn't forget that. She had to be careful how she approached these topics.

He sat up straight. His chest pushed out. He clearly didn't like the implication. "I didn't see it, no. Not Tammy, not the others. And Sara, she wouldn't let me be. She kept telling me I wasn't the Kenny she remembered. I didn't want anything to do with the old life. People change. I changed. She wouldn't let it go."

His breaths came in short, sporadic bursts.

Frankie thought she might have to order the paper bag after all.

Maybe it was time to ease up with the questions. "Look, I'm not blaming you. No one is blaming you. If you didn't know she was stalking you, you're as much of a victim in this as everyone else." She reached across the table and grabbed his hand again, trying to reassure him. "You were right to tell me."

He took a moment and gathered himself. Squeezed her hand and offered a slight smile. His thin blond hair blew in the light breeze. "I really didn't know anything until you connected all the dots. You really are a woman who gets her man."

Frankie sat there, stunned by the news he'd given her. Perry was Mary Campbell. Betty Sue had never mentioned Perry's last name; otherwise, maybe Frankie would've put it together sooner. "Mary has admired you since the day she met you. But is her obsession that she wants to be *with* you or that she wants to *be* you? It seems to me that it's the latter—that she wants the life you have, the attraction of women you get—but it never succeeds because she isn't fully male. She can't fulfill the promise, so she alters them physically to look like her."

Yes, that was it. The removal of the breasts wasn't to make the woman virginal after all, but sexless, like she was. And it explained the lack of physical sex. Yet ...

She thought about what Dr. Whitman's girlfriends had said, how he'd longed for a perfect wife, how he said he was a virgin, waiting for the right woman. She stilled, swallowed the hard lump that suddenly formed in her throat. *No.*

She removed her hand from his and took a sip of wine. When she set the glass back down, she asked, "Do you happen to have a recent photo of Mary?"

He stared mournfully at the space where their hands had embraced. "No."

Frankie glanced across the ripples of water, the boats lining up for the sunset. "Well, it doesn't matter. I should have one in a couple of days. At least I hope to." She turned back to him. "Did I tell you I have a new witness? She called me while I was in Baltimore. Says she knows where to find Mary and knows what she looks like."

He snapped from his daze. "What? A witness? To what, exactly?"

Frankie pretended not to notice the whitening of his knuckles from the extra pressure he applied to his wineglass. "She's a friend of Rory Spencer. Says she met Mary once when Rory and Mary dated. See, the individual who courted Rory wasn't a man but a woman. Rory was a lesbian. I didn't understand at first, but now, after what you've told me, that makes perfect sense."

"When will you meet with her? I'd like to be there," Dr. Whitman said.

"I appreciate it, but no, that wouldn't be a good idea. She was very afraid. Wouldn't even provide me other details on the phone. She wants to meet at this old house outside Spartanburg where she thinks Mary might've taken Rory. Who knows, if I'm lucky, there may still be evidence."

Frankie kept it to herself that the witness was a ruse, a plan she had to lure Mary. Even now she suspected the woman was nearby as she and Dr. Whitman spoke and would be watching Frankie's every move, if not Dr. Whitman's.

The whites of Dr. Whitman's eyes were huge. He looked like a man in need of a pen to click. "That's great news."

He stared across the lake into the violet-and-orange swirls of sunset, his thoughts seeming to drift like the gentle laps against the deck. Small, involuntary twitches highlighted his forehead, as if he was troubled. "I hope you don't take this wrong, Agent Johnson, but if what you say is true, Mary has been watching me all along and obsessing with those I take an interest in, and now we're having dinner. You and I."

His pale-blue eyes greeted her in sad contemplation.

She held his gaze. "This is true."

Dr. Whitman abruptly scooted his chair back just as the waiter approached to take their order. "I can't do this."

"Where are you going?" she asked, appearing dismayed.

"You're right. Death does follow me. And now, by having dinner with you, I could be putting you in great danger. If she's watching, she'll see that I'm leaving, and maybe, just maybe, that will keep you safe."

He apologized to the waiter and walked away, leaving Frankie at the table, alone.

Safe? She didn't think so. But that was exactly what she'd planned.

CHAPTER 43

Two days later, Frankie departed her house for the first time since meeting with Dr. Whitman. She walked to the car on legs like stilts, keeping an eye out for strangers. The nerves weren't an act. If she was right, Mary would come for her today, and there was little doubt about what she had in store for her.

She slid into the driver's seat and fired the ignition. The roar of the engine made her feel commanding, in control of the situation, but only for a second. She kept an eye on the rearview mirror as she pulled away. Though nothing stirred, it did little to ease her anxiety. She could feel Mary now, stalking her, as she had no doubt done countless times in the past few weeks, maybe longer. Like that time standing across the street from her house at night. Or sitting on a nearby park bench uptown, eyes hidden behind bumblebee glasses.

She shivered.

The drive south on I-85 to Spartanburg seemed unusually long, the rolling green hills and occasional homes passing in a slow, repetitive motion. Maybe it was her own heightened awareness, or just paranoia, but she was certain every driver she passed turned and stared in her direction, as if they knew what dark and sinister journey she was headed into. Across the state line, the previously hazy sky thickened into an ominous gray soup. Hurricane Isabel had made landfall on the South Carolina coast the day before, and the remnants were steadily moving inland.

The house the realtor had recommended for her fake meeting with the new witness was five miles out of Spartanburg, on a parcel of land eerily similar to the one where Anna Jamison had been murdered. Frankie now understood there was a pattern to the houses Mary chose—they resembled her childhood home. After her dinner with Dr. Whitman, she'd called Betty Sue, the foster mother, to learn all she could about Perry and Mary's family history and looked at the land online, which Mary, as Perry, still owned. It sat on a ten-acre spread outside Barnwell, South Carolina, and there wasn't much of the house left after the fire, but an old barn remained, and she couldn't help but wonder ...

Is that where Mary will take me?

She had to believe so.

When she arrived at the abandoned property, she drove the car as far down the dirt lane as it would go, which was still well back from the house. From the back seat, she grabbed her black raincoat and slid it on. The pockets were loaded with the things she would need, including rope, a pocketknife, and a syringe. She couldn't take the gun; if she did, it would look like she was expecting more than a scared witness. Instead, she slid it under the driver's seat and placed her cell phone beside it. At least if anything went wrong, Ben and Vicks—once they came to their senses—would be able to locate her.

She just hoped they didn't wait too long to discover she was missing.

Outside, she checked her watch and scanned the area, searching for her supposed witness. Seeing no one, she began the long trudge to the house. As the weeds and thorny brush grasped at her jeans, a light rain started to fall. Small flies swarmed around her face, and grasshoppers sprang from deep in the brush. The cicadas, robust this year, screamed from the nearby trees, mirroring the screams inside her head.

Up on the porch, she was careful to avoid the rotted boards and the railing, which had seen better days. The door was open. As she slid inside, what natural light remained quickly vanished, and she cursed herself for not bringing a flashlight. Without the light, she could make out only the shadows of objects: a rusted stove, a pile of old books, a half-gnawed chair. She could hear the scurry of little legs across the floor and felt them run across her shoe. With a voice she hoped sounded confident, she called for her witness. "Valerie?"

The increasing wind howled a cold response.

She rounded the kitchen corner into the living room, trailing her fingers along the left wall as a guide. She quickly retreated them, however, when she imagined the hand that could suddenly appear and seal its grip around her wrist. She steadied her breathing, attempting to slow her pounding heart, but it was futile. The farther she inched inside the house, the harder it beat, until she was certain its dynamic pulse would give her away.

A large strand of her hair broke free to grace her right cheek and she jumped, batting it away. She stopped and leaned against a wall, catching her breath.

Why was she so damn jumpy? What made this situation any different than the hundreds of times she had staked out a fugitive or raided a house? She already knew the answer. One, she was alone. Two, she was not the hunter—she was the hunted.

She mumbled, telling herself she knew what she was doing, that this was a good plan, the right plan. With renewed muster, she called out again. "Valerie? You here?"

A creak in the floorboard. Then another.

"I don't think she's coming," said a voice from the darkness.

Frankie's knees locked. At once she knew the voice, but she couldn't move. Her plan had been to lure Mary to this place, but this wasn't the voice of a woman.

His footfalls thumped across the floor. Three, four steps. Slowly he appeared from the shadows, his eyes intent upon her. Dr. Lawrence Banks. "I'm sorry. I didn't mean to frighten you. I know you said to stay away, but I couldn't."

"What are you doing here?" she asked. "How did you know about this place?" She felt her voice crack. "Only the killer we're seeking would know about this place."

"I followed you." He took another step. "Don't be frightened. It's me."

He reached for her, but Frankie stepped back. "Nobody followed me. I know. I watched. I waited."

"Maybe not close enough. Maybe not long enough."

"Very close."

"I kept my distance."

She kept stepping back until she had nowhere to go. She'd unwisely worked herself into a corner, dark and dank. Outside, thunder rumbled and the rain intensified. The musty odor of wet wood permeated the house. "You shouldn't be here."

They both turned when they heard a scratching sound, like that of a cat clawing a post, or a piece of old furniture being moved across a wooden floor.

"Ah, maybe it's Valerie," Lawrence said. "The witness who can identify your killer. Good timing. Let's call her in." He yelled over his shoulder. "Valerie? Is that you? You can come out now." When there was no answer, he shouted a second time. "Valerie?" The whites of his eyes glowed large in the dark.

Frankie fumed. "Stop it. You know it isn't Valerie. It isn't her because she doesn't exist. It was a ploy. I created her just for you and Mary. I knew whoever showed up would be the real killer."

"And guess what?" she said. "You're here. She's not."

Lawrence tilted his head, an odd grin on his face. "What?"

"I made Valerie up. There is no witness."

He appeared taken aback. "Frankie, I'm here to help you, protect you. I simply followed you. Don't get paranoid on me."

Frankie shook her head. "You're lying. You've always been lying."

She gripped the items in her pocket: the rope, the syringe, the pocketknife.

His grin faded. "You know I love you, don't you?" he said. "From the moment I saw you." He took three steps forward until he stood in front of her.

Frankie huddled in the corner, trembling, breaths shallow. With a deft hand, she removed the cap on the syringe in her pocket, felt the sharp tip. "No, I don't believe you."

"Yes, you do. And you love me too. I know it. I can see it in your eyes."

She slid the syringe from her pocket and held it at her side as he caressed her cheek and leaned in to kiss her.

"I just want you to know," she said, when their lips were just an inch apart, "I'm doing this for your own good." She stabbed his thigh with the syringe and emptied the contents into his bloodstream.

His head lobbed toward his leg. "What the—?" He lurched forward and back, then tripped over suddenly useless feet and went down hard, breaking an old table and chair in the process.

Frankie removed the rope from her pocket and quickly secured his hands and feet. Lawrence moaned and tried to sit up. He glanced up with those long feathery lashes and appeared to be barely hanging on, like a man dangling from a ledge with just his fingertips. "Frankie, why? Don't do this. It's not safe."

She stood up and tucked the remaining rope and used syringe back in her pocket.

He wriggled and twisted against the rope. "What have you done to me? What have you done?"

Frankie peered down, fire licking her nerves. "Shut up. You need to shut up now."

She leaned over him and allowed the pocketknife to slide to the floor.

She whispered. "You know what to do."

CHAPTER 44

Frankie rushed from the old house, the rain pelting her face. Lawrence's anguished shouts continued behind her, like the distant cries of a coyote. She felt bad for leaving him, but wanted to get away as fast as she could.

Once inside the car, she glanced back, half expecting to see him, or Mary, running after her, but there was only the grayish-blue streaks of rain and her heavy breath fogging up the glass. She thought for a moment that she saw movement at the opposite corner of the house but dismissed it as the wind, bending the tree limbs with growing gusts.

She cranked the engine, threw the car in reverse, and stepped on the accelerator, mowing down the overgrowth in reverse straight to the road. Around her, mud and debris flew until her tires hit pavement. Only the horn of an approaching SUV saved her from crossing the highway and taking out her entire back seat.

Frankie slammed on the brakes and shifted into drive. Another approaching car honked as she pulled wildly into the road, losing a hubcap in the process. Undeterred, she sped across the country roads at seventy miles per hour.

The rain continued to increase in intensity, the outer bands of Isabel carving their way northwest. The wind increased too, whistling through unseen gaps in her window. The storm was coming in much faster than anticipated. She suddenly wondered if the weather would interfere with her plans. She hadn't seen Mary at the house, but that didn't mean she wasn't there and hadn't done exactly what Frankie had expected her to do.

A mile later she got her answer.

Two miles from the highway interchange, the engine light came on and the Dodge began to sputter. As it died, Frankie coasted it to the side of the road and put her flashers on. She tried to start it several times, but the engine only grinded.

Her heart thrummed a petrified dance in her ears. *This is it.*

Having spent the last three days reanalyzing the crime scenes with Mary Campbell and her abduction of the victims in mind, she knew now—this was how it happened. The cars. Each of the victims had experienced car trouble before their disappearance. Anna and Rhonda at the mall and, she was certain, Jeanne at the coffee shop.

With that knowledge came further insight. When Anna had experienced car trouble at the mall on Saturday, a man with thick glasses had come to her aid. But the elderly couple who'd reported seeing the man only assumed it was a man because he was helping with the car. That man was actually a woman—Mary.

That Mary had abducted Anna Saturday and not Sunday—as they'd originally believed—explained a great deal. It meant Mary was with Anna at the bar that night when Anna told her friend she was leaving her fiancé for another man, and it meant she was with her the next day at her apartment when she forced Anna to write her good-bye letter and pack a few things. It meant Mary had abducted Jeanne Tuesday morning at the coffee shop and followed her around at the conference, making sure Jeanne did exactly as she instructed—like attend Lawrence's session and flirt with him afterward to make him a suspect.

Frankie wondered about the control Mary exerted upon the victims to do exactly as she told them, and could only assume her threat went beyond hurting the women individually. Women would do most anything to protect those they loved, so Mary must've expanded her threats of harm to families and friends; otherwise, Frankie had to believe, the women Mary abducted would've resisted or asked someone for help. Mary must've told them she was watching and listening at all times and that if they didn't do as she instructed, a loved one would pay the price.

Frankie saw the headlights of a vehicle approach in the rearview mirror. The lights slowed, veered off the road, and came to a stop. A human form in a yellow rain slicker exited the vehicle and ran to the side of her window. The individual had the drawstring of the hood pulled tight, but Frankie could see a tuft of blond hair off the individual's forehead. Was it Mary? It had to be.

Frankie slid the window down, but only a crack.

"What's the problem?" the voice yelled above the wind.

"Won't start," she said.

"Pop the hood."

Frankie did as the person asked, then thrummed her fingers on the steering wheel. Did she really want to go through with this? It would be easy to grab the Glock and end it right here, but feared if she arrested Mary now, it would be too soon. There was no more direct physical evidence to tie Mary to Anna than there was for Dr. Whitman, and there was more to the puzzle to uncover. No, she had to continue.

The person ran back to the window. "I think I know what it is. I have something in the car that might help. I'll be right back."

Frankie studied the human form running to the car. Betty Sue's words rang in her ears. *Perry left school. He lived and worked above a garage for a time.* A mechanic's garage, where he'd clearly learned a thing or two about cars. Perry, who was actually Mary.

The person returned to work on her engine. Made the motion for her to try to start it. She did, and it didn't.

She thought again of the phone and the Glock beneath the driver's seat. Hoped against hope that Mary would take her car and not leave it there on the side of the road. She wished for the umpteenth time that she could figure out a way to take her phone and weapon with her, but she couldn't think of a single place on her person that Mary wouldn't search. She'd proved smart about the cell phones in the past, and a gun was too difficult to hide.

The individual ran to the window. "Let me try, do you mind?"

Frankie took a deep breath. In her right mind, she would never do what she was about to do. She could hear Ben's words of warning, a promise not to do anything crazy.

Too late, Ben. Much, much too late.

She rolled down the window just enough for the person to get his arm through and leaned far back in her seat. The Taser rendered her motionless in an instant. The door was unlocked in another. And the next thing Frankie knew, she was out of her seatbelt and moved to the passenger seat with her hands and feet bound.

The person quickly rummaged through the glove box and beneath the seat, finding the phone and the gun, and Frankie watched, immobile, as the individual tossed both into the ditch outside the driver's window. She heard the engine crank and felt the car do a U-turn. When she was able, she turned to look at the driver. "Oh, it's you."

"Yes, it's me."

"Where are we going?" she managed to ask, although she already knew.

"Home, sweetheart, home." Mary Campbell smiled. "Wait until you see what I've done with the place. I think you'll like it."

CHAPTER 45

Ben saw the smoke rising over the hill. The call had come in from the closest neighbors, more than half a mile away, who'd reported seeing it as they drove up the long, winding road. The fire was struggling to survive beneath the thunderous rain, as if the elemental gods were fighting an epic battle.

Ben jumped out the door as Tommy, who'd decided to join Ben after the call about the missing woman had come in, brought the car to a lurching stop. Ben halted only long enough to grab a flashlight and ran toward the house. Tommy followed suit, shouting excited words that got lost in the wind. Two officers and an EMT crew had already arrived on the scene, and the sirens of the fire trucks weren't far away.

One of the officers blocked their path. "Whoa. You can't go in there."

"You don't understand, there might be a woman in there," Ben shouted.

"A woman? Who?"

"Mandy McCay, the missing woman from Charlotte."

He held up a hand. "I know who she is. What makes you think she's in there?"

Ben fidgeted, frustrated at the questions. "Look, I don't have time to explain."

While the officer spoke into his radio to notify the arriving crew of Ben's claims, Ben circumvented him and kicked in the front door. A brief burst of flame erupted, then quickly died, leaving a smoky but visible path through the house. Covering his mouth with the corner of his FBI jacket, he rushed in, choosing to take action now and apologize later. Tommy followed behind like a loyal dog.

Inside, the smoke immediately stung his eyes as flames climbed the walls and snaked their way across the ceiling. Ben swept the flashlight from corner to corner, looking for the unsub's setup. "Clear," he yelled to Tommy as he ran from the living room into the hall. "Clear," again as he raced between two bedrooms.

Next to a third bedroom, a rumble like thunder sounded above them, and a section of the top floor suddenly collapsed. Ben jumped back, pushing Tommy to the floor, and shielding his own face from the spraying embers. "It's no good. Go back!"

Coughing and sputtering, they scrambled through thick, gray smoke pouring from an unseen opening, only to realize the front entrance was now blocked. Around them the walls groaned, as if bearing some great weight that they could no longer stand.

"It's going to fall," Ben yelled through the crackling inferno. He grabbed Tommy and shoved him toward the back of the house and the kitchen.

They burst from the utility door into a yard with a sloping hill. The steady rain made quick work of the soot and ash in their eyes and soothed their throats. Tommy bent at the waist, gasping for air. "She's a goner if she's in there, boss."

Ben shook his head and wiped a wet sleeve across his face. "I don't think she's in there. Maybe this is just a random fire." He saw the first fire truck arrive, wheezing up the last of the road. As soon as a second truck arrived, he caught sight of the cellar, a white cement cutout on the side of the house. He nudged Tommy. "Look."

He ran over and touched the metal door. It didn't feel warm. He told Tommy to stand back and yanked it open, waiting for smoke to billow forth, but none did. Instead, a musty, moldy smell spilled out, like an old jar with coins in it. The flashlight guiding their path, Ben and Tommy navigated the stairs. As soon as Ben's shoes made contact with the floor, he felt them sink into an inch of mud. Surrounding them were walls of concrete blocks crumbled by weight and age, and a sole basement window, where rain seeped in through the cracks.

"There!" Tommy yelled, pointing to a far corner.

To the right and behind the stairs, the missing woman lay on a gurney with nothing but a thin sheet covering her. Her arms had been neatly folded across her chest and her long, dark hair spilled toward the floor. Ben and Tommy, unable to stand under the five-foot-high ceiling, maneuvered beneath the pipes to her side. Ben checked for a pulse. Though she appeared to be sedated, she was unharmed and alive.

Ben removed an IV from her hand, scooped the young woman up into his arms, and told Tommy to lead the way. Tommy rushed up the stairs and cleared debris, making sure there was an open path. Once outside, Ben ran to the front of the house, where he met the firefighters and the EMTs, who quickly took Mandy and assessed her condition. Ben noticed that the fire crew, with the help of Mother Nature, had already made progress in containing the blaze.

Tommy put his hands on his knees and took several deep breaths. Ben clapped him on the back. "We got her. We saved one," he said.

The fire chief walked over to where they stood. "Not too bright, running into a burning house, but I can't argue with the outcome," he said.

The fire crew continued to douse the remaining hot spots. One of them came out holding something in his hand. "Didn't take long to figure out what started this one."

With Tommy looking over his shoulder, Ben examined the device. "A timer?"

"Yep. Part of an incendiary device set to ignite next to a pile of clothes soaked with gasoline. Easiest arson I've ever had to call."

"Don't forget attempted murder," Tommy said.

Ben regarded the house through rain-soaked eyelids. He frowned. Arson was part of the MO of this unsub, but not until he'd completed his task. Why would he set the fire before performing any surgery on his latest victim? And why set it remotely? Had Dr. Banks decided there was too much attention on the case and aborted his mission?

Ben felt a tightening in his gut. He looked at the fire chief. "I need to go back in."

The chief narrowed his gaze. "Just the cellar. Make a note of what you touch."

Tommy followed. "What are you thinking?"

Ben didn't answer. He'd been in too much of a hurry to get to the missing woman before to analyze the place, and now he needed to take a harder look. With the flashlight, he scoped the room, first returning to the corner where they'd discovered the victim. Other than the gurney and the IV pole, there was no medical equipment. No generator. No lights. No surgical tools. There was a tiny table adorned with a single rose, but no chairs, food, or wine. And instead of an assortment of clothes strung across a makeshift clothesline, a single dress hung from a small pipe. Ben retrieved it and held it up in front of him.

"Not really your size, sir, if you don't mind me saying," Tommy snickered.

"Not Mandy's size either," Ben said. To be certain, he was no expert on the female form, but growing up with four sisters had taught him plenty. The victim in this case was not a size six, but he knew who was. He'd seen her wear this dress before, on many occasions.

Frankie Johnson.

His heart began to hammer. Frankie's words echoed in his ear, how she thought the unsub was targeting her. Poems left for her, clothes missing. And how Jeanne's crime scene wasn't right, that the unsub wouldn't set fire to the place until he'd spent his time with the victim and buried the body, how Jeanne's case was all too convenient. The unsub had *wanted* them to find Jeanne. And now Mandy.

He noticed a small envelope on the table. He grabbed it and removed a single piece of paper from inside. It was a poem: "She Walks in Beauty." As he read it, he felt his entire body reverberate, like when the race cars passed by at close distance at the track. His pulse gunned and surged, pumping fury and anxiety and guilt into his engine all at once.

"No," he said.

He thundered up the stairs and ran to the front of the house, hoping the ambulance was still there. He shouted to the driver climbing into the front seat. "Wait!" He slid through the mud. "How long do you think before she regains consciousness?"

"Her eyes are already open. Trying to mouth a few words."

"I need to speak to her." He ran to the back and rapped on the double doors. The EMT sitting with Mandy swung them open, and the smell of sterility permeated the air. Mandy was on her back, eyelids fluttering, her head lobbing from side to side.

Tommy finally caught up and joined him.

Ben stepped in the back and took her hand. "Mandy, I'm Special Agent Ben Andrews. I need your help. It's very urgent." He snapped his fingers at Tommy to give him the photos. He held them up. "Please, just tell me which one. Which one of these men abducted you?"

He watched as her eyes took in the two photographs in front of her, her breath fogging up the respirator mask. She glanced at one, then the other. She stared up at Ben, dark-brown eyes like a mink's fur, and blinked. He turned to Tommy. "Did you see? Which one did she blink at?"

"I don't know. I couldn't tell."

Thunder rumbled and the wind howled, hurling rain against the outside of the ambulance. With an unsteady hand, Mandy reached out. Her eyes shifted from the photos to Ben, to Tommy, to a barely breathing EMT caught up in the drama. Then, with a bloody and broken fingernail, she tapped.

Ben turned the photo around to face him. His stomach lurched and landed with a thud. There were no words for what he was feeling. He would never forgive himself if something happened to Frankie Johnson.

"Tommy, get on the horn and get us a helicopter."

"Sir? A helicopter? There's a storm ..."

"I don't care," Ben yelled. "I don't care, Tommy. Find me a damn helicopter, and now!"

CHAPTER 46

rankie woke lying on a gurney surrounded by wooden walls and a room filled with lighted candles. A thin blanket covered her, but it did nothing to prevent a damp draft from drifting beneath and chilling her to the bone. The scent of hay and rain was strong, reminding her of the trip across Maryland post-storm. Outside, lightning flashed and the wind raced. The outer bands of Hurricane Isabel had made it inland.

Keeping still, she tried to organize the earlier events in her head. She remembered encountering Lawrence and leaving him in the farmhouse. Remembered fleeing in her car and it breaking down. Remembered feeling the odd combination of fear and relief when she'd seen Mary, then the Taser and the long ride south in heavy rain, barely conscious. Then an injection to "help her sleep."

How long had she been out?

She quickly raised her head to look at her heaving chest and blew out a sigh of relief. Mary hadn't begun preparing her for surgery yet. There was no IV in her arm, and she was fully clothed. Knowing she needed to clear the fog from her head as fast as she could, she breathed in deep, getting as much oxygen as she could to her brain. Mary wasn't in sight.

When she looked up, the ceiling seemed to vanish into darkness, but the occasional lightning strikes revealed a pitched roof, maybe twenty feet high, and the back wheel of an old tractor beyond the door to her room. She was most definitely in a barn. *The* barn. Mary's childhood home.

She'd been correct about the location.

She glanced to her side, taking stock of her immediate surroundings. The candlelight gave her a fair view of the walls, dark wooden slats about eight feet high. On a shelf in the corner were items she recognized—panties, bras, and camisoles missing from her home. Two of her dresses hung from a strung rope and several pairs of shoes sat on the floor, including the ones she'd worn here.

Good. She'd be able to grab them upon her escape.

But first she had to make that happen. As expected, Mary had restrained both her arms and legs to the gurney.

She settled back and let her mind clear, knowing that for the next several hours now, she had to play her role perfectly. One of her mother's quotes popped in her head: *An ounce of behavior is worth a pound of words.* She certainly hoped her acting could live up to that standard. It was critical for her to gain Mary's confession. Without it, the physical evidence that linked her to Anna and the other missing women could prove inconsequential. They needed to know what she'd done and why, and where she'd buried the other bodies. Then Frankie needed to make it out of here alive so she could expose the true nature of the relationship between Mary and Dr. Whitman. If she didn't succeed, the deaths of several women—including possibly her own—might never see real justice.

Into the darkness, Frankie called out. "Hello?" Her voice sounded foreign.

The wind screeched a hollow response. The rain battered the outside walls.

She tried again. "Hello? Mary? Are you here?"

This time the response was a faint clink of metal. And wheels. Rolling.

Near the opening, an image emerged, but remained outside of the stall. She wore blue scrubs, a hair cover, and a surgical mask, and the sight of her froze Frankie to the bone. On the cart before her was a tray full of surgical tools, including an obsidian scalpel. Frankie caught her breath, at once vastly aware that those tools were for her.

"What are you doing awake?" Mary asked. "You shouldn't be awake yet."

She continued to push the cart inside, the squeaky wheel ever turning—like nails screeching down a chalkboard.

Frankie squirmed beneath the restraints as her pulse quickened, fearful of Mary injecting her with more sedatives or worse, give her a full anesthetic. The day before, Lawrence had told her there was no drug that could block the effects of anesthesia, so preventing her from administering it in the first place was the only solution.

Mary stopped the cart near Frankie's feet and tinkered with the instruments. One by one, she straightened each tool and set them equidistantly apart. Frankie thought about the preciseness found at Anna's crime scene but missing at Jeanne's, and she wondered if Ben had discovered a similar scenario with the new missing woman or if he'd discovered her yet at all. She also questioned if Lawrence had contacted Ben yet, and if a plan to intercede in this setup, if necessary, was in the works.

Would Ben listen and come to help her once again, as he had with Lianna Wakefield's killer? Or would she be on her own? He'd warned her that if she went rogue, she'd better be prepared to go it alone.

She took a deep breath. *I am. I'm ready. I can do this. So let it begin.*

"Mary, could you stop what you're doing for a moment and come talk to me?"

The woman's hands paused and her head tilted, but she remained where she was.

"I want you to know, ever since I learned the truth from Kenneth, I haven't stopped thinking about you. I can't imagine what you've gone through or how you must feel. If we're going to be together, it's important I understand what you went through, don't you think? Will you sit with me and tell me about yourself?"

Mary remained quiet, both gloved hands now running over the instruments as if they were precious children. But she was thinking, Frankie could tell. When she didn't offer anything, Frankie changed tactics. "How about if I tell you what I think happened, and you can tell me where I'm wrong?"

Frankie lay back, stared at the vast ceiling amid the flashes of lightning, and began.

"I think Mary was a bright child, alert for her age. She knew very young that something wasn't right with her. At school, she discovered she didn't like the games the girls played but enjoyed flag football and tag with the boys. At home, she wanted to work the farm and learn to drive the tractor, like her brother Perry, but her parents kept insisting she do things like cook and clean, and she grew resentful.

"Her parents grew concerned, but the doctors and the teachers told them not to worry. She was just a tomboy and it was a phase she would grow out of once puberty hit. Her parents probably demanded additional supplements from the doctors, those special vitamins Mary always took, trying to hurry the process. But Mary knew it was more than just being a tomboy, because internally, she felt different. She felt like the wrong sex.

"Imagine her parents' horror when she told them that she felt like a boy. That she wanted to wear boys' clothes and do boys' chores, and worse, that she was attracted to girls. It had to be an embarrassment to them, pure horror over the possible exposure of their daughter's condition and the choice they'd made for her. I mean, they were very religious people, devout Southern Baptists. Daddy was a minister and Mom a Sunday school teacher. What would be seen as a transgender child wouldn't set well with the congregation."

Frankie paused, taking a few breaths. She could see Mary had stilled as well.

"The worst part was, Daddy thought he could beat it out of her. She wasn't succumbing to God's will. The devil was putting evil thoughts in her mind. Maybe she was even possessed by a demon. She wasn't normal, and her parents wanted normal.

"But Mary didn't know what normal was, and as the days and months passed, she came to despise her parents and her brother, who joined the other kids in making fun of her in school. And this continued for many years."

Frankie glanced at Mary. Though Mary's head was lowered, she gave a slight nod.

"When she was twelve, she discovered her birth certificate in a baby book. Twin, it said, but not fraternal. It said identical. At first, she didn't understand, until she saw the baby's original name was to be Gary and not Mary, and on the line indicating the sex, a haphazard *FE* had been typed in front of the previous *MALE*. Mary didn't understand, so she took the items to her parents and demanded answers. That resulted in another lashing, then being locked in the crawl space until Mary promised to never mention it again."

Frankie knew this part to be true after speaking to Mary's surviving grandmother, who'd told her of the incident as well as other atrocities.

A tear fell from Mary's eye, verifying the story as well.

"Soon after that incident, when she was thirteen, her mother informed her that she'd be going in for some surgery—to make her a full woman. It was a rite of passage, she said, as if all little girls underwent these things at this age. It would resolve Mary's confusion and, more importantly, solve her parents' problems."

Frankie put herself in Mary's place now, lacing her words with bitterness, letting it drip like sap from a long untapped tree. She wanted to take Mary back to that most hurtful time, to the child who'd endured the taunts, the shunning, the hatred.

"Most people get to make their own choices in life, but not Mary. For her, others decided her fate. She must've felt extremely trapped, with no way out.

"One day, Mary decided to have no more choices made for her. She knew she would never make it out of adolescence and into adulthood living as someone she was not, so she made a plan. Everyone knew Mary was the bad seed—the rebellious, devil-inflicted child. It would make sense that she was smoking in the basement and fell asleep, and it would make sense that Perry was out in the woods, doing what boys do, when the fire started. She just had to wait for that one night. That one very special night.

"Mary let them burn."

Frankie quieted and let the howling wind speak its own truth for a few minutes. She kept a close watch as Mary turned her back to her and wrestled with her emotions. It wasn't a lie to say Frankie felt a deep empathy for her. She couldn't imagine the pain, the mental battle she'd gone through her entire life. What would she have done under such circumstances? What would anybody?

"I bet this barn here, this was Mary's favorite place to come as a child. I bet she would climb to the loft and sleep in the hay. I bet she stole cigarettes and stashed them there. I bet she even kept a *Playboy* magazine or two to look at the girls."

"I didn't know whether to love them or hate them." Mary's voice broke.

Frankie lolled her head to the side. She'd gotten Mary to speak. That was progress. Up until this time she'd referred to Mary in the third person to distance her identity from that of the person she used to be. Now it was time to switch to first person, to speak directly to the individual in the room, not to the memory of the past.

"I understand what made you who you are today. Other people—your parents, the doctors—they made choices for you they shouldn't have. They forced you to conform to their wishes and what made them comfortable instead of asking you what you wanted."

She tilted her head to the side so she could see Mary. "So you need to understand too—you can't make those you love conform to your wishes either. You, and Kenneth, can't alter the bodies of those you desire without their consent."

"Kenny makes people beautiful," she said, her voice almost childlike.

"Kenneth has spent his entire life changing people into what they want to be because they fear being accepted for who they are. Don't you see the irony in that? You more than anyone should understand how wrong it is to not let the women you pursue have a choice."

Mary's brow furrowed beneath the surgical cap. She shook her head. Frankie's intent had been to plant confusion, and it was working.

"I need someone who looks like me. They won't understand what it's like to be me unless we're the same. I know. They run. They all run," Mary said.

"They run because you change them into an image you want instead of accepting who they are." Frankie closed her eyes briefly to say a little prayer before she opened them again. Mary was standing near her now, having moved from the foot of the bed.

"If you love me, then you will love me just as I am. I don't need to change. Isn't that what you've wanted your entire life? Someone to love you just as you are? Please, Kenneth, come out. It's time to remove the mask."

CHAPTER 47

With his back to her, Mary, aka Dr. Kenneth Whitman, removed the gloves, mask, and hair cover and folded them neatly on the surgical tray. His hands reached up and loosened several pins and the wig slid off, the shoulder-length blond hair now sitting in a pile of its own. He rubbed his hands through his natural hair and turned. His face was flushed. "When did you know?"

"During our dinner at the lake. I suspected earlier, but after our meeting, it became clear. The way you spoke of Mary's discovery was very personal. Also, you mentioned once that you'd helped Emily with her car, and once I knew that was how your love interests were intercepted, I knew you and Mary were the same."

It had actually been more than that, including the details Whitman's girlfriends had provided and Betty Sue's explanation of the photo she'd shown Frankie. When Betty had tapped on the photo and said he didn't like to get his picture taken, she'd been referring to Perry, but Frankie had assumed she was speaking about Kenneth. And why not? Frankie knew the boy in the photo only as Kenneth. She hadn't yet known the whole story, that not only had Mary become Perry after the fire, but she'd taken Kenneth Whitman's identity on the way to college.

He closed his eyes. It had to be a relief after all. Someone knew the truth.

She pulled at the restraints. "Can you undo these, so we can talk properly?"

He looked at her warily.

"I'm not going anywhere in the middle of a hurricane."

He undid the ties. She slid off the gurney and walked around to get her blood flowing and casually slipped into her shoes. As she did, she checked out the area surrounding the stall. She couldn't see the entire barn by candlelight but saw that other rooms had been prepared for her.

"Could we have some wine and sit where it's warmer?" she asked.

She'd do anything to get away from that gurney—and those tools.

He led her to the makeshift kitchen, where he uncorked one of the bottles of wine. She noticed it was a Malbec, one taken from her house. He retrieved a blanket and wrapped it around her shoulders. She thanked him.

Outside, the rain, wind, and thunder roared.

"This is home," she said. "Was it difficult coming back here?"

"Yes and no. I knew I would return eventually. When the time was right." He sighed deeply. "I'm so relieved you're here."

He reached across the little table and brushed a strand of hair from her face. She blamed her shudder on the cold and pulled the blanket around her tighter.

"You know, when everything with Anna went wrong, I was so angry," he said. "I couldn't understand how God had led her to me, only for us to be torn apart. But now it's so clear. It was all to lead me to you. You, an FBI agent, would never have come into my life if things hadn't gone wrong with Anna."

He leaned closer, his breath grazing her face, his eyes wide and restless like a child's. "Isn't God amazing?" He stroked her face, like he was petting a prized dog.

She underwent a slow and torturous melting.

"How many women did God grant you?" she asked, trying to control the crack in her voice.

"Ten. But you are the final one. This is it. I finally found my wife."

Ten. Which meant they were still missing some.

"Tell me their names," she said. "I want to know them all since they ... brought us together. Who else besides Anna, Emily, and Melanie?"

In addition to the three Lawrence had found and Rhonda Stewart, Whitman gave her the names of three others, including the one who'd come up on the ViCAP alert at one point but Frankie had dismissed because she'd died in a hit-and-run accident. Now, Frankie realized, she'd died trying to escape. Sara Phillips and Jeanne Mapleton, on the other hand, weren't on the list.

It was at that moment, as he spoke of his girls, his pale-blue irises fixated on her, that she realized the true depth of his erotomania. It was more than just a method to rationalize his behavior; he truly believed these women were gifts to him. Destined for him. Despite his strict religious upbringing—which she'd thought would cause a contentious, if not outright hostile, relationship between him and any higher power—he believed God was helping him.

"What was it?" Frankie asked. "How did you know that I wanted you? Something I said? The way I looked at you?"

"Both. You were so subtle in expressing your interest at the office that first day, I wasn't sure I was reading you correctly, but then I saw you on television a few days later. You were attending a press conference with that old sheriff, and you looked right at me. Then, when it was over and everyone else walked away, you glanced over your shoulder one last time just to make sure I saw you. I knew then you were the one."

Frankie told herself to keep breathing. To think that such an innocent gesture could be so misinterpreted in the mind of an erotomaniac was beyond frightening. She wondered what Anna, Emily, and the others had done to earn his attention. Had it been a simple greeting? A smile? An offer of goodwill? And what had it cost them?

Their lives.

"When I saw how much time you spent thinking about me at home, writing about me on your wall that night," he said. "I got so excited. I wanted to stay outside and watch but ... I had to take care of business."

She nodded. "Miguel Herrera?"

"I couldn't let him ruin it for us. I knew we had to be together."

Frankie closed her eyes. He was the unknown nurse. Of course. He would've had access to whatever he needed to pull off such a plan, including whatever drug he'd used to initiate Miguel's sudden respiratory failure.

She felt her blood boil.

"You set up Dr. Banks, too, didn't you? To get him out of the picture?"

Whitman did an eye roll. "He kept meddling! I couldn't get him to stop. And he wanted your attention. I couldn't allow that. No. So I followed him at the conference, and after he stopped at the café, I waited for the perfect girl. It didn't take long. She came in minutes after he did with her conference badge on. It was a sign. I felt badly about her, but it was necessary under the circumstances. He was trying to lure you away from me."

Frankie observed his animated movements through the eyes of her education in psychology. His personality seemed to vacillate from the person she knew as Dr. Whitman to one with undertones of Mary. Adulthood and childhood. It was as if, in this new role of being two outed individuals, even he wasn't sure who he was.

"And the new missing girl? Was that you also?"

"I needed to keep your work partner busy. He's annoying, that one."

When he stood to get more wine, she clenched her fists and gritted her teeth. He'd killed Jeanne Mapleton and possibly another woman for no other reason than to remove obstacles between them. First Lawrence, then Ben.

He returned to refill her wineglass. He grinned, near giddy.

"Can I ask you something?" she asked. "Just one more thing. What happened to the real Kenneth Whitman? Did you ... do to him what you did to Sara Phillips?"

His grin increased. "You mean kill him? It's okay, you can say it. He deserved it. I told him in confidence about my condition, and he told all his friends. He was part of the group that attacked me that day in the bathroom, and he laughed right along with them. He always thought he was better than everyone else. Smarter, stronger. But in the end, I was the smarter one. The stronger one."

A wave of nausea passed over her. He was fully in Mary mode now.

"Is he, like the others, buried somewhere?"

He waved her off. "Why does it matter?"

"It matters for their families. Even Betty Sue. To have closure. Maybe you could write them down—who they are and where they're all buried—and mail it to the field office. To Ben."

"They're already documented. All of them. In a box I keep in my office, where I also have ... other reminders. Once we're together, they will find it." He gathered some items then left the room. "I'll be back."

Together? What did that mean? She didn't want to be together.

Where in the hell were Lawrence and Ben? Had the storm delayed them? Was Ben in denial, refusing to help? Had the Bureau wrapped up Lawrence in an intense interrogation instead of listening?

That would be like them.

It didn't matter. Her time was up. Now that she knew the evidence that they needed was in Dr. Whitman's office, she had to get the hell out of this barn.

Rising, she poked her head around the corner of the stall to see where he'd gone. To her dismay, he was back in the room with the gurney, once again organizing the tools on his tray. And the blond wig was back on. Her heart did a deep dive.

Oh hell no.

It was then that he saw her standing across the barn, observing him.

"What are you doing?" he asked.

He came out of the stall, holding the obsidian scalpel.

She stammered. "I, uh, need to use the restroom. I'm just going to go—"

Then she took off.

CHAPTER 48

His scream was like that of an animal. Frankie crouched behind the tractor, then rushed for the barn door. She pulled and pushed with all her strength, but it was well secured, as expected. Feeling him closing in, she scrambled right, navigating around items she could barely make out in the dull glow of the candlelight. Lawrence had said he'd loosened some boards in the southwest corner in case there was no other way out, but she had no idea what corner that was. In the middle of the dark barn, she had no sense of direction.

Should've asked a few more questions about those boards.

The first corner she reached was blocked by a variety of tools—rakes, shovels, and pitchforks. It didn't seem likely that Lawrence would block her exit with such things, but she slid her hand between the items anyway. A spider web the size and complexity of a small city enveloped her arm, but this was no time for cowardice. She pushed her weight into the boards. They didn't budge. Tried again. Nothing. She yanked her arm back and caused a shovel to career sideways into the other tools, creating a domino effect of clangs and clatter.

Behind her, Whitman screamed Frankie's name again, as if in mourning. As it pierced the shadows, Frankie clamped her hands over her ears, waiting for the dreadful sound—like a lamb at slaughter—to stop.

"Why are you running?" he shouted. "You know how very angry that makes me. You're the one who chose this. For you, for me, for us. You said you accepted me, and I you. You're a liar, just like the rest of them."

Frankie's blood ran cold. He suddenly sounded dramatic and juvenile, more like Mary than Kenneth. Was this what happened when his girls betrayed him? All that rejection came forth—Mary's parents, the kids at school—and surfaced the angry child.

She darted lengthwise down one side of the barn on hands and knees until she reached the next corner. The candles flickering in the opposite stall where she'd fled created elongated shadows out of objects and forms, dancing like ghosts toward the ceiling. Seeing odd shapes of arcs and chains, her gaze trailed up, and she nearly lost control of her bowels. Hanging above her were an assortment of butchering knives and tools, clanging together like the devil's windchime. There was no way in hell Lawrence had picked this corner.

Staying low, she crept along the dirt floor, doing her best to remain in the shadows. There were only two corners left, and one was a locked room with a loft above it. It made sense that Lawrence might've loosened the boards in the corner nearest the stall Whitman had prepared for her, but how was she supposed to go back there now? What had seemed like a good idea at the time now appeared futile. Frankie could see Whitman standing over there, just waiting for her to return.

He knew there was no way out. He'd made certain of it.

What am I going to do? She didn't want to die in this place.

She paused behind two oak barrels for a moment. Somewhere above her near the loft, the roof was leaking, delivering thick drops on her head. She wiped the water from her face, then peered high above.

If the rain was getting in, it meant there was a hole up there.

Frankie was sitting there, feeling her heart pound against her chest, when she heard him gathering items and muttering scripture. This was followed by the sound of liquid sloshing from side to side and a much-too-familiar smell.

Gas. He's pouring gas.

Oh my God. Oh no.

With scant breaths, she peeked through the crack between the two barrels to get a partial view of him. His agitation was clear, his face twitching, his eyes dark. The blond wig flowed over his shoulders. "I'm not going to let you go, my love," he yelled. "You're the one, Frankie. I've waited for you my whole life. If we must die, then we die together."

She sat back. *Jesus, he's going to burn us alive.*

Panic ripped her heart. This wasn't supposed to be how it went down. She was supposed to keep Whitman talking while Lawrence contacted Ben. Together they would come to her rescue, as Ben had done once before in the Carolina mountains. If for some reason Lawrence couldn't convince Ben or things didn't go as planned, then she was to make her escape through the loose boards in the corner of the barn. But so far, plan A wasn't materializing, and plan B wasn't working, and she had no plan C.

I have no frigging plan C!

Ben's words about how she'd better be prepared to finish the job alone haunted her. From *we* to *me.* She had to do this on her own.

She looked to the barrels and up at the loft. A wooden ladder hung from the side, but two-thirds of the rungs were gone or splintered, and those intact were nearer the top. Still, she thought it might be possible to reach them if she climbed on a barrel and jumped for it. It would expose her location, but what choice did she have? Dr. Whitman was going to kill her just as he had Anna Jamison, just as Mary had her parents and brother—with fire.

She climbed on top of a barrel and had started to jump when she heard it, a rip, like the tearing of a sheet in half, followed by a crackle and a pop, and flames appeared. She watched the single trail of fire spread and thought of a circus, how the flames formed a perfect circle.

For a moment Frankie imagined Anna sprinting through the meadow, trying to escape, and knew at once how she'd felt. Panicked. Frantic. Running for her life in a last-ditch attempt to live.

No, God, no. I was so close.

She leapt from the barrel and grabbed the last rung on the ladder. The dry wood splintered and gouged her hands, but thankfully held her weight. She pushed off the side of the wall of the locked room, then launched forward, curling up so her feet would catch the rungs of the ladder higher above her. She hooked her feet on the inside of the rails and used the side to hoist herself up.

Whitman headed her way. He stood in the middle of the barn with his arms spread wide. "There's no way out, love. The wood will collapse and the rain will pour down, but it will be too late. The smoke, the flames, they will engulf us. But at last, we will be together in a life free of pain and agony."

He grinned. "This is it. Frankie, my love. You can't outrun fate."

She heard a large snap and briefly shielded her eyes. Just as he predicted, the smoke poured forth, thick and choking. Flames lapped ever higher on the walls. Wood popped and embers sparked, igniting new fires. Frankie's eyes burned and teared. She coughed.

Grunting, she fought to pull herself up and over the side of the loft. A ray of hope ignited when she realized that what hay remained there was soaked. The boards beneath that hay, however, were rotted, and several were already missing. Through one gaping hole she could see Whitman looking up at her.

"It's no good, my love. You won't make it."

Yet he climbed on the barrel, preparing to come after her.

She had to hurry.

She quickly tested each of the boards. Balanced her weight between the two sturdiest ones and scrambled to the far side of the loft. Above her there, the wind whistled through unseen gaps in the window and water poured in through the leaky seals. She looked for something to shatter the glass and grabbed the remains of a splintered board. She held it above her head and began to butt the window.

Behind her she heard a loud snap and, turning her head, saw part of a stall collapse and the beams above it catch fire. Embers flew. Whitman had now proceeded to the ladder, looking far more concerned than before. She butted the window again and again until it shattered.

The smoke followed the open air and poured in her direction.

Frankie coughed and gasped, trying desperately not to breathe in. She jumped for the window ledge. It wasn't much higher than the chin-up bar in her bedroom, and she made it on the first try. Shards of glass cut her hands, sending blood trailing down her arms, but she barely felt it. She was a ball of adrenaline now, the fight and flight of survival fully activated.

She heaved herself up until she had both arms through. She leveraged her toes against the wall to help her push. *So close, so close.* When she had both shoulders through, she felt his hand latch upon her ankle.

Frankie screamed into the pouring night. Behind her, another beam fell. It wouldn't be long before the roof caved in. She kicked at Whitman with her free leg as he pulled on the other, all the while hanging by her sternum on the ledge, refusing to give up. She could see glimpses of Whitman balancing precariously on the loose boards and could tell he was fighting an epic battle of his own, torn between realizing the end was near and struggling to believe his dream could still come true. His face contorted into nightmarish shapes.

He yelled her name as the fire began to lick at the floorboards of the loft. The popping and cracking grew in intensity, and despite the rain lashing her face, she could feel the searing heat and sparking embers on her legs. She took one last look behind her as a far section of the barn began to crumble.

She glanced at the man holding desperately onto her ankle. She felt badly for him and the life he'd lived, but she wasn't about to die as his bride-to-be. She leaned into her arms and used her core strength to pull up as far as she could, then with her free leg stomped down on his extended forearm until she heard the bone snap. His hand fell free of her ankle, and the last image she had of Kenneth Whitman—of Mary—was of him falling through the boards of the loft to the burning floor below.

With the weight gone, she freely pulled herself through the window. The heat and smoke increased behind her, choking and blinding. There was nothing she could do now but jump. She might break a leg or something even worse, but at least she'd have a chance.

As soon as her legs cleared the window, she slid headfirst down the tin roof, slick with rain, then tumbled off the side of the barn. Every bone and organ in her body shook, as if inside a baby's rattle. She landed in the tall grasses with a sickening thud and immediately gasped for air. A searing pain emanated from her shoulder and right hip, but she didn't care. Right now, she was free of the smoke and fire. And alive.

She turned her face up toward the barn's loft, wondering if Whitman would appear in the window. Even with all the pain he'd caused, she didn't want him to die. He'd suffered in his own right, and this wasn't how it was supposed to end. She was thinking about calling out for him when his final words broke the flames—now fully engulfing the barn—her name, followed by the question she could never answer. "Why?"

Trembling, she pulled herself to her feet and began to limp forward, away from the barn and the embers and those horrific sounds she would not soon forget. Near the highway she could just make out the dim glow of headlights as they turned onto the road. She struggled to make her way across the field but collapsed the moment she reached the end of the meadow, diving head first into the muddy road. She glanced up through the pelting rain to see the headlights getting brighter, and in the sky above, she heard the whir of approaching blades.

CHAPTER 49

B en coasted his black Mercedes down the tree-lined street. It was mid-July and
the summer haze had settled in, making everything feel like it moved in slow
motion. A block away he could see the little brick bungalow encased in late-
day sunlight and Frankie sitting on the front porch. As he pulled up to the curb, her
gaze followed him, although she never altered the gentle sway of the swing. In her
hands she held a glass of tea and took a sip—nursing it, nursing herself and what
must be her considerable wounds. Minor physically, but emotionally, who knew? What
he hated most was to have been a part of the damage.

She didn't stir when he stepped from the car. Didn't curse him or tell him to go to
hell when he walked up the five steps and sat on the porch with his back against the
rail. She only did as Frankie often did, offered hospitality. "Tea is in the fridge. Harder
stuff in the top cabinet." Her arm was still in a sling.

He declined, but thanked her. Unsure of where to start, he sat with his head bowed
and played with his keys. He was certain she was examining him, his submissive body
posture, sitting lower than her, begging at her feet like a dog that had done a bad deed.
Maybe she felt his humiliation. He hoped so. It was easier to show it than to say it
aloud.

"I heard you'd been released from the hospital. I thought I'd give it a week before
I visited. Two bad guys and two hospital stays. You're creating a trend." He sighed.
"How are you?"

"Okay. No worse than when I got stabbed. Dislocated shoulder. Otherwise, bruises
mostly. I'll recover."

The stabbing. The other incident that she wouldn't have had to endure if he'd just
listened a little earlier and acted a little quicker. "Emotionally?"

A deep sigh. "Oh, that. Well, I'm still working through the process. Where I made
mistakes. How I got involved with a potential suspect. Why I allowed my feelings to
come into a case." She started to say more but stopped.

Ben finished it for her. "Why your good friend Ben would sacrifice you to the Hoover gods."

She studied her tea. "Yes, that too."

His heart caved in a little. "I wish I could offer you an answer. But I can't. Not yet. It seems I have my own processing to do, lessons to learn." He felt his emotions surface, burning his skin. He knew his chest and face were red. "When we took off in that helicopter, I was so worried. I just thought ... here we go again. I fell for the misdirection a second time."

"A woman was missing. You had to look for her, misdirection or not," Frankie said. "I heard you found her alive. That's a win."

"Yes, but I almost lost you in the process. Again." A lump sealed off his voice. "When Tommy and I rushed in that house and I saw your dress and that note, a little piece of me died. Whitman abducted my partner right under my nose and he let me know it." He winced at his own words. It was hard to hear.

"Well, I didn't fare much better. My biggest fear since I botched the serial rape case was making a bad decision that resulted in the harm or death of another victim, and then Jeanne died while I slept. Her death haunts me. Every night it haunts me. That look in her eyes, when she gazed into the camera and pleaded for help."

"You did everything possible to find her."

She glanced out over the neighborhood, slightly shook her head. "Maybe, but I can't stop thinking, if I'd just asked the right questions during that first encounter with Whitman, detected his erotomania sooner."

"Frankie, don't. Don't beat yourself up. You're a great profiler. You had all the right elements from the beginning. Your analytical skills, your insight, your ... instincts. They're your strengths," Ben said.

She raised a hand to the sun and squinted. "Instincts? B, is that you?"

He swung his head, laughed. "Yes, I admit it. As much as it pains me, your instincts played a big role in solving this case."

"I don't know," she said, resting her head on the back of the swing. "The only thing I do know is I'm tired. I don't want to profile anyone for a while. I just want to believe people are who they really say they are."

He nodded. Her dream seemed like a nice place to be. "You certainly had faith in Dr. Banks. How did you know he wasn't the killer?"

She chuckled. "Oh, believe me, after your interrogation, I had my doubts. I questioned how I could be so wrong, so completely blinded, and when you said a witness had come forward with Melanie, that really threw me. But by then I'd started to put the pieces together about Mary and Dr. Whitman; I just needed to complete the puzzle. And finding Rhonda Stewart did that."

"That witness was paid to come forward by Dr. Whitman. Just another one of his tactics to buy time and distraction."

Frankie nodded. "Figures." The porch swing resumed swaying. A soft breeze blew from the southwest. "I didn't sleep with Lawrence that night, you know."

Ben cringed. He wanted to cover his head with a bucket. "I'm sorry I didn't believe you. I'm sorry about a lot of things."

"Well, what was it that Paul Boese once said? *'Forgiveness does not change the past, but it does enlarge the future.'* And, circumstances as they were, I don't blame you. Not for questioning my involvement with Lawrence, anyway. I fully expect to get a slap or two from the OPR."

Her words of forgiveness lifted his spirits, if only a little. It didn't matter how long it took her to let him back into her life, as long as there was a chance for reconciliation. "It's good to have a little rebellion on your profile. Shows them you're willing to do what's necessary. I could use a few demerit badges."

She cocked her head. "I don't know," she said. "Vicks told me you twisted more than a few arms to take up that helicopter in tropical storm winds. That should at least give you a gold star."

He flashed a grin. "I did, didn't I? Never thought I'd consider practically assaulting a security guard a proud moment." He stretched out his legs and sighed. "Did they tell you? About the items we found in Whitman's office? The personal effects?"

"Vicks did. And I saw the press conference. He said there was evidence pointing to ten women, plus Sara Phillips, Jeanne Mapleton, and the real Kenneth Whitman. More than a decade of a killer going unnoticed."

"They already discovered four of the bodies, including Melanie's and Rhonda's, and the Florence, South Carolina, police dug up a long-ago report of an abandoned car taken to impound that was registered to a Perry Campbell. We think that's when Mary abducted the real Kenneth Whitman. A construction crew found a body years ago who has remained a John Doe. They think it may be him."

"Wow. Well, I'm glad they're making progress."

Ben stared out over the neatly landscaped yard. He noticed some newly planted zinnias and hyacinths. Gardening therapy. He stood, feeling as if he had taken enough of Frankie's time. He would check in on her but give her the space she needed to work things out. He had his own introspection to do.

He walked over and offered a hug. "I want you to know, I will never, ever question your judgment again. I hope you'll come back soon. It's lonely there without you sizing me up and keeping me honest." He planted a kiss on her cheek. "Plus, this New Patriot group is up to no good. We need you back in the fold."

"I'm going to hold you to that," she said. "The judgment part."

"I'm counting on it." As he stepped off the porch, a silver Lexus pulled behind his car and parked. Ben squinted into the sun before turning back to Frankie. "Looks like you have a visitor."

CHAPTER 50

Frankie watched Ben stop to shake Lawrence's hand and briefly speak to him before he departed. It was a good gesture, and when it occurred, she knew one day that the three of them would be able to put this behind them. They'd be having dinner, or playing cards, and someone would call Ben a Hoover or tell Frankie that instincts were like farts and they'd all get a good chuckle. Frankie, though, would always be a little more cautious, and a lot wiser, for the ordeal.

As Lawrence strolled up the stairs and snuggled next to her on the porch swing, she realized how happy she was that he was there. Seeing him had always brought a little flutter of her heart, but this time it delivered something deeper—a sense of relief. He wasn't everything she'd imagined—he wasn't perfect—but who was? He'd been deceptive about his past, yes, because he'd witnessed something horrible and had been falsely accused of taking part. Deceptive about his mother, yes, because she'd been an abusive addict and had died a violent death. Deceptive about his name, because he wasn't proud of his past. He wore shame and bled guilt, all yes, but that didn't make him a killer.

"How'd it go with Ben?" he asked.

"Good, I think. We'll get past this."

"And Vicks?"

Frankie sighed. "Well, I'm missing half an ass cheek and a month's pay, but he says he'll go to the mat for me with OPR. Might be awhile before he assigns me a case again. Might have to say a hundred J. Edgar Hoovers and polish a closetful of shiny black shoes to make it all look official, but at least I'll still have a job."

"Just fifteen more years to that pretty gold watch."

Frankie raised an eyebrow. "Government issued. Just one of thousands."

"Special."

He squeezed her hand and they rocked the porch swing in silence for a few moments. It was good to feel the movement, the weight of them together, as they swayed forward and back.

"Have I said thank-you lately?" she asked.

He sighed. "No." Wounded.

She felt a smile curl her lip. "Then I'll say it again. Thank you, Dr. Lawrence Banks. I truly appreciate all the help you gave me on this case, but I'm especially thankful for your trust. You didn't have to go along with my crazy plan, but you did."

"Crazy is right. Whitman could've killed the both of us."

"But you were such a good actor."

"Yeah?"

"Yeah."

He squared his shoulders and cleared his throat. "Well, you know, we doctors get a lot of real-life drama. People sick, people cured. People coming back from the dead. I'm a natural." His grin stretched from cheek to cheek.

"The fall into the table and chairs was a little over the top," she said.

He looked incredulous. "What? That was classic. The clutch of the chest, the stagger, the knee going down." He shook his finger at her. "I've watched my share of old movies to know that was good stuff."

"A tinge excessive." She chuckled.

"Excessive? You want excessive?" He raised the leg of his shorts to reveal a deep-purple bruise. "This is from you jabbing that syringe of sugar water into my thigh. And this ..." He turned his wrists out. "Rope burns."

She examined the raw skin. "What, did I hurt you?"

He pointed to a red spot. "Right here. A little."

She took his hand and kissed it.

He turned his jaw out. "And here."

She planted a kiss on his cheek.

He turned to look at her. The comedy fell away. "But mostly, right here," he said, placing both hands across his heart. "I don't know what I would've done if you hadn't believed in me, or if catching Whitman hadn't gone down as planned. If you hadn't made it out of that fire ..." He choked up, glanced away.

She started to speak but stopped. Could she trust the words she was about to say? She wanted to. She wanted to believe them with everything she'd buried within that small, tight space within. "I can fix that too."

He studied her, his dark chocolate eyes fixated. "This one might take longer, you know. Might require more than a few days and nights. Might require months. Even years."

Frankie warmed. "I think I'm up to the task."

"You're sure?"

233

"I'm sure." She stood, and he helped her across the porch. "I just have one request," she said.

"What's that?"

"Promise not to write or recite any poems to me—ever."

"What about those expressing my dying obsession with you?"

She issued him the laser daggers.

He laughed. "Got it. The poetry books are out."

"Also ... one more thing. Promise to tell me the truth and nothing but the truth from now on, so help you God?"

They walked inside, and Lawrence shut the door behind them. "I do."

***

Thank you for reading The Art of Obsession. Reviews help authors by providing social proof to other readers. Please leave a review of this book on Amazon here: https://bit.ly/ObsessionReview

ACKNOWLEDGEMENTS

Many thanks to the FBI Media and Public Relations divisions for answering questions regarding this novel. Thanks to Rachel Keith for editing and Nick Castle for a fantastic cover design. Thanks to Melissa Yahr and Melissa Ammons, proofreaders extraordinaire, and to my entire Advanced Reading Team for early reads and reviews. You are the best!

This book is a work of fiction and is not intended to reflect on any actual persons in local police departments or federal agencies.

ABOUT THE AUTHOR

LORI LACEFIELD writes suspense thrillers that keep you turning the pages late into the night. Her Women of Redemption series features heroines who may not be perfect, but who perfectly kick-ass when given a second chance. Titles include *The Advocate*, *The Fifth Juror*, and *The Tattoo Artist*. Lori also writes the Frankie Johnson, FBI Local Profiler series. Titles include *99 Truths* and *The Art of Obsession*. You can read more about Lori at www.lorilacefield.com. Sign up to receive news, enter her latest giveaway, and receive a FREE novella at https://www.lorilacefield.com/news-and-giveaways.html.

Made in the USA
Las Vegas, NV
19 February 2024